The Ways of Heaven

The Ways of Heaven

A Maine Girl's Struggle to Keep Her Faith
Through Unrelenting Tragedy

Michael Gervais

The Ways of Heaven:
A Maine Girl's Struggle to Keep Her Faith Through Unrelenting Tragedy
2024 © Michael Gervais
ISBN 979-8-9916786-0-5

Cover photos by Michael Gervais
Note: The inset on the cover and photograph of the young girl on the title page are of an unknown person meant to represent Annie Goodwin. The daguerreotype is owned by the author.

All newspaper clippings are from the *Gardiner Home Journal* unless otherwise indicated. All images are photographed by the author from items in the author's private collection, unless otherwise indicated here:

Page 7: Maine Maritime Museum, Sewall Family Papers

Page 47: McCord Stewart Museum

Page 72: New York Public Library, Robert N. Dennis collection of stereoscopic views

Page 75: Wikimedia commons, Vol. 2 of *Robertson's Landmarks of Toronto: A collection of Historical Sketches of the Old Town of York from 1792 until 1833, and of Toronto from 1834 to 1895*

Page 119: The Christmas Tree (from *Harper's Weekly,* Vol. II) after Winslow Homer, The Metropolitan Museum of Art

Page 197: New York Public Library, I. N. Phelps Stokes Collection of American Historical Prints

Page 263: Wikimedia Commons, *Battles and Leaders of the Civil War* Vol. 4, "The destruction of the *Albemarle*"

Laurel Dodge, editor
Cover and book design by Lindy Gifford, Manifest Identity
Michael Gervais, publisher

To my parents

Raymond Lawrence Gervais,
who overcame poverty and prejudice to
provide us with a life of opportunity.

Pearle Edith Sullivan Gervais,
whose loving heart drew down many
graces from the Divinity.

The Ways of Heaven

by Charles Swain

Secret are the ways of Heaven, yet to some great end they tend.
Often some affliction given, proves a blessing in the end.
Let no vain impatient gesture question the diviner will,
But in Faith's immortal gesture, wait thy mission and be still!

That which is the deepest sorrow often proves the inmost good;
They who build upon tomorrow, build on ground not understood:
Lose not then thy trust in Heaven, take its counsels like a friend.
Often some affliction given, proves affection—in the end.

—Gardiner Home Journal, June 21, 1860

Contents

Detail from map of Kennebec County, Maine, 1856

Preface

My great-grandmother, Gertrude Nelson, lay dying in a hospital bed in Houlton, Maine, some two hundred miles from our Northern Avenue apartment in Augusta. I was a month shy of my second birthday and sleeping soundly in my mother's arms. Suddenly, I pulled myself up, wrapped my arms around her, and gave her a big bear hug. Then, just as swiftly, I slipped back into a deep, undisturbed slumber. Mom was overcome by a strange sensation and knew that something unusual had just transpired. Five minutes later the phone rang from the hospital. Her dear grandmother had passed five minutes earlier. I had delivered Gertrude's final embrace.

Encounters of this type at the hour of death are not unusual, and in light of the story I'm about to tell, they become an important feature. But what is their purpose? Are they heralds of an eternal afterlife, or are they strange but natural occurrences yet to be explained by science? One thing is certain, their timing is flawless.

When my wife, Carrie, and I purchased our 1840s cape in Chelsea, Maine, in 1995, I was inspired to do some research on its original owners. I learned through Helen Taylor's *Chelsea Maine History*, which serendipitously was published that same year, that our home was originally owned by a sea captain and farmer named John Andrew Goodwin. He and his wife Sarah (Kean) had seven children: Charles (b.1845), Annie (b.1849), twins Franklin and Johnny (b.1852), twins Isabella and Sarah Lilly (b.1857), and Andrew (b.1863).

I wanted to find out as much as I could about the family that first owned our home, and a logical step was to visit the local graveyards. I ventured over to the Chelsea Heights Cemetery, which was the closest burial ground and a likely resting place for members of the Goodwin family. On arriving, I noticed that the older stones were towards the back, so I parked in an open spot and walked slowly down the path, taking note of the engraved surnames. About two hundred feet down the path, I was greeted by a tragic scene. There stood stone after stone of the family Goodwin, each with a heartbreaking epitaph recalling unspeakable sorrow. Yet, from among all those hallowed stones, one was missing—someone who lived, someone who was there, someone who saw it all, someone who wept before each and every grave—Annie Goodwin.

A chill ran down my spine at the realization of what this girl must have endured. What does such unabating grief do to one's faith, one's sanity, one's perception of life's purpose? Were Annie's painful losses heralded by phenomena like my mother experienced at the time of my great-grandmother's death? Did they extend to her some similar bittersweet solace?

For years, I nurtured the idea of penning out this true-life story within the context of a historical novel. The question was whether such an undertaking was worthy of the time and motivation needed to see it to completion. Then the pandemic arrived, providing me with plenty of time. The energizing motivation, however, came about quite differently and in a mind-boggling fashion.

After collecting historical facts and designing a rough outline, I committed the whole idea to prayer. I asked for confirmation that I should begin this multi-year enterprise. On the evening of July 14, 2020, while still in the process of gathering tidbits of relevant data, I decided to make a routine online search for Annie's maternal grandparents, James Kean and Isabel Turner. At the very top of the first page of results was this heading: "The James Kean and Isabel Turner family Bible, for sale." I was shocked! What were the odds? I immediately purchased the large Bible, which had not resided in our home since the last year of the Civil War.

The Kean Bible is full of artifacts: fragments of clothing from deceased loved ones, four-leaf clovers, prayer cards, newspaper clippings, and a small hand-written note. To top it all off, I discovered that Grandma Isabel lived with Annie until her death in 1881. The final entry of Isabel's passing was likely penned into that Bible by my protagonist's own hand.

So, who was this Annie Goodwin, formerly an obscure name amidst the dry and dusty records of time? She wasn't a Lincoln, a Stowe, or a Frederick Douglass. She was an ordinary person, born in a small Maine town, smack-dab in the center of the most turbulent days of the 19th century, trying to make sense of her world.

Now that her story is complete, I cordially invite you to enter, through the doorway of time, the world of Ann Elizabeth Goodwin.

Michael Gervais, September, 2024

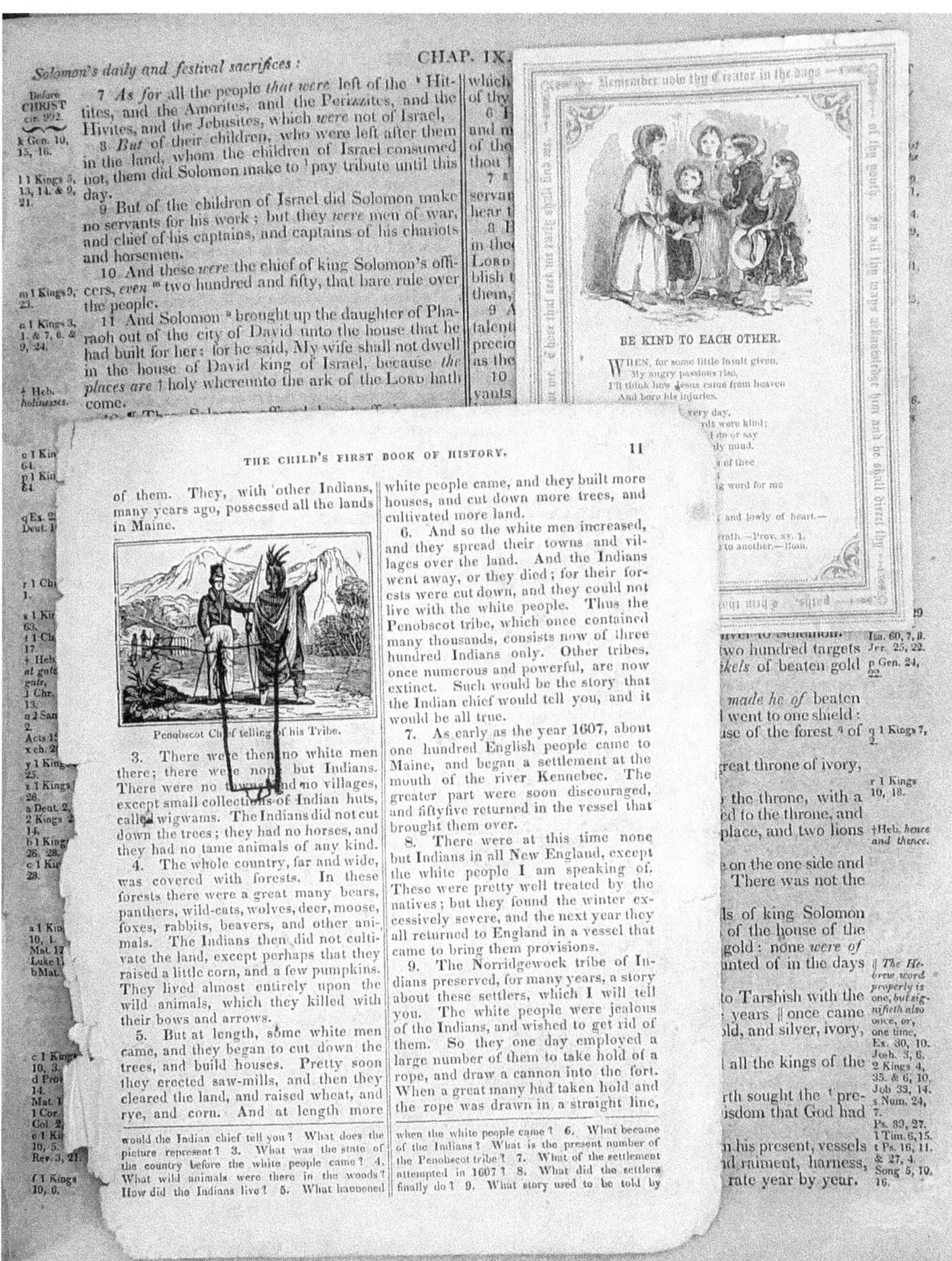

Memorabilia found in the Kean family bible.

rom off
hath given
nath given
Deut. 28,
15. 68.
ovenant of the
ou, and have
yourselves to
RD be kindled
ly from off the
He
them God.
all the tribes of
d for the elders
for their judg and for
a Gen. 33,
18.
esented before
all the peo ith
our fathers the
b ch. 23, 2.
ld time, even the
father of
c Gen. 11,
braham from
roughout all the
d Deut. 26,
d, and gave
Esa
ss it But
h G
i Gen.
20.
k Gen. 36, 8
serv
16
that wa
17 Fo
up, and
the house
in our sigh
we went, a
passed:
18 And
people, eve
therefore w
God.
19 And
serve the
God; he
sms.
20

Introduction

Bath, Maine, August 1900

There was a loud knocking at the front door of our home at 32 Oak Street in Bath. I scurried down the stairwell to find a middle-aged gentleman standing outside the entrance holding a brown paper package under his arm. I opened the door and greeted him.

"May I help you?" I asked.

"Are you Annie Elizabeth Goodwin, daughter of Captain John Goodwin, of Chelsea?"

"Well, yes, Goodwin was my maiden name, and John was my father," I replied.

"Happy to make your acquaintance, ma'am. My name is George Walker. I'm the current owner of your old homestead in Chelsea. Truth is, I've been tryin' to locate your whereabouts for some time now. Not many folks 'round there remember your family. So many have passed on, it seems."

"Indeed," I replied, extending my hand in welcome. "Please, come in and be seated. Would you like some coffee or tea?"

"No thank you, ma'am," he replied. I don't plan to take much of your time. I've come to give you something that I believe to be yours." He set the package on the tea table.

I fetched a pair of scissors and cut the twine that bound the parcel. The size and weight of the items inside seemed familiar. "It couldn't be," I muttered. With mounting excitement, I tore open the wrappings and several cloth-bound, musty-smelling booklets tumbled out onto the tabletop.

"My journals!" I gasped. "Oh, my dear God! They've been missing for thirty-five years!" I exclaimed, shaking my head in disbelief. "Looks like they're all here, too! All twelve of them! Where did you find these?"

"Well, ma'am, my wife found 'em up in a dark corner of the attic, up over the summer kitchen. They've been sittin' there for some time, given their condition and all. Wonder the squirrels didn't have 'em for lunch."

"Looks as though a couple of them tried," I smiled, holding up one with a chewed corner.

"I thought these were gone forever," I continued, in a reminiscent daze.

"Everything was in such turmoil. When I discovered they were missing, Mr. Kebler, the new owner, let me explore every inch of the old house, but I couldn't find them. So how did they end up in the attic?"

"Well, somebody found 'em and had the common sense not to chuck 'em. There's been one other owner, Joe Patterson, mayor of Augusta. He didn't move into the house after Mr. Kebler left, instead he rented the place out to tenant farmers. Place was a wreck when we got it. It took a lot of fixin' up."

"Sometimes I miss the old place. So many memories … Ghosts."

"Yes, ma'am. When I began tryin' to find ya, I wandered up to Chelsea Heights to see if you was among the livin'. Long row of stones, ain't it?"

"Truly," I replied, my voice quavering.

"Well, happy to see you're on this side of the turf, Ma'am," he replied, with a wink and a smile.

Tears were welling up in my eyes as George headed towards the doorway. "Thank you so much, Mr. Walker, you have no idea what this means to me. God bless you, sir."

"And you, as well, ma'am." And with a gentlemanly nod he took his leave.

———

I returned to the parlor and set the booklets upon my lap. Lying before my astonished eyes was my entire childhood! The journals, which I began in 1858 when I was nine years old, extended continuously through February of 1865. As I sat there flipping through the pages, forgotten memories jumped out from the past: Charlie and his inappropriate antics, Eli's visit, the two-horse ferry, Edith Sullivan's wisdom, our terrible grief and serendipitous blessings, and my desperate search for an answer to life's most important question. Though I couldn't wait to begin reading, I felt a deep foreboding over the painful passages that I would have to revisit.

Now, at fifty-one, I was ready to journey back to my childhood with a perspective that only time and reflection can yield.

Part I

Chapter 1

A Whale's Tale

—

*S*ome of my earliest remembrances are of the old salts, whalers, and mariners who visited our home on those long-ago summer evenings, all of them friends and acquaintances of my father. The yarns they spun in the parlor were full of omens, fantasms, and specters, which grew more terrifying as the rum-consumption increased throughout the night. Ten-year-old Charles and I hid in the dark on the second story landing, where we hung onto every word that drifted up the stairwell. The spine-chilling tales, like malcontent spirits looking for a place of repose, filled our minds, and our eyes went wide with wonder and fear. We were too bewitched to even think of sleep. But eventually the party broke up, the spirits dissipated, and we needed rest. My brother went off to bed, but being only half my brother's age, I was greatly affected by the fright given me by those tales. More often than not, I ended up crawling into bed with my parents. It wasn't long, though, before I learned to distinguish between the accounts that had some basis in truth, and those that were merely the result of too much alcohol.

Papa's tales, however, were different from the others. His were of such a character that their accuracy could be verified by living souls, by family members, by friends of the family, or sometimes, by friends of friends of the family. There was always a moral to be comprehended in their telling, making them a bit like the parables of the New Testament. They solidified a notion into a fact or a popular myth into undeniable truth. Often, their content was full of clairvoyance and the supernatural.

My first encounter with such an other-worldly event arrived from Father's telling of an episode which occurred during his courting years. When I placed my hand upon the illustration I had made on the first page of my long-lost journal—a drawing of a storm-battered whaleship surrounded by fog with a ghost-like figure hovering near—the memory unfolded before me.

Father had called Charles, my mother, and myself to join him in the parlor. Mother, who had just rocked my twin brothers to sleep, entered the room with the peaceful glow of victory on her countenance. The sun was setting, casting long shadows across the floor as the solemn ticking of our tall clock added a sense of the fleeting nature of time and of earthly life. The large maps used during a recent voyage to England lay neatly rolled up in the corner of the room. Father put a match to the whale oil lamps on the mantel, hinting at the essence of the narrative to come.

Without warning, Charles broke the enchanting atmosphere. "Hey, Sis. No yappin' durin' his story! Got it?"

Papa corrected him. "Charlie, you were always interruptin' stories when you were her age. Let 'er be."

Looking over at me with a smile, he added, "You can ask all the questions ya want, dear."

"Papa, don't tell her that! We'll be here 'til first light!" growled Charles.

Momma jumped into the mix. "Charlie, how do you expect your sister to learn if she doesn't ask questions? She's a bright young lady."

"Bright!" exclaimed my brother. "She's denser than a two-by-four!"

Mama gave my brother a hard look. "Charles Andrew Goodwin! That's enough outta you!"

"You don't believe me? Anyone happen to notice the holes all over the front yard? Guess who dug 'em?" asserted Charles, pompously. "That bright young lady."

"Because you lied to me! You brat!" I yelled back in my own defense.

Charles scoffed, "I told her Papa was a pirate, and whenever he returned from sea he buried his treasure in the front yard. Dumber than a bag of rocks I tell ya."

"One more unkind word and you'll be spending the rest of the night in your room, 'til first light!" Mother said.

"Children, I haven't seen ya for three months, and I've missed ya terribly. Can we all get along now?" pleaded Papa.

Charles nodded in compliance and I relented as well, but not without a lethal glare at my infuriating sibling.

"Papa," asked my brother, in a more courteous tone, "could you tell us the story about the fog?"

"Yes, Papa," I chimed in. "Charlie says it's a good one."

Father smiled, "Well, 'tis quite unusual, but a bit scary for ya, Annie."

"Papa, please?" I begged. "I promise I'll go straight to my own bed. I won't bother you and Momma."

Father chuckled, "Well, we'll see about that." He then winked at Mother, lit his pipe, enthroned himself in his soft, plush wing chair, and began the tale.

"Have ya ever watched the fog slowly creepin' up from the Kennebec in the evenin' hours?" he began in his best "old salt" accent. "Low down, it leaves Hallowell landing, gradually risin' and troopin' a ghostly procession up the ravines, up the steep embankment into Chelsea Heights graveyard, and spreadin' out over the vast plateau? It has a great charm for the one who observes it closely. What fantastic shapes it assumes: a vast conquering army marching in formation; billowing smoke rising up from a great conflagration; a wide lake covered with rushin' waves, flooding the whole valley of the Kennebec, the tops of the hills standin' out like islands, lashed by a furious surf!"

"Papa, what is fog?" I interrupted.

Charles rolled his eyes in disgust and blurted, "It's a cloud, Annie. A low cloud."

"I've seen fog before, Charlie, but what's it made of?"

"This ain't a science lesson, Sis," grumbled Charles. He then turned to Father and pleaded, "Papa, please make her stop yappin'! She's gonna ruin the story."

Papa responded with patience, "It's water vapor, dear, like when Momma boils water in the kettle."

After noting my satisfaction with his answer, he continued, "As you're well aware, the families of whalemen and merchant mariners are always watchin' the sky, for the weather, fair or foul, holds the lives of their loved ones in its embrace. They're always making, out of the most common, natural phenomena, omens favorable or ill as their emotions rise and fall with the passage of time."

"Now," continued Father, whispering in a suspenseful voice, "some folks believe that if a loved one dies at sea, the fog will creep its way to their doorsteps, rise up, become animated and reveal the face of the dead one!"[1]

His chilling words made me shake with fright, and I leaped right into my momma's arms.

"John, you're frightening this little thing to death! She's not one of your shipmates, she's your six-year-old daughter," Momma declared.

"I'm not scared," said Charles, with a dismissive tone. "I've heard all about that spooky face comin' outta the fog. It's just an old legend, Annie. Don't be such a sissy."

Maine Line Telegraph,
BETWEEN
BOSTON, PORTLAND, BANGOR AND CALAIS, WITH INTERMEDIATE STATIONS
Connecting with lines to all parts of the United States and British Provinces.

Bath, June 2nd 1854

By Telegraph from Calais

To Clark & Sewall

The Macedonia will be at Eastport Seventh. Send crew of ten men. —

Jno. A. Goodwin

Telegraph message form Capt. Goodwin requesting crew members for his 1854 journey to Great Britain.

"Charles, apologize to her or you'll go straight up to bed!" growled Father.

My brother sighed, "Sorry Sis."

"Go ahead with the story, John, but take it easy on the phantoms," Mother insisted, tempering her words with a smile.

Father waited until we had all settled a bit, took a big puff on his pipe, and continued with the saga.

"Well, children, your momma, at the ripe age of twenty, couldn't make up her mind about whether she wanted to marry an ol' sea dog like me or not. Her pappy was a seaman and she hated his long absences; wasn't sure she wanted to spend the rest of her life like that. She seesawed back and forth on the marriage question 'til I got fed up and signed onto a whale ship for a two-year journey. Let's just say, it wasn't the smartest decision I ever made, and it was my first and last time on whaler.

"Of course, whalin's a mighty dangerous enterprise. Not only are ya out in uncharted waters, but one of them behemoths can split a tiny whaleboat in half with a flick of its tail or might stave in the bow of a sea-goin' vessel, which was the unfortunate fate of the *Essex* a few years ago. But I was young and foolish, and like all young and foolish men, I believed myself to be immortal. So I left Hallowell for Nantucket. There, I boarded a ship by the name of *Maria,* which was bound for the South Pacific. It was captained, appropriately, by a man named Fisher.[2] Figured with a surname like that, I had nothin' to fear.

WANTED,

IMMEDIATELY, 15 or 20 Young Men to go on whaling voyages, to which good lays will be given. Also Carpenters, and Blacksmiths, wanted. All clothing furnished on credit of the voyage. For further information call at the WASHINGTONIAN HOUSE, Gardiner. August 15, 1844. J. TOWNSEND.

"'Twas smooth sailin' with a good catch 'til we rounded the Horn on our return from the Pacific. There, we hit a gawdawful storm, a typhoon, really. The vessel banked so much that the yardarm was touchin' the waves! We all thought we were doomed, and frankly, it would've been my ticket to the Pearly Gates, save for a strange encounter.

"I was securin' the whaleboats when a fierce gust whipped me into that frigid ocean! Now, I can swim fairly well, but 'twas near impossible to stay afloat in that violent, icy surf. There was no visibility, and I was completely disoriented. Couldn't even see the ship. My body was growin' numb from the cold and I was 'bout to go under for the last time. So I began to call out your mother's name in a wild panic. I could truly feel my soul slippin' away from my body."

At this point, Father motioned with a nod, and Mother continued the story.

"Well, children, at the very moment this was taking place, some seven thousand miles away, I was sleeping in Grandpa's hayloft. 'Twas early September, when the evenings are cool with fewer insects about. I'd taken a book, a lantern, and a thick quilt to camp out in my nest, as I called it.

"Anyway, while experiencing a peaceful sleep, I was awakened by terrifying screams coming from outside, below the loft. I stood up trembling, and stumbled to the open hay door and gazed down. An immense fog had gathered that resembled a raging surf, and there, as though swimming in the midst of it, was your Papa, begging and pleading for me to save his life!

"I stood dumbfounded, unable to move a muscle as his shrieks continued. Finally, I came to my senses and noticed a bailing rope that was attached to a beam. I grabbed it and tossed it out the opening as a lifeline. The next thing I knew, a morning sunbeam was greeting me. I awoke in the same position I was in when I fell asleep the evening prior. It was all just a terrible nightmare. So, I got up, brushed the hay off me, folded my blanket, and proceeded down the ladder.

"While I was eating breakfast, your grandpa came in and asked me a question that shot through me like a lightning bolt, 'Sarah, why was that rope hanging out of the hay door? Hope you're not using it to climb down from the loft? You could've hurt yourself.'

"I nearly fainted. It wasn't a dream! I was filled with the unspeakable fear that I had witnessed my beloved's death. I told no one and continued to suffer a double agony of grief in my heart. John had ventured to sea because of my foolishness, and divine justice had allowed me to witness his last moments on this earth. How I loathed myself.

"I scoured the papers to find any bits of information about lost vessels. Hope was but a flicker in my dismal world. I busied myself, as best I could, throughout the day, but nighttime always brought on dark thoughts and imaginings. The image of that helpless hand reaching out of the tumultuous fog was always before me along with the echo of John's last woeful cries. The very things that had once made life beautiful became poison to my soul, a stark reminder of what I'd lost.

"One day, a neighbor came by and informed me that a whaling vessel out of Nantucket and its entire crew had been lost near Cape Horn. My heart was in my throat until I read the article and discovered it was not the *Maria*. I felt as though I was losing my mind. The bleak winter months with their long dark nights and frigid cold days didn't help matters. Nothing brought me any joy.

"In late February of the following year, while feeding our livestock and feeling sick at heart, I climbed to my nest in the loft. I hadn't been up there since that fateful night. The lantern and the rolled-up quilt still waited there, and even the imprint I had made in my bed of hay was unaltered. I sat down on a bale and began to weep. An hour or so went by, and having drained every last teardrop, I realized I needed to get back to my chores. The pigs were making a racket, awaiting their feast of slop.

"As I started back down the ladder, I heard a thumping sound coming from the hay door. Assuming it wasn't latched tightly, but fearing to go near the thing, I balked. 'What a coward you are, Sarah Kean!' I said to myself. 'Afraid of a wooden door.' So I plucked up my courage, climbed back up, and wandered over to check the inside latch. It was firm and tight. As I walked away, another loud thud echoed from that same place. Now, I was curious. Crows, perhaps? Squirrels?

"I lifted the latch and stealthily cracked the heavy wooden portal to about an inch. I peered through the slit and swoosh! My face was covered with wet snow! It startled me so that I inadvertently let the door swing wide open. I then moved to the center of the doorway and was assailed by another slushy projectile that promptly removed my bonnet! My eyes were blurry from the snowball and dazzling sunlight.

"'Sorry, Ma'am,' my assailant exclaimed. 'Your papa told me I could find ya here.'

"As my watery eyes cleared, I was able to make out the form of a young man wearing a wide-brimmed hat and sporting a full, bushy beard. At first, I thought him to be our new pastor. Then he lifted his arms as though pleading, and shouted, 'Sarah! Throw me a lifeline!'

"Well, children, I nearly fell out of the loft! It was your Papa!

"I tossed that very same bailing rope out of the portal and climbed down into the embrace of my dear husband-to-be. There was no doubt in my mind anymore. And as you know, I did make my way to the altar with this old sea-dog."

Mother smiled, got up off the sofa, and gave her husband a big kiss on the forehead.

"I thought it might take a miracle to get 'er to tie the knot," laughed Papa. "And I was right!"

I sat there wide-eyed at the amazing story I'd just heard.

"Papa, when you were in the water, did you see her throw the rope from the loft?" asked Charles.

"Yes, Charlie. But I couldn't see where she was. I just knew it was Sarah. Truly, I don't remember how I got back on the ship. Some of the crew found me on deck after the *Maria* righted herself. After that brush with death, I was delirious with fever for a week."

Overcome with wonder, I raised my hand to ask a question.

"What is it, Annie?" chuckled Father, enjoying my scholarly manners.

"How far is seven thousand miles, Papa?"

"It's very, very far."

"Like going to Portland?" I asked, for I couldn't imagine anything further away than that.

"Oh, no, Dear. More like goin' to Portland a hundred times."

"Oh my," I gasped. "How did Momma ever throw the rope so far?"

There was a roar of laughter from my dear brother, who exclaimed, "God, give me patience!"

"Well now, Charles Andrew Goodwin," said Mother, "how did I throw the thing to the tip of South America? Would you like to explain it to her in your all-knowing wisdom?"

Charles mumbled something under his breath.

"It was Divine intervention, dear, and nothin' but," proclaimed Papa. He then re-lit his pipe and smiled. "Your momma threw the rope, but God made sure it reached me."

I remember penning this story into my journal. I was nine at the time. Mother insisted that I preserve it "for posterity." She believed that such events needed to be documented and the writings would prove valuable as a means of reflection. I will never forget her prophetic words; "We are given these blessings so that when our faith has been tested with long suffering and our hearts have been broken in grief; we may yet cry out, 'I believe!' It is then we shall see His unfailing mercy descend like dew from the heavens."

Chapter 2

In the Beginning

$\mathcal{I}$ came kicking and screaming into this life on May 18, 1849. My christened name is Ann Elizabeth Goodwin. As a young girl, attempting Spencerian script, I practiced penning my name upon almost every page of my journal and quickly came to prefer the two-syllable "Annie" to the shorter form, "Ann." It flows more musically with the other two names, don't you think?

I hail from the small town of Chelsea, Maine, which was previously part of Hallowell. Our little hamlet was incorporated in 1850, the year after my birth, providing me the opportunity to jest, "I was born in Hallowell, now live in Chelsea, and I never even moved a smidgen." My father, Captain John Andrew Goodwin, purchased 40 acres of land with a house and barn in 1844[3] when he and my mother, Sarah Turner Kean, were married.

Our home was modeled after those on Cape Cod, a New England style that is still very popular. Let me give you a guided tour. As one entered the house through the front door, there was a sitting room, sometimes called a living room, to the left, and a parlor to the right. When a death in the family occurred, the exposition of the body took place in the formal parlor, and the sitting room was where the "living" congregated, hence "the living room".

The main stairwell of the house ascended against the parlor wall, and a hallway to the left of the stairs provided a straight shot into the kitchen. Upon entering the kitchen, there was a small guest room to the left, where Grandma resided after the death of her husband. To the right was the mudroom entry and another stairwell leading to the second level.

The chambers on the upper floor, as well as the three lovely west-facing dormers were added in the mid 1850s, as our family grew in size. There was a walk-in closet on the top landing of the main stairwell and directly to the

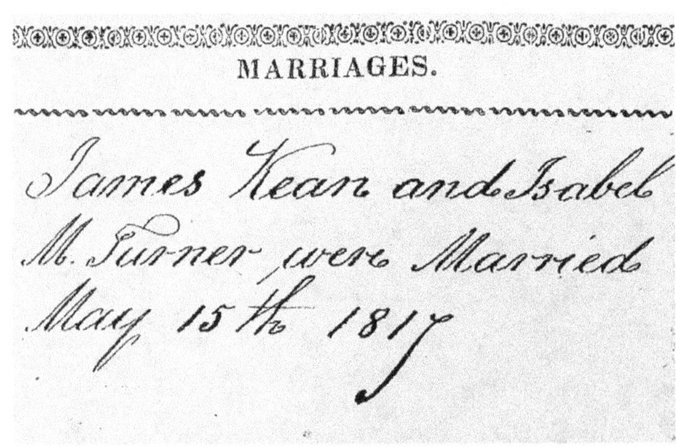

Spencerian script from the Kean family bible.

left of that was my cozy bedchamber, where all three of us girls slept. Adjacent to my room was our parents' master bedroom, complete with dormer and another north-facing window. There was a narrow walkway extending from my doorway past my parent's room to a little sewing nook, located beneath the dormer above the stairwell. To the right of the second-story landing were two more rooms, one with a descending stairwell leading to the mudroom and another larger abode directly off the landing. This one was complete with a third dormer and a south-facing window, the boys' room, as we called it.

The most poignant joys and sorrows of our family played out in the summer kitchen. This was a room on the ground floor extending off the back of the dwelling, that some referred to as an "ell". The summer kitchen connected the main body of the house to the woodshed, outhouse, and barn, and served as a birthing area for all the Goodwin children. When necessary, it became the family infirmary. It was there that I drew my very first breath, and as I remember all too well, it was where many others drew their last.

Like many Maine towns in the 1840s, Chelsea was a farming community. From the Kennebec River eastward, the land rises sharply for about a half mile until it reaches a rangeway that extends for another mile and a half. Our homestead farm was built on that stretch of more or less level ground. Behind it lay rolling fields that continue for a quarter mile, followed by another ascending group of hills that outline the horizon to the east.

What distinguished the southern Kennebec region from other rural areas was our connection to the sea. Hallowell,[4] situated twenty-five miles upriver from the coast on the tidal waters of the Kennebec River, was a true port, where goods from all over the world could be obtained. Many of the farmers, my father included, were seafarers, whalers, and merchant mariners as well. These hearty and brave "old salts" farmed the land near the river for a season or two and then went off to sea to provide for their ever-growing families.

Though a whaler's take from a good catch might be enough to provide for his retirement, the voyages were dangerous and could last in excess of three years. A ship's haul might consist of tons of baleen and hundreds of barrels of whale oil, with the most treasured commodity being spermaceti.[5] But to obtain these valuables, men risked their lives. Some returned to the sea even after terrible disasters. Three survivors of the whale attack upon the *Essex* later signed on to another whaling ship that was built right here in Hallowell.[6]

Though a merchant mariner, like Father, might net less than a whaleman, at least the cargo wouldn't drag his whaleboat for miles on a "Nantucket sleighride," smash the hull into splinters, or send it to the bottom of the sea if the harpoon-line became entangled. With transatlantic voyages lasting only three or four months, Father took fewer risks. Stateside journeys were even shorter, a month or so, at most. Nevertheless, I hated his absence.

My physical appearance during my early years was quite similar to that of my younger sister, Bella. I was thin, with wavy, light-auburn hair, and had freckles adorning my nose and cheeks, a gift from Grandpa Kean's Irish ancestors. As I grew to adulthood, reaching my towering height of five feet, five inches in my bare feet, my hair became a darker brown but it still retained some reddish strands that stood out in direct sunlight. My eye color morphed from light blue to green, depending on the amount and type of lighting in my surroundings. This anomaly continues up to the present, though I find I must hide them behind reading glasses these days. My likeness would probably not have adorned the fashion advertisements of the day; however, I did manage to turn a few heads back in my prime. Generally, I paid little attention to fashion except during my courting years, but I always dressed respectably.

Some of my very first and fondest memories are of sitting outside with Charles, my eldest brother, on early spring nights, listening to the enrapturing chorus of peepers that inhabited a small marsh beside our home. Every once in a while they would abruptly cease their singing, enhancing the silence of the starlit night. Charles, who enjoyed exploiting my ignorance, told me that they had stopped because "the frog maestro" summoned them to do so with his baton. Naturally, I believed him and went so far as to wade into the swampy muck to get a glimpse of the amphibious conductor in action!

Is The Planet Mars Inhabited?—The opponents of the doctrine of the plurality of worlds allow that a greater probability exists of Mars being inhabited than in the case of any other planet. His diameter is 4,100 miles; and his surface exhibits spots of different hues—the seas, according to accurate observation, appearing to be green, and the land red: The variety in the spots, it is thought, may arise from the planet not being destitute of atmosphere and cloud; and what adds greatly to the probability of this, is the appearance of brilliant white spots at its poles, which have been conjectured to be snow.

In part because Papa was a mariner, I became fascinated by the stars, the motion of the moon and planets, and in particular, the clouds and the weather that they often foretold. At five years of age, I could identify almost any cloud in the sky and predict the weather better than the almanac. Their morphing formations fascinated me to no end, and I would sometimes lie out in our field for hours, looking up at them as they lazily floated along in the azure heavens.

As a youngster, I drove everyone crazy with questions, and many of them involved theological inquiries of the unanswerable genre, such as: "Who made God?" or "How can God make things out of nothing?" or "How can God be everywhere?" Grandma told me that my inquisitive nature was one of my best attributes and the mark of a scholar. She cautioned me to beware of those who pretend to have all the answers, especially when it comes to religion. Her warning was well-timed and I was prepared to do battle with the foe of pretentiousness whenever it reared its ugly head. One such skirmish took place when I was beginning my third year of Sunday school.

My first two years of religious instruction at the Old South Church were enjoyable. Our teacher was the pastor's wife and she loved teaching children, having class discussions, and talking about her faith. Unfortunately, she and her husband were transferred to another district and we were without a pastor for a few weeks. Our substitute was a newcomer to Hallowell, a man who didn't seem to like anything besides intimidating and belittling youngsters. He was about fifty years old, had a scruffy beard, was balding on top, and sported greasy gray curls along the edges of his forehead. Let's just call him Mr. Down-Wind, because he had the most horrible breath one can imagine! He was a pompous, dogmatic drill sergeant who couldn't tolerate being wrong about anything, let alone find his own intelligence challenged by a child's inquisitive mind.

A YOUNG LOGICIAN. A friend of ours, up-town, has a little fair-haired youngster theologian of some four summers, who, after being, the other day, for some time lost in thought, broke out thus:

"Pa, can God do anything?"

"Yes, my son."

"Can he do everything, pa?"

"Yes, dear."

"Could he make a two-year-old colt in two minutes?"

"Why, he wouldn't wish to do that, Freddy."

"But if he did wish to, could he?"

"Yes, certainly, if he wished to."

"What! in two minutes?"

"Yes, in two minutes."

"Well, then, he wouldn't be two years old, would he?"

On our first Sunday school class of that fall session, having never set eyes on me before, Mr. Down-Wind seated me directly in front of his podium and in close range of his stinky breath. His squinty eyes scrutinized the classroom over his wire-rimmed spectacles, and like an eagle honing in on its prey, he came in for the kill.

"Young man. What is your name?" he croaked, pointing towards a young scholar.

"Jonathan, sir," the boy replied, shyly.

"Stand up when you address me, Jonathan."

"Yes, sir," he replied, nervously stumbling to his feet.

"So, Jonathan, I would like you to name one thing that God cannot do."

After a few moments, the boy responded, "Sir, I can't think of anything that God cannot do if He so wished."

"Correct! Jonathan is correct. There is nothing that God could not do if He so wished," Mr. Down-Wind declared, with unbridled arrogance. "Let's continue. Can God turn the Kennebec River into dry land?"

"Yes," a few in the class murmured.

"I will ask this again, and I expect a response from everyone this time!" he ordered.

"Can God turn the Kennebec River into dry land?"

"Yes," replied the intimidated class in unison.

"Of course He can. Scripture is clear about God's ability to do anything, and I need you to remember that…" He lost focus as his eagle eye fixed itself upon another student.

"Miss!" he yelled, pointing at Ruth Whittier. "Sit up straight! Now!"

"Your parents have all encouraged me to use this if necessary," he said, brandishing the disciplinary switch that had been lying on his podium. "Don't make it necessary!"

At this point I was starting to think I would rather be beaten mercilessly with that willow branch than endure another moment of his breath! Dear Lord, it was like something had crawled into that cavernous orifice, died, and was decomposing there. The louder and more agitated he became, the more the stench penetrated our tiny classroom. The torture dragged on for another grueling forty-five minutes, interspersed with sarcasm, threats, and ridicule. I was praying fervently that this ogre wouldn't call on me, as I couldn't be held responsible for what might come out of my mouth.

During the last fifteen minutes of Sunday school, Mr. Down-Wind challenged us to come up with a theological question that he couldn't answer. It was clear he was convinced by his own self-righteousness that there wouldn't be any.

A little girl named Emiline, who sat directly behind me, raised her hand, was acknowledged by Mr. Down-Wind, and stood humbly beside her seat waiting for permission to ask her question.

"Go ahead," he responded.

"Well, sir … why did my little sister have to die so young? Hannah was only three," Emiline inquired, with a pitiful tone.

"The wages of sin is death, my dear!" he blared, completely insensitive to the child's grief.

"Are you saying my baby sister sinned?" she asked, her voice quavering.

"Of course not! But sin *is* the reason for her death. Mark my words! Maybe someone in your family sinned, or even one of your ancestors from years ago. Your sister's death was punishment for that transgression," he uttered, coldly.

The little girl sat down, looking as though she might burst into tears.

I was incensed! Did he really believe this hogwash? I was going to have to challenge this impostor.

I turned to Emiline and whispered, "Don't listen to him. He's a dolt! God is love, Emiline."

"Miss!" barked Mr. Down-Wind, glaring at me. "If you have something you'd like to add to our discussion, I'd be delighted to hear it. If not, then face forward and keep your mouth shut."

I sat there, quietly fuming. Suddenly, an ancient paradox that Charles taught me popped into my mind. Risking the wrath of Down-Wind and his whip, I decided to take the challenge. Biting my lower lip, I raised my hand.

"Yes, Miss. What is it, now?"

I stood up and stared, unflinchingly, at my target. "I have a question for you, sir.

"Procede then. We've only a minute left."

"If God can do anything, can he make a boulder that he cannot roll?"

There was dead silence for what seemed an eternity. Down-Wind's face turned beet red, so much so that I thought his head might explode! Then he grabbed the switch and I hightailed it out of the room as fast as my little legs could carry me! "Come back here you cursed brat!" he screamed.

Meanwhile the entire class erupted in a chorus of laughter, as Down-Wind tripped over the door jam, landed splat on the ground, and his glasses and willow whip took flight! In the commotion, the other children scurried out the back door, escaping into the refreshing, sweet-smelling September air.

There were so many complaints from students and parents that Down-Wind was terminated immediately by the church elders. Thankfully, within a few weeks our beloved Reverend Rogers acquired the position of pastor at the Old South.

Chapter 3

The Truth of the Matter

Before introducing the other members of my family, I'd like to give my opinion about the whole subject of introductions. In polite society, it's proper to give a description that flatters the person being introduced, their accomplishments, schooling, important friends, and social status. How very boring! It's not that one should avoid mentioning these glittery attributes, but they only represent a kernel on the cob, so to speak.

Pretend you've been invited to hear a lecture by a well-known orator. He is introduced as follows: "I have the distinguished honor of presenting to you, Dr. I. M. Splendid. He holds a PhD in Mathematical Science and Astronomy, has held posts at both Harvard and Yale, and is currently touring the country, giving lectures. Here he is, Dr. Splendid!"

Now, let's hear the same introduction, but with a little more truth added: "I have the distinguished honor of presenting to you, Dr. I. M. Splendid. He holds a PhD in Mathematical Science and Astronomy, which he was given in compensation for his wealthy family's donations to the institution. He has held posts at both Harvard and Yale, but was fired from both for excessive carousing and is currently unemployed and touring the country, giving lectures to make ends meet. His wife has temporarily banished him from the household. Here he is, Dr. Splendid!"

Now, honestly, which of those introductions is more interesting?

A silly example, but you can see my point. I've learned that we are all more than our accomplishments. We are full of imperfections, idiosyncrasies, sufferings, joys, contradictions, and nagging faults. We are considerably flawed and beautifully unique, all at once! Mindful of this, I will reconstruct the personalities of those who made up my family through anecdotes and stories that show them in their true light, so that you might be properly introduced.

What was it like to have a father who commanded the high seas? Men of that genre are often the object of stereotypical thinking: "They are all drunkards, loud and boisterous, hard-shelled, mean-spirited, godless, tyrannical fathers and abusive husbands." Yes, I have known a few who were like that. But those deplorable traits are not relegated only to sea-faring men. Any person can be a brute, male or female. My father was not of that character. Father, Papa, or Captain John Andrew Goodwin,[7] which was how Mother addressed him when exasperated, were some of his titles. The most popular term of endearment (used by us children, and occasionally, Mother) was "Mon cher Papa," a French phrase that quickly alerted him that we were up to something.

One needed only to glance at him to know he was a man of the sea, tall, stocky, and broad-shouldered. He had a loud, compelling voice, developed by years of shouting orders. When angry, he could sound like the trumpets of the Almighty during the battle of Armageddon! Should one of us misbehave, his face would get bright red with rage and his iconic beard would take on a disheveled and frightening appearance … you'd better listen up, or else! Or else what? Well, you might encounter more scolding, be threatened within an inch of your life, or silently glared at, but the very worst fate—and all of us children agreed—was to be sent to Mother! This was the final and most horrific form of punishment. If you were sent to her, you had better be prepared to lose some enjoyable activities for an extended period of time. The threat alone usually did the trick and rarely needed to be carried out to produce its intended results.

I did see Papa get so furious once that he paddled Charles's behind. It did no good, though it probably made Father feel better. My brother feigned some remorsefulness, and a few crocodile tears trickled down his face. Then he hid himself away in the woodshed and laughed himself into a frenzy until his stomach ached far more than his bottom.

What was his crime? Well, it all started in August 1855, when Father noticed that there were groundhogs burrowing and eating the lettuce in the garden. Ten-year-old Charles pleaded with Papa and was given the auspicious job of ridding the field of the varmints.

My brother had been learning to shoot Grandpa's[8] Brown Bess musket, which last saw service during Maine's involvement in the War of 1812. Prior to that, it was taken from a fallen British soldier during the Revolution, or so the story goes. Anyone using this antique needed both patience and luck to successfully discharge it. The beast weighed a ton and was quite inaccurate, even when fired at close range by an experienced soldier.

> BLEW HIS ROOF OFF. A correspondent writes us that an honest but not over-cautious old farmer, living in Winslow, had a keg of powder for blasting purposes, which he kept in the attic of his house. Going up to fill a bottle from it one night, a few weeks since, he got his candle in contact with the powder and an explosion took place that knocked the old fellow several times his length, and deposited the roof of his house in the yard.

Charles,[9] as strong a little farmhand as ever there was, could barely hold the thing in a horizontal position for more than a few seconds. Grandpa told us that a good soldier could load and fire three shots per minute. With Charles, it was more like three minutes per shot. First, he had to measure and load a fixed amount of gunpowder into the barrel, then he'd take a musket ball, wrap it in a greasy lint patch and ram it down the barrel. After that, he had to "prime the pan" with a small amount of powder, flip the frizzen back over the pan, cock back the lock (once, into safety, then again, into firing position), hoist and steady the cumbersome artifact, and finally, sight the target. Ready! … Aim! … "Fzzzztt" … but no bang! Flintlocks seemed to misfire more often than not. It's a wonder that we ever won our independence with those infernal things! Of course, King George's men also shouldered the same mechanical nightmares, and this was one of theirs.

I was present when Charles first loaded and fired the gun by himself. My dear God! He nearly blew off his left foot! It was hilarious and frightening at once. The second time was more successful, as he missed his foot by about five yards. I told him he should rest the gun on the fence to stabilize it. At first he pretended to hate the idea, no doubt, because it was mine. But, eventually he tried it and found it effective. One problem was solved, but there was a larger one to confront. Groundhogs, dumb as they may be, are not gonna just quietly "assume the position" and wait 'til the gun is loaded, pan is primed, and the musket is stabilized. Needless to say, once he was ready, there were no varmints anywhere to be seen. Poor Charles. Oh well, he'd try a new trick tomorrow. He was not one to quit and considered the day a triumph for having kept both feet attached to his legs.

The next day, Charles realized the futility of shooting groundhogs and came up with a new scheme that he'd read about in some adventure book. He decided to take one of Father's small, square seining nets and set a trap for the unsuspecting critter. He placed the square net on the ground, tied each corner with a piece of twine, and attached the four loose ends to the top of a small poplar tree, which he bent to the ground. Finally, he affixed a pull-string, fastening it to a small stake that anchored the contrivance in place. This was no easy task and there were several disasters along the way, but eventually he got his functioning trap. Then, having obtained some fish, lettuce, and leftovers from the evening meal, he placed it all in the center of the net in hopes that Mr. Groundhog would come out for lunch. These animals are generally herbivorous, but they will occasionally eat grubs, snails, and other delicacies of animal origin. Just to make sure that the net was concealed, he covered the exposed portion with a thin layer of dirt. Once his foe was on the netting Charlie would yank out the stake and the tree would do the rest of the work, trapping the prize in the net.

More than once, we had to chase the cats away from the culinary delights prepared for our chubby friend. The waiting was tedious and we were beginning to wonder if our ploy would work at all. But at high noon the groundhog popped its paunchy body out of the hole and started to sniff the air. He waddled over to the concoction in the center of the trap. Once the unsuspecting victim was squarely planted over the net, Charles gave the pull-string a strong, firm yank and the groundhog was airborne.

"Got him!" yelled Charles. The poor creature was struggling frantically but to no avail, and my brother was beside himself with excitement! However, there was a part of his scheme he'd not accounted for. What to do with the animal once trapped?

I screamed at him, "What do we do now, Charles? Please don't kill him!"

"I won't hurt him, Annie. I'll take him far away, into the woods out back."

"No, Charles! We've got to do something now! He's starting to chew through the net!"

"I've got a great idea," my brother assured me.

Charles cut down the struggling beast and carefully held the upper part of the net so as not to get bitten or clawed. "Hey, Annie," he said, "let's put him in the kindling box and make something to carry him in. Maybe we can use one of Momma's apple crates."

The kindling box, which resided in the summer kitchen, had a latch on it, so the groundhog couldn't escape on its own. Little did we know that the prisoner would soon have an accomplice! We deposited the rambunctious culprit into the box, secured the latch, and proceeded to the barn to create a rodent-removal rig.

In the meantime, Mother, who had come into the summer kitchen to cut up some greens for dinner, heard a queer scratching sound coming from the kindling box. Naturally our young hounds, George and Martha, were sniffing at the lid and barking in response to the groundhog's clamor.

MUMMIES PUT TO USE.—Egypt has three hundred miles of railroad. The first locomotive run, mummies were used for fuel, making a hot fire. The supply of mummies is said to be almost inexhaustible, and are used by the cord. How little could the ancient Egyptians have dreamed of being put to a use like this!

"What on earth?" Mother asked under her breath, "Did Charlie put one of the cats in there again?"

In the meantime, Charles and I had finally located some nails, a hammer, and an open apple crate, when we heard the earth-shattering scream. We stampeded into the house and entered upon a scene that could only be rivaled by the last moments of Pompeii! Dogs racing, knocking over chairs, smashing into walls, leaping over furniture; Mother running with a meat cleaver like a mad-woman, and shrieking oaths I'd never heard before! Eventually, the hounds cornered the critter in the woodshed, but it slipped under the outhouse door and entered that odiferous "Throne Room," as we affectionately called it. Well, at least the flying blob of fur was contained! Now we had to catch the criminal and put him on trial for his crimes.

Father came running in and wanted to know what the ruckus was about. After a brief summary, given by our semi-incapacitated mother, Father turned towards Charles and put the question to him, "Did you have anything to do with this, Charles Andrew Goodwin?"

My brother tried to explain, but Father glared at him in such a way as to make him envious of the groundhog's fate. "I'll catch him, Father ... I promise!" stammered Charles.

Charles gently opened the outhouse door and peered in. And there he was, perched on the seat of the two-holer, sitting on his haunches like a fat, furry pot-belly stove! On seeing Charles, he instinctively dove into the left hole, probably expecting the pleasantries of his burrow, only to plop into a nauseating soup of human waste!

"Oh my God! The critter's in the shitter! The critter's in the shitter!" yelled Charles. "He just fell in! What are we going to do? We've got to get him out! He's gonna drown in the shitter!"

Our neighbor, Beth, who had been tending my three-year-old twin siblings, entered the shed with the boys. Unfortunately, little Johnny and Frankie had overheard Charles's expletives and were giggling, taking turns chirping, "Crittah in the shittah ... Crittah in the shittah." Hilarious belly-laughs followed each citation.

Mother was not amused. "Thank you Charlie," she growled, "for teaching my babies some new rhyming words!"

Meanwhile, Papa had come up with a plan. "OK, Charles, go get my sturgeon net, and get it, NOW!"

My brother returned immediately with the net, but it was far too wide to fit through either hole. So Papa and Charles removed the entire plank and set it aside. As we squinted down into the dark, malodorous depths, we spotted our arch-enemy paddling frantically among the floating globs of fecal matter. Papa tried to reach the beast, but the net handle was a foot too short to make the catch. After several tries he turned and looked at Charles with a sinister grin.

"No ... No, Father ... I'll do your chores for a week! I'll be nice to my dumb sister! I'll do anything you want!" But negotiations were off the table.

Father gave Charles the net, and picking him up by the ankles, lowered him into the smelly, dark netherworld.

"How is it down there, Charlie?" I teased in retribution for calling me dumb.

"Shut up, Annie!" he barked back.

Finally, after a few unsuccessful tries, Charles snared the groundhog, and Father hoisted him out of the mire along with his squirmy goo-covered prize. My brother was as white as a sheet and gagging like he was going to puke up a horse! But, after a few deep breaths of fresh air he was much revived.

"Charles," said Father, looking sternly at my brother, "do ya have any idea how tempted I was to let ya go for a swim with your buddy?"

In the aftermath, there was a huge mess to clean up, including a broken oil lamp and the shattered cups, saucers, and dinner plates destroyed in the mayhem. The groundhog was sentenced to death by firing squad, but chewed his way through the net and escaped before Papa could get the musket ready. Charles had worked hard to earn his "token spanking" and never regretted a single moment of the whole escapade.

Ladies and gentlemen, my big brother, Charles Andrew Goodwin!

Chapter 4

Frankie and Johnny

I was taught a handful of little prayers when I was small. My first prayer, one you may have learned as well, went like this: "Now I lay me down to sleep, I pray the Lord my soul to keep. If I should die before I wake, I pray the Lord my soul to take." Though I never thought much about it then, I now believe it to be a frightful prayer for little children to recite, especially right before they fall to sleep. In the 1850s, death seemed to be all around us, lurking in the dark around every corner. Nearly every home had lost a child or two by some dreadful disease. Sometimes, entire families were wiped out when an epidemic hit the area. The reaper was always in the wings, waiting to make its swift, unwelcome appearance.

My twin brothers, Franklin Davis Goodwin and John Davis Goodwin, were born on November 28, 1852, when I was three and Charles was seven. The Davis name was derived from my uncle Franklin Davis,[10] who married Momma's sister, Mary Ann Kean.[11] John was named after Papa. These two were fraternal twins, as different as night and day. Johnny had dark hair like Father and Frankie had light auburn hair like my own. Both were highly intelligent, but little Johnny was the risk-taker of the two and for that reason had to be watched constantly.

One of Johnny's memorable escapades took place a month or two after his second birthday. None of us could find him anywhere in the house, and Mother was frantic. We were aghast to find the wooden top to the well removed and lying on the ground nearby. Mother, the first to reach the shaft, peered in. "Thank the Good Lord, he's not in there!" she exclaimed, with relief. But where could he be? We were all yelling his name at the top of our lungs. Soon, Father joined the rescue party.

On entering the barn, we heard a clatter coming from somewhere above us. Suddenly, a flock of vexed barn swallows swooped down towards us, coming within inches of our heads! Because we had just come in from the bright sunlight it took a few moments for our eyes to adjust to the shadowy lofts. Suddenly we heard it, that ominous giggle coming from the heavens above! The little monster had climbed a ladder and was standing nonchalantly on a high, narrow beam. With arms flapping like a bird, he yelled, "Pa-pa, look! Birdie." Father gasped and started immediately up the ladder to try to coax his prankish namesake back across the beam. Meanwhile the barn swallows continued making angry, threatening circles all around us, as Johnny continued to laugh and flap his "wings," slowly tiptoeing his way over to Papa. Just as he got within Father's grasp, the little imp turned around and proceeded back to the center of the beam, tweeting and mimicking his avian companions.

Without a second thought, Papa stepped out onto the beam, which was barely as wide as his boot, inched his way over, and grabbed Johnny's hand. Together they moved carefully back toward safety as the rest of us held our breath. Finally, the two stepped onto safe footing, the solid floor of the upper level of the loft. With his risky mission accomplished, Papa gave the little boy a big hug and a stern warning, "Don't you ever do that to us again, you little demon!" Well, he never did that again, but he found other creative variations on the theme to keep us in a state of panic much of the time.

Little Frankie, however, was of a totally different character. He loved to play with the dogs and cats, and was always gentle with anything newborn. We could trust him to occupy himself when he was alone, even for several hours. If he was told to do something he would do it, and you wouldn't have to ask him twice; it was his nature. Unlike his twin, he would never attempt anything deliberately dangerous, and always asked permission to do new things. Frankie adored his adventurous twin, and would gladly give up his favorite toy if Johnny wanted it.

One of my fondest recollections of Frankie was when Mother came back from market with three wooden boxes full of new Mason canning jars. She was tired and decided to leave the task of storing them until morning. When she came downstairs the next day she found all the jars neatly stacked and thanked me for putting them away.

"Momma," I replied, "I didn't put those away. It must have been Charlie or Papa." But before we had time to ask them, Frankie arrived on the scene, ran into the pantry and pointed at the jars. He was grinning from ear to ear with pride. He must have come down very early, as no one had heard or seen him do the work. Mother picked him up and smothered him with kisses.

One beautiful afternoon in late April, the twins, Momma, and I rode into Gardiner to attend a spring fair on the commons. There were several types of exotic animals, a few monkeys, two beautiful macaws, and a huge boa constrictor which Frankie adored. We were even allowed to pet the formidable creature! There were lots of tasty things to eat and drink and a variety of games to play. A military band serenaded the crowd from the gazebo. But the highlight of the afternoon was a hot-air balloon, piloted by a friend of Father who worked at the Pittston shipyard. Overall, we had a splendid time.

From *Harper's Monthly,* 1862

On the train ride back to Hallowell, we all started feeling a bit under the weather. By the time the ferry had carried us over the Kennebec to the Chelsea side, we had painful stomach cramps and nausea. We'd barely made it home before we found ourselves dashing for the outhouse. Mother and I jumped on the two-holer with only seconds to spare. But the twins, unfortunately, never made it to the chamber pots that our babysitter had laid out for them, poor things. Afterwards, Momma and I felt somewhat relieved, but still queasy. The twins, however, continued to go and go. At first the whole incident seemed rather humorous, as we believed our plight to be nothing more than a quick bout of indigestion, or at worst, a mild case of food poisoning. However, by the second day the symptoms had become worse for the twins, and a dangerous situation was brewing. Dehydration had begun to take its toll on their tiny bodies. Their sunken eyes were surrounded by dark circles and their skin was beginning to wrinkle. Despite our best efforts, we were unable to get them to keep any liquids down. It was frightening to helplessly watch the malady progress from bad to worse, and from worse to desperate.

I was too young to grasp the severity of the crisis, never dreaming it might come down to a life-and-death struggle. However, Momma wasn't under any such illusions. She slept with the twins in the bed chamber directly above the parlor, where Johnny and Frankie cried and mumbled deliriously throughout the night. They even began to suffer painful muscle spasms that came on without warning, especially during those rare moments of much-needed rest.

At dawn, on the third morning of their illness, Papa entered the sickroom and Mother greeted him, a heap of soiled bedding in her hands. "Oh John, I fear the boys have something far worse than food poisoning!" she exclaimed, in a panicked tone that was clearly not meant for my vigilant ears to overhear.

"Calm, dear one. Tell me." he asked.

Mother blurted out her dread in a frantic, gasping crescendo, "They're both having these awful milky runs! I've had to change the sheets twice since last evening. The poor things are just too weak to make it to the chamber pot! It's pitiful. They're not holding anything down. They've got cholera, John, I'm sure of it! We need to fetch Doc Davis." Then, within a big sigh, she whispered, "I'm very, very frightened."

"Sarah, dear, don't worry, they're tough little boys. They take after this hardy old sea dog. They'll be just fine. But, it can't hurt to have someone with medical expertise around. I'll go into town and fetch the doc, but ya need to get some rest! Let Beth take over with the boys."

"No! I can't. They need me," she insisted. "And John, if Davis isn't available, fetch Ellen. She'll know what to do. She's treated cholera before."

"Of course. Should I get anything for the twins while I'm in Hallowell?"

"No. Just come back as quickly as possible," Mother replied.

Papa gave Mother a gentle, reassuring kiss on the forehead, hitched up the wagon and left for town.

Cholera epidemics had assailed New England in three waves between 1832 and 1866. We were now ascending the crest of the third. Father, unable to find Doc Davis returned with Ellen Springer, Mother's cousin, who was a highly regarded midwife with many years of experience in the Chelsea-Hallowell area. She was bluntly honest, confirming that it was indeed cholera that was squeezing the life out of my little brothers. But she was determined to do all she could, volunteering to stay with us for the duration. Her medicinal supplies consisted of aromatic concoctions of spearmint and camomile, as well as several types of juices, which would only be helpful if her little patients were able to retain them.

The fear written on Momma's face and those of the other adults, penetrated deeply into my own heart. When you're little, your emotional world is governed by those around you. Their joy becomes your joy, and their worry becomes yours as well, even if you don't understand why you're afraid. My mind was on heightened alert and I eavesdropped on every conversation within earshot, listening in for that dreaded word again: cholera. The frequency and intensity of the hushed remarks told me that something serious was afoot. One night, I jumped into bed with Mother, who was, once again, with the little invalids.

"Annie, dear. You've got to go back to your own bed. Get some sleep, sweet one; it's midnight," she said, lovingly.

"Momma, I just can't sleep. What's gonna happen to the twins? Are they going to die?" I whispered.

"I think they'll recover, dear. The midwife is right here with us. Ellen knows what to do to help children get better. She even managed to get a little tea into both of them tonight," she reassured me.

"But why didn't we get sick like the boys?" I asked.

"Well, it's like other illnesses, dear. Remember when we all had that stomach complaint last year? You and I had it bad, but the boys only had mild cases? It's the same with this."

Despite Mother's reassuring words, I felt the knots in my stomach tightening. "Momma, I'm so scared. Can I sleep here with you, near the boys?

Mother then got up, took me by the hand, and walked me back into my little room across the hallway. Then she sat down on my bed and took my hand in hers.

"Annie," she began, "we have to remember that God is with us. He loves us and He's always watching over us. Remember, not even a little sparrow falls to earth without his knowledge."

"If He loves us, why are my brothers so sick? Can't He make them better? He healed lots of people in the Bible."

"Of course He can, dear. He can do anything He wants to do."

"Why wouldn't he want to?"

"Well, sometimes he allows things to happen that seem bad at the time. But later, sometimes years later, we begin to understand that it was for the greater good."

CHOLERA PREVENTED BY SALT WATER BATHING —It is well known among the medical profession that persons who are in the frequent habit of salt water bathing, are seldom if ever attacked with cholera, or other diseases incident to warm weather, and a relaxation of the physical powers of the body.

"But how can letting my brothers die be for the good?" I insisted.

"Well, dear, God knows what's best for us in this life. We have to have faith that if He takes away something that we treasure, He does it for a reason. Our souls and those of our loved ones go on forever, and we will see them again," she explained.

I wasn't convinced, but I gave her a big hug regardless. After returning my hug, Mother retired to the boys' chamber, leaving me alone with my thoughts, and some of those thoughts were disturbing. For the first time, I was beginning to have nagging questions about God's existence and the afterlife. How could the death of a child be anything but evil, and why would a loving God permit it?

The following morning, little Johnny spoke his first intelligible sentence in two full days. A feeble little voice whispered, "Momma, I'm hungry." We were filled with joy and relief! He was able to hold down the assortment of liquids that provided the necessary nourishment for his recovery. As soon as we were sure that he was clearly out of the woods we gently moved him, and his small cot to the summer kitchen. But little Frankie was not improving at all. On the contrary, his pupils had dilated, his breathing and pulse were rapid, and his hands and feet were turning blue. Sometime, just after noon, Ellen called Mother and Father aside, informing them that their little boy had gone into shock and the outcome was now in the Creator's hands.

Shortly after that dire prognosis, a violent thunderstorm rolled in with winds that shook the walls while hail the size of musket balls hammered the windows. A small glass sidelight in our front entry was shattered by a chunk of ice. It was as though nature had conspired with the dark forces in an overture of impending doom. The knots in my stomach continued to tighten. Finally, at about two-thirty, the rain stopped, the black clouds parted, and the sun began to shine through. The barnyard was full of melting hail pellets that sparkled and shimmered in the bright sunlight.

"You see, Annie," proclaimed Mother, "light has conquered the darkness, after all."

I was relieved for the moment. But soon an ominous silence, more terrifying than the storm, enveloped the household. We waited, hoping against hope for a glimmer of life to appear on Frankie's emaciated countenance. During the marking of those painful moments my little room became a sanctuary. I knelt down and prayed fervently at my bedside, then ventured to see if any meaningful change had occurred as a result. Then I would return to my "chapel," only to perform the same ritual time and time again.

The bedchamber was now full to capacity. Grandma and Grandpa Kean, Mamma, Papa, Ellen, Beth, Charlie, myself, and even our dogs waited silently at the foot of the bed, tending to the frail form who had given us so much joy. We had now replaced all conversation with painful, quiet glances, which spoke more intensely than words. The death watch had begun.

Around three p.m., Frankie's breathing became more shallow, and shortly after, the unmistakable death rattle began. This distressing development went on for a short time and then, all at once, he became quiet. A little after four in the afternoon, Ellen positioned a looking-glass near his nose to check for breathing and then checked his pulse. For the next few minutes she continued to repeat the procedure. Finally, with a painful grimace, she turned towards us, saying, "I'm sorry. Your little boy is with the angels now."

At that very moment, a bluebird fluttered noisily and landed on the open windowsill. It perched there calmly as though paying its respects and then took flight, back into the azure heavens. It was Tuesday, 4:20 p.m., May 6, 1856. My sweet, kindhearted little brother was dead.

I stood there frozen. How could this be? Just a few days ago, I was playing marbles with him in the barnyard. He was so full of life and laughter and goodness. Why would God take him? Why would God take someone who brought so much joy to our world? Why?

I suddenly threw myself on his little body, grabbing and shaking him by his lifeless shoulders. "Get up!" I shouted, refusing to let go of him. "Get up, Frankie! … Please, God! Please get up." Father pulled me away and hugged me as I struggled and screamed. Finally, after a few minutes of wailing I gave in, exhausted from the ordeal, and we hugged and consoled one another in the unity of our shared loss. Even nature reached out a kind hand, as a solitary late afternoon sunbeam fell gently on Frankie's peaceful face. His suffering was over.

Chapter 5

Death-days and Flowers

I must have aged ten years in the days that followed. I was not yet seven but I felt like an old woman. My thoughts were dark and my heart was broken; the magical world of childhood had collapsed before my eyes. Reality, with its fleeting moments of joy and its lengthy intervals of sorrow, began to set in.

On Tuesday evening, Papa and Charles constructed the small coffin that would house Frankie's remains. To make his body appear to be in gentle repose, they placed his tiny form on soft, cushioned fabric overlaying some hay. He was then brought into the parlor for the viewing.

Commonly, wakes and funerals were held in the homes of the deceased. There was no need for announcements in those days, as word of mouth was faster than the telegraph in our small community. A few relatives were at sea, but most lived nearby and received notification within twenty-four hours. Those attending would bring food, baked goods, or other tokens of good will for the grieving family. Frankie's ceremony was set for Friday, May 9, at the end of the customary three-day grieving period, to be followed by graveside prayers and burial.

At that time, odd traditions and superstitious beliefs abounded with respect to the passing of a loved one. Often, people would draw the curtains and stop the clocks at the exact moment of death. Mirrors would sometimes be draped with veils to prevent the spirit of the deceased from getting trapped within them. Some families made sure that the corpse was carried out of the house feet first in order that its spirit not look back and summon another family member to accompany it to the grave. A few families even turned their photographs and portrait paintings face down to stop any other relative from becoming possessed by the soul of the dearly departed.

Thankfully, our family wasn't superstitious, and our customs were simple. We held a three-day wake, displayed a wreath on the front door sporting a ribbon with Frankie's name embroidered on it, and wore traditional black clothing during the days leading up to and including the burial.

Once my brother's body was at rest in the parlor, there was one other task that needed to be initiated, contacting a daguerreotypist to capture an image of my little brother *in the slumber of death.*

Daguerreotypes were one-of-a-kind images, not reproducible like those that would soon follow. Earlier versions involved a minute of sitting time, and the camera obscura lens was opened for the duration in order to absorb the necessary light. Any movement would blur the image. Often, an iron neck brace had to be placed behind the subject to make sure that no perceivable motion occurred. Therefore, most daguerreotypes were very somber things, as maintaining a serious face was the best way to ensure a clear image. The morbid postmortem photos, as they were so aptly named, were not only somber but downright creepy!

At the time, photography was in its infancy and every grieving family wanted a memento of their departed one. Mourning rings and brooches, made from locks of hair from the dead, had been popular for centuries. However, to actually own the true likeness of a person was a remarkable novelty, and thought by many to be the most meaningful way to immortalize the deceased. These "death-dags," as I called them, may have helped some folks remember their loved ones, but the ghastly images terrified me! I wanted nothing to do with having to look at a photographic image of my dead brother every time I gazed over at the mantle. I wanted to remember the beautiful, loving boy that he was in life!

My abhorrence of these enframed nightmares came from the macabre extremes that some folks went to in order to obtain a photo. One variant was for a grieving mother to hold the dead child as though it was sleeping, an unthinkably cruel torture for a bereaved mother. Another was to pry open the eyes of the deceased, dress the body in formal attire, and prop up the corpse in a chair in order to make it appear alive. I saw one of these at a friend's home, once; those dead eyes looking straight ahead into my own, I couldn't sleep for a week!

There were daguerreotypists close by, but we were not in any condition to seek them out. However, our helpful neighbor, Mr. Blanchard, located Mr. Thomas Thwing, a photographer from Gardiner, and inquired as to his availability. Much to my dismay, he was available, and arrived at about two o'clock that day. He took three exposures and promised to select the best of the three to encase. Then, after less than an hour, Father escorted him to the ferry.

During this interim, Johnny's health was improving. He was able to move around a bit, but was still very weak and needed to take frequent rests. The poor child was unaware that he would never play with his best friend again. Mother was the one to break the heart-wrenching news to the little boy, who immediately demanded to see his brother. Father reluctantly carried the fatigued child into the parlor, where his brother lay in state. He ran to the side of the coffin and tapped several times on Frankie's lifeless hand.

"Why doesn't he wake up, Papa? He won't wake up!" He then looked at each of us in turn, as if waiting for an explanation. Silently, big tears began to run down his little cheeks as the irreversibility of the situation took hold. He ran into Papa's arms, crying and wailing as we surrounded him with hugs.

I took the little mourner aside in an attempt to help him understand what had happened, *using a seven-year-old's version of theology.*

"Johnny, our little brother is dead, but his spirit will live on forever and ever," I said.

"What is a spi-wit?" he asked, wiping the tears with his shirtsleeve.

"Well … it's the part that we love. All the happy things we remember, his laugh, the things he liked to do, all those special things that made him our Frankie," I responded.

"Does a spi-wit have eyes? Can he see me?" he questioned.

"Yes, Johnny. He can see all of us, but we can't see him. He's in heaven."

"I wanna go to heaven wite now!" he demanded.

"Oh, my sweet little brother," I exclaimed, giving him a big bear hug. "Heaven is the place where God lives. Everybody is happy there. There's no pain or suffering or sadness. But you can't go there until God says it's time, and not a minute before. And it's not time for you to go, Johnny."

"When will it be time?" he asked, between tears.

"When God comes to get you, like he did Frankie," I responded, stroking his hair.

"Did Fwankie see God come to get him?" He inquired.

"Yes, he saw God the moment he left us."

"Did you see God, too, Annie?"

"No. But a bluebird landed on the windowsill the very moment Frankie died. I think his little soul followed it straight up to heaven."

Johnny sat quietly for a minute or two. Then he walked over to the tiny coffin, lifted his deceased brother's hand and kissed it affectionately. He turned to me, imparted a look that said, "Thank you," and Papa escorted him back to his bed.

After that conversation, I felt a sense of disquiet that stemmed from my uncertainty about an afterlife, and having presented heaven as a fact to my grieving brother. True, there was the bluebird's timely appearance, but did it really mean anything? When I asked Momma how she knew I'd see Frankie again, she responded, "It's all written in the Good Book, Annie. It's God's word." But I was a hard sell, even as a little child. Franklin's death triggered the onset of a crisis of faith that would hound me for years. But my quest for a resolution would have to wait. The funeral preparation was at hand.

Thursday was a blur of activity in preparation for the guests. Many kind neighbors stopped by with food and bouquets of flowers, thus encouraging Mother to escape from her isolation and redirect her thoughts from grief to appreciation. Beth kept the place tidy and attended to other needs, while my grandparents, Uncle James, and others rotated in shifts during the round-the-clock wake. I attempted to engage little Johnny in games and other activities in order to brighten his spirits, but being greatly fatigued from his battle with cholera, he couldn't endure more than a few minutes of recreation.

As Friday morning broke, clear and bright, I lay there in my bed thinking that this was the last day I would ever see Frankie's earthly face. As I looked in on Johnny, who was sleeping soundly, I could see all of Frankie's favorite toys neatly arranged on the shelf, right where he had last placed them with his own tiny hands. The morning sunlight, dispersing through the window panes, illuminated the picture book of wild animals that he and I had spent hours perusing and discussing. All his little things were there, but he wasn't.

As an overwhelming sorrow engulfed me, I realized that my grief was but a shadow of Johnny's. Franklin was his best buddy in the whole world. They spent almost every waking moment together. I approached the bundle of blankets that wrapped the tiny sleeper, bent over and kissed him on the forehead. As I did so, I whispered, "I will never ever abandon you, Johnny. I will be everything that Frankie was for you."

Beth arrived early and cooked us a wonderful breakfast. Even Mother was up and back in command of the Goodwin crew, determined to greet the day without surrendering to any outward signs of her inner sorrow. Flowers adorned every niche of the parlor, bringing life to an otherwise morbid day. As I sat there with Charles, lost in memories, little Johnny entered and lovingly placed Frankie's wild animal book in the casket to be buried with his brother. That tender moment left me breathless, and its image has remained with me throughout the years, as though it were yesterday.

At mid-morning, the newly-taken daguerreotype arrived by parcel and Father positioned it as the centerpiece on the parlor mantle. The plate, itself, was enshrined in an elaborate brown *gutta-percha* case which was outwardly adorned by an embossed sleeping lion—one of Frankie's favorite animals! Glass covered the fragile plate that closed against a velvet green cushion for safe storage. The photographer even managed to appease my disgust by capturing my brother's likeness in a gentle, closeup image, eliminating any sign of a coffin. Frankie did truly appear to be sleeping.

Reverend Rogers,[12] from the Old South[13] in Hallowell, arrived promptly at noon and spent the better part of an hour consoling our grief-stricken family. He was a joyful soul who was dearly loved by everyone who knew him. His mere presence brightened the gloom with an aura of hope.

Once everything was ready, the Reverend summoned the mourners to gather in the parlor and began by recounting a true story that occurred after his grandfather's death.

"Well," he remarked, "I don't like preachin' to people 'bout things that are so high and lofty that nobody here on earth can understand them, or probably even cares to understand them."

There were a few muted chuckles from the crowd.

"Whenever possible, I like to relate examples from my own personal experience that help confirm what this Good Book says about the issue at hand, which in this case is the passing of little Franklin.

"Unfortunately, as is too often the case, I am called upon to officiate at a funeral and assist the poor souls who are grievin' and strugglin' to make sense of their loss. That said, it is exceedingly more burdensome when the deceased is a youngster, one so recently full of laughter and life. So, I will do my best to recount an event that brought me to understand death in a whole new light, and played an instrumental part in leadin' me to become a man of the cloth, as they say.

"When I was but a couple years older than little Johnny, here, I lost my dearest friend and confidant, my grandpa. He loved to sit and smoke a pipe in his high-back, Revolutionary War armchair, upon which he had installed rockers. I loved going to his house. I would sit on his lap and we'd tell jokes, laugh, read stories, and talk about God. We always ended our time together with a prayer or two. Of course, I asked lots of questions. One day I asked him if God could stop time from passing. After a few moments of quiet thought, he answered, 'That there's one of the most mind-boggling questions anyone's ever asked me. And frankly, I don't know how to even begin to respond.' Grandpa was always honest, and he never tried to make up answers to things just to sound smart.

"Well, anyway, one day Grandpa got real sick and couldn't rock me anymore. The evening before he left this world, I stood at his bedside and he spoke these words to me: 'I'll see you again, you know.' The next morning Momma told me Grandpa had passed during the night. I was beside myself in grief. I couldn't sleep, didn't want to eat, and I was mad as hell at God … 'scuse me, but 'twas the truth.

"It was the dead of winter when he passed, and the night after the funeral there was a ferocious nor'easter. Grandpa's body had been taken to the crypt for safe keepin', 'til the spring burial. I went to bed, as I imagine you good folk will do as soon as this is all said and done. But I couldn't sleep even though I was unspeakably tired. Suddenly, I smelled something very, very familiar, a pleasant aroma that had wound its way up the staircase into my bedchamber. It was the odor of tobacco from Grandpa's pipe! No mistakin' it! Nobody in my family smoked. So, I ran downstairs as fast as my feet would carry me. And there by the door stood Grandpa! I could not believe my eyes! He just stood there and smiled at me, with the most heavenly grin I ever saw. I hightailed it upstairs to get Momma, but when we got back there, Grandpa had vanished.

"You're all probably thinking 'twas the imagination of a sad little boy, and that would be a reasonable assumption 'cept for one minor detail; my good parents and my big sister all smelled the tobacco that night, and its scent lasted 'til sunrise! The door to the outside was still locked, and there were no footprints anywhere to be found in the newly fallen snow. So, if any of us had entertained any doubts about the reality of an afterlife, they were removed that night.

"So, my beloved, Jesus says, 'I go to prepare a place for you.' Do I believe it? I would stake my life on it. I'm sure Grandpa will be very happy to keep little Frankie amused until we join 'em. God bless you all."

At about two-thirty in the afternoon, the mourners reassembled and made their way down the road, escorting the horse-drawn wagon with Frankie's tiny coffin. Father and Charles sat at the helm. Mother, her parents, little Johnny, and I rode in a separate, borrowed carriage behind Father. When we arrived at the graveyard,[14] we walked down the well-trodden path to where the Goodwin-Kean burial lot silently awaited Frankie's remains. Only our lovely, eighteen-year-old Auntie Belle, who had died of consumption the year before, was entered in this lonely place. Her remains would now be joined by the company of her nephew, Franklin. The tiny grave had already been dug, and after a few heartfelt prayers, my little brother was lowered into the ground. Charles, Johnny, and I each threw a rose onto the coffin, and two of Father's friends shoveled the dirt back into the grave. I'll never forget that eerie hollow sound of each clod of earth hitting the casket, echoing the emptiness of our own hearts.

Then the mourners dispersed, a few at a time until our family alone was left at the gravesite. Poor Mother, in her black dress and veil, was transfixed. All I could think of was Jesus' mother, Mary, at the foot of the cross, unable to change what must be. After a time, Father gently put his arm around her and escorted her back to the carriage. No one spoke on the ride back to the farm and even nature seemed to be cooperating out of respect; the air was still, the birds were silent, and all we could hear was the sound of the carriage wheels turning and the horses' hooves keeping time.

———

The next few months were difficult ones, especially for Johnny. I'd often find him alone, sitting on his bedroom floor, playing with some of Frankie's toys. He was beginning to show that deep sensitivity that Frankie had demonstrated in such abundance. Seemingly overnight, he became more thoughtful and less impulsive. I actually began to miss the old unpredictable "risky" side of him, and was never quite sure if the change was a healthy one or not.

I did my best to fill Frankie's shoes and Johnny seemed to appreciate my efforts. I climbed trees, played soldier, caught worms for fishing, went on adventures in the woods, and even tried to trap a bobcat that had been after our chickens. One evening, Johnny asked me to help him build a survival shelter out in the woods. I tried to help, but nothing I did was right. The branches were too small, the area I chose was too open, and there wasn't enough cover to stop the rain from coming in.

Suddenly, he turned and glared at me with a scowl. "Stop it!" he yelled. "Just stop it!" There were tears in his eyes.

"What did I do?" I asked, bewildered.

"I want Fwankie!" he screamed, at the top of his lungs.

My first emotion was rage. I had spent the last three months doing everything to be the companion that I thought he needed me to be. I'd given up hours of my own valuable playtime and devoted them to him! I had joined in all of his escapades, trying to be a stinky, snotty, snake-catchin', mud-covered boy!

"Finish this stupid shelter yourself," I spouted, and walked away in a huff. When I reached the house, I pounded each step of the stairwell to make sure everyone in Chelsea was aware that Princess Ann was not pleased! Then I jumped on my bed and cried in loud, wailing yelps, in hopes that Mother or Father or *somebody* might validate my piteous charade. But no one attended to Her Majesty's distress. Finally, I gave up the drama.

As I lay there nursing my bruised ego, a warm breeze entered by the open window and whispered calming thoughts, mysteriously disarming my pride. I began to understand that Johnny was right; I wasn't Frankie. As the pleasant aromas of late summer soon lulled me to the brink of repose, my mind's eye was visited by a series of concentric circles of light beginning from the periphery and moving inward. They began to wrap themselves around a central figure that, at first, I couldn't recognize. After a few moments the center came clear; it was Frankie's smiling face. Before I had time to make sense of it there was a gentle knock at my door.

"Annie," came a sad whisper, "I saw-wee."

I got up, opened the door, and wrapped my arms around my lovable little brother. "I'm sorry too. I know I'm not Frankie, and I could never take his place. I just wanted to help you."

"I wuv you, Annie."

"I love you, too, Johnny."

I had spent so much time and energy "being Frankie" that neither of us had fully mourned his death. Thanks to our little confrontation, the floodgates of grief opened and we spent the rest of the evening remembering the wonderful little boy who had so touched our lives.

Chapter 6

The One that Got Away

U.G.R. We learn from "official sources" that the Underground Railroad, a big branch of which runs through this city, up to the Canadian frontier, has been doing an unusually large business this year. Some days the "train" takes a dozen at a time, and the aggregate business of the year is counted by hundreds. One gentleman, who is ranked among the high-toned, conservative Democrats—a sustainer of the fugitive slave law, the Nebraska bill, and the Pierce and Buchanan administrations, on principle—is regularly called on for his subscription when funds are needed. His sober and invariable reply is this: "Give money to help the fugitive slave escape? Not a cent! It's illegal, and against the compromises of the Constitution! Send him back to Virginia! Send him back—and here's a five dollar bill to help pay the expenses of returning him back to his master!"

—Gardiner Home Journal, Nov. 10, 1859

Mother, Momma, or Sarah[15] (when we needed to get her immediate attention) was the heart of the family. She was of medium height, lightly framed, and blessed with the handsome features of Grandma Kean. Her hair, which she usually kept in a long single braid, was golden in her youth. Through the years it had darkened to an acorn hue and was salted with snow-white strands. Her eyes were a pale blue, with one anomaly; there was a touch of brown pigment in her right eye. Grandpa Kean used to brag, "That was my contribution!"

One could easily be fooled by Mother's delicate appearance. However, her personality was formidable: strong, loving, firm, and truthful to a fault. She despised prejudicial attitudes towards people of different races, religions, or skin colors and would speak out boldly to anyone who crossed the line. Sarah Goodwin was known as a practical abolitionist who confronted bigotry where it often began: at home. She spent many an evening reading the immortal *Uncle Tom's Cabin* to us, exposing the evils of slavery. Mother advocated for the mentally ill and those with mental retardation, as she had a younger brother, Jimmy,[16] who was labeled "the village idiot" for his inability to learn. It was probably through witnessing such injustice that she developed such sensitivity of heart. If there was a cause, she was the effect! Although a believer in equality of the sexes and women's suffrage, she was unflinchingly traditional in another way; she saw her life's mission as being mother, care-giver, and moral-educator of her children.

A good academic education was high on her list of priorities. So, unless there was a dire emergency on the farm, we were being schooled. That "good education" meant developing an inquisitive mind, employing common sense, and acquiring a keen notion of right and wrong. She believed that the advancement and preservation of our democracy was grounded in those skills.

Eighteen fifty-eight proved to be an indelible year for the Goodwin family. Charles started his eighth and final year of grade school; I, my fourth; and Johnny, his first. In that same year, our one-year-old twin sisters, Bella and Lilly,[17] toddled their way into this big mysterious world as Grandpa Kean[18] took his final steps into eternity. However, the most unexpected turn of events resulted from some late-night angling near the ferry landing. The "fish" that Charles and I landed on the evening of May 28 was of quite a different species.

The two of us were trying to catch some of those big, fat catfish that inhabit the bottom of the river and are most likely to be caught during the hours after sunset. The moon rose full during the early twilight hours, and the weather had been unseasonably hot and humid during the week prior. It was the perfect time to catch the cooling river breeze and maybe even tomorrow's dinner.

We had been fishing for about an hour when I noticed something moving on the water right along the shoreline. Could it be a moose? I pointed it out to Charles, and we both remained quiet so as not to disturb whatever it was. As the object got closer, Charles came to the realization that it was a rowboat, but no one was rowing. It was just floating along on the incoming tide. On closer inspection, we made out the form of a slouched human figure, who was struggling to propel the craft with a long stick against the shallow margin. We were both curious and frightened at once, but my brother had the presence of mind to call out, "Hey … Ahoy there, captain!" When there was no response, he added, "You ain't gonna make it to Canada with that stick!" Charles's humor was his best weapon against his own fear.

Apparently, my brother's comment struck a nerve. The skipper sat straight up on the seat and continued to inch his way towards us. Finally, the figures of "boat and captain" came to rest on the shore a few yards south of our fishing spot. Cautiously, Charlie made his way through a small patch of brush, coming within a few feet of the craft. I stayed behind, frozen with apprehension and wonder. The moonlight cast an eerie outline on both figures, protracting the moment, until a hoarse voice from the boat finally broke the silence.

"Canada … Yez, sir … Canada," For the first time we were hearing a dialect we had heard only once before. It was slave talk, which Mother had done her best to simulate in her many bedtime readings of *Uncle Tom's Cabin*.

A young, black, teenage boy staggered his way out of the boat and onto the shore. In one great emotional explosion, he blurted out all his hopes and fears in rapid succession. "I'm Eli, sir … please don't turn me in … I begs ya. I come up on da railroad, ya know … not da train, sir … d'underground? Weez 'scapin' from d'Crowley Plantation … d'as a bad place …" Eli gasped as though being strangled, and then burst into tears. "Sophie …"

I moved trancelike through the brush to join them, still dumbfounded by what was happening.

"There, there, my friend," spoke Charles, as he extended his hand, pulling Eli up the embankment. "You're safe now. And we're gonna figure out how to get ya to Canada … no more frettin'. Our Momma knows all about that railroad. Let's get ya some food and dry clothes."

Charles then made the introductions. "I'm Charles Goodwin, and this here is my sister, Annie."

Eli bowed his head, reverently, and gently shook our hands.

The three of us then trod the mile and a half toward home. Eli talked continuously, often pointing to the North Star, which seemed to encapsulate all his dreams. And we listened, fully absorbed, as the fictional world of Uncle Tom became three-dimensional reality before our eyes.

It was nearly 10 p.m. when we approached the farm. Mother was in the parlor. From a distance, we could see her through the window reading the newspaper. Charles, with his usual wit, asked me to run ahead and prepare her for a surprise.

I sprinted to the house and entered the parlor. "Momma, Momma, you've got to see what Charlie and I caught down on the Kennebec."

"Is it a sturgeon?" she asked, wide eyed.

"Oh, better than that!" I exclaimed.

There was a short anticipatory silence. Then Charles arrived at the doorway.

"Hear ye! Hear ye!" Charles bellowed, as though announcing royalty. "It is my distinguished pleasure to introduce to you, Master Eli, direct from the Crowley Plantation in South Carolina!" Eli slid out of the shadows behind Charles. Mother's Kennebec Journal dropped to the floor and her mouth nearly followed suit! Standing before her stood a handsome young man, about Charles's age, with deep ebony skin, a water-soaked shirt, worn-out trousers, and bare feet. He sported a beautiful shy grin that reflected a lifetime of catering to white folks and trying to avoid their wrath.

"Eli, welcome!" said Mother, who rose from her chair to greet him warmly. "Please, sit here on the sofa. You look exhausted."

"Annie, would you please bring in some bread, butter, and preserves for our guest. He must be starving!" Mother exclaimed.

I grabbed a lantern and proceeded to the pantry. While completing her request, I had a wonderful thought, followed by a complementary sense of poetic justice. I was a white girl about to serve food to a runaway slave. Such irony! My eyes filled up with tears as I walked back into the parlor, and unable to see properly, I tripped over the blasted rug! The food and cider went everywhere. Eli jumped up and asserted, "Missy, let me clean dat up!"

"NO!" I blurted out, then immediately softened my voice, "No Eli, please sit back down. Thank you for offering, but it's my mess. I'm sure you're used to cleanin' up after white folks, but you won't be a slave in our house." I walked back towards the kitchen to get some towels when I heard Eli comment, with a somewhat choked-up voice, "Well, I'll be! I know d'ere be kind white folk, but you take da cake, Miss Annie!"

Charles alerted Grandma and Papa, who joined us with great interest. After I successfully replenished the refreshments and navigated the rug without incident, we conversed for a short time and then retired for the evening. It was clear that our guest was bone-weary, and there would be plenty of time for questions once he got some rest.

The next morning he bathed himself in the woodshed and donned some of Charles's old clothing and a pair of shoes. He asked to help out around the farm, but due to the Fugitive Slave Act,[19] which was in force in Maine, we would need to be extra vigilant. Bounty hunters were coursing up and down the Kennebec, looking for runaways. The river towns of Maine were among the last stops on the Underground Railroad before the final leg of the journey to Canada. A brief glimpse of Eli or an innocent slip of the tongue could send him back to his master in shackles, or worse. In the meantime, Mother began making contacts for his safe passage to freedom.

During the day the young refugee took precautions to stay out of sight; but when darkness fell, he and Charles ruled the night! They fished, played hide and seek amidst the shadows, and went on those nocturnal adventures that young men seem to enjoy so very much. Charles taught Eli everything he knew about astronomy: why the moon has phases, the reason the North Star never seems to move, how the seasons are brought about, and a myriad of other scientific truths. This young fugitive, with no formal education, learned and absorbed everything as if he was born to be a scholar. Needless to say, Charles and Eli quickly became best buddies and referred to each other thereafter as blood-brothers.

Initially, Eli was very tight-lipped about his personal experiences. We assumed that this was due to the pain of having to relive those events.

However, there was one occasion during Eli's first week with us that provided me the sacred privilege of observing the young man's soul in all its tenderness and gravity.

Early one evening, having drawn a few buckets from the well, Charles initiated a full-scale water war in the backyard. I was soaked to the bone as we chased each other around in a fit of unbridled lunacy. Eli had been quiet, solemnly sitting on the back steps, overlooking the commotion.

After a while, I invited him to join us. " Eli! Come on!" I shouted gleefully, but to my utter shock, the poor, young boy started to cry uncontrollably. My brother and I stopped our foolishness and rushed to the side of our distraught friend.

"Tell us, please, Eli, what is wrong?" begged Charles.

"I's sorry … I's so very sorry … I can't." He stood up quickly and ran into the house. Neither of us pursued him. We somehow sensed that we had just witnessed an expression of pain that was far beyond our understanding.

It was nearly a week later, during dinner, that Father asked Eli if he might recount his escape from slavery. Up until that point, we hadn't inquired about the matter, sensing that it was more than he could bear to relate. At first, Eli declined to answer Father's question, but after the meal, he surprised us all by reversing his decision.

"Ya know, if y'all wanna hear da story … I's ready ta tell it."

"Wonderful," exclaimed Father. "Let's all go to the parlor. Leave the dishes, Annie, they can wait. After a few minutes of settling in, the Goodwin family gathered in the sitting room, solemnly waiting to hear the long-awaited saga of Eli's escape from slavery.

"Da reason I's 'fraid ta tell y'all is 'cause I know I's gonna cry. But … I's gonna cry no matta when I tells it … makes no diff'rence. Cry now … cry later. So's I's gonna cry now, if d'ats all right wit y'all."

"Of course, dear," said Momma. "We understand."

"Well ma'am, reckon it's time to face da fire. But … da story gotta be told, cuz so many's done so much fo' me ta be here wit you kind folk.

"Let me see … Well, we'd been concoctin' dis plan fo' nigh one year wit' d'underground. Me an' five udda slaves planned d'escape from da plantation. 'T'all began afta' da Sunday evenin' service, out behind d'Big-House, back aways in da woods. T'was Auntie Raya, Uncle Billy, four-year-old Lydia, and my nine-year-old sissa, Sophie."

Eli bit his lower lip, turned his head away, and looked wistfully out the window in silence for a moment. Then, turning and looking directly at Charlie, he remarked with a quavering voice, "Some mem'ries hard on da heart."

After firming up his resolve, he continued, "Da conducta', Boss, was a freed slave his-self. He had us all meet by dis 'normous live-oak tree. Everyone knowed where 'twas in da woods. Da tree's covered wit moss and big 'round as dis here room!"

"Did ya take any provisions with ya?" asked Father.

"Well … we hadda travel fast t'void da dogs and da slave catchers. But, yes sir, we done take a little food an' drink, but only da clothes on our backs. But … Hallelujah! D'Almighty stirred up a big ol' lightnin' storm, wit' hail, wind, and rain dat kept ol' Massa's attention durin' da chaos. 'Twas like da great deluge in Noah's time … wonder da little animals didn't line up two-by-two," he chuckled.

"By mornin', weez on our way to Philly in a rickety ol' steamer named da *Sout'ern Cross*. Once arrivin', we wuz 'scorted to da home of a Quaker minister … Had an odd name, Pickett or Piggott … I ain't quite sure. But, dis Quaker man was part-owner of a schoona' called da *Silver Gull*.

"D'interestin' part 'bout da *Gull* was d'at it flew da 'Stars and Stripes' as well as da 'Palm tree and crescent moon' o' Sout' Carolina. Dis was all contrived by d'Underground to deter bounty hunters from suspectin' a hold full o' runaways. Now, d'is pius ol' reverend was not committin' da sin o' deception, as y'all might surmise … by flyin' dat palm tree flag, d'at is. 'Cause his partner was, indeed, from Sout' Carolina, makin' da whole ente'prise righteous in da sight of d'Almighty."

We all had a good laugh at Eli's wit. Charles and he had different skin colors but their humor was of the same hue.

After a few moments of playful chatter, I inquired, "So what was it like on the ship?"

"Well," continued our guest, "durin' da voyage we spent mos' o' da daylight hours below deck, so's not to give ourselves away. But, at night we come up t'catch da cool breeze and try t'relax from all da troubles.

"We tarried in New Yo'k, fo' a short time to get supplies dat we couldn't find in Philly. D'en we headed fo' Maine. At Portland d'ey unload a couple tons of slave-picked rice, da proceeds goin' back to da Quaker man to help finance his Unda-Water-Railroad. The skippa' also paid a sho't visit to d'Abyssinian Meetin' House,[20] which is da centa fo' d'Underground in dis here state. Careful not to be seen, he made 'is way back to da ship. Any slip-up would mean jail time for da crew … big fines, loss of da vessel, and we slaves bein' returned to da plantation, where da lash would greet us … if we wuz lucky! Sellin' us Sout' or even da hangin' tree might be da punishment. No matta, weez be spoilt goods and branded wit da red-hot iron, jus' like cattle."

"That is so cruel!" I exclaimed.

"Yes, but da way dey figures it, you's a runaway and you's gonna run again. If d'ey brand ya, folks see da mark! Yep, sho' is cruel … but 'member, we ain't people, weez property … d'eir property! If da horse branded, d'hey know who belongs to … da nigga's branded, d'hey know who belongs to. Jus' da same. No differ. We no betta d'hen d'animals.

"Good Lo'd! Here I is, preachin' to da choir! Y'all know slav'ry ain't no picnic. Anyway, where was I? Oh, yeah. D'en we sail up da Kennebec, very slowly. We need t'arrive unda cover o' darkness t' keep us safe from d'unfriendly eyes."

Eli continued to describe the ascent of the *Silver Gull* up the Kennebec. Her destination was Hallowell, where the refugees were to connect with Israel Weeks[21] who would arrange the final leg of the journey to Canada.

I'd learned from Momma that Israel had been a part of the Underground Railroad for years and owned a white-pillared mansion in Vassalboro which resembled the "Big House" of a Southern Plantation. His home was reputed to have an escape tunnel that led from the shore of the Kennebec, under a road, and into a secret room. The chimneys were painted white with black trim on top, a symbol that the owners were "friendly to the cause." Just in case the chimneys were not noticed, there was a lawn jockey statue in front of the mansion, another Underground Railroad sign.

Eli explained that it was dusk as the *Silver Gull* turned the final bend in the river as the lights of Hallowell flickered in the distance. Out of nowhere, a smaller, steamer vessel with lightly-armed federal officers, accompanied by bounty hunters approached, demanding to search the vessel.

Eli detailed his escape, "We wuz all up on da deck ... plannin' fo' meetin' Massa Weeks, and was caught off guard! D'ose slave catchers must'a been tipped off or somethin' ... cause d'ey knew weez on board! As d'officer climbed on deck I bade Sophie jump off d'udda side of da boat, cause weez bot' fair swimmas. We jump toget'er into da dark water. I swam like I's nev'a swam befo' and reached d'is side in 'bout four o' five minutes. I wuz fit to drop and couldn't hardly get ma breath. D'en I look fo' Sophie ... I call and I call ... but she no answer!"

Eli's voice choked up, "Oh, my God, why You fo'saken me?" The boy collapsed into such a fit of anguish that Momma pleaded with him to stop. But after composing himself, he insisted on finishing his story.

"I wait d'ere all night and all d'at next day in d'woods, 'cross from Hallowell town. I found d'is ol' rickety row boat, half sunk in d'water and pulled it outta da muck so's I could find Massa Weeks, upriver. I was hope'n an' plead'n wit God to see dat lovin' little Sophie 'gain ... but I guess Jesus, He want her t'himself ... Jesus, He good ... He no want 'er suffa' no mo'. But why He no' take me? I's a sinna ... not Sophie ... She good ... kind ... do anyt'in' fo'ya, don't matta if you's black o' white ... 'Tiz all my fault ... my fault!"

Our family was in tears, hugging and consoling poor Eli. Now I understood why he ran off so grieved, after watching brother Charles and *his* nine-year-old sister splashing and romping about in the dooryard. So many memories, so many hopes and dreams, gone! Swept away by the foreboding, indifferent currents of the Kennebec.

That night I had a terrible dream. I was Sophie! I sensed the futility of paddling against the river currents and the terror of being sucked under again and again until I went down for the last time. I awoke gasping for air with my pillow covering my face! I was relieved to find myself in my own bed, but the terror of that nightmare gave me even greater empathy for Eli and for his poor little sister in her last moments.

A few nights later, as Eli was sitting on those same back steps, deep in thought, I approached him.

"You're thinkin' about Sophie, aren't you?" I asked, quietly.

He nodded and put his head down, "She come t'me at night in my dreams. She tell me she happy, dat she's waitin' fo' me on d'utta side. Don'know d'ats really her o' jus' my 'magination tellin' me jus' what I wanna hear."

There was a short pause, as I searched my mind for some profound words of comfort. "I'm so very sorry, Eli. I wish I could help. You must have loved her very much."

I realized, immediately, how insipid my words sounded. They were far from the sagacious condolences I'd hoped to convey.

Eli took no notice of my *faux pas* and continued. "Yes, love each udda we did. Well, weez fight sometimes ... jus' like ev'body do, like you an' Charlie. But we don't mean nuttin' by it."

"Yeah. But I surely would grieve over Charles, too, if anything were to happen to him," I replied.

Again? Oh my goodness. Mumble and fumble. How would my hypothetical feelings help Eli to cope with his loss? They wouldn't, of course. If only there were a Ben Franklin maxim for awkward moments such as these.

Yet, as before, Eli just overlooked my blabbering. "Yup. But weez gotta move on, don't we? Jus' don'know z'actly how ta do d'at."

"Grandma Kean says that 'time is the healer of all wounds,' and she's had a heap of wounds in her lifetime," I spouted.

Suddenly, Mr. Franklin whispered in my ear, "Wise men speak because they have something to say; fools, because they must say something."

Finally, Eli opened up the opportunity for me to engage in real dialogue. "I'm sure d'at time will help ... but don't make it no easier when you da *cause* of d'ose wounds."

"Eli, you know that you had no choice. If you'd left her on that boat she would have been sent back to a horrible life of slavery. She would have been beaten, branded, and God knows what else."

"Do we really know d'at, Annie? She's jus' a nine-yea' ol' girl taggin' along wit da rest of us. P'haps d'ey jus' take 'er back wit no punishment t'all. D'en 'least she be alive."

"Eli, how would you feel if she hadn't jumped off the ship with you? When you reached the shore, you'd know she was still onboard with those terrible slave catchers. Wouldn't that be worse than knowing you tried your best to save her life?"

There was a long pause in the conversation as we listened to the sounds of the crickets and watched the barn swallows sailing above our heads.

The sun had dropped behind the hills of Hallowell, but was still casting its departing red rays on the eastern horizon.

"Ain't it som'in' d'way d'evenin' sky got d'at red glow, Annie?"

I nodded in agreement, relieved that Eli was able to shift his attention to something less painful.

"Charlie, he tell me 'bout d'at. He say d'at b'cause d'air act like a prism. He show'd me one d'em prisms on da lamp in d' parlor. He done held it in d' sunlight. Made d' rainbow on da wall! If ya hold d' prism wit' da red at da bottom of da rainbow, it's kinda like when da sun go down in d' evenin'. D'en da blue an' da vi'let come when da sun up above, like in da daytime."

"Well, I never heard that before, but it makes sense. My brother knows a great deal about science," I replied, feeling slightly jealous of my brother's knowledge.

"I'll say he does! I learn lots from d'at boy. He's my dea' blood brudda. Did ya know? We swore d'oath! We's bruddas fo'ever! I never dreamed da white boy wanna be my very own kin."

"Eli, I don't think Charles ever dreamed a black boy would ever wanna be his very own kin, either. It's pretty special," I responded, with a delicate smile.

He continued, "Speakin' o' d'at, how's you like t'become my blood sissa? I reckon Sophie done approve o' d'at … y'all very much alike, 'cept d'color o' da skin."

"Oh, Eli! I'd love that!" I exclaimed. "But you gotta know, I'll never be another Sophie. I tried to be Frankie, once, after he died. That didn't work out. I could never replace her in a million years, if that's what you're hopin' for. Charlie says I'm nothing but a clumsy, annoying, imp … and my worst fault is … I ask too many questions. If you can put up with all that, I'd love to be your blood sister."

"Oh, I recken I can put up wit' d'at. T'ain't so bad. Weez all clumsy … annoyin. How ya gonna learn if don't ask questions? Now I ask da question … d'yall wanna runaway nigga as yo' brudda?"

I clasped his right hand between both of mine, and exclaimed, "Eli, don't you ever call yourself that horrible name again, you hear! You're no nigga! You are a human being, as good as me, Charles, or any other person in this world!"

"I believe d'at is so … but once ya been tol' d'lie ova and ova 'gain … well, starts soundin' like da truth."

He turned and hugged me, shaking with joyful emotion. That evening seemed to be a turning point in Eli's attitude. He now had a family, again.

———

Happily, Eli chose to remain with us for several months while Mother tutored him and made arrangements with Mr. Weeks to get him safely to

Canada. Although he spoke in traditional slave dialect, his vocabulary was extensive. The desire to learn to read and write consumed him. His memory was sharper than that of any person his age that we had ever known. Perhaps because, as a slave, forgetting even minor details could mean punishment.

Unlike the way I learned to read, Mother taught him the sound of each letter. For example, the letter P makes the sound "puh" and W makes the sound "wuh", and so forth. He learned to sound out words using this simplified strategy. We also bought him a small dictionary, in order that he might understand the meanings of the more complicated words that he encountered. Never was there a more enthusiastic, dedicated student or a more empathetic, hard-working teacher. Asking for assistance didn't come easily to this former slave, who had been taught not to speak to white folks unless spoken to. Mother gave him confidence in himself, a commodity that Southern slavery had tried to suppress and extinguish. But he was able to break those chains as well.

St. John, NB, ca. 1860s

Too soon came the day of Eli's departure. We understood that with the fugitive laws in place we might never see him again. Yet, there was a glimmer of hope; *Uncle Tom's Cabin* had awakened many, and the issue of slavery was beginning to eat away at the hearts of compassionate people. Perhaps someday, the pathway to freedom would open for everyone..

By the time he left us in early November, Eli had learned to read and write with confidence. The night before he departed to the Farwell Mansion in Vassalboro, he read us a letter that he had written in his own hand.

My dearest family,

I have never known such love and hospitality from people, either black or white, that compares with what you have given me here. Charles; my brother, if you hadn't said the word "Canada" on that fateful night, I'd probably still be floating on the Kennebec.

Annie, you taught me, that first night that you fell flat on your face, to get right back up again and do the right thing. And ... although I lost my Sophie, God rest her, you've become my little sister now. Grandma Kean, Captain Goodwin, young Johnny and you sweet little girls, Lilly and Bella, you've made me a part of a family again. Finally, Mrs. Goodwin, ... rather, 'Momma', you have been a true mother to me. You've given birth to my soul ... the gift of being able to read, write, and figure out my way through this crazy world. I know I am loved. On my arrival in Canada, I will legally make your surname my own. God bless you all!

Eli Goodwin

Four days later, Eli would become a free man as he penned his new name into the immigration register at St. John, New Brunswick, Canada.

Chapter 7

Old Pete

Now, no man can develop a true manhood who does not love the things that he does. No man does anything that marks him as masterly except it be done by a certain inspiration into which the whole should enter. A man that paints, hating his business, never is an artist, and never can be one. A man that is a teacher and hates teaching, making drudgery of it, can never be an inspirational teacher. A man that is a true workman in any sphere must work by a stimulation which comes from the actual enthusiasm of loving the thing done. A man that obeys moral laws without loving them is like a man who walks within the walls of a penitentiary.

—Rev. Henry W. Beecher

Those were the final words of a sermon by the abolitionist Henry Ward Beecher, a famous clergyman and the father of the writer Harriet Beecher Stowe. I had just turned ten years of age in the spring of 1859, and my search for truth was becoming more intense. I'd had a deep desire to find the answer to my questions about God and the afterlife ever since Frankie's death. I took advantage of every opportunity to engage in religious discussions or events, and Reverend Beecher coming to the Old South privileged me yet another opportunity to pursue my quest.

Reverend Beecher had agreed to come to our area in July to preach a three night revival. Mr. Beecher requested a rural setting and it was decided that the event would be held in the field across from my schoolhouse in Chelsea, where the County Road and the Ferry Road intersect. The schoolhouse was the perfect venue because it provided a quiet, reflective setting, free from the noisy clatter of city streets.

I volunteered, along with several other children in my Sunday school group, to go door-to-door and hand out informational fliers about the revival. After our Sunday school class, we were commissioned to go out in pairs, just like the Apostles! I recruited Emma French,[22] our blacksmith's daughter, who was a friend of mine and a year and a half my junior, to work with me. Due to the fact that we were both novices at this sort of thing, we would need to practice our invitational approaches. So, we stood on the front steps of the church to rehearse what we were going to say as we greeted people on our route.

"Okay, Emma, you start," I beckoned, not wanting to break the ice myself.

"No thank you, Annie. You're the elder."

"Elder? By only a year! You're the one that everyone thinks is so very adorable. You'll have their attention before you even open your mouth. You've got that magic touch," I answered.

"Annie Elizabeth! Are you jealous?" Emma teased.

"No. ... Well, maybe a crumb," I admitted, with a smile. "It's just that whenever we're around adults they dote over you like you're a newborn baby, and I become invisible. It's a bit annoying," I made sure to speak the truth, but kept my tone light and playful.

"It's just 'cause I'm tiny for my age! I hate being this small. Do you think I'll grow, or end up a Lilliputian?" Asked Emma, with a touch of vulnerability in her voice.

In that moment, my jealousy subsided and I realized that Emma had some insecurities of her own.

"Of course you'll grow. Look at your parents, they're taller than mine. You're gonna be a head above me in no time," I replied, setting my hand gently on her shoulder.

"I hope so. And I don't like being doted over like a baby," she said.

I cocked one eyebrow in response, staring the truth out of her.

"Well ... maybe I like it just a little," she admitted.

"Of course you do," I laughed. "Who wouldn't? Anyway, all I meant is that you have a natural talent, a gift for getting people's attention. So, give it a go."

"All right, If you insist." She began, "Ah ... good morning. My name is Emma French and this is my friend, Annie. Are you on the narrow path to heaven, or running straight down the highway to hell?"

"Emma! You can't say that to people. Your papa would tan your bottom," I shouted.

"Pastor uses the H-word a whole lot," she reasoned.

"Yes, but he's preaching a sermon. You can say 'hell' all you want if you're a preacher. God gives you special permission when you're ordained. But we're not preachers. We're just inviting folks to a revival," I explained, as I drew figures in the dirt with a stick.

"You're right. Why don't you show me how to greet 'em. You've always had the gift of gab, at least that's what Momma says." Emma grinned.

"Well, you must thank your Momma for her kind regards," I replied, feigning offense.

"We both have our gifts, don't we?" said Emma.

"I suppose. Okay, I'll give it a try," I said, surrendering. But let's just invite 'em to the revival. Then God can send 'em … you know … wherever he wants."

"All right," chuckled Emma.

"Here I go." I whispered and then cleared my throat. "Good morning. My name is Annie Goodwin and this is my friend, Emma French. We'd like to invite you and your family to a tent revival with the famous Reverend Henry Beecher."

"That was great, Annie. But I want the gift of gab, too," Emma replied.

"Okay, you tell 'em when and where it will be held then hand 'em a flier."

"Agreed," said Emma. Then we sealed the accord with a handshake.

The next morning, John French escorted us by wagon to the landing where we were ferried across the river to Hallowell to begin our mission to save souls. We started on the north end of Second Street and handed out fliers to several families. There was no one home at a few places, so we simply slid the pamphlet under the doors. At one of the larger dwellings, a kind and stately woman opened the door, and we ran through our script in the parlor. After praising us for our well-rehearsed oration, she offered us apple cider and some freshly baked cookies, which we gladly accepted. But as we were devouring the goodies, she admonished us not to visit the house directly across from her doorstep.

"Forgive me for saying so," she whispered, pointing through the window, "but the man that lives in that house over there will have nothing to do with God or religion. He's an atheist! He won't let you within ten feet of his property, especially with that religious material of yours. Steer clear of him. You don't want to meet with his wrath!"

If that good-hearted lady knew anything about me at all, she never would have challenged me to avoid that house. Papa called it "headstrong." Call it what you will, but I took her warning as an invitation, a mission within a mission, a crusade! Stampeding horses couldn't keep me from knocking on that man's front door!

We thanked our hostess for the advice and treats, and then continued on the west side of the street. Along the way, I gave Emma a rudimentary course in world religions.

"Hey Annie, remind me what she said about the man across the street?" asked Emma.

"That he's an atheist," I responded. "Someone who doesn't believe in God."

Emma gasped. "I thought everyone believed in God."

"Not everyone. Father knows a man from India who prays to many gods," I replied.

"You mean like the Egyptians in the Bible?"

"Yes. Just like them. There are all kinds of different religions," I explained. "And there are many different churches, too! Baptists, Catholics, Methodists.

Papa likes to say, 'There's lots of colored eggs in the henhouse but the yokes are all the same.'"

"That's right. And Jesus said, 'My yoke is easy!'" Emma exclaimed with glee.

I tried to suppress a giggle, but it quickly erupted into an all-out, stomach-aching belly laugh. My puzzled friend just stood there with a questioning look. After trying to explain the pun, which ensured that it would lose every ounce of humor, I realized the moment was lost, so I just moved on.

"So, Emma," I continued, "what do we do about that atheist? If we don't knock on his door we're not doin' our Christian duty. What's the worst thing that can happen?"

"He could shoot us!"

"Emma, no. That's against the law … He could yell at us or threaten us. That sort of thing happened to Jesus all the time. People got angry at him but that didn't stop Him, now, did it?"

"Ah … Annie, it did stop Him. They crucified Him. Besides, Jesus could run across the Kennebec, but I can't."

I chuckled, "Look, when we get to his house you can stand far behind me. I'll introduce myself, and then, if he's real angry, you can run to the next house."

"No, I'll be brave … I'm just a little terrified inside," she explained.

We finished the west side of Second Street and started working our way back down the east side. Finally, we made our way to "that house." I walked right up to the huge front door and lifted the heavy brass knocker. It came down with a crash that echoed throughout its spacious chambers. We waited anxiously for nearly a minute, which felt more like an hour. No one answered, and with a sigh of relief, we agreed to move on to the next dwelling.

"It's not our fault if no one's home," I thought, with some relief. We started to walk away and had only taken a few steps, when the door opened behind us, followed by a roar!

"What the hell do you want!" boomed the voice.

Emma was frozen in place, but I forced myself into a half-turn to face the "beast." The man was a Goliath! He had a massive build and sported disheveled hair and an immense beard that would have made Father's look like chin-stubble.

I plucked up my courage, answering him with a soft, shaky voice, "Sir, I am Annie … and this is my friend Emma, and…"

"I didn't ask you who you were, nor do I give a damn. State your business, then get off my property!"

Though I thought my heart was going to jump out of my chest, I ignored his frightening curses and responded, "We'd like to invite you to a revival meeting in Chelsea. The famous Reverend Beecher will be our speaker." By then Emma had turned around and meekly attempted to hand him a flier.

"Listen here," he growled, pointing towards the sky. "We're all floatin' around in space on a piece of rock. There ain't nobody out there, ladies! Nobody that gives a goddamn about any of us!" He paused in his tirade for a moment, and then added, "If there is a god, he ain't a god of love and I want nothin' to do with him!" Then, glaring furiously at Emma, he barked, "Go peddle your nonsense somewhere else." With that, he slammed the door in our faces.

Emma burst into tears, and I jumped to her side to console her. Neither Emma nor I had ever witnessed so much anger, especially towards God. Rather than feeling afraid, my Irish temper was flaring. How dare he be so rude to a couple of young girls! Poor little Emma was in hysterics, and it was all my fault for choosing pigheadedness over wisdom. We sat on that fiend's sumptuous granite doorstep for a good five minutes until she was able to regain her composure.

"Hey, Emma," I preached, "Blessed are they who are persecuted for my sake,' says the Lord. We just got a great big blessing."

"I don't feel very blessed," my friend sniffled. Just as I was helping her up, the door opened again and a soft, gentle, and very deep voice spoke. "Girls?"

It was the monster, himself! I grabbed Emma's hand and we bolted for the sidewalk."

"No, wait! Please." The man then raised both arms as though surrendering to the sheriff. "Please don't cry anymore. I can't bear it." His voice trembled with emotion as we stood there, dumbstruck. He then sat down on the top step, his facial expressions betrayed much suffering. Emma and I apprehensively inched our way back towards him, stopping just close enough for a quick get-away.

He continued, with much emotion, "When this little thing here started a-wailin'," he said, pointing at Emma, "I heard the cries of my own little girls. Ya' see, children, me and religion used to be friends. Then, that 'God of Love' took my two babies from me," he said, his voice quavering. "They was 'bout your age. But, just 'cause my little ones are gone don't give me no right to be cruel to ya. Ain't no hope for me ladies, but I will take one of those papers of yours, out of respect for your kindness toward an old cuss like me."

Emma handed him the flier, and I saw his big calloused hand was shaking when he took it.

"By the way," he added, "they call me Old Pete." A big, solitary tear trickled down over his weather-worn features. He gave us a warm smile and closed the door.

"Oh, my," exclaimed Emma, "I can't believe he came out and talked to us, as kind and gentle as a lamb!"

"Yeah," he must have gone through so much pain, losing both of his little girls. And where's his wife? I wonder if she's dead, too."

"I just hope we did him some good," sniffled Emma.

"I think we did. Looks like his little girls spoke to him through you. It's that magic touch of yours, Emma."

We continued on our trek and finished up a little before noon. Father met us at the ferry landing, and we rode back home in our buckboard wagon. We took the longer route, which gave us time to discuss our encounter with Old Pete.

"Let me tell ya what I know about him," said Father. "Peter McKay was the skipper of a whaler out of New Bedford. He and I used to keep company now and then. But when his girls died of diphtheria, both within a couple of weeks, he took to the drink; very heavily, I might add. Eventually, his wife, June, left him and went back to her family in Massachusetts. Pete's a very good man who lost heart. It happens, ya know. But all things considered, I'm right proud of you two! What ya did today might have helped that old salt in ways we'll never know."

Thursday evening arrived, and a large tent, complete with lengthy log-benches had been set up in the field. A few good-Samaritan women brought cider and cold water to keep the attendees from passing out in the summer heat. Emma and I walked the quarter-hour stretch from home and arrived just before 7 p.m., the official beginning time of each of the three services. I must admit, we were disappointed to find that there were only about fifty in attendance.

Reverend Beecher's topic that night was *Getting to know the Lord through scripture*. It seemed to me that this was a common theme used by every preacher on the planet, but little did I know, he was going to show us a way of interacting with scripture that none of us had ever experienced before.

"Good evening, everyone," he began. "Thank you all for coming out on such a dreadfully hot evening. Many thanks to the good ladies who have mercifully brought us refreshments! My topic tonight, *Getting to know the Lord through scripture*, has three stages to it. Reading, imagining, and encountering. For most of us, reading has been the limit of our reflection on the Holy Word. And that is a good thing. But, tonight you are going to learn to move much deeper into the experience.

"First, I want to thank the youngsters for helping me to get the word out. They've all been quite busy going from door to door over the past few days. So, I'll ask you children to choose your favorite scripture story for a demonstration."

Almost every hand went up, but luckily, mine was the first.

"Yes," he said, pointing to me. "What is your favorite story, my dear?"

"Ah, I'm not sure if it's my very favorite, but the last supper, sir," I replied.

"The last supper," he repeated. "And what's your name, young lady?"

"Annie, sir. Annie Goodwin."

"Well, thank you, Annie. That's one of my favorite scripture stories as well. Let me ask the assembly … Is there anyone here who isn't familiar with that famous scene from holy scripture?"

He gazed about for a moment and continued. "Good. Then step one is completed! You are all familiar with the story from reading it, and you're likely familiar with elements of the setting as well. So we'll proceed to the next two stages, imagining and encountering. Close your eyes, please." He waited for a moment as the people settled in.

"*You* are now at the Lord's last supper with his disciples. You are sitting beside Jesus, not in a chair, but reclining at a low wooden table as was customary in the first century. The fragrance of freshly baked, unleavened bread is in the air, along with the aroma of wine. There is also the smell from the oil lamps that hang about the room. Their flames are casting eerie shadows that dance on the walls and ceiling of the structure. The disciples are cheerful, laughing and talking about the events of the day, the miraculous cures they have witnessed. Suddenly, the Master raises his hand and the room becomes quiet. Jesus is about to speak. Outside, a dog is barking in the distance and you can hear the footsteps of a small group of Roman soldiers passing by, their light armor clinking with each step along the stone pavement.

"Jesus speaks. 'Truly, I say to you. One of you is about to betray me.' The expressions on the faces of the disciples become serious. 'Is it I, Lord? Is it I?' each echoes. Confusion and fear fall like a dark shadow. Soon the room becomes silent again with anticipation. Jesus remains calm. Then He turns to you, alone … looks deeply into your eyes, and speaks to you. What is his message?"

There was a hush over the assembly that lasted for about five minutes, as the reverend let each person ponder his question. Then he said, "You may all open your eyes now."

I could hear many remarking on how wonderful the experience had been for them. As for Emma and me, we loved the encounter, and couldn't wait to try it again at home.. Though, I must admit I was uncomfortable with what the Master said to me.

"What did Jesus say to you, Annie?" whispered Emma.

I was embarrassed, so I just said, "I don't know. I need to spend more time in prayer. What did he say to you, Emma?"

FEMALE SUFFRAGE. Henry Ward Beecher has declared in favor of female suffrage. He says that "every miscreant, if a candidate for place, would be blasted before the vote of woman." But many a miscreant, when a candidate for the place of husband, finds very little difficulty in getting himself elected by a woman's vote. And isn't likely that women are quite as careful and conscientious in voting to fill that interesting place as they would be in voting to fill the public offices? [Louisville Journal.

"Oh, he thanked me for bringing all these people here tonight!" she replied, with quiet jubilation.

"That's wonderful, Emma! We'll have to pray this way again, when we get home. That way we don't have to rush," I remarked, making it seem like lack of time had been a problem for me. But the truth was, my message had been an immediate and clear one: "*Why do you doubt Me, Annie?*"

Friday night had better attendance. There were more than one hundred there on that equally hot and humid evening. Reverend Beecher spoke about finding God in nature. He said that in order to experience the fullness of God's majesty in the natural world it is necessary that one must "not think in words," but simply sit in awe of divine creation. I had no idea what he was talking about until he gave an example.

He explained it this way, "Have you ever just gazed up at the sky after a thunderstorm and seen a brilliant rainbow that you weren't expecting? That very moment, before any words come to mind, is what I'm talking about. That moment of awe … that moment of appreciation before thoughts began to intrude … the soul's initial impression of unspoiled beauty. That's what I would call pure thanksgiving and praise."

Ironically, that evening, nature gave us the gift of mosquitoes, and they were as thick as honey. At the conclusion of the lecture, one old farmer raised his hand and said, "These 'skeetahs … well, they're a part o'nature, too, Mr. Reverend. The way I sees it, when one o' those things lands on my arm, even before any thoughts come to mind, I swat that blood-sucker! Then follows pure thanksgivin' and praise!"

On Saturday night, there were too many people for everyone to fit under the tent. Fortunately the weather cooperated, the air was somewhat cooler than on the previous nights, and the airborne "servants of Beelzebub" had disappeared. The reverend's topic that evening was forgiveness.

He asked each of us to look around at those standing beside us and those throughout the assembly. Then he admonished, "Is there anyone here, in this congregation, that you haven't completely forgiven? Is there anyone anywhere that you haven't forgiven? Hanging onto a grudge is like taking arsenic and expecting the other person to drop dead." Laughter rippled through the crowd and Reverend continued, "I'm not sure who said that, but it's very much true. Another analogy would be two wrestlers holding each other to the ground; neither is free. Even the one who has the upper hand has to use all his force to hold down his opponent. Again, neither is free. And they will never be free until they let go of each other. The same is true in the spiritual life."

During the break, Father came over to Emma and me and said, "Girls, there's someone here I'd like you to meet. Follow me." We tagged along like a couple of puppy dogs until we got to the open field behind the tent.

There was a man, standing back to us, looking towards the sunset. Papa tapped him on the shoulder. It was Old Pete! Em and I stood there with our mouths hanging open like a couple of fools.

"Mr. Pete," I said in astonishment, "you're here!"

"Now, girls. Don't you be thinkin' I'm turnin' religious or somethin'. I was just sittin' around that big old house of mine and needed to get some fresh air. Thought this would be a good place to do it." He winked at Father. "Truth be told, I wanted to thank you for bein' so brave the other day. After I lost my youngins I couldn't stand the sight of children, 'specially little girls. But, after I got done yellin' and screamin' at you two, I felt just awful. I said to myself, 'Pete, what the hell has become of you?' Not quite sure how it happened, but like the reverend said, I let go of somethin' big and terrible. I believe my soul has finally dropped anchor into a tranquil sea."

After this encounter with Old Pete, I often wondered what it must have been like to live in such loneliness, to be in a state where everything that was once hopeful is now dark and void, where sounds of happy children crush the heart, where even the thought of joy brings on sorrow. How does one keep faith when all is taken away?

Chapter 8

The Fightin' Irish

Several Irish girls at work in one of the mills in Lewiston, pitched into Miss Ingalls, a Yankee girl at work in the same mill, one day last week, and nearly beat her to death. Had these Irish girls been black, what a hue and cry our Copperhead[23] papers would have raised, and ten chances to one, if every negro in Lewiston had not been mobbed. No one, however, will think of holding the Irish, as a body, responsible for the act of these girls. Why then in one case more than in the other?

—Gardiner Home Journal

My interest in new forms of prayer grew, following the revival. Emma, her brother Charles, Eliza Blanchard, and I would assemble together after school, to practice the type which the Reverend had so masterfully employed during the first night. I would fetch Grandpa Kean's big Bible, and each of us would choose a section from the text. Then we would close our eyes and try to imagine the biblical context of the passage.

One afternoon, I chose to be the soldier standing near the cross on Calvary. My thoughts went something like this:

I'm suffocating in this stifling armor, the sun is beating down and I can hardly breathe. I'm anxiously awaiting three prisoners sentenced to death. I wonder what their crimes are that Pilate has judged them worthy of such brutal torture. There they are, the condemned, trudging up the incline. It's dusty and a large crowd is following, and making a great din. I dread having to witness this cruel form of capital punishment again. Once witnessed, it can never be forgotten. But I drew the short straw … It's my turn. I'll think of Rome, my family, and my home; that should help distract me from the horror.

One of the accused is covered with blood; his garments are red from the merciless beatings he has just endured. I see His face. He looks familiar. Where have I seen him before? He gazes up at me with kind eyes, full of anguish and resignation. I know him! This is no criminal! It was he who healed our Centurion's servant by a simple command. I witnessed it! I must help him, but

I'm forbidden to leave my post. If I interfere, I'll be crucified right beside him. I'm such a coward!

My heart is pounding as though it might burst through the armor on my chest. They're now stripping this holy man of his clothing and laying him on the wood. I can't watch. I know what's coming; it's all too vivid in my memory. The executioner is picking up the hammer and those horrible nails. Now they're positioning the first against his hand and raising the hammer. BANG! BANG! BANG!

I screamed and opened my eyes wide, frozen in terror! I had not just imagined the hammering, I had heard it with my own ears!

"What's wrong, Annie?" yelped Eliza. "Are you OK?"

"I heard them hammer the nails in!" I shrieked.

Instantly, there was another BANG! BANG! BANG!

"There it is !" I screamed.

Father burst into my room, hammer in hand, and two nails between his teeth. Removing the nails, he said, "Sorry dear, I'm puttin' shelves in the walk-in, did I frighten ya?"

"Almost … to DEATH!" I gasped in reply.

By the time I had finished explaining what had happened, the other three monastics had broken their vows of silence and were rolling around on the floor in fits of laughter. After all was said and done, I was never again able to read or listen to that scriptural passage without having the jitters.

Eighteen-fifty-nine was a pleasant year from what I remember. The Goodwin clan was prosperous, the harvest abundant, and most importantly, we were all healthy. There were eight of us living under one roof: Momma, Papa, Charles, Johnny, Bella, Lilly, and yours truly. Mother had invited Grandma Kean,[24] who was now suffering from rheumatism, to take up residency with us, as well.

The one-room schoolhouse which we attended stood on the northeast corner of the intersection of the Hallowell Road, also known as the Ferry Road, and the County Road[25] that ran parallel to the river. In those days we had two school sessions. The summer session usually started after spring planting, extending from June into September, and the winter session started after the last harvest, roughly from November through late March. These intervals varied from year to year, as they followed the needs of our rural community. During the summer session, female teachers were employed, to accommodate a student body made up of younger children. Male teachers[26] often taught the winter sessions, to better deal with the more rambunctious older boy scholars, who had been needed for intensive farm work during the summer session.

In late May, Charles completed his eighth-grade year of schooling, fancying himself quite a grown man. He intended, like many rural male "graduates," to further his education on his own and eventually take command of the farm. My brother would have become a stellar candidate for Bowdoin College, had we the means. However, he continued to read extensively and was quick to show off his cerebral prowess, sometimes to the point of being an annoying know-it-all! His passage into intellectual self-worship left Johnny and I as the only Goodwin scholars at the school, at least until the twins were old enough to join our ranks.

Though our schoolhouse was rather small for the thirty-six children enrolled, absences were common, upwards of half the class could be missing on any given day. We walked to school, rain or shine. However, when the roads were snow-covered, Johnny and I would attach long ropes to the front of our sleds and hitch a ride with sleighs heading in the direction of the schoolhouse.[27] We'd cast the rope to the occupants and they'd haul us in tow. More than once, the person holding my rope lost her grip and I plowed into the gully, head first.

Our teacher was Miss Octavia Hunt.[28] She lived on the Winter Road, which branched off from ours, about a mile east from our farm. She was kind, intelligent, and uncompromising in her quest for equity. We were expected to display our best efforts and she promised us, in return, her best efforts to educate us. That education was both academic and social, because Miss Hunt wanted us to become good, informed, and responsible citizens.

She was much esteemed, in large measure because she showed respect to everyone. If Miss Hunt was talking with you, she gave you her undivided attention regardless of whatever distractions might be occurring in the classroom. Never did she hit a child or threaten to do so.

Now, there were a couple of boys I would have flogged with a bullwhip if I'd been her! And it was all because of a newcomer from the Emerald Isle.

Irish folk had been settling in Maine since the 1600s. My own Great-Grandpa Kean had immigrated from County Clare, Ireland, in the mid-1700s. In preparation for the arrival of our own Irish scholar, Octavia did her best to educate the class about the disaster that had recently forced so many of the Irish from their homes. In 1845, the year brother Charles was born, a destructive fungus wiped out more than half of Ireland's potato crop. This catastrophe became known as the "Irish Potato Famine." The Galic name for this disaster was *An Gorta Mor,* the Great Hunger, and it was far more complicated than just one failed crop. In fact, the famine had lasted for four years, and as a result, immigrants from Ireland began to pour into the United States by the shipload. Most of them were desperately poor and willing to do almost any task for less money than local workers were willing to accept. Greedy factory owners, happy to get the same work done for less compensation, exploited the situation and often replaced locals with the newcomers causing anger and resentment.

Our new scholar, Michael Sullivan, was an infant when disease took the lives of his parents. After acquiring enough money to buy passage, his grandparents brought the child here in 1851. His grandfather died of cholera, just about the same time that Frankie passed away from the illness, and now Michael lived alone with his grammy. The boy was just about as Irish as they come. He had red hair, a face full of freckles and a stocky "farmer" build. He was twelve years of age and had a reputation of not taking insults to his Irish heritage lightly. It was rumored that he had been expelled from his previous school for fighting.

On his arrival, Miss Hunt had us each stand, walk up to our new classmate, tell him our name, and shake his hand. All went as planned until our class clown, Mary Hale, approached Michael and decided to use her surname first, and with a chuckle, introduced herself as "Hale Mary[29]." This was followed by a burst of laughter from some of the boys who thought it fine sport to make fun of the newcomer's Catholic faith. Ms Hunt called Mary over to lecture her, privately.

As I approached Mr. Sullivan, I put my head down in shame at the behavior of my classmates. When I reached him, I looked up and whispered, "Sorry." After that, I extended my hand, curtsied, and in a normal voice, declared, "Annie Goodwin. Pleased to make your acquaintance."

From that moment forward, he and I quickly became friends. Though boys and girls were separated in the classroom, he would always seek me out during our noon break or play with me at recess. He was a good-hearted young man and seemed about as normal as anyone else for being Irish Catholic.

Unfortunately, there were two numbskulls, George and Billy, who were determined to push Mikie over the edge. They tripped him "accidentally" when he walked by their desks, whispered nasty things under their breath, and sometimes stole his lunch! One time, they replaced his meager meal with two rotten potatoes, a cruel reminder of the blight that had taken the lives of his parents. They continually ridiculed the religious medal of the Virgin Mary that he wore around his neck. However, in contrast to all of their recklessness, the two were very careful not to do anything in the view of our teacher.

After a while, I became furious with all the bullying. I begged Michael to speak out and tell Miss Hunt what was going on, but for some reason he wouldn't, nor did he want others to come to his defense. I found myself growing frustrated with his continual tight-lipped secrecy. We were becoming close friends and it bothered me that he didn't trust me enough to tell me why he was expelled from his old school or why he refused to defend himself from those two trouble-makers! One chilly afternoon during recess, I decided I had had enough, and I threatened never to speak to him again unless he confided in me.

"I'm embarrassed, Annie. You're gonna think I was to blame," he mumbled nervously.

"Michael Sullivan," I fumed, "you know me better than that! We've both seen what those two dummies are doing. Why won't you tell Miss

Hunt, or simply let me do it?" In my frustration, I began kicking pebbles at Mikie's feet.

"Ya know very well why not! I don't wanna have to leave this school, too!" He paused for a moment and added, in a whisper, "I'll tell ya why I got kicked out … but not word of it to anyone. Anyone! Folks 'round here just love spreadin' Irish dirt."

"I swear on the Holy Bible, I won't tell a living soul!" I whispered in earnest.

"Oh, come now, people swear on the Bible for any ol' thing. Then they print it in the Hallowell Gazette!" he retorted.

"So, how many things do I have to swear on?" I asked, but I already knew the answer. I sighed and finally resigned, "All right, I swear on Frankie's grave."

Mikie paused, placed his index finger against his lips, and looked up at the clouds, as though awaiting a celestial nod from Saint Patrick. Then, looking back at me, he declared, "That'll do."

"It had better!" I snapped, feigning disgust. "And what were you looking at in the sky, anyway?"

Mikie didn't answer, but gave me a smile.

We wandered over to a bench, brushed off the light snowfall, and sat down together, away from the eager ears. "Well," he began, "there's always someone who wants to start a row with me. It's like my red hair says 'come punch me, I'm Irish.' Anyway, there was this one lad at my second school who hated me from day one."

"Did you go to a different school before that?" I asked.

"Yes, sad to say, I did. Anyway, I was a youngun when I was at the first school, and the boys and girls were much kinder. Went there for five or six years. Then it closed down for a season, and Grammy taught me for a year or so. Then she decided to send me to the one at Togus Springs. She heard there were some blokes there 'bout my age. Thought I might find a friend or two."

"That's where you had all the trouble?" I asked.

"Yep," he continued. "Trouble seems to find me no matter where I hide. Anyhow, this fella, Clem, taunted me just like our two rascals. I can take that kinda malarkey, and it rolls like water off a duck. But, ignorin' his mischief made it worse. Trouble really started when Jenny, a girl he had his eye on, took a likin' to me. That really got his goat. He and her weren't nothin' but friends, but he thought I'd moved in on his territory, and vowed to take revenge. And that he did!"

"Were you two officially courtin'?" I asked.

"No. Goodness no! We weren't courtin' officially or unofficially! We was friends … and that's it. Now, what *she* may have thought might be a different story. But I made it quite clear that I had no such intentions."

"So, what happened?" I prodded.

"Well, it seems that someone wrote a letter, put my name on it, and stuck it in Jenny's coat pocket. When we entered class, after recess, she reached in and pulled out the note. Clem grabbed it outta her hands before she had time to open it, and read it to the entire class!"

"What did it say?" I asked, wide-eyed.

"Well, let me put it this way ... it was the most vile and filthy thing you ever heard. And Mr. Jones just sat there in his seat, hands behind his head like he was enjoyin' a good laugh. He never stopped Clem. For God's sake, there were little ears present! 'Twas like he wanted a reason to get rid of the new Irish kid, and he'd found it," Mikie explained, shaking his head.

"What did you do, Mikie?"

"I looked over and explained that I had nothin' to do with the letter. 'Sir,' I said, 'I would never write such a vile thing!'" Then, from out of Clem's mouth, came a muted snicker, and before I knew it, I was on him like flies on a dung heap. I pounded him to a pulp, which was a stupid thing to do. Got myself expelled. And now I'm here, and that's why I'm tryin' not to get into a fight with those two monkeys."

"Didn't Jenny try to help you?" I asked in disbelief.

"She tried to stick up for me, but Mr. Jones had already made up his mind. Everyone knew 'twas Clem that wrote the letter. Course, it wasn't the note that got me expelled. I broke the kid's jaw. Stupid ... stupid."

"Well, you had to do something. I'm infuriated just hearing about it," I remarked.

"It's over now. I just wanna move on. Sometimes you gotta pay a price to get an education," he explained.

Mikie's self control was nothing less than heroic. However, it wasn't long after disclosing the events at his old school that things boiled over at ours.

Chapter 9

Grammy Sullivan

*O*ne afternoon, after having been excused for the day, the two instigators approached Michael, who was talking with Eliza and me. George, the worst of the two came right up to Mikie and looked him straight in the eye, nose to nose, and whispered, "I'd rather have a nigga in our school than a goddamn Mick."

I watched, but Mikie said nothing and turned away. Then Billy grabbed him by the arm and whipped him around, looking him straight in the eye again. "Ain't you gonna say nothin' you stupid horse's ass?" Again, Mikie was silent but continued to stare Billy down. I saw a vein begin to bulge on his temple and realized that he was struggling to hold back his rage.

George jumped back in, "Is it true that your momma and papa died from eatin' a bad potata? Hmm? That's what'cha call the luck o' the Irish. Couldn't tell a rotten 'tata from a good one, huh? Musta been pretty stupid … just like their offspring. Why don't you fight us, right here an' now, you freckle-faced coward!"

"You 'fraid to fight us, ain't ya?" mocked Billy, in a whiny voice.

"That's right, Billy," taunted George. "He's probably gonna go right home and cry on his Grammy's shoulder 'cause that old Irish pig's all he's gut now!"

That was the very moment when George parted ways with three of his front teeth, and Billy dropped to the ground after a single punch to the bread basket. For a moment, the maleficents simply stared at Mikie, wide-eyed and gawking. Then, no doubt realizing they'd messed with the wrong Irishman, they turned and raced home as fast as their legs could carry them.

Yours Truly was outraged! Looking at George's three bloody teeth lying on the ground, I screamed after him, "Hey, George! You forgot your teeth!"

After we had calmed down, I explained to Miss Hunt everything that had happened. She vowed to have Billy and George expelled from our school immediately, which made me feel overjoyed. Finally, some justice! But oddly enough, Michael simply said that he didn't want that, claiming:

"They already paid the price for their crimes. I don't think they'll give me any more trouble, ma'am. I've a hunch they could use an education."

I'd rarely seen such astonishment and admiration on a teacher's face than on that of Miss Hunt in that moment. She was so impressed by Mikie's ability to forgive. Fortunately for all of us, those two demons never did return to our school.

Over time, I became Michael's most trusted friend; so much so that he even let me call him "Sully," his deceased grandfather's nickname, which only the "elect" were allowed to use! We both enjoyed discussing current events happening around the world, and Miss Hunt continued to stir those interests by bringing in the most up-to-date newspapers.[30] Through the articles and editorials, one could almost hear the ever-intensifying tremors of a volcano that was about to split our country in half.

Some folks brushed off those rumblings as nonsense. After all, most of the contents of these papers had to do with far-away places, and therefore were not our problem. Until recently, Boston had been a bumpy, two- or three-day ride by coach. And South Carolina? That might as well have been India! But, by 1859, one could be eating breakfast in Hallowell on the Kennebec and dining that same evening in Boston overlooking the Charles. A trip into the deep South would take slightly less than two days, and locomotives could now travel nearly a mile a minute! Those troubles, which had once seemed so far away, were moving closer to home.

Another topic that Mikie and I often deliberated, was the existence of eternal life. Of course, this kind of question was typically initiated by me, but Mikie was always an eager participant in our dialogues.

"Sully, do you ever wonder about your momma and papa?" I asked with a smile, as we were walking home from school.

"Yeah. Think about 'em every single day. Can't remember their faces, though. I was a wee 'un when they died. You're lucky to have an image of Frankie," he remarked quietly, as though lost in thought.

"Guess so. Honestly, those death-dags are repulsive things. Just lyin' there, stone-dead. That's not how I want to remember him," I explained.

"Well, at least you can see his face whenever ya like. More than I can say."

"True," I admitted.

"Yes," Mikie sighed, then glanced up at the sky as he so often did. "But I will see 'em again, some day."

"How do you know? Maybe this is all there is," I retorted.

Mikie continued to look up to the heavens, as if there was something up there looking back at him. "Annie Doubtin'-Thomas Goodwin! Didn't know you were an atheist," he teased.

"I'm not. Just wanna be honest about my doubts. I've been strugglin' in this muddle ever since Frankie passed," I admitted, realizing that this was the first I'd officially admitted it to another person.

"Well, maybe God *wants* ya to struggle in the muddle," Mikie replied. "If ya knew everything, what good would yer faith be?"

I let out a heavy sigh. "I guess. Maybe I just think too much. But I refuse to live my life believin' a lie. Most folks just accept what they're told. I can't do that. Just can't."

"Ya need to talk to my gram. She'll straighten ya out, right good!" Mikie admonished.

"And try to convert me from my evil, Protestant ways, I imagine," I said.

"Never!" he replied, defensively.

"Sorry. Just makin' a dumb joke. Papa's always teasin' me about being friends with you. Thinks I'm gonna end up in a convent."

Mike chuckled. "Well, rest assured Gram would never meddle in that convertin' malarkey. You ain't gonna lose anythin' by talkin' to her. In fact, you'll end up a better Protestant than ever, most likely, and she'd enjoy it, too. She'll talk your ear off about this stuff."

One Friday in early December, Sully invited my brother Johnny and me to come over to visit. It was never easy to get time off at the farm. I had to go through a chain of command starting with Mother, who had recently found out she was with child again. The twins had been difficult deliveries, and she had been cautioned about the risks of another pregnancy at age thirty-nine. However, she was feeling well and her friend, Angela, along with her thirteen- and fourteen- year-old daughters, were visiting for the weekend. The two girls generously volunteered to help out in any way they could. (Undoubtedly, Charles's handsome presence provided some motivation.) In any case, Momma gladly accepted their offer.

I then went off to find Papa who was in the barn, repairing our sleigh.

"*Mon cher Papa*, can Johnny and I visit the Sullivans, tomorrow?" I asked. "Michael's grandma has invited us and Momma's already agreed."

"Well now, if she says yes, what do I have to say in the matter?" he replied with a wink.

"Thank you!" I cheered, giving him a quick peck on the cheek.

"You're welcome dear. Kinda like the reverse of the army, ain't it. You start with the commander, then you work your way down to this old foot soldier!"

"You're the commander, Papa!" I replied, eager to stay on his good side.

"You know better than that Annie Elizabeth! I'm only the commander when I'm at sea." Father continued, "So how do ya like our sleigh? Been workin' on the wooden bed. Most of the boards were quite rotten. Wouldn't want'cha to fall through when we're dashin' through the snow!"

I laughed, "No, that wouldn't be pleasant."

There was a short pause, then Father continued, as if it were an afterthought, "So … ya takin' a likin' to this Sullivan boy, eh?"

"Not in that way, Papa," I replied, rolling my eyes. "I'm only ten years old for heaven's sake!"

"Yes, but you're a handsome ten, and ya look thirteen, and you're as smart as I was at twenty. You're gonna catch somebody's eye pretty soon," Papa warned, shaking his head.

"Well thank you *mon cher* for that noble compliment," I replied, with aristocratic flair. "But we're just good friends, and Edith is a sweet old lady. I've seen her a few times when she's picked him up at school. You know, Mikie's had to put up with a whole lot of mischief from some of our local hellions."

There is a woman in the lunatic asylum at New York who thinks that the Roman Catholics are trying to build a cathedral on her stomach, and who goes to bed every night with a club to keep off the Papists. She ought to be admitted into the know-nothing lodge without a ballot.—*Providence Journal.*

"I don't doubt it … bein' Irish and Catholic. Sad how some folk ain't welcome 'cause the color of their skin, their religion, or where they're from. 'Cept for the Indians, we're all from somewhere else. Makes no sense, does it?"

I nodded in agreement.

"Well, you go ahead and have a good time. Just don't come back a cloistered nun, ya hear?" He chuckled. "I'm gonna want grandchildren in my old age."

"Oh, Papa!" I exclaimed in a mix of exasperation and good humor.

———

Mikie arrived to pick me up at about 10:30 the next morning. The wagon jerked and rocked as we traveled up the steep hill to his grandmother's place. The muddy wagon tracks from the previously warm day had frozen into deep, rock-solid, furrows. These were the kind of road conditions that could snap a wheel right off its axle if the driver wasn't attentive. Nevertheless, we enjoyed the unpredictable bounces and jolts and arrived with no mishaps.

The Sullivans lived in a small farmhouse, eastward about halfway between our home and Togus Springs. The Togus Springs Hotel, which opened in June of 1859, quickly became a popular resort during the early 1860s. The establishment was so well frequented that our road became known as Chelsea Avenue[31] as a result. The waters there were rumored to possess curative properties for "anything that ails ya." It was likely the peaceful setting, more than anything else, that helped folks recover. Nevertheless, the spa's notoriety put our little town on the map for a brief moment.

Mrs. Sullivan was an intelligent and jovial, down-to-earth, octogenarian with a magnetic personality and delightful Irish brogue. Though slightly hunched over with age she maintained a healthy, deliberate gate, and her features bore a youthful beauty that radiated an empathic quality attesting to much heartache and perseverance. Her snow-white hair was always neatly tied in a bun and her clothing plain but immaculate. In her prime she must have been one of the most captivating gems of the Emerald Isles! She welcomed Johnny and I with a smile and some warm hugs.

After helping her cook and consume a delicious early afternoon meal, I had the opportunity to talk to her at length. We had much in common. She was a devoted abolitionist and had written several anti-slavery editorials for the Kennebec Journal using the clever pen name, "Freeman Riley." Talented female journalists were still being snubbed by many newspaper editors, so women writers disguised themselves with male names.

During our candid conversation, Edith told me of a vivid dream that she'd experienced on the evening of October 16. She dreamt that she was walking along a foggy road. As she wandered, she began to meet scores of negroes trudging silently past her in the opposite direction, many of them carrying shovels and hoes.

"At first, I reckoned d'ey were farmers," she remarked, in her charming accent. "I asked one of 'em, 'Where're ya goin', so many of ya?'"

The young man lifted his head, and looked at me, pitifully, sayin', "To bury da dead, ma'am."

"What dead?" I asked.

"All d'em young boys, ma'am … all d'em young boys."

"Da dream ended, and I came to wit' a start. Couple days later, found out d'at John Brown tried and failed to start a slave uprisin' in Virginia. 'Twas all happenin' whilst I was dreamin'!"

"What do you think it means?" I asked, thoroughly intrigued.

"Oh, Annie, a great tempest is a gatherin'. We must pray for da soul of our nation."

After a moment of silent reflection, probably sensing my uneasiness, she smiled and remarked, "Let's talk about somethin' a little lighter. Could I get ya a cup of coffee … or are ya not allowed?"

"Oh, I'm allowed," I replied, with a grin.

"Good. I'll brew it up."

As she was preparing the coffee, I gazed around and noticed what looked like a small guest room off to my left. Within, I could see a statue of Mary with prayer beads wrapped around the praying hands. There seemed to be several candles surrounding the little sanctuary, some paper pictures and other items as well. I was trying to be discreet with my gawking, but was caught red-handed.

"Yep, dearie, I'm a Roman Cat'olic, a rare bird 'round d'ese parts. Here ya go," she said, carefully handing me the hot drink.

"Oh, thank you. And please excuse me for being so nosey."

"Curious, ya mean," she responded, with a giggle. "A questionin' soul is halfway to becomin' wise. But let me put yer first query to rest. I don't worship da Blessed Virgin," she remarked, with a big smile, "or statues, for d'at matter."

"I was quite sure you didn't," I responded. Then I paused for a moment, for fear of asking something she might view as offensive.

"Annie, dear, I can read your t'oughts like a book," asserted Edith. "D'ere's nothin' you could ask d'at would ruffle me feathers. Speak yer mind, young lady!"

"I was wondering," I began, hesitantly. "How should I put this? Why do you have … have a statue of Mary … ah … " I stammered.

"Why not one of our Lord, instead?" asked Edith, finishing my question. "Or, better yet, why any statues at all?"

"Yes, ma'am," I responded, meekly.

"Oh, da statue's but a memento, dear, like a photograph of a loved one."

"Guess they didn't have daguerreotypes back then, did they?" I quipped, smiling at the thought.

"No, 'fraid d'ey didn't," laughed Edith. "Let's go into me little shrine and I'll explain a few t'ings." I followed her to the small adjacent room, and she continued, "Cat'olics believe d'at we can seek da Lord's help in many ways. Are ya familiar wit' the weddin' at Cana in da Good Book?"

"Yes ma'am, I know that story."

"Annie, let's not be so formal. Call me Edith. You're a friend of da family. Anyone who would stick up for Mikie must have a good heart."

I looked down at the floor with a timid grin, "I can't stand prejudice, ma'am … Edith."

"Nor can I, as ya know. OK, where was I? I would forget me brains if d'ey didn't come wit' da package! Oh yes, da weddin'! Let's see what ya remember from Sunday school. When da caterers realized d'ey were outta wine, what did d'ey do?"

I thought for a moment. "They went to Mary?"

"Aye, d'ey did! And where did she go afterwards?"

"To Jesus."

"Correct again! Do ya recall what Mary said to her Son?"

"She told Him that they'd run out of wine."

"Ya do know your scripture, young lady. Bravo! And what was his response?"

"It was … rather like … 'Why are you bothering me? My hour has not yet come' or something like that."

"Somet'in' like d'at is right! A wee bit rude of Him to speak to his own mot'er d'at way, don't ya t'ink?"

"Yes, I've always felt uncomfortable with that verse."

"And ya should, unless He wanted us to see a *deeper meanin'* in d'at reprimand. Do ya remember Mary's response?"

"Yes. She told the caterers, 'do whatever He tells you.'"

"And what did He do?"

"He changed water into wine."

"And dat, my dear," concluded Edith, " is why we Cat'olics like to ask Mary for help. She goes to da Source, twists her Son's arm a smidgen, and gets da job done!" Edith exploded with laughter at her own, simplified conclusion.

Now, feeling more at ease, I posited, "Don't you believe that we can go directly to Jesus?"

"Of course! Askin' da saints is but an option." Then, appearing to change the subject, she asked, "What do ya t'ink happens when we die?"

I wasn't ready to reveal my struggle with faith, but was grateful that she had opened the door for future reference.

I replied, "At the very moment little Frankie died, a bluebird landed on the window sill. I've often thought it was guiding his soul back to heaven."

"Oh my! I'm so sorry for yer loss. But, what a godsend at such a crucial moment! And have ya ever asked Frankie's assistance from above?"

"Well, I asked him to guide me to help Johnny."

"Dat's what we're talkin' about! Death doesn't break da bonds of love. I hope me simple examples make sense. Wouldn't want ya to t'ink I'm away with da fairies!" she declared, with a joyful cackle.

Thus closed the first of many encounters with this lovely woman. I could never have imagined what a powerful role she would play during the dark years that were looming on the horizon.

Chapter 10

Munky Funk

A Canine Tollman—We had a paragraph sometime since, about a wonderful dog owned by Fuller, of the Chelsea Ferry, that he knew so much that he could be trusted to make change for passengers and could detect the least disposition in any one to dodge toll. He got run over last week, by a four horse team in an attempt to open the ferry gate, in order that it might pass through. He was rolled out as flat as one's hand. He recovered from this and resumed his duties. Yesterday, he came into the ferry-house with a very knowing look, wagging his tail in a very waggish manner, and placed in his master's hand three one-dollar bills that he held in his mouth. He had picked them up after a careless teamster had passed, and with becoming honesty, handed them in. Such conduct merited some reward, but the ungrateful teamster didn't give him a cent.

—*Gardiner Home Journal*, Jan. 13, 1859

In early April of 1860, an exciting local event took place. The drawbridge that had been under construction for the last four years, linking Hallowell and Chelsea, was completed! Up to that point in time, you either crossed the river by ferry, or you rode to Augusta or Gardiner to access their covered bridges. People from all over central Maine turned out for the opening. The piers were constructed from Hallowell granite and reached a height of 16 feet. The drawbridge section was an open, wooden structure made of hackmatack, a hard, sturdy, and water-resistant wood used in shipbuilding and for railroad sleepers. The piers were built parallel to the shore in order to better accommodate the tide's ebb and flow.

Tolls were reasonable.[32] If you were on foot it would cost a trime[33] to pass into Hallowell and another back to Chelsea. Horse and rider were charged a half-dime. If you were in a wagon the toll would be assigned by the number of horses you were driving: one horse, twelve cents; two horses, fifteen cents; and four horses, twenty cents. Those going to and coming from public worship, military personnel with baggage, and fire-emergency crews could pass and repass at no charge. The fact that people no longer

Chelsea-Hallowell bridge, ca. 1860.

had to take a ferry to cross the Kennebec meant that those wishing to go to the popular Togus Springs resort in Chelsea could do so with ease. A road[34] had been specially constructed about a third of the way up the hill, heading northward and branching off the Ferry Road, allowing travelers a more gradual but longer route to the County Road. No doubt, the horses appreciated the detour, and I, for one, was thrilled with the bridge! Let's just say that the ferry and I were not on friendly terms.

My distaste for the ferry, and all things associated with that contraption, began with an incident that took place in November five years earlier. For those who are not familiar with the two-horse ferry, let me acquaint you. Ours was a riverboat-type barge powered by two horses walking along a single round tread-wheel system and facing in opposite directions. The only section of the tread that was exposed was in the horses' stalls; the rest of the rotating device and its system of gears were below deck. Two six-foot paddle wheels on either side propelled it through the water.

It all began on a beautiful Saturday morning in November of 1855. Father, Charles, and I had gone to Hallowell to do some shopping. The crossing from the Chelsea side was uneventful. After we finished our errands, we boarded the 9 a.m. ferry, aptly named the *Munky Funk*. That name alone should have been enough of a warning! Anyway, ex-Governor Hubbard was on board along with many other passengers. I believe that the dignitaries were all attending the launching of a vessel on the east side.

When we reached the halfway mark on the Kennebec, there was a loud crack, as though a huge tree branch had just broken! The sound came from right under our feet. Suddenly the paddle wheels stopped turning and the boat made a sharp turn south. The tide was moving out quickly, and we along with it! The ferry had now become a 64-foot piece of driftwood heading to who-knows-where. People were yelling and screaming for help, but how do you stop a multi-ton boulder cascading down a mountain? Captain Beeman tried to calm us with his authoritative voice, and promised that we would be unharmed. Not everyone believed him and a few broke into the Lord's Prayer. A little help from above couldn't hurt. By then, Papa had picked me up and was holding on tightly to Charlie's hand.

"Papa!" I screamed, "What's happening to the boat!"

Charles piped in, "Something broke! The wheels aren't turnin'!"

Papa tried to calm us down, but we could hear the worry in his voice. "It's all right," he soothed, "We're gonna be just fine. She's still afloat!"

The vessel was now adrift and completely at the mercy of the accelerating currents. People were moving chaotically from one side to the other, much to the captain's dismay. "Stop that movin' around!" he yelled. "Stay put!"

We were now traveling at the speed of the outgoing tide, which was faster than usual due to an overnight swell of rain water. The wayward craft was on a direct collision course with protruding boulders that jutted out near a small island off the west bank of the river!

"Papa … we're gonna crash into that island! Look at those rocks! We're gonna die!" I screamed in terror.

Father wrapped his arms around Charles and me. The three of us sat down on the deck and leaned against the rail post to prepare for the impact. But before we ever reached the boulders, we slammed to a crackling, crunching stop. Because of Father's quick thinking, we were not thrown overboard or injured. Others did fall to the deck from the impact, but the wooden barriers put a stop to anyone taking a November swim. The horses toppled over and one broke the side of its stall, nearly crushing an elderly woman. But Captain Beeman, with no time to spare, courageously pulled her out of harm's way! We'd hit a rock-laden shoal, and the hull began taking on water from the jolt. The captain ordered us to stand closer to the resting end of the stranded vessel as the other end sank. He assured us that as soon as the tide was out we could all wade to the island and wait for help to arrive. Miraculously, no one was severely injured and everyone, including the horses, made it to shore safely. Within a couple of hours we were, thankfully, back home!

That very day, this article was printed in the Hallowell Gazette[35]:

Mr. Editor:

The ferry boat "Munky Funk" of about 75 tons burdon, which piles between this city and Chelsea this morning about 9 o'clock in crossing the Kennebec at this place, full of passengers, (ex-Governor John Hubbard amongst them) broke some of the machinery when in the middle of the river. In her disabled condition she drifted with the rapid current until she brought up on a shoal just above Herring Island and sank.

We are happy to learn that owing to the prompt exertions of Capt. John Beeman at their head, that no lives were lost and all the passengers were safely landed. It is supposed that the boat will be raised and repaired at the cost of something less than $1,000.

The boat was recovered, repairs were made quickly, and within a week, the floating death trap was ready for its next adventure; an experience of which I was not planning to partake!

I contrived every ploy imaginable to avoid another ferry ride. I feigned illnesses by putting soot under my eyes, complained of an aching stomach, pretended to vomit up food, and forced myself to lie in bed all morning, moaning and groaning (which was boring beyond belief!). My scheme actually worked for a short time, but Father and Mother caught on quickly. But my most creative stunt, my final attempt to avoid the *Munky Funk*, took place about a month after our ill-fated voyage.

I planned the whole thing out as carefully as possible, using all the creativity and resourcefulness a child could muster. Saturday morning was our usual day to travel to town. So coming up with an instant illness on that day was no longer working. I decided that Friday morning would be the best time for me to contract smallpox, or Munky Pox as I thought of it.

On Thursday, I ate nearly twice as much as usual, because I knew the next day would be one of fasting, as my illness progressed. On Friday morning the dreaded symptoms suddenly came upon me as I was walking into the kitchen. Momma was sitting on a stool, stirring up a mixture of milk and eggs in a large bowl.

"Mother, I'm sorry but I really don't feel like eating breakfast. I have a bad headache, and I think I have a fever," I said, in my well-rehearsed, fretful tone.

"Hmm. Let's see," she replied, holding the bowl under her left arm and placing her right hand on my forehead for a few seconds. "Well, there's no fever. Why don't you rest awhile and see if the headache goes away."

"Very well. I hope you didn't make anything special for me."

"No. We're having French toast with maple syrup. Charles would never let that go to waste. He'd eat all our portions if he could."

"Oh … that's my favorite, too. I wish I felt better," I drawled, in a melancholy voice.

As I trudged upstairs, I was fuming! "This was the wrong day to get sick," I thought. "Why didn't I wait 'til after breakfast to come down with something? No French toast! No maple syrup! Stupid, stupid, stupid."

Early that afternoon a miracle happened; Mother received two visitors who stayed for several hours, giving me plenty of time for more machinations. When I was sure that the coast was clear, I snuck into my parent's room and opened Mamma's box of toiletries. There were all kinds of oils, salves, and creams for skincare, as well as brushes to apply the concoctions. After experimenting with the oils I realized that my face looked sweaty, and when applied to the forehead and hair, I truly looked stricken with some god-awful fever. Now, all I needed were a few ghastly red spots and voilà—smallpox!

Time dragged by slowly. Whenever Momma came up to check on me I positioned myself facing away from her and pretended to sleep. That worked, as she merely peeked in and then silently closed the door. Finally, the clock chimed eleven, and in the stillness of the night, I crept down to the pantry, groped around on the shelf, and grabbed a jar of preserves. I returned to my room, and placed the "pox" under my bed. At first light, I sat before my small vanity, took out a pen, dipped it into the jam, and began to dot my greasy face. The color spread out slightly over the oiled surface of my cheeks and forehead and looked quite convincing. When I finished my "death-mask," I retired to bed again.

Finally, early Saturday morning, the door opened gently and Mother walked quietly over to my bedside. As soon as she got a glimpse of me she shrieked a blood-curdling scream. "John, Annie has the pox! Oh, my God … John, go fetch Ellen. Quickly! Keep everyone away from her room!"

"Oh no," I thought. "I've overdone it."

I was really in a pickle! I had not only succeeded in my artistic endeavor to look sick but also appeared to be at death's door with a highly contagious disease. This wasn't what was supposed to happen. Now, Ellen would be here in an hour's time, the play would be over, and I might even get a spanking! Lord knows, I'd worked hard for it.

I could hear the tumultuous scurry of footsteps up and down the stairwell. "Stay away from your sister, Charles, she's got the pox!" yelled Father. "Get the little ones downstairs and open all the doors and windows on the top floor to air the place out! I'll go hitch the wagon."

"What a mess I've got myself into. Should I just confess?" I asked myself in a panic. "The whole household's in an uproar and they're gonna find out anyway. I can't let Father go all the way to Ellen's house for a feigned illness. Oh dear."

Without any warning, Charles came bounding into my room, sat down on the foot of my bed and looked at me. I mean, *stared* at me. Intensely!

Two-horse ferry boat

"Charles, what are you doing in here?" I howled. "Don't you know I'm sick?"

"Really? Hmm … " he responded, calmly and cryptically.

"Didn't you hear Father?" I asked, with concern. "You need to get out of here before you catch this!"

Momma followed Charles into my room in an anxious flurry, covering her face with a handkerchief. "Charlie! What on earth are you doing?" she yelled. "Your sister's got the pox … and you're gonna catch it, too!"

"Hmmm," he grunted again, unmoved by her warning and still staring at my face. "I want to catch this malady of hers, Mother. Then I can avoid cleaning those smelly stalls."

Momma stood there, frozen, wide-eyed and mouth agape. "This is no time for your jokes, Charles!" she exclaimed.

My brother reached over, stuck his index finger in one of the "pox pustules" on my forehead, and retrieved some of the slimy ooze. He walked to the window to examine the foul-looking secretion. He squinted, held his finger in different positions, observing every angle like a mad scientist, and then proclaimed, "Holy smoke, Annie! I never knew smallpox had seeds. Maybe that's how it spreads." And he put his finger in his mouth, consuming the oily discharge with a satisfied smirk.

Mother gasped and collapsed onto a nearby chair, fanning herself with her hand for fear of fainting. Meanwhile, Charlie broke into a fit of hysterical laughter. Needless to say, Momma didn't need smelling salts to bring her back to awareness. Her facial expressions went from sheer terror to all-out wrath. She glared at me furiously and stormed out of the room.

"John! John!" she hollered, quickly descending the stairwell, "Annie pulled another fast one on us!"

I looked at my brother with tears running down my cheeks, "Papa's gonna give me a lickin'!"

"When was the last time *you* had a lickin'?"

"Never, but this time I've earned it," I whimpered.

"Annie, if anything, you've earned an award. Your performance was first rate! Hell, Shakespeare would be impressed!"

"Don't cuss. It's not funny. How'd you figure it out?"

"Simple," he responded, with a cocky air. "I was lookin' for Grandma's preserves, noticed the jar was missing and, heck, everyone knows you been playin' sick on Saturdays. So, I summed it all up to simple mathematics: raspberries plus Annie equals no Munky Funk. But smallpox was a bit overboard, don't ya think?"

Needless to say, I wasn't given an award, nor did I get a lickin'. But that afternoon, Papa dragged me, stomping and screaming at the top of my lungs, to the ferry! After a few more excursions I managed to contain my embarrassing outbursts. But it wasn't until the completion of the new bridge that I was able to take a long-awaited sigh of relief.

Chapter 11

"Belle!"

*Weep not for her! She is an angel now, and treads the sapphire floors of
    Paradise;*
*All darkness wiped from her refulgent brow; Sin, sorrow, suffering, banished
    from her eyes:*
*Victorious over death, to her appear the vista'd joys of Heaven's eternal year:
    Weep not for her!*
*Weep not for her! Her memory is the shrine of pleasant thoughts, soft as the
    scent of flowers,*
*Calm as on windless eve the sun's decline. Sweet as the song of birds among
    the bowers,*
*Rich as the rainbow with its hue of light, Pure as the moonshine of an autumn
    night: Weep not for her!*

        —*Gardiner Home Journal*

As the spring of 1860 commenced, our circumstances were better than ever. Our farm continued to thrive economically, so much so, that in June of the previous year, Father purchased 100 acres of land that lay directly across the road from us and extended north to the Augusta line.[36] The area was mostly fields, but it also had a wooded section sporting a small pond and a stream that fed out of the nearby marshlands. He was planning to use a portion of it for our needs and rent the rest to tenant farmers.

Lilly and Isabella were growing and demonstrating their very unique personalities. Bella was clearly my sister, both in personality and appearance. Though her hair was of a lighter hue than my own, our features were similar, complete with the freckled nose. She demanded to know everything immediately, if not sooner. One endearing habit of hers was to bring me a flower, a bug, a coin, a picture, or some other treasure, and silently leave it on my lap, expecting a thorough explanation. She would then put her hands on her hips and look up at me, inquisitively, expecting to learn its name, geographic origins, scientific qualities, and relevance to the human race! If my answer happened to be insufficient, she would entreat every member of the family until her curiosity was satisfied. Whether it be the hatching of a Monarch butterfly or a shooting star blazing a trail across the heavens, her questions were intelligent and challenging.

The girls were born on Easter Sunday, April 12, 1857. Sarah Lilly, or Lilly, as she preferred to be called, was a true Easter lily. She was as beautiful as the sun catching the dew on a forest dawn and adorned with wavy blonde hair that was nearly white in color. Characteristically, she loved everything about the season of spring: the melting snow, the budding leaves, the returning birds, and especially, the nightly chirping of peepers that typically began their yearly spring chorus on (or near) her birthday. Her fondest longing, during that glorious season, was for the blossoming of the lilacs that Mother had planted in the front yard; their aroma was irresistible to the little girl. She was a giggly little flower, who, like Johnny, found everything to be funny. It didn't take much to get her howling; a silly face, a strange vocal noise, or a cat pouncing on a nearby table would do the trick. She loved to cuddle and enjoyed my "hovering-tickle-troll." I would lift up my hand, hovering like a wiggling spider, and then drop it gently on her head as she lay in her bed. She would try to push it away, laughing with that belly laugh that only a three-year-old can demonstrate to perfection.

Johnny was no longer the "powder keg" of the household. He, like his older brother, had begun to develop a deep curiosity about the cosmos. Father gave him an old nautical telescope, with which, on a clear late winter evening, we were able to observe the great nebula in Orion's belt. On another night, we observed the hazy, oblong outline of Saturn; but there was too much humidity to view its rings. Johnny was able to explain how the 23 degree tilt of the earth, in combination with its rotation and revolution around the sun, defined the seasons. We were all amazed at how closely he was able to calculate the very moment of the moon's rising over the hills to our east, as well as the rising and falling of the visible planets and constellations. He was aware that light travels at the incredible speed of 186,000 miles per second, and he would never pass up an opportunity to flaunt his astronomical wizardry in front of anyone who would listen. In spite of his brilliance, he was an empathetic child with a generous heart, very much like the little twin that preceded him into eternity.

A cup of coffee is a sure barometer, if you allow the sugar to drop to the bottom of the cup and watch the bubbles arise without disturbing the coffee. If the bubbles collect in the middle, the weather will be fine; if they adhere to the cup forming a ring, it will be rainy, and if the bubbles separate without assuming any fixed position, changeable weather may be expected.— Try it.

Charles, at fifteen years of age, was maturing into a tall and handsome young man. More than a few young ladies had taken notice of that fact, including my ever-faithful companion, ten-year-old Emma. Unfortunately for her, she was little more than a fly buzzing around my brother's head.

At one point, in exasperation, she blurted out, "He'll notice me in a few years, but I won't give him the time of day!"

"Emma," I replied, sympathetically. "My parents are five years apart, just like you and Charlie. Give yourself a few years and he won't be able to take his eyes off ya."

"Well, I'm not waitin' around for any boy, not even your brother."

"Good," I asserted. "There's lots of fish in the sea."

"Yeah, but I'm afraid my net has a big hole in it," she quipped, with her impish grin.

True, my big brother could be a know-it-all, a show-off, and to my displeasure, show an agnostic indifference to matters of faith. But he was quickly becoming a kind and insightful young man. Though he was four years my senior, Charles was now my cherished confidant and I, his. He was my mooring against the difficulties, challenges, and changes of our unpredictable world.

Within the span of my brief eleven years, the railroad[37] had become a regular form of transportation in Hallowell. Steam engines powered many industries, locomotives, and some ocean-going vessels. The telegraph now connected most of the country with instant access to information, as an unending stream of new inventions flooded the market from every conceivable avenue. Technology was evolving at a breathtaking pace, and in many ways, our lives were better for it.

But there was something else happening in the country that was paramount, more important than useful gadgets or scientific breakthroughs. America was outgrowing its moral adolescence, and that coming-of-age would have dire consequences for the nation. The volatile emotions around the slavery issue were polarizing. Even at the tender age of ten, I could hear the approaching thunder in everyday conversations and newspaper articles. Were we truly on the brink of civil war?

My biggest worry was Charles's "war is glorious" attitude. Every afternoon, he would take Father's new caplock rifle and practice the techniques of a soldier, skillfully loading and firing the proverbial three-rounds-per-minute, and in short order, he was becoming an excellent marksman. He stated, firmly, that if war broke out over *the peculiar institution*, he would be the first to volunteer. I reminded him, (in order to soothe my own fears), that there wasn't a war and he couldn't enlist until he was eighteen, which was yet three years down the road.

One evening, as the family gathered in the sitting room, the topic of the possibility of going to war over slavery was introduced by Charles. Up to that point, Father had said little about it so as not to give us cause for alarm. I later penned his veiled but prophetic words in my journal.

Civil war would be the height of stupidity! Armed conflict today would be nothin' less than suicide. There are guns that can fire several shots in a few seconds and cannons that can reach targets miles away. Entire cities would be leveled. Artillery and vast numbers of troops can be moved hundreds of miles, overnight, by rail, and steam-powered warships can reach their destinations in no time. Civil war is too frightenin' a prospect for civilized people to give serious mind.

I was taken aback at how much "serious mind" Father had given the situation and how closely his thoughts echoed the dream that Mrs. Sullivan had shared with me back in December. After hearing his words, there was an eerie foreboding that tainted the everyday comings and goings of my young life.

In early May of 1860, Mother, at just six months pregnant, went into labor. Once again, Ellen Springer was summoned to our home. There was nothing that could be done to arrest the process, and the infant, a baby boy, was stillborn. Mother was made very disconsolate by the sudden loss. She had wanted another little boy after Frankie's death, but it wasn't to be. We decided to name the child and allow Johnny, himself, to do the honors. The name he chose was Davis Franklin, a reversal of the name of his deceased twin.

Father wrapped the baby in a cloth and placed him in a small wooden coffin. He thought it best for us children not to view the remains, but that didn't set well. We demanded, under threat of insurrection, that we should see our brother! Reluctantly, Father gave in, but forewarned us that the fetus did not look like a newborn baby.

As father unwrapped the swaddling, my lips trembled. Baby Davis Franklin, curled in fetal position, was about twelve inches in length and weighed nearly two pounds. Johnny and Charles were the first to see him. Neither said a word, but by the expressions on their faces, I knew they weren't prepared for the experience. The twins gazed in wonder at the doll-like features, the bald head, and the translucent skin. Lilly was frightened by all the "roots" that were showing under the skin. Charles explained that those were veins, and that skin usually covered them up once babies were old enough to be born.

"Do we have banes, too?" asked Bella, our resident scientist.

"Veins? Yes, we certainly do. Here, let me show you," I replied, rolling up my sleeve. "See those blue lines on my wrist? Those are my veins. They're like drain pipes. They help the blood move through my body when my heart pumps."

"Look, Annie. I have some too, just like yours!" she exclaimed, excitedly, pointing to her wrist.

Then Lilly piped in with the sudden discovery of her *own* circulatory system.

"Do we have them everywhere?" asked Bella.

"Yes, but we usually can't see them. They're covered up."

"Do I have them in my feet?"

"Yes."

"In my eyeball?"

"Yes."

"In my bones?"

"Hmm. I think so. Bones grow, so they have to have blood."

"Is there another place where we can see our banes?"

"Yes. There's lots of them under your tongue."

The "Child of a Thousand Questions" tore off to find a looking glass, allowing the rest of us to spend a few more minutes in quiet reflection with the brother we would never know in this life. I was most struck by the tiny hands; beautiful, well-formed, delicate hands that would never hold a book, write a love letter, or catch a baseball. Why would a loving God allow an innocent baby to die, especially after taking Frankie? The infant's death added another layer of doubt to my struggling faith.

Since our Congregational Church and local government had no rules as to how to dispose of a miscarried child, we took matters into our own hands. All of us, save Mother, gathered 'round the coffin which was less than a foot in length, and took turns saying a short prayer. Then, following Father out into the field behind the barn, we buried Davis Franklin Goodwin in a small grave, placing a large fieldstone over the spot. A few days later, Johnny and Charles carved DFG on it.

Mother had lost a great deal of blood during the miscarriage, but her health seemed to improve over the next three days, as the bleeding and cramping subsided. However, in the middle of the night, at the beginning of the fourth day, there came a blood-chilling scream from my parents' bed chamber. Charles, Johnny, and I, shaken from our sleep, came running into the room followed by the twins. Mother was sitting on the edge of the bed, doubled over in agony.

Father, donning his clothing, ordered, "Take care of Momma! I'm getting Ellen." He then rushed to the barn and hitched up the carriage, making a quick dash for the midwife. Time was of the essence.

Johnny and the girls were horrified to see their mother in such a state, and Charles had to physically restrain Bella and Lilly from overwhelming the poor woman. My brother did his best to usher the three children to Grandma's room, while trying at the same time to reassure them. Lilly could be heard screaming all the way down the stairwell, "Mumma, Mumma … I want my Mumma! I wanna see Mumma!"

Somehow, Bella broke loose from Charles's grip and bolted back into the bedroom. I grabbed her, just in the nick of time! Picking her up in my arms, I scurried down to the first floor.

Upon reaching our grandmother's room, Charles and I briefly explained the evolving situation. How very traumatic it must have been for that poor old woman to have to sit there with three distraught children, while her daughter lay in agony, directly above her. But being a soul tried in the arena of suffering, she promised to entertain the children as long as was necessary.

We returned, breathless, to find Momma in the same state as before.

"Mother, what's happening," I asked, terrified.

"Oh, dearies … It feels like someone's cutting me open with a knife," she replied, flinching and grimacing in pain.

"Mother, you're bleeding!" blurted Charles, noticing a few small drops of blood on the floor. "What should we do?"

Without warning, something snapped in my brain, and I fell to my knees, crying uncontrollably! Mother might die right here in front of us! I couldn't think, I couldn't move, I couldn't breathe … I felt paralyzed. The idea of living without her was more than my mind could accept. What would happen to the twins? What would they do without their "Mumma"?

"I can't do this! It's too much! Oh, God! Not Mother!" I raved, in repetitive frenzied sobs.

"Annie, get up and get yourself together!" barked Charles, shaking me forcefully by the shoulders. "Now's not the time for you to fall apart!"

Somehow, his angry bellowing and rough hands jolted me back from my drift into hysteria.

"Momma, I'm sorry. What we can do to help," I begged.

"Help me get back into bed, please" she stammered.

With me on her right and my brother on the left, we gently lifted her.

"Oh, my God! I just can't do it," she gasped. "Something's just not right. Oh…"

The pain was too much for her to right herself and she slumped back into her previous position.

"What do you mean?" I pleaded, on the verge of utter panic. "What's not right?"

"It's the pain, Annie … it's not like anything I've ever had before."

"Is it worse than having a baby?"

"No, but it's all in one place, on my left side … not like contractions. It's worse when I try to stand. Let's see if I can roll onto the bed in this position," she said, grimacing, as she leaned to her right.

Maintaining a near-fetal position, Mother was able to lie back down on her right side, without further agony. We laid a pillow under her head and covered her with blankets. Charles fetched soap and water and cleaned up the patches of blood on the floor. Within a few minutes, she was able to slowly straighten herself out on the bed into a more comfortable position. The sharp, stabbing pain had diminished to a dull throbbing ache.

"We've gotta let her rest," said Charles. "Ellen'll be here soon."

"You might wanna check on the little ones," suggested Mother, in a calming voice. "They're frightened. Tell them, I'm all right. I'm gonna be just fine."

She then caressed my head in her usual playful manner. At that moment, the mantle clock struck two. "Oh, my! It's so very late. You children need to get some sleep and stop worryin' about me. Momma will be just fine. We Keans are tough!"

"We'll go get Johnny and the girls back into bed," assured Charles.

"Thank you, dear," said Mother, with a sigh.

—⁓—

Ellen arrived with Father a short time later. Within an hour she had assisted Mother with her medical expertise, bathed her, dressed her in clean garments, and instructed us on how to care for our beloved patient. She would need complete bed rest until further notice. Warm, damp cloths should be applied, hourly, over the affected areas to bring down the swelling, and cold towels on the forehead for fever.

She explained, "It's not uncommon for inflammation to occur after miscarriages. Because the affected area is inside the body, it's more difficult to treat than if it were outside."

Though none of us was aware of it at the time, Ellen had called Father aside and informed him, "Your wife's condition is life-threatening. Let us hope and pray we can keep the infection from spreading. She's still young enough to fight it off."

Over the next forty-eight hours, Mother seemed to be improving. Just when hope of recovery was on the horizon, there was a sudden turn for the worse with the onset of a deep throbbing pain in her lower abdomen. Alarmingly, the pain was not confined to a specific location, and that was not a good omen. The infection was spreading! This new phase of the illness was heralded by a chronic, generalized, and escalating torment, accompanied by a spiking fever. My poor mother went from profuse sweating to uncontrollable chills. With my ears affixed to every adult conversation, I overheard whisperings of childbed fever, and I knew it was a killer.

The next three days of her illness were terrifying. Mother moaned, screamed, and thrashed around in her bed. She frequently called out for Father in fits of delirium and complained of horrific headaches that no amount of cold-presses could alleviate. There was also a foul-smelling stench of infection, which Mrs. Springer tried to manage by cleansing the affected area and then burning sage in the bed chamber.

Along with Charles, Papa, and Ellen, I attended to her frequent needs, and did my best to imitate their stoic approach to her unbearable suffering. Then, I would flee to the hayloft alone and weep, often falling asleep there from exhaustion. Even now, forty years later, nightmares from those disturbing scenes still visit me.

Thankfully, laudanum was prescribed and it afforded some relief. As the minutes, hours, and days ticked onward, things became more manageable for us, but that wasn't a good sign. Mother was no longer having uncontrollable fits, nor was she complaining about her suffering. But, her fever was raging as the infection invaded the other organs of her body. Once in a while there would be a soft moan or she would raise her arm in an involuntary fashion. Early one morning she softly spoke our names and even seemed to recognize us when we were in the room, giving us a morsel of hope.

"Momma, can you hear me? Just squeeze my hand if you can," I pleaded. There was a gentle press of her feverish hand against mine.

"I love you so much," I whispered. "I'm sorry that you're so ill. But you're going to get better. I'm going to pray and pray until the Good Lord hears me."

At that point the dear woman looked into my eyes, and lightly shook her head to the contrary.

"Mamma, you can't give up. You've got to be that 'tough old bird' like you said."

This time, she shook her head decisively, and seemed to emit a gentle smile of surrender. Every member of the family spoke to her that afternoon, and it was clear that she was aware, though unable to speak. Then she drifted back into the antechamber of eternity.

A MIRACLE IN MAINE. The Spirit Guardian of this city affirms that Dr. Caleb Thomas of Camden, "a very powerful healing medium," by the laying on of his hands has restored to the use of her senses a lady of 27 years of age who has been deaf and dumb from her birth. The name of the lady is said to be Mary Hews, and her residence, Cooper's Mills, in the town of Whitefield. We suggest that some of our Kennebec friends investigate this miracle. [Bangor Courier.

Our marvelousness is hardly up to the point of soberly investigating the proposed case.— Nevertheless we hereby request any of our subscribers in that vicinity to report what they know about it.

She may have surrendered to her fate, but I had not given up on her recovery. I had heard in a sermon once, that if you had enough faith and didn't doubt, that whatever you asked for in prayer would come to pass. But did I have enough faith for God to raise my dying mother? Or, perhaps my faith was already corrupted by all those nagging doubts? Was I, sinfully, putting God to the test? It didn't matter to me at the time, and I had nothing to lose. I decided to command her to arise, like Jesus did with Jarius's daughter when he summoned her from the dead." I told no one of my plans, so as not to be discouraged by their comments about my "religious foolishness," which I'm sure would have been forthcoming.

That night I knelt, prayerfully, at my mother's bedside. I could feel the dreadful fever radiating from her body, like a human furnace, from several inches away. How much she must have been suffering! I whispered in her ear, "Arise, Mother, in the name of Jesus." I waited. Nothing. No miracle, no movement, no response of any kind. I wasn't ready to give up that easily and I did the same thing every night, as the flame of life dwindled to a flicker.

Over the next couple of days the early signs of death began to appear. Her breathing was more shallow and rapid and her pulse was weak. Her features were sunken with a grayish pallor. Undaunted, I continued to try to summon her back from the grave.

On the night of the 17th, Dr. Davis from Hallowell paid us a visit. The entire Goodwin family surrounded the bed with the exception of Sarah Lilly and Isabella who were downstairs with Ellen. The doctor confirmed our fears; the end was very near. In my mind, I repeated the words, "Arise, Mother, in the name of Jesus," over and over, but I was too overwhelmed for any words to escape my lips.

Suddenly, Momma opened her sunken eyes and with a peaceful expression, as though greeting a welcomed visitor, spoke her last word, "Belle!" Then her eyes closed, she took one last breath, and her head turned slightly to the left. Sarah Goodwin[38] was gone. It was 9:25 p.m., Thursday, May 17, 1860.

A deafening silence came over the room as Dr. Davis checked her pulse and breathing, confirming what we already knew. We stood quietly there for some time until Father broke into uncontrollable sobs and fell to his knees. I had never seen my dear Papa weep so much! This big, strong sea captain with a bushy beard and weather-worn complexion from doing battle with so many ocean gales, collapsed to the floor like a little child, helpless. We all followed in an explosion of grief, releasing all the compressed emotion that had been bottled up for the past two weeks. Grandma Kean sat there stone-faced, staring out the dormer window, as one little tear escaped from that wrinkled, marbled visage. We embraced and consoled one another until there was, again, silence in the room.

Father, after regaining his composure, asked me to relieve Ellen, so that the twins could say goodbye to their Momma. Lilly burst into tears at the sight, as I expected she would. She was so distraught that I needed to take her out. We sat together at the top of the staircase and hugged silently for some time. Finally she asked, "Did Momma say anything, Annie?"

"Yes, dear. She spoke one beautiful word, 'Belle,'" I replied. "I think Auntie Belle came to take her to heaven to be with Frankie."

I couldn't help wondering if I was propagating a fantasy or a fact, but the grieving child needed some assurances. Truthfully, I was the one who needed certitude. Sarah Lilly, as yet, had no such misgivings.

Poor little Bella. She seemed to understand the finality of what had happened, demonstrating a maturity beyond her years. When the three-year-old entered the room she stood there for a second, observing everyone, as though she wanted to make sure that those present were all right. Then, she walked over to the lifeless body and imparted a beautiful kiss on her mother's cheek. She didn't wail and cry as one might have guessed.

After escorting the twins back down to Grandma, feeling emotionally drained, I returned to my place at the top of the stairwell and buried my head in my hands. It was past midnight when I finally retired. As I lay in my bed, the window wide open with the beautiful scents and sounds of springtime floating, paradoxically, on the gentle breeze, my thoughts began to drift. As I started to merge into slumberland, something nudged its way into my consciousness. I couldn't quite make sense of it at first. It was nothing of great importance, but something I wanted to remember; an event of sorts. It was now Friday, the eighteenth. Suddenly, I remembered it was my birthday.

"What eleven-year-old forgets her own birthday?" I mumbled, addressing the chorus of peepers that were chanting endlessly in the marsh.

"One who has just lost the person who gave her birthdays," came their immediate response.

"Wonderful!" I reflected, cynically. "I can celebrate it with a wake, a disturbing post-mortem photograph, and the burial of the dearest person on earth. The merriment never ceases around here."

"Charles couldn't have said it better," chirped the amphibious choir.

I could feel the onset of tears welling up again, but repulsed it by sheer stubborn will.

I had no sooner finished my swiftly dissolving soliloquy, when the door creaked open. It was Bella. She entered, and climbed into bed with me. Then came Lilly, followed by Johnny. We hugged each other and cried until the rising of the silver, waning crescent moon; after which, we fell into an exhausted repose.

Chapter 12

That Tangle of Threads

When a loved one passes, it's as though a violent storm or a devastating fire has engulfed your world. Once the shock dissipates, you must take inventory of what still remains. Some irreplaceable structures are gone, other possessions are damaged but can be repaired, and a number of things remain as they were, but their personal importance to you has changed forever. Death has a way of altering what we value and how we value it. For example, Grandma lovingly cut a piece of cloth from the nightgown that Momma was wearing when she died. She then placed the shred in the family Bible as a remembrance. I wouldn't trade that priceless icon for a twenty-dollar gold piece! It's a sacred relic, a memory beyond monetary value.

Friday, May 18, 1860, bloomed radiant in springtime glory, in stark contrast to the funereal mood that pervaded our little world. On that very day, a divided country learned of Lincoln's nomination for president, but the event bore no import amidst our grief. Even my eleventh birthday passed without notice. It was just as well. "Happy birthday" would have seemed more like cruel mockery than a thoughtful greeting. The clocks, all silenced at 9:25, preached a silent but eloquent sermon on the foolishness of temporal vanities. The lifegiving heart of the family was dead.

Over the next two days we greeted mourners, kept a round-the-clock wake, and tried to maintain our composure amidst the whirlpool of emotions that threatened to do us in. Thanks to our generous neighbors we had an abundance of food which we shared with our guests. Unexpected visitors came in from all over, and even Mr. Weeks, who aided Eli's escape, paid his respects. Mother was greatly loved and the outpouring of sympathy was a consolation for us.

We all express grief in different ways, and most of us have known someone who used ill-timed humor to momentarily deflect their own pain. That was Charles's defense against a broken heart and he was the master of it. The deeper the grief, the more outlandish his antics. The gloom surrounding us was as thick as mud, providing the perfect environment for my brother to distribute his "appropriately" inappropriate levity. He lost no time beginning his mission, and his first target was me.

On Saturday morning, I was arranging flowers in the summer kitchen when my brother entered. "Hey Annie," he quipped, "Tom Thwing is here."

"He's early," I responded, in a distracted manner. "Just as well. Sooner he gets done with those morbid photographs of Mother, the better."

"Yeah, then we get to face the camera. Those portraits should be even more ghastly," replied Charles.

His attempt at humor did not work on me. Charles could see I was teary and about ready to break down again. "Come on Sis, Mother wouldn't want us to fall apart. You and I need to be the strong ones this time ... especially for Papa. He just lost the love of his life."

I looked at Charles, threw my arms around him, and exploded with such huge sobs I could hardly breathe.

"Annie ... Smile for me."

"There's nothing to smile about."

"You know what Ben Franklin would say: 'Trouble knocked at the door, heard laughter, and hurried away!'"

"But trouble didn't hurry away, Charlie. It came in, stole our mother from us, and took up residency," I muttered, my voice trembling.

"Well it ain't gonna stay long. I'm gonna get a smile out of everyone or I'll give you each a silver dollar."

"You don't have that much money," I responded.

"Yeah ... but I ain't gonna lose!"

"Charles, this is our mother's funeral. Your foolishness won't be appreciated."

"And what makes you think I would do anything foolish?"

"You're Charles Andrew Goodwin."

My brother picked up one of the flowers and playfully swatted me across the face. "I demand satisfaction! You have insulted my honor!"

"Not funny. I'm exhausted, grumpy, and sick at heart."

Unwisely ignoring my emotional state, he continued, "I challenge you to a dung duel. Choose your weapon: cow, horse, or dog?"

"Damn it, Charles! What's wrong with you? Momma's corpse is lying in the next room, people are here to pay their respects, and you want to play court jester? Make yourself useful," I snarled, discourteously shoving a bouquet of flowers into his hands. "Take this into the parlor."

"I've lost the battle, Sis, but not the war," he proclaimed with a smirk, proceeding to carry out my orders.

Eight-year-old Johnny was his next victim. The little boy was lost in sorrow, and no one had been able to get the grief-stricken fellow to respond to anything. All he wanted to do was sit there, looking at Mother's worn out features. And I had promised myself to be his champion, but I could never be his mother.

Charles didn't let failure discourage him. He saw his humor as a crusade against the dark forces of grief and despair. At first he tried the "dung duel" approach, but got nowhere with that, not even so much as a sideways glance from his brother. Then he put his arm around Johnny and hugged him. I could see that the wheels in his head were turning. This was not going to end well.

Suddenly, Johnny erupted into a fit of laughter, startling the newly arrived guests with the incongruous outburst. Charles was smiling from ear to ear and shot me a wink. "Success!" he mouthed, with an air of conquest.

Father was furious. He literally dragged the pair out of the room by their collars, threatening them with hellfire. But, that was the end of it. Mother wasn't there to carry out their sentences.

When I caught up with my brother, I asked him how he had worked such a miracle with Johnny. He replied, cryptically, "You'll find out soon enough."

A short time later, there was a break in the clouds and our photographer was able to take the postmortem photos of Mother. Our family then assembled for the portraits of the living. We decided to use the sitting room, with its large, ornate sofa as the centerpiece for the group pictures. I, for one, was relieved not to have to stare at my dear mother's remains during our sitting.

After many adjustments of lighting, movement of curtains, positioning of the camera, and posturing of people, we were ready for the first plate. Thomas admonished us not to smile or move our bodies, as the camera would need a few seconds to absorb the appropriate amount of light for a good image. He said he would give a three-count before he opened the lens cap.

There we were in our black attire, quiet and solemn, frozen like statues in a deserted mausoleum. Our grief was so heavy that it could have been measured in pounds.

Finally, everything was ready and Thomas began the count. "One … Two …"

"Three!" came an alarming, high-pitched squeal from behind the sofa! "Critter in the shitter!"

Mr. Thwing gasped, looking up from his camera in shock! All eyes fell on Charles, who maintained an air of smug satisfaction. There followed a deafening, anticipatory silence, as Father glared at his son with such indignation that I thought Charles might be the next postmortem photo. Suddenly, Grandma burst into uncontrollable cackles and the sitting room exploded with laughter. Even Papa, who had not smiled in two weeks, was caught up in the moment. Hilarious mental images resurfaced; those of Charlie being lowered into "fecal paradise" and Mother screaming like a banshee, storming through the house, wildly brandishing a butcher's knife to do in her roly-poly foe.

Our photographer, although he had no idea what was happening, seemed to find this display a breath of fresh air amidst the leaden sorrow. It took us a few minutes to regain our composure, as one of us would either break into a smile or start giggling during a pose.

———

By early Sunday afternoon there were so many mourners that the pastor thought it best to have the gathering in the front yard. The people of Maine often say, "If ya don't like the weatha, wait a minute," and we found the words to be true. The previous day had been dreary and overcast, with temperatures in the forties, but the day of the burial turned out to be exceptional, with temperatures in the mid sixties! Beautiful, fluffy, fair-weather clouds drifted lazily from the west and a gentle breeze brought the essence of springtime to our senses. Charles brought out chairs for the elderly mourners, and the younger guests either sat on the doorsteps, on the grass, or remained standing for the service.

Once everyone was assembled the sermon began. "Remember," the reverend admonished us, "while we're sayin' good-bye on this side, our loved ones are comin' to greet us as we cross over to the other. Death is the bridge, and our dear Sarah Goodwin was greeted on that bridge by her beloved sister, Isabella! Those with whom we associate and love, here on earth," he declared, "will be the very ones with whom we share eternity."

"In God's world, there is a complete reversal of how things operate. Here, we are heartbroken; there, we are rejoicing. Our limited time here ends; there, it begins, never to cease. Here, there is decay; there, only perpetual perfection.

"How many of you ladies have ever embroidered or stitched a sampler or a decorative piece?" Many hands went up. "Good. Let's pretend you're a little child sittin' on the floor and watchin' Mamma perform such a task. All you can see from your position is the frame of the embroidery. You see her push the needle through the underside. To you, it's a mixture of colors and hangin' threads and criss-crosses that make no sense at all. You tell her that she is makin' a big mess! She laughs and turns the piece over so you can see the top. You are amazed! Before your eyes is a beautiful garden scene done in intricate detail.

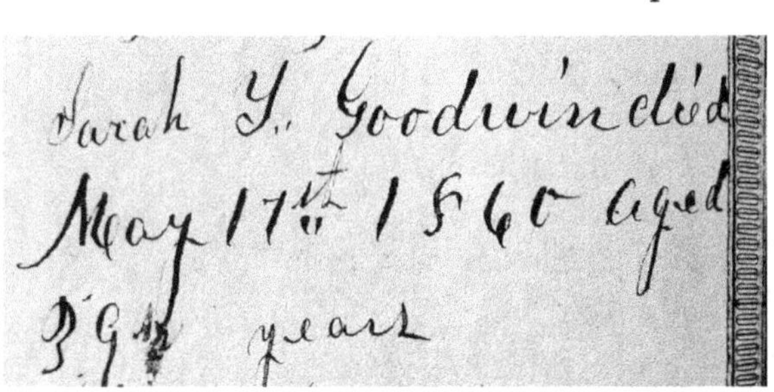

Entry of Sarah Goodwin's death in Kean family bible

That, my dear friends, is how it is with God. We are like the little child sittin' below the Master's work while we're on this earth. It appears a tangle of unrelated, random threads, or in our case, random events. But in the end, if we keep the faith, we will see the other side of the sampler and will understand the whys of the haphazard under-section of the cloth. Our lives, as they unfolded, will then make perfect sense. All things work together for the good, for those who love God."

Later that day, I penned everything that I could remember of this contemplative analogy into my journal. I could never have imagined how often I would refer to it on the dark road ahead.

After the burial, once the friends and relatives dispersed, Papa and the rest of our family retired to the sitting room. Grandma went to bed, overcome with exhaustion. I had been so concerned with my own emotions that I hadn't really taken time to think about how much grief Father must be enduring. We all cuddled around him on the sofa. Even Charles displayed raw, unmasked emotion, no longer using his sense of humor to insulate his heart. Father didn't say anything at first, but we could see from his eyes, reddened by tears that had flowed in solitude, that he was suffering deeply.

"Well, children," he said, "we're gonna be all right, ya know. We've got each other ... and the good Lord above."

"But what about you, Father?" asked Charles, with a tenderness he rarely exhibited. "You've lost the love of your life."

"Yes, Charles," replied Father, choked up with emotion. "The Lord giveth and the Lord taketh away. I'm thankful to have spent those last sixteen years with my beautiful Sarah." His voice broke.

The dam finally collapsed in a deluge of tears. The twins wrapped their tiny arms around Papa's neck, kissing his whiskered face over and over again. Charles, Johnny, and I cloaked ourselves in a human tangle of grief, hugging one another in howling bursts of emotion. After a few minutes, the sobbing stopped, the tears died to a trickle, and there remained only stillness in the room. Even the clocks stood in reverence, having retained their quiet settings to the minute of Mother's departure.

It must have been close to a half an hour before Johnny broke the silence. "What will we do now, Father?"

Papa smiled and looked at each one of the worried faces surrounding him.

"We will do what Mother wants us to do. Carry on with our lives. One foot ahead of the other, moment by moment," he spoke, calmly.

"Children, I can't lie to ya," he continued. "There'll be difficult days, when we hurt inside and miss her greatly ... as we do now; moments when we feel like we can't even breathe ... but that'll pass. A time *will* come when we'll remember the good things: the joy, the laughter, the tender moments, and ..." Papa looked at Charles with a smile, "even that dastardly groundhog. Those memories will crowd out the sad ones. I promise."

About an hour later, Mrs. Sullivan and Michael arrived to pay their respects.

Once again, Edith invited Johnny and I to come for a visit and Father assented. She thought it would be beneficial for us to get away for a spell. "Ya know what d'ey say in Ireland?" she asked, with a twinkle in her eye, "If ya have no time for yer health today, you'll have no health for yer time tomorrow."

Chapter 13

Checkmate

$\sim$

On Monday, Father carted us up the hill to the Sullivan's home. He had decided that we needed a housekeeper and was planning to head back into Hallowell to put an advertisement in the Gazette.

"What do you two think about hirin' a housekeeper to keep the ship afloat?" he asked.

"I can do the job myself, Papa," I responded, confidently. "We don't need anyone else."

"No, Papa!" spouted Johnny, "No one can ever take Momma's place!"

"Johnny, that's not what Papa means," I responded, gently trying to defuse his angst. "He's just saying that we need extra help, especially with the twins. They're too young to have lost their Momma … Heck, we all are," I added.

"Yes," sighed Father, in somber reflection. "Did ya notice the twins at the gravesite? Shouldn't have taken 'em. My fault."

"Papa, they begged to go. They would have screamed bloody murder if we hadn't let 'em come," I replied, in his defense.

"But they were lost, poor little dears. Sarah did everything for 'em. They didn't need to see their Momma lowered into the ground. What kind of father am I?"

"A kind one," I replied. "You did the right thing."

"Do ya really believe that?"

"Yes, Papa. with all my heart."

Father paused the wagon for a moment of silent reflection. He wiped away a stray tear with his shirt sleeve. Then we proceeded on our trek to the Sullivans.

As we approached the crest of the hill, Papa spoke again, "Annie, dear, ya might have to take on a few extra chores. And Johnny, you're gettin' to be a pretty big boy, and I can pair ya up with Charlie. But to do Momma's work, you'd have to be home every minute of every day. And neither of ya's givin' up your schoolin', period! Mother sure wouldn't approve. She wouldn't even want ya missin' today! That's why we need someone with good housekeepin' skills at the helm, twenty-four and seven."

Johnny and I sighed at the exact same moment, bringing a smile to Father's face.

"What about Grandma?" chirped Johnny.

"Oh, my. She can hardly take care of Grandma, let alone those two little urchins. If she had to entertain Bella and Lilly all day long, she'd come unhinged," replied Papa, puffing away on his pipe and musing at the thought of such a catastrophe.

"Grandma loves those two urchins, Papa," I asserted.

"Yeah, Papa," added Johnny, in solidarity.

"Goodness, yes! She loves 'em. But she's done her time on the battlefield of babies and toddlers. She's sixty-one. Can you really imagine her chasin' those two up and down stairs, runnin' through the house and gallopin' through the field? You have a better imagination than I do. And we need someone who can do all that, plus tend to all the other duties 'round the house."

Johnny and I nodded in reluctance. Father was right, but it didn't feel right. It had only been four days since Momma's passing.

⸺⸻

When we arrived, the boys took off into the woods to do some hunting with homemade bows and arrows, and I went into the house with Edith. Naturally, Mrs. Sullivan enquired as to how the family was getting along after Mother's tragic death.

I simply responded, "We're adjusting. It will take lot's of time, I'm afraid."

Edith could sense that I wasn't up to reliving the ordeal, everything was just too fresh. She intuitively changed the subject, offering that balm to calm any storm—coffee!

While waiting for it to brew, I happened to notice she had a chessboard with its pieces arranged for a match on the parlor table, and I asked her if she knew how to play.

"Oh, certainly, dear. That's me favorite pastime," she replied. Do ya play, Annie?"

"No, but I always wanted to learn. Charles had a friend from school who played, and he used to come to the house with his board and pieces. The horse was my favorite. I watched 'em play, but they always ran me out of the room."

"Well, me dear," responded Edith, "we have da whole afternoon. I'll show ya how da pieces are set up and how each one moves durin' da game. And, yes, da horse is a sly one. He's captured many a queen for me."

"Is the queen important?" I asked.

"Important? Oh, my! She's da most powerful piece on da board, I'll explain all in a bit."

"Isn't the King powerful, too?"

"Hmmm. Powerful?" she chuckled, "His power resides mostly in his protectors. But once he's captured, da game's over. Here's yer coffee," she added with a smile.

After dinner she began teaching me the basics of the game. Edith took great care to demonstrate the moves of every piece, informing me there would be an exam when she finished her instructions. Finally, she got to the queen. "The queen is da most powerful piece on da board. She moves horizontally, vertically, and diagonally for as many empty spaces as ya wish. However, she cannot move like d'at elusive knight. Her job is to take as many pieces from d'opposition as possible, diminishin' his power. But, once ya lose yer queen, if yer rival still has his, yer chances of winnin' are slim."

I then proceeded to take my examination and passed with great marks! After describing a few more details—such as castling, check, checkmate, and stalemate—we played our first game. Mrs. Sullivan said she would help me win and would coach me through the process. The first game was a bit confusing, but I managed to see its objectives more clearly. During the second game, I became more confident, and by the third, I felt secure enough to ask her to play a real game with me and let me lose, and I was sure I *would* lose!

We were well into the match, and I was quite proud of my skills, when Edith captured my queen with her knight. Stunned by the unexpected loss, I was struck with a tidal wave of emotion and began to weep like a baby! I ran out of the room and outside onto the porch steps, where I sat with my face cradled in my lap. Mrs. Sullivan ran out after me.

"Oh, dear, I'm so sorry. Y'er nearly an expert! A few more matches and you'll be winnin' me every time!" she declared, assuming she had stepped on my pride.

I was so ashamed and embarrassed that I could have melted into the ground. It wasn't about the game of chess. It was about the game of *life*.

"Oh, Edith, I'm not upset that you took my queen. I'm upset that God took my queen." Again, I burst into great sobs of anguish.

Mrs. Sullivan gave a compassionate sigh, "Oh, dear." She sat beside me and hugged me with great tenderness, allowing me to speak without interruption.

I tried to blurt out my thoughts between nose-sniffles and gasping breaths, "I saw my whole life in that last game. When you took my knight, that was … little Frankie. And when you took my queen … that was Momma."

I looked up at Edith, and continued, "We are all pawns, Edith. We live. We die … with no rhyme or reason. Now my king is without his queen to protect him. And the kingdom … what happens to his little kingdom?"

I then whispered, answering my own question, "In a few years, the game is over. We all surrender … death wins … checkmate."

After a few moments of silence, my insightful mentor asked me a question that got to the heart of the matter. "What do ya want, Annie?" she whispered.

"What do you mean?" I replied, leaning against her shoulder. "I want to get control of my emotions. I'm sorry."

"That's not what ya want. We all grieve, it's very normal. What are ya lookin' for? Put yer t'oughts in the oven and let em bake for a bit."

As I sat there, feeling the throbbing of my own heartbeat, hearing the birds twittering in their springtime glory, and sensing the warm breeze blowing a few loose strands of hair against my face, it became clear to me what I wanted.

I looked up at that beautiful old soul, "I want to be sure, like you are, that something beautiful exists beyond this life. It's always on my mind. I want to know that Auntie Belle really did come to take Momma to heaven, and that the bluebird on the windowsill was God's angel, taking Frankie's soul to eternity. I want to believe, but I'm more stubborn than the doubting apostle Thomas. Even when I *do* see with my own eyes I still doubt! I'm such a mess."

Edith chuckled, "You're not a mess, Annie. You're grievin' a great loss, dear. And yer on a quest to find an answer to da most important question of 'em all! Once ya find d'at answer, it'll make all d'ose ot'er disturbin' t'oughts bow in submission."

"I want to have faith like you, Mrs. Sullivan," I replied.

"Well now," she responded pensively, "d'ere's a measure of fait' given to everyone, ya know."

"I'm not sure I have any faith," I sighed.

"Sure ya do! When ya sat down to play chess, ya had fait' d'at da chair you were sittin' in wouldn't collapse, didn't ya?" she asked, in her jovial Irish brogue.

"That's different," I replied. "Sitting on chairs, time and again, helps us trust that they won't collapse when we sit down."

"But, how's d'at so different? Fait' builds on repetition, as well. Wit' each grace comes a little more trust 'til ya can sit on it without fearin' a collapse," she chuckled. "And you've had some blessin's, have ya not?"

"But maybe they're just coincidences. Charles thinks they are. Birds land on window sills all the time. And it's possible that Mother was just simply remembering Auntie Belle at the moment she died."

"True," said Edith, "but don't ya t'ink da timin' was flawless?" She continued," Have ya studied statistics, Annie?"

"No, I don't think so. I'm not even sure what it is," I replied.

"It's da study of da odds of somethin' happenin'. Like findin' a needle in a haystack. Or one chance in a million of findin' buried treasure. D'at sorta t'ing."

"Yes, I know what you mean."

"OK d'en. Let's figure da chances of a bluebird landin' on yer sill at da very moment of yer brother's passin'. How long did da bird sit d'ere?"

"A few seconds, at most," I answered.

"And how many times have ya seen a bluebird on d'at very sill?"

"Never. I saw a few in Augusta, once. They have a touch of orange on their breasts; Eastern Bluebirds, I believe," I answered thoughtfully. "I've never seen one at our farm."

"D'at's what I'm goin' on about. Couple da bluebird landin' wit' da one-time incident of yer brother's passin' and d'odds would be one in a billion! Of course da skeptics will argue d'at concurrent events are still just coincidences. And I would counter-argue d'at coincidences can be ot'erworldly as well as natural; da dictionary doesn't exclude supernatural in its definition. Me point is, da more d'ese events occur, one after anot'er, da more likely d'ere is a "Mind" behind 'em."

"That makes sense," I replied. "It separates the ordinary from the extraordinary, but not necessarily from the divine."

"So, y'er lookin' for somet'in' where ya don't have to do da math," she chuckled.

"I guess. Perhaps I'm hoping for too much."

"No, my dear one. God is great. Ask boldly!"

Every time I spoke with Edith I gained deeper insight into life's many mysteries. I like to think that I helped her, as well. I was becoming a granddaughter to her, and she, another grandmother to me; a person with whom I could converse about anything without fear of being judged. I was accepted as a Protestant and was treated as her equal. Judging others was pure foolishness in Edith's book. One of her favorite expressions was, "Only God knows the heart." To me, that means that we never know what others have suffered or the internal battles they are experiencing. She gave me a little prayer card on forgiveness which I tucked away in Grandma Kean's bible. It was uncanny how our meetings always seemed to foreshadow the next step in my life's journey.

BE KIND TO EACH OTHER.

WHEN, for some little insult given,
  My angry passions rise,
I'll think how Jesus came from heaven
  And bore his injuries.

He was insulted every day,
  Though all his words were kind;
But nothing men could do or say
  Disturbed his heavenly mind.

My Saviour, may I learn of thee
  My temper to amend;
And speak the pardoning word for me
  Whenever I offend.

Learn of me, for I am meek and lowly of heart.—Matt. xi. 29.
A soft answer turneth away wrath.—Prov. xv. 1.
Be ye kindly affectioned one to another.—Rom. xii. 10.

Original prayer card from Kean family bible

Part II

Theresa Gervais

Chapter 14

Humility

It is worth to remark that soon after Paul was converted, he declared himself, "unworthy to be called an apostle." As time rolled on and he grew in grace, he cried out, "I am less than the least of all the saints." And just before his martyrdom, when he had reached the stature of a perfect man in Christ, his exclamation was, "I am the chief of sinners."

—*Gardiner Home Journal*, August 23, 1860

Early on Wednesday morning, a middle-aged, well-dressed woman arrived by coach at our doorstep. She said her name was Louisa Ricker[39] and that she was interested in the housekeeper-nanny position that a "Captain John Goodwin" had advertised. I invited her into the sitting room and told her I would alert Father as to her arrival.

Moments later, Papa entered, trailed by the rest of the Goodwin tribe, all hoping to get a glimpse of our prospective nanny. Louisa was slight and stately, with long, brown, gray-streaked hair ascending into a high wrapped bun, which added to her already considerable height. She held her head erect at all times, presenting an ever-observant air. Her clothing was not pretentious but neat, and her face betrayed a serious tone, complete with brow wrinkles. She briefly introduced herself to us children as a possible housekeeper, with what I thought to be a somewhat condescending air. She then had the audacity to usher us out of the room, as though already in command, perhaps a strategy to impress Father. Whatever the case, after a one-hour interview, Papa decided he liked her philosophy and hired her on the spot. She agreed to begin work on "Monday next," which would give her ample time to collect her personal belongings.

I didn't express my initial apprehensions, as I realized that first impressions can be misleading, tainting what might otherwise become an agreeable relationship. However, Charles and I did inform Father that we thought he was making a hasty decision. His response was that of his usual, nautical wit, "The defeatist will complain about how the ship is off course, the dreamer will hope the vessel will simply right herself, and the pragmatist will take the wheel. Without a proper helmsman, the ship will never get back on course!"

As I left the room, I said to myself, "That is true, Father. But what if the crew is driven to mutiny?"

Father decided to temporarily rearrange our sleeping quarters in order to accommodate Louisa. He decided to offer my small but pleasant bedroom to Grandma Kean, who was a private person and needed her solitude. Papa, Charles, and Johnny would be cabin-mates in the large, west-facing room on the corner, and the master bedroom went to us ladies. Miss Ricker now had the entire bottom floor to herself. If, during the night, someone got sick or needed the nanny, they could go down to her room without disturbing the rest of the household. Louisa would be near the kitchen and woodshed, which would facilitate her tasks of preparing breakfast and firing up the stoves. Father assured us that we would not need a nanny forever, perhaps only until the harvest was complete.

———

Louisa arrived with her bags on a rainy Monday morning, and I was given the less-than-joyful undertaking of showing her around the house. After she had unpacked her belongings in the guest room she began wandering, looking for anything she could find to complain about.

"Oh dear. There's so much dust on the piano keys, it's a wonder the thing still works."

"Well, only Grandma plays, but she does so rarely. Her arthritis causes her great distress," I responded.

"It's no wonder! Some of the keys are stuck," she observed, pressing down on a few, randomly. "The poor woman has to push twice as hard to get any sound out of it; there's undoubtedly some grime clogging up the mechanics."

I bit my tongue, locking my thoughts up in the prison of bad inclinations that I'd learned about in Sunday school.

Every piece of furniture, every piece of molding, and every utensil in the kitchen was found unfit to support human life. The dishes and cooking pots were poorly arranged for efficient use. There were lint-balls in every corner and mud in all the entries. On and on went the litany of fault-finding.

At one point she looked at me and asked, with a haughty grimace, "It's obvious why the captain hired me; this place is quite untidy. Doesn't anyone around here know how to clean?"

I tried to hold my tongue again, but a few thoughts were released on good behavior, "Well, ma'am this is a farm, we do have pets, and there is mud in the fields at…"

Louisa interrupted before I could finish, "That's not what I asked you; I don't want excuses. The place is filthy!"

I felt my Irish temper starting to boil over. I'm sure my hair was beginning to turn ginger as well. "I assume you realize that my mother has recently passed and we have had more pressing things to think about than lint-balls and dog hair," I declared, liberating a few more "badly-inclined" inmates.

"Yes, I'm sorry about your loss, missy. But cleanliness is next to Godliness and I'm sure all this squalor didn't help your mother's malady, " she added, with a know-it-all air.

"My mother died of childbed fever, not from dust on the piano," I growled.

"Well, that response was a bit discourteous. Didn't anyone teach you to respect your elders?" she demanded. "Your father gave me the job of disciplinarian, and I won't be spoken to in such a manner."

"*You* are not my mother! And all you've done, so far, is complain about the condition of our home, which, by the way, has been host to a crowd of mourners coming and going for the past two weeks. Respect is earned around here. Don't expect much of it from me if you start insulting us!" I could feel the veins in my face pulsating, as the doors of the "prison" burst open, welcomed by my unruly mouth.

"Well, you are quite a feisty little thing aren't you, missy?" she retorted.

"I am not 'Missy.' I am Annie. Annie Elizabeth Good-Win!" I bellowed, meeting her stare without wavering.

Louisa placed her hands authoritatively on her hips. "Well, Annie Elizabeth Good-Win, we're not off to a very pleasant start, are we now,"

"No we're not!" I snarled, placing my hands on my hips, in a mock gesture. "And I suggest you remember that *you* are the one whose job it is to clean this 'filthy' place." I walked out, slamming the kitchen door behind me.

Ignoring my angry exit, Louisa yelled, "Where do you keep the broom around here, young lady?"

"Oh, it's probably hiding under a pile of dog hair. Find a shovel and dig it out!" I hollered back, sarcastically, as I stomped up to my room.

After a few minutes of fuming, I began to feel terrible about what I had just done. Oh, how I wanted to "clean her plow," as Father would say. But I felt like a hypocrite. Suffering the self-inflicted wounds of guilt and sorrow, I realized I had not achieved a victory by being rude. My dignity had been defeated by my own sharp tongue. After a few moments of thought, I went back down to find Miss Ricker and apologize. She was sweeping the kitchen floor. Apparently, she had done her shoveling."

"Miss Ricker," I began, "I came down to apologize for my rude behavior. I don't want us to be enemies."

"Very well. Thank you, Annie," she said, as she continued to her task without ever glancing up at me.

I waited there for an inkling of remorse on her part, but it never came. I went to my room with Grandma's big old family Bible, which held the little prayer card that Edith had given me about forgiveness. After reading it over several times, I made a resolution to try to overlook Louisa's rudeness and temper my childish tendency to react.

A Sunday-school in Bangor has been inciting its pupils to insane emulation in committing verses of Scripture to memory, and one poor little girl ten years old has managed to learn nearly fourteen hundred in six months. The foolish torturers of infancy have presented her a Bible for her success. [Boston Advertiser.

As spring turned to summer that year, things smoothed over between myself and our housekeeper. I tried to find likable things about her. I thought, at first, we might have some degree of accord around Christian topics, as she could quote scripture, chapter and verse, like a preacher. She considered herself a solid Christian woman who believed solely in the Bible. But because she had never found a church that completely agreed with her interpretation of scripture (and she detested the word *interpretation!*), she didn't go to church at all. Our theological discussions were enjoyable until I questioned the reasoning behind some of her beliefs. Then things always deteriorated quickly.

One afternoon, while preparing dinner, we had a discussion around my very favorite spiritual topic, the afterlife.

"Miss Louisa," I asked, "do you ever talk to your dead loved ones or ask them to help you?"

"What kind of foolishness is this, Annie? Of course I don't talk to them. They're asleep until the Day of Judgment. Scripture's very clear about it. One Thessalonians 4 says, "For if we believe that Jesus died and rose again, even so, those also which sleep in Jesus, will God bring with him.""

"But, perhaps the word 'sleep' means 'to be at peace' rather than just snoring away on a heavenly couch until the last day," I remarked.

"That's pure nonsense. The Bible says *sleep*, and it means *sleep*."

"How can we really be sure of that? Mrs. Sullivan tells me that the first scriptures were written in Greek, then Latin, and finally in English. Some words don't translate easily. For instance, did you know that the French word *voilà* has no English counterpart? So, couldn't it be that 'sleep' is just another way of talking about death. Certainly, a dead body appears to be sleeping, but the spirit could be playing chess with St. Peter," I quipped.

"Annie, you mustn't assume the Bible means something different from the literal word. You must never ever interpret! Anyway, Mrs. Sullivan is a heretic. She's a Catholic. They worship statues!"

"That's not so! I've had several conversations with her about…"

Louisa interrupted, "And they pray to the saints, rather than God!

"But…"

She interrupted again, "And they worship Mary! If you're not careful, she'll try to convert you, too. If that happens … you're damned."

I sighed. I couldn't bear to have that dear old lady belittled, but I knew arguing never worked with Louisa. Suddenly, an interesting scripture passage came to mind; something I had previously discussed with my Irish friend.

"Miss Ricker, I don't wish to argue with you. But, in light of our discussion, there is a scripture passage that I'd like you to explain to me."

"That's my area of expertise, dearie. What passage did you have in mind?" she asked.

"Do you remember Jesus's response to the good thief on the cross? When he asked Jesus to remember him when he came into his kingdom?"

"Of course I remember it. Luke Chapter 23: 'Verily I say unto thee, today thou shalt be with me in paradise.'"

"But Miss Ricker," I paused, weighing my words carefully, "Jesus didn't say, 'Today thou shalt be sleeping soundly with me in paradise,'" did He?'

"No! But let's not split hairs. It means the same thing."

"*Voilà!*" I exclaimed in jest, raising my eyes and hands to the heavens in dramatic fashion. "That's an interpretation!" I snickered, awaiting the coming wrath.

"Get thee behind me, Satan!! Luke 4:6!" she barked, scowling.

That was the end of the discussion! Maybe I was imagining it, but I think Louisa's grimace turned into a gentle smile a few minutes later. Perhaps she really didn't hate me as much as I thought.

Our housekeeper was somewhat of a mystery to all of us. I made the mistake of asking her about her past and she bluntly retorted, "That is none of your concern!" Even after several weeks, we knew little more than on the day she first arrived. When her work for the day was finished, she would retire to her room and disappear until morning. Sundays were completely devoted to prayer and reading scripture. Save for an emergency, all meals and chores for that day were finished on the previous one.

In spite of her abrasive personality, she attended to her duties with near-military precision, and with great attention to detail. Charles referred to her as "Lieutenant Louisa," but not to her face, of course. She did a commendable job of managing the household and keeping our battle-weary ship afloat. Father was pleased, so much so, that he gave her an increase in salary. Louisa was competent and dependable with the little ones, but never seemed to allow herself to bond closely with them. The mothering instinct seemed to be missing in her, so it became my role by default.

I did learn a great deal about myself by living with someone whose view of life seemed at odds with my own. My ability to tolerate differences in character was growing and my childhood tendency to react to the smallest slight was disappearing. Miss Ricker was giving me the experience I needed to voice my opinions calmly in the face of resistance. She taught me the valuable skill of not taking offense, even when offense was

"Mr. Douglas I cannot look at you without thinking of a passage of Scripture."

"What is that?" asked Douglas, good humoredly."

"'The way of the wicked is short,'" responded Lincoln, and fainted away.

The crowd applauded tremendously, but Douglas was not to be outdone. Waiting until Lincoln revived, he quietly said :

"And you remind me, Mr. Lincoln, of another passage,"

"What is that?" asked Lincoln.

"'How long! O Lord, how long?'" responded Douglas.

From the Lincoln/Douglas debates

intended. My own beliefs were becoming refined in the furnace of repudiation and contrary opinion. I was even beginning to look forward to those, often challenging, conversations with our housekeeper.

At the time, "the fair sex" was beginning to venture into areas previously occupied by men, but not without resistance. Oddly, there was a sizable population of women, as in Louisa's case, who balked stubbornly against the idea of women moving outside of their traditional roles. Of great interest to me was that young ladies were beginning to move on to high school and college; a dream that I hoped would come to fruition for myself.

One day, while we were working outside in the garden, Miss Ricker started a conversation concerning a woman's purpose on the planet. I knew this was going to be a puritanical quagmire, but I couldn't resist the challenge.

"I believe a woman's place in this life is in her home, as a good wife and mother. She has the God-given ability to bring children into the world. Your own mother was an excellent example of that if I'm not mistaken, Annie. What do you think?" asked Louisa.

"I couldn't agree more. That was Mother's vocation. But there are many things that I'd like to do before I settle down and have a family, such as travel across the country, see the Pacific Ocean, and meet people from different parts of the globe. There's plenty of time for all the rest," I replied.

"Annie, with all due respect. Even at your tender age, you're well-aware that *time* is something we are never guaranteed. You could be dead tomorrow. The purpose of our lives, as women, is to rear children. That *is* our vocation!"

I was tempted to ask her—if that is what she thought—why was she still *Miss* Ricker, unmarried and childless? But since that would have been excessively rude, I held my tongue. However, it did raise the question in my mind, given her strong opinions on the subject.

Louisa continued her sermon. "The earlier we begin, the more the blessings of family life we get: the joys of watching our children grow to adulthood, and someone to care for us in our old age."

"But that didn't work out for my poor mother, did it?" I replied. "She never reached old age. However, as you say, we're not even sure about tomorrow. So why not experience as much of life as possible while we're here? I want to go to college and learn all I can about everything!"

"Whatever for?" replied Louisa, chuckling under her breath. "To be an over-educated wife and mother? For what purpose? Most men wouldn't think of courting a woman who's better educated than they. It's not the way it's supposed to be."

"So, women should remain stupid so they can find a husband? That doesn't make sense. And who says it's not the way it's supposed to be?"

"A woman needs to be docile and submissive to her husband, as Paul tells us in the Good Book. The husband is the head of his wife, and if she's the more educated of the two, how would that work out?"

"My mother was anything but docile and submissive to Father, and they had a good marriage. She was better educated than he, as well. Besides, Paul was preaching two thousand years ago. Don't you think he might see things differently today?" I responded, transforming my declaratives to interrogatives, so as not to turn our conversation into another dead-end argument.

"Annie, the Bible doesn't change as society changes. We must adhere to what is written, word for word. We've had this discussion before. You need to give it some serious thought."

I paused for a moment, collecting my thoughts. "Doesn't Jesus tell us, if our eye leads us into sin we should 'pluck it out,' or if our hand causes us to sin to 'cut it off'? Is that to be taken as written?"

"Well … of course not! He was speaking in hyperbole," she stammered. "Are you trying to trip me up again with your worldly logic?"

"Oh no, ma'am," I replied, respectfully, as I could see she was getting agitated. "I'm just trying to point out that one can't take *everything* in scripture literally, or we'd neither be able to hold the Bible with our severed hands nor read it with our missing eyes!" I replied, reveling in my Charles-like wit.

Again, I paused, trying to remember another scripture passage. "Also, I learned in Sunday school that Paul told slaves to obey their masters. Does that mean that Jesus would approve of slavery?"

"No, Annie. Paul didn't want to interfere with the customs of the people with whom he was speaking."

"Yes, I agree. When in Rome, do as the Romans! I think that's how it goes," I said.

"Actually, he was in Ephesus."

"Well, then … When in Ephesus, do as the Ephesians. That's what I was trying to say about women being submissive to their husbands. That was the custom at the time. I think Paul would see things differently today. You know … When in America, do as the Americans."

"Annie, if you don't change your way of thinking," she pointed her finger at me, "I'm afraid you will end up in hell, alongside all those who challenge holy scripture!"

"Miss Ricker, I'm not trying to challenge anything. I just want to understand our different ways of thinking, that's all. A friendly difference of opinion. And I don't really believe that God would ever send me, or anyone else, to hell for asking questions. Doesn't He command us to seek that we might find?"

That ended the conversation as usual. Miss Ricker remained silent for the rest of our time in the garden. There seemed to be some invisible barrier that was raised every time I, or any of us for that matter, tried to have a heartfelt conversation with her. She allowed us only into the shallows.

Chapter 15

Only God Knows the Heart

One day in early August, Father pulled up into the yard in the wagon with a long white rectangular object lying on the bed. As I got closer, I realized that it was Mother's marble headstone, which had been newly engraved. I ran to alert the rest of the family, and we stood there respectfully, reading the words and remembering that beautiful soul: "Sarah T., Wife of Capt. John A. Goodwin, Died May 17, 1860, Aet 39yrs. 11ms., A devoted wife and affectionate mother, Into Thy hands I commit my Spirit, Thou hast redeemed me O God of truth."

Unexpectedly, Lilly went over, stood on her tiptoes, and kissed the stone. And then, even more unexpectedly, Louisa looked over at me and a big silver tear slid down her face. That was the very first time I'd witnessed anything resembling unscripted emotion coming from her. Something deep inside had just escaped, small though it was, revealing the depth of the soul within.

After dinner and without any forewarning, Miss Ricker announced her immediate resignation from her housekeeping job. She would leave as soon as she could find a suitable replacement. Papa was furious! She had agreed to stay on until November 1, the harvest was just around the corner, and she had recently received a considerable increase in salary. In addition, we were all beginning to settle into the routine which she had designed with such efficiency. Her excuse was that she had received a letter from her widowed sister Joanna, who lived alone in Boston and requested that Louisa come live with her. Charles and the three youngsters seemed indifferent about her leaving. Only Papa and I were outwardly disappointed.

That night I found it impossible to sleep, and my tossing and turning was keeping the twins awake. It was early August in Maine, hot and muggy. My clothing stuck to me as though I'd gone swimming in them, and there was one very annoying, soon-to-be-dead mosquito who thought buzzing in my ear was its mission in life. After permanently putting the beast out of commission, I washed my sweaty face and decided to retire to the first floor where the temperature was ten degrees cooler. Grabbing a candle from the

mantle in our bed chamber, I crept quietly down the stairwell. The clock
in the parlor struck one o'clock as I entered the sitting room. I blew out the
flame and set the holder on the side table and stretched out on the cool,
soft sofa.

As my eyes adjusted to the darkness, I noticed some lamplight flickering under the doorway of Louisa's room. In those days, everyone was
justifiably worried about a fire starting from an unattended candle or kerosene lantern, and our cats were notoriously given to knocking tapers to
the floor, lit or otherwise. Kerosene was my worst fear as its flames must
be smothered; water will simply spread the conflagration. Many a night, I
would wander through the house like a malcontent ghost, making sure that
there were no wicks left burning.

Without a second thought, I headed over to Louisa's room to extinguish the lantern. I presupposed she'd fallen asleep and forgotten about it, a
crime of which Grandma was a habitual offender. But, as I neared the door
I could hear the muffled sound of weeping. Had it been anyone but Louisa,
I would have simply knocked and gone in, but she never allowed anyone
to invade her inner sanctum. For a moment I stood there, frozen, trying to
decide. Finally, I chose to act.

I knocked gently. "Miss Ricker, are you OK?"

She opened the door, wiping her eyes with the sleeve of her nightdress.
"What are you doing up at this late hour, Annie?"

"Oh, I was very hot and couldn't sleep, so I thought I'd try my luck on
the sofa. It's much cooler down here. Anyway, I noticed your lamp was on
and I was afraid you might have forgotten to turn it out. I was about to do
so when I heard weeping coming from your room."

Louisa gave a heavy sigh and sat back down, gazing through the window into the darkness. "Well … I … ah …" she mumbled, stumbling to find
the words.

"Miss Ricker, I wasn't trying to spy on you," I asserted, trying to dispel
the awkwardness we were both experiencing. "I was just wondering if you
were all right?"

She looked at me and forced a light smile. "Annie, as you may have
guessed, my life has not been an easy one."

"If you'd like to talk about anything, I'd be happy to listen," I replied.

"Well, dear, I'd prefer my privacy right now. But thank you for your
concern."

"I understand. I'll leave you to your thoughts, then. Good night."

"Good night, Annie. And thank you."

I quietly closed the door, and headed back to the sofa.

A short time later, Louisa opened her door into the dark sitting room
and whispered, "Annie, are you still out here?"

"Yes, ma'am."

"I *would* like to speak with you, if you're not too tired."

"I'm awake. I'll be right in."

I reentered her bed chamber and took a seat beside her. Louisa sighed a heavy sigh of resignation, and began unraveling her story.

"I was a month shy of five-years when Momma died," she began. "There were four of us children, two boys and two girls, and I was the youngest. We grew up near Amherst on a dairy farm."

"Mamma died of consumption and it was a long, painful illness. Once she became bedridden, Papa took to heavy drinking. He was never violent, but I remember many a night when Joanna, the boys, or I would find him passed out on the floor. Somehow he'd manage to drag himself out of the house to milk the cows before sunrise. Then the whole cycle would start over, drinking all night, up at four, and farming all day. Joanna, the oldest of us, became our caretaker as well as his.

When Mother died, Papa purchased a beautiful headstone made of slate, as most of them were back in those days. We all went to the cemetery to watch our neighbor Jonas Lynch and the groundskeeper put the heavy slab in place. Then, just like Sarah Lilly, I went over and kissed that cold, black stone." At this point, Louisa's voice quivered but she continued without losing her train of thought.

"Early the next morning, the same Mr. Lynch came to our home asking for Papa, but we couldn't find him. Jonas was puzzled, as Father had promised to help him set posts for a new fence. After our neighbor left, we discovered that our brothers, who had been doing their regular chores, hadn't seen Papa either.

By then we were fearful for his whereabouts and began frantically searching the property. As we were walking back towards the house, Joanna spied something far across the field. We ran as fast as our legs could carry us. When we got there, we found Father lying on his side with a whiskey jug nearby. "Papa, get up! You shouldn't drink so much!" I commanded.

"Joanna, sensing something was seriously wrong, knelt down beside him and turned him over."

"Annie," Louisa glanced up at me with a grimace. "Papa had blown his brains out! The pistol was lying under him!"

Miss Ricker began to sob inconsolably, and I pulled my chair beside her, holding her hand as she wept.

After regaining her strength of will, she continued, "Our lives were shattered. Joanna and I ended up at an orphanage in Connecticut for a brief spell, and the boys were taken to another. Thank God, we were reunited when Uncle Nate, who lived in Portland, agreed to take us in.

My brothers say Papa was a selfish coward, and they never forgave him. A preacher told me it's the type of sin that sends a man straight to hell. The thought of Papa burning forever terrified me," she remarked, bowing her head with a sigh. "So, I made my bargain with God. I promised Him I would never marry, never have children, and pledged my life to

His service alone, under the condition that he would save my father from
eternal damnation."

"Oh, Miss Louisa! God would never send your Papa to hell. Never!" I asserted. "If you've forgiven him, I'm sure God will! His forgiveness is greater than ours."

"Yes. But what about God's wrath, Annie?"

"Miss Ricker," I replied, "didn't Jesus say, 'Father, forgive them, for they know not what they do'"? Your papa didn't know what he was doing. It was the alcohol and grief that pulled the trigger."

For the first time, Miss Ricker didn't admonish me for my interpretation, and a period of silence gently settled over us.

At length, Louisa became tranquil and reflective. "You know, Annie," she remarked, altering the flow of her thoughts, "I remember your telling of the bluebird on the windowsill and that of your mother's last word. I too experienced something other-worldly when I was fourteen. I took it as a sign that God had accepted my self-offering. Of course, only Joanna believes the story. I tried to tell my brothers, but … well, you know brothers."

"Yes, I do. Charlie says I'm a few cards shy of a full deck," I jested.

"Well, I guess *my* insanity is safe with you," she affirmed, with a pleasant smile. "Let's see … Yes. A few months before my mother's passing, she and I strolled the spacious fields together to find the very first dandelion of the season. Papa loved them. I finally found a beauty, picked it, and with great excitement, walked back home to give it to him. I'm not sure if he loved it as much it seemed, but he went on and on about the treasure I'd given him.

"That's the kind of person he was … before all the drinking and sorrow," she sniffled.

"Anyway, nearly a decade later, I gathered the courage to revisit Amherst. I went by our old farm which was under new ownership. I could have stopped in, but my ambivalence got the best of me, too many memories, too many phantoms. But I did make it to the cemetery.

"As I walked that lonely path of the burial grounds, I was struck by the sparsity of foliage, compared to how I remembered it. Fewer trees, fewer bushes, and many more tombstones, as one might expect after a decade.

"I began searching the rows of headstones for our family plot, starting on one end and moving down the length, then back again. By the time I reached the fifth or sixth row, I sensed that I was getting close. Perhaps it was the lay of the land, the ancient oak tree, or the pattern of stones that dotted the area, but something called forth a feeling from deep within. As I moved ahead to the top of a small knoll, I noticed a man, about a stone's throw away, seated on the ground leaning against a headstone.

"I couldn't make out his features, but when he detected my approach he stood up, turned calmly toward me, tipped his wide-brimmed hat politely, and walked away towards an open field. At that very moment, being a tall, clumsy fourteen-year-old, I stumbled over a tree root. After regaining my balance, the man had vanished from sight. He'd disappeared like vapor! There was no place for him to go, just a few small headstones and then open pasture."

"That's uncanny," I whispered, wide-eyed.

"Yes. And when I reached the stone on which he'd been reclining, I found that it was Momma's. And there were nine freshly picked dandelions leaning against it!" Louisa was trembling with emotion.

"Oh, my God!" I gasped, in a hush.

"Papa had been dead for nine years!" she exclaimed. "I've tried to make sense of it. Perhaps it was all a bizarre coincidence. But the timing was perfect, and the dandelions weren't an illusion. Would you like to see them?"

"Most certainly," I answered, as though I was about to view the Holy Grail.

Louisa then opened her Bible and showed me the pressed, dried, and crumbling fragments of all nine flowers, allowing me the privilege of holding one.

"I feel honored," I voiced, gazing upon the remnants of that other-worldly event.

"The event was too personal to share with those who would simply tear it apart, but I knew you'd understand."

I nodded, in distracted agreement.

"Can I tell you something?" she asked. "Annie?" she nudged me when I did not reply.

"Oh … of course … I'm sorry. It's all so amazing. Please continue," I replied, having come back to the present moment.

"I must confess, like you, I pondered whether it was a natural event or a true miracle. I nearly drove myself crazy with the ambiguity. In the end I accepted it as a sign, and along with it, a literal understanding of scripture—a place where ambiguity has no entry."

"I understand," I said, then paused in reflection.

There followed another few moments of silence, broken only by the hooting of an owl in the distance.

Then Louisa's eyes met mine.

"Please don't leave us, Miss Ricker," I whispered. "We need you."

"Oh, but John would never take me back. He was angrier than a hornet in a bonnet."

"He's just blowing off steam. Trust me, he's quick to forgive. Please reconsider." I said, entreating her.

"You knew that Joanna's letter wasn't the reason for my sudden resignation, didn't you?"

"Yes, ma'am."

"You're a perceptive young lady. Please don't mention any of the things I've told you. I don't want folks pitying me."

"Of course, cross my heart."

She gave me a hug and said, "I think it's time for bed. I've got to get up in a few hours and make breakfast. I'll need to get back in your father's good graces."

I smiled, "Thank you, Miss Ricker."

"Oh, thank *you*. It wasn't a coincidence that you showed up when you did."

"The timing?" I replied.

"Yes, the timing," affirmed Louisa.

As far as I am aware, Louisa never wavered from her strict, literal understanding of scripture. Yet, something changed on that hot summer night; our adversarial relationship made an about-face and turned into mutual respect, understanding, and trust. Our conversations became richer and less guarded, and smiles were more frequent. Louisa stayed with us until December, after which, she left for Boston to join her lonely sister.

Chapter 16

The Writing on the Walls

On Tuesday, November 6, 1860, Abraham Lincoln was elected the sixteenth president of the United States. What that would mean for our divided nation was yet unclear. Father and all of his friends had cast their ballots for him. I remember being quite disappointed that women were not allowed to vote, and said so on many occasions. In fact, since women's suffrage was discussed so often, Miss Hunt asked the older children to write a short essay for or against it. Not surprisingly, the split of pros and cons went completely by sex.

I decided to interview several men and explore their opinions on the subject in my essay. Students were given a week to finish and then we read our papers aloud in class. My essay went as follows:

Good morning, class. I chose to write my essay about the reasons men don't think women should have the right to vote. I asked six different gentlemen the same question, "Why shouldn't women have the right to vote?" I will give you their responses and the examples they gave to back up their opinions.

The first said, "Women are affected by waves of sentiment. Their minds move and change like the wind. One day they're Republicans and the next, Democrats. They are too unstable to vote with any degree of competence." I asked him to give an example to back up his opinion. He could not.

The second said this, "Birth and marriage rates are decreasing at an alarming pace according to the census. If women bother themselves with politics they will want to get more involved, and families and marriages will suffer." I asked him to give me some evidence to back up his assumption. He could not.

The third said this, "Women are extremely impressionable. If they found a candidate that they thought was handsome, they'd vote for him. If they found a candidate with an amiable personality, they'd vote for him. Once there is a notion in their heads, reasonable or not, they will follow that notion to the end." I asked him to provide some evidence. He could not.

The fourth said this, "Women have too much intuition based on feelings.

They do not have the logical reasoning power of men to make good choices at the voting booth." I asked him to back up his opinion with proof. He could not.

The fifth said this, "The female mind's deadly logic is destructive. Ask any married man! Think what her logic would do to an election." Since this person was, in fact, a married man, I asked him to give me an example. He could not, or perhaps, dared not!

Upon hearing this line, Miss Hunt chuckled. Then, I continued:

> Woman should have a right to do anything which she can do well,—anything that it is fit for any one to do. Instead of spending their time upon worsted dogs, and other frivolities of fashionable embroidery, the daughters of wealth should be taught to live a useful life. In all the great questions of interest to the human race, woman should have a voice. She has none now in deciding them ; nor has she any purpose in life. When the young man attains his majority, he has a plan of life arranged, his occupation or profession chosen ; but his sister's life is aimless —her future a blank.

Dear scholars, the opinions of these gentlemen are all built around excuses that are as fleeting as the smoke from their pipes. Not one of them could think of an example to back up his opinion. The reason they couldn't come up with evidence is that there is none.

In closing, I would like to say that I did interview one other man, and he said this, "Women should definitely have the right to vote, they are citizens of this country, too." I asked him if he could provide any evidence as to why they should not vote. He could not.

The defense rests, Your Honor.

I smiled, looking towards Miss Hunt.

I'd like to say there was thunderous applause, but really, only the girls clapped. But that was good enough for my vanity.

———

According to the newspapers, because of Lincoln's election, some southern states were on the verge of leaving the Union to create a new country rooted in slavery. Up until the "Rail Splitter's" election, most of us children had never even heard the word *secession,* but now the talk of it was everywhere. Few Americans were clairvoyant enough to envision the armageddon that was about to be unleashed on our soil; a test that would mortally threaten the five most hallowed words of our Declaration of Independence, *"All men are created equal."* Could the United States,[40] *"or any nation, so conceived and so dedicated,"* endure such a test?

———

Soon after the election, we received one of Eli's frequent letters stating how elated he was to learn that an abolitionist was going to be in the White

House. He was grief-stricken upon hearing of Momma's unexpected death, and wanted, so very much, to visit our family again. There was hope for this reunion only if Mr. Lincoln would repeal the Fugitive Slave Act. I wanted to inform him that Old Abe, who was an abolitionist at heart, would probably not change the fugitive slave laws at the moment, as such an action would hand the southern states another reason to pursue their secession insanity. So, I avoided that topic and voiced my hopes that things would soon change.

And change they did! On December 20, 1860, South Carolina, Eli's home state, seceded. It was expected that many more slave states would soon join ranks, leaving our new president with an enormous dilemma. What were Lincoln's options? Would we go to war with the South to preserve that unity of states? Might we become two countries? The possibilities started many a conversation at our supper table during the cold December nights of 1860.

"Father, what do you think? Are we gonna have a civil war?" I asked.

He cleverly avoided a direct answer by rerouting the conversation. "For what it's worth, this is my personal opinion, in a few years slavery's gonna die out, all by itself. It won't be needed any more. And all these comin' troubles will have been for not."

"How so?" asked Charles, in a puzzled tone.

"Charles, why does the South have slavery?" asked Father.

"To do the work in the fields, pick the cotton and rice, and work the farms, I guess."

"That's right," remarked Father. "Look at all the inventions that are comin' to pass these days. The telegraph, railroads, steam engines, reapers, all these things are doin' the job of hundreds of men. You don't need a pony express when you've got a telegraph; you don't need hundreds of wagons and horses to pull heavy loads when ya gotta railroad; and ya certainly don't need slaves in the field when ya got huge reapers that'll do the job in a fraction of the time. When I was a young boy all these things didn't exist. And there are more inventions on the horizon."

"So, you're saying they'll replace the slaves who are now doing the work?" asked Charles.

"Precisely!" he declared. "Why would you wanna buy a hundred slaves for a hundred-thousand dollars or more, if you could get machines to do the same work for a couple thousand? That just doesn't make financial sense, now does it?"

"Well, I don't know," Charles replied. "Most of these big plantations own many families of slaves. They've been there for generations. So there's no need to buy more. Slave owners not only own the slave but all its descendants forever and always."

"That's true, son. But why continue to keep many slaves, feedin' 'em, clothin' 'em, and rulin' over 'em … incurring their righteous hatred, for what must cost tens of thousands of dollars, when you can buy a couple machines, hire a few farm hands, and save yourself the grief and the cash?"

"Papa," I jumped in, "when the cotton gin was invented they said that would end slavery, too. Instead the farms expanded, increasing the need for more slaves to work the gins."

"That's a fair point, Annie," Father answered.

Johnny jumped in, changing the subject, "Father, would you have to go fight if there's a war?"

"I don't think so, son. We've just lost Mother, rest her soul, and I have to maintain the farm … and you children couldn't run it by yourselves, not yet anyway." Father paused thoughtfully, "I don't think they'd call me into active service. But I could help locally, if they needed me. So, Johnny, don't worry your head about that, OK?"

"Father," I said, "Mrs. Sullivan had a frightening dream that she told me about. She believes there is going to be a terrible war and thousands of young men will die, and that it will go on for years."

"Annie, you have to be careful with dreams. They can portend the future, but not very often. As old Scrooge says, they can be the result of a piece of undigested beef!" he replied, with a laugh.

"Let me tell ya 'bout a dream that scared me just about out of my wits, to illustrate my point. When I was a young lad, about Johnny's age, I dreamt I was sittin' in front of a Gypsy fortune teller. She wore a witch-like hat, and the room was very dark. She was gazin' at an object on the table in front of her. Then she looked up at me with fire in her eyes and said, 'Three months from this very day, John, *you will be dead*!' I woke up from my sleep in a panicked sweat. I marked the time of the dream and began to count the days. Finally, I got to the 'last day of my life' and awaited the end to come. The clock on the mantel was tickin' away my last few seconds on this earth and …"

"Did you die?" asked Bella, with a serious look. There was a roar of spontaneous laughter that hadn't been heard in our house for a long time.

"No dear, I'm still here," he laughed, giving his little girl a big kiss on the forehead.

"That's good, Papa," she replied, with a sigh of relief.

—⁓—

The Christmas celebration of 1860 was but a shadow of the feast it would become over the next three or four years, but it was quickly gaining momentum towards that end. Not yet a national holiday, it acquired customs that had been previously practiced at other times during the month. The Dutch celebration of *Sinterklaas* (Saint Nicholas Day), celebrated on

December 6, gave rise to gift-giving and *Santa Claus.* In 1860, adults more often exchanged presents on New Years' Eve or the following day. However, a popular and influential poem written in 1823, called *A Visit from St. Nicholas,* better known as *The Night Before Christmas*, helped bring together the traditions that are now so familiar. The little ones were already hanging stockings on chimneys *"with care, with the hopes that Saint Nicholas soon would be there."* Children, from toddler-age right up through twelve years, partook of this exciting event in order to receive goodies from that jolly old soul. Like today, greeting cards were exchanged, a large noonday meal was prepared to share with relatives and friends, and of course, the singing of carols had always been part of the season.

———

Christmas and New Year's without Mother were weighted with emptiness, but we resolved to make the holidays enjoyable anyway. On the 23rd, Father took us out into the woods, with a small sled trailing behind, to find a Christmas tree. We eventually found a seven-foot spruce that was both elegant and full. When we arrived home and attached it to its wooden base, we found an additional surprise; a bird's nest was resting in its branches about half way up. We let the tree thaw in the summer kitchen overnight, and the wonderful smell emanating from its branches filled the house.

Our family tradition was to wait until Christmas Eve to decorate the tree and then to keep it up through New Year's Day. Some folks trimmed theirs earlier, which was a risk, as trees dry out quickly and become fire hazards. On the morning of December 24, we carried the tree into the parlor, base and all, and placed it in the corner. We had a few beautiful and fragile blown-glass bulbs that Father had purchased in England. Those we hung from the higher branches as the cats loved to assail anything dangling from the tree.

Our favorite activity was illuminating the branches of the spruce. President Pierce's candle-lighting of his White House tree, a few years back, popularized this precarious custom. What could possibly go awry by putting two dozen open flames on a dry tree inside a wooden house? Some people tied the tapers to the branches with strings or wire, while others used candle wax to fix them to the tree … not to be recommended! Father concocted a small round tin holder to encircle the base of the candle. He punched small holes for wires that wrapped around the tree branch, holding it firmly in place. After attaching twenty of these to the tree, he placed the small candles in them. We made sure that the candles, themselves, were only large enough to last for an hour or so, and a couple buckets of water were kept nearby for any emergency. Every winter local newspapers reported homes in the area that had burnt to the ground from candle flames igniting unattended trees.

From *Harper's Weekly*,
after Winslow Homer

After we had trimmed it with garland and long strands of cranberries, Papa read us *A Christmas Carol* by the famous Charles Dickens. "Children," he said, "I'm afraid I won't be able to do justice to this story like your Momma could. But, I'll do my best." I could see tears in his eyes when he started to read. But he composed himself, put himself into the characters with intense verbal and facial expressions, captivating his audience from beginning to end.

After we had finished listening to the tale, Father brought out the Nativity scene. This set of figurines was ceramic, fragile, and very old. It had been in the Goodwin family for two or three generations before it was given to my parents for a wedding gift in 1844. It was said to have been manufactured before the Revolutionary War and was probably of French design. The set included the three Magi, two shepherds, a camel, Mary, Joseph and the infant Jesus. Lilly was delighted to be the child selected to place the infant Jesus in the little wooden bed with its straw mattress. Grandma Kean, who played our poorly-tuned piano with some skill, found her book of Christmas carols, and we all sang with her until late into the evening.

The last event, before we hung our stockings from the mantel, was Grandma Kean's recitation of *The Night Before Christmas*, which she'd memorized. Sometimes she had to repeat the whole poem in order to satisfy the wide-eyed excitement of Johnny and the twins. Every sonorous

119

phrase was pure magic! They wanted to know everything about St. Nick, so we had a discussion as soon as Grandma finished.

"Grandma, is it true that St. Nicholas knows if you've been bad?" asked Bella.

"Yes, dear," she replied, going along with the spirit of the night.

"But how does he know? Does somebody tell him?"

Lilly piped in, "His elves travel all over the world, from house to house. They watch the little children all year long … secretly"

"I've never heard that one before," chuckled Grandma. "Who told you that?"

"Charles," asserted Lilly.

"Now there's a reliable source," I said, under my breath.

"Bella's been bad!" exclaimed Lilly. "She's gonna have coals in her stocking!"

"No, I'm not! You put a dead June bug in the olive jar! I bit into it and puked! *You're* gonna get the coals!"

"That *was* disgusting!" I said with a grimace.

"But creative!" quipped Charles, ever on the lookout for pranks he could play on me.

Johnny was laughing so hard that he fell off the chair and rolled around on the floor holding his aching stomach!

"It's not funny," growled Bella, pouting. "I'll never eat olives again!"

"But Bella put a live pollywog in my cider!" retorted Lilly. "She deserved it!"

"I just wanted to see if it liked cider," she said, with exasperation.

Knowing Bella, her excuse was probably an honest one.

A yelling match broke out between the two, and Papa had to come to the rescue. "Girls, girls, this is Christmas Eve. You don't wanna let St. Nick hear ya fightin' like that, now do ya?"

"No Papa," they replied, in one voice. They quickly became calm but the questions continued.

"Did you ever see St. Nick, Grandma?" asked Johnny.

"No, I never have," she replied. "Have you seen him, Captain?"

"Oh, goodness no. Only a very few people have caught him by surprise."

"But how does he get down the chimney?" asked Bella, with a puzzled look.

"He flies down, like it says in the poem," I answered. "He has to be very, very fast at his work. After all, there are millions of boys and girls, all over the world, that he has to visit."

"I wanna see him! I'm gonna stay up all night and listen for his sleigh!" exclaimed Lilly.

"Me too," shouted Bella. "I wanna see the reindeer."

"Count me in!" bellowed Johnny.

Father smiled and said, "We'll see how long this lasts."

As expected, the little girls and Johnny were fast asleep in a big pile on the sofa some time after ten. So much for the St. Nicholas vigil. Papa carried Lilly, then Bella up to their room and tucked them in. Fortunately for the rest of us, they didn't wake up. Johnny, however, being aware of the twins' removal from the sofa, did awaken enough to ask if St. Nick had arrived. I answered in the negative and escorted him to bed.

As the hour approached midnight, Papa permitted Charles and I (for the first time ever, and probably because Momma wasn't here to stop it) to have a small glass of wine to welcome in Christmas 1860. And welcome it, we did! Finally, after becoming so silly from the "fruit of the vine," wrestling like a couple of three year olds and nearly knocking over the irreplaceable Nativity scene, the captain commanded us to go to bed. And to bed we went.

The night was short. Johnny and the twins were up at dawn and had already gone down to the parlor to see if St. Nick had come. Lo and behold, he had!

"Annie, Annie, get up! Get up! The stockings are full!" yelled Bella and Lilly, as they jumped up and down on my bed.

"OK, girls, I'll be right down," I replied, half awake. The twins then took flight to retrieve their treasures.

By the time I arrived, the girls had already assembled their spoils across the braided rug. Jellies, tops, hair ribbons, paper-wrapped candies, and doll clothes fueled their unbridled excitement. St. Nicholas cleverly remembered to give them each the exact same things. Apparently, he remembered the infamous Christmas tantrum of 1859.

My own stocking held a sewing kit, a new journal, pencils for writing and sketching, hair ribbons, and some beautiful mittens.

Johnny received a top, marbles, preserves, and a toy gun. However, he was quite confused to find a lump of coal at the bottom of the stocking. He looked as though he wanted to cry.

Grandma, instinctively aware of his thoughts, jumped in. "Johnny, coal, along with all those other gifts, is a sign of good luck."

"Oh," he replied, "I thought it was a warning."

"No, silly," she remarked, rubbing his head playfully.

Father, with a glimmer of mischief in his eyes, interjected, "Hey there Little John, I found something outside that must've fallen out of that jolly ol' fella's sleigh. And I think it's for you."

Papa left the room momentarily and came back holding the mysterious object behind his back. "Close your eyes for a moment, and no peekin'!" Johnny followed the instructions with great anticipation.

"All right, you can open 'em up!" he announced.

"Oh my goodness! That piece of coal really is lucky!"

Father then handed him his very own percussion fowler, complete with birdshot, powder, flask, and caps.

"Papa, let's go out and shoot some turkeys! I saw ten of 'em out back this morning," he shouted, ecstatically.

"I'll go out with ya in a bit, son. But first we're gonna have the talk," responded Papa.

Charles rolled his eyes in typical fifteen-year-old fashion.

"What talk is that, Papa?" asked Johnny.

"It's the *this is not a toy* talk. There's responsibility that comes with ownin' a gun.

"Of course, Papa. Thank you so much! I love it!"

"Thank St. Nick," replied Father, with a wink.

I was truly grateful for all the love and kindness shown by everyone. Yet, there was a sense of melancholy tugging at my soul that morning. Once everyone had left the room I began pondering my upcoming twelfth birthday and reminiscing on the past year. Next Christmas would be the last time I would hang a stocking on the chimney with the youngsters. In ensuing years, I would join Charles and the adults on New Year's Eve to exchange gifts. How quickly time seemed to be passing. Paradoxically, it felt like an eternity since I had last seen Momma's beautiful smile. Christmas wasn't the same without her, nothing was. And what surprises would 1861 have in store? Mercifully, the future doesn't like to give up her secrets until it becomes the present.

Chapter 17

The King of the Golden River

We went back to school on Wednesday, January 2, 1861, a very cold and blustery day. Over half of the children were absent, mostly due to illnesses, which were common during the winter months. Our teacher was vigilant when it came to coughs and sneezes in the classroom. Many severe illnesses started with similar, mild symptoms. Influenza could start with a slight fever and cough, pneumonia could begin with a slight fever and cough, diphtheria could present with a light fever and sore throat, scarlet fever could start with a light fever and sore throat, or any of these symptoms could be the prelude to nothing more than a mild cold. Yet, even wintertime colds could get out of hand. Octavia didn't take chances. During school hours, children with possible symptoms were quarantined in the small back room, where there were two cots and blankets prepared for such occasions. Octavia sent notes to parents urging them to keep their children at home if they were sick. Most listened, but some didn't.

By the second week of class in the new year, on the day Mississippi seceded from the Union, three children from two different families in our schoolhouse came down with sore throats and fever during the afternoon and had to be quarantined. Miss Hunt seemed somewhat alarmed due to the speed at which the malady came on. I was worried too, as one of the children was a close playmate of both Lilly and Bella. The next day the three sick children were absent and another young boy came down with similar symptoms during our morning session. He was quarantined. It seemed that every time a child got sick a new state left the Union; this time it was Florida.

On Friday, there was a rumor going around that the three children, who became ill on Wednesday, had diphtheria. This was a real concern, but Miss Hunt tried to keep us calm by reminding us it was only a rumor, and that diphtheria is not always severe. When we all left for home, I thought to myself, no one got sick today and no state seceded. Progress! However, on arriving home, Charles informed us that Alabama had "dropped out of the game." That evening, Bella developed the dreaded symptoms that I had hoped we could all avoid.

The next day, her sore throat was worse and the fever was continuous. The unwelcome news came to Father via Mr. Blanchard, who knew the families whose children had gotten sick at school. It *was* diphtheria! My parents had survived it as youngsters, but Charles nearly died from the illness when he was an infant. I, too, contracted a mild case when I was eight, but soon recovered.

All the schools in Chelsea were temporarily closed, in order to curtail the spread of the disease. Doctor Davis and Ellen were both summoned to Bella's bedside, confirming what we already knew. Though no one besides my sister was stricken in our family, we all imagined we had symptoms at one point or another. Lilly was sure she had a fever and complained about every little ache and pain as though she was at death's door! The concern was understandable. Previous outbreaks in Kennebec valley had claimed the lives of two out of every ten who had contracted the disease. Survival from the illness, for the elderly and very young, was a metaphorical flip of the coin.

After the doctor had seen Bella, he gave Father this advice, "Give her plenty of bed rest and whatever liquids you can get into her. She will probably lose her appetite for solid food, so applesauce and soups are something you might try. Your mother-in-law and the younger two children should avoid her completely while she's ill. As for you, Charles, and Annie, I would spend only the amount of time necessary to meet her needs. No lengthy stays!"

"We've all had this thing at one time or another," stated Father, with a little too much self-assurance.

Doctor Davis gently admonished him, "That may be so, John, but continual exposure can make transmission more likely, even if you *have* had it before. Diphtheria can be deadly."

"Very well, Doctor," replied Father, reflectively. "We will be careful."

REMEDY FOR DIPTHERIA. The Hallowell Gazette gives the following recipe for the cure of diptheria. It is a simple one and easily tried, and if it should do no good it can do no harm. It is said to be effectual however :— "Take a common tobacco pipe, place a live coal within the bowl, drop a little tar upon the coal, and let the patient draw the smoke into the mouth and discharge it through the nostrils.— The remedy is safe and simple, and should be tried whenever occasion may require. Many valuable lives may be saved, our informant confidently believes, by prompt treatment as above."

Oh, how I desperately wanted to be with Bella. I loved that little girl! I saw so much of myself in her and that cursed disease would not keep me away. So, I began to concoct a scheme.

Ellen stayed late that night, to nurse and comfort my frightened sister. Isabella had been moved to the far end of the summer kitchen next to the stove, which we kept running because the nights had been bitterly cold and her symptoms were always worse after sunset. What sleep she could get was troubled due to her inflamed throat and spiking fever.

Once everyone was asleep, I lit a candle and quietly crept down the stairs. I turned into the parlor, tiptoeing so as not to be overheard, reprimanded, and sent back to my room. From there it was a straight shot through the kitchen and into the ell. I could hear the poor little girl tossing and turning, trying to get comfortable. Then she saw me walking towards her in the candlelight. The woodstove was very hot, so I cracked a window open and adjusted the damper as quietly as possible, expelling some of the excess heat. Then I pulled a chair over to her beside and sat down. Bella struggled to right herself, but I readjusted her pillow and motioned for her to lie back down.

"What are you doing down here, Annie?" she whispered, in a raspy voice.

"I want to be with you," I whispered in reply. "Don't talk. I'll just sit here awhile and you just try to get some sleep."

"Didn't you hear what the doctor said? You could get this, and it's awful."

"I am not going to treat my sister like an outcast. I love you. If I get it, I get it!"

"You could die, Annie. I don't want both of us to die." She began to cry in muted gasping sobs.

Borrowing some of my brother's wit, I replied, "Well, you're not going to die. But if you did die, are you saying you don't want me to tag along with you? Am I that much of a bore?"

"Oh, stop it, *Charlie*," she wheezed, forcing a smile.

"You've gotta think cheerful thoughts, Bella."

"I try, Annie. But I'm scared."

"No need to be scared. Papa, Charlie, and I have all had it, and we're still here."

"But Charlie nearly died."

"He was only a year old. You're older, and older children get better more often than babies do."

Bella sighed and we both sat there quietly for a few minutes.

"Annie," she said, "will you read to me?"

"Of course, what would you like?"

"*The King of the Golden River.*[41] I love that book."

"Is it in your room?"

"Yes, it's on the shelf next to the bed."

The King of the Golden River is a Styrian legend from Austria. (Styria is a southern state in Austria.) I was surprised that Bella had ever heard of it, but she must have been listening when I read it to Johnny. I finally located it, crept silently back downstairs, positioned the candle in a place that allowed me the best lighting, and began to read.

"A secluded and mountainous part of Styria there was, in old time, a valley of the most surprising and luxuriant fertility. It was surrounded on all sides by steep and rocky mountains which were always covered with snow ..."

Normally, Bella would have been asking me to explain the meaning of the unfamiliar words, and there were a good number of them. But she was exhausted and had little voice left to converse. So, I paraphrased much of it. Before I had finished the first chapter the little girl was asleep. I placed the book by her bedside, kissed my fingers and placed them on her feverish head, and took off to bed.

The next morning, Father confronted me, forbidding me to get that close to Bella again. He had seen the book at her bedside and put the pieces together. I begged him to allow me to sit on the other side of the room and read to her, and he reluctantly agreed. So, that's what I did for the next four or five days.

During that period the illness became alarmingly worse. Breathing had become difficult as the airways were becoming constricted, and this was most serious. In those days, if the throat closed up, a tracheotomy (without anesthesia!) was the only option, and it was rarely successful due to infection and the trauma it inflicted on the patient. Dr. Davis was against such a last-ditch procedure. He believed that the operation killed many who might have survived without it.

I was deeply distraught by her condition, but continued to carry on as though all was well.

One afternoon, sensing my distress, our midwife admonished me, "Children often get all of these symptoms before they recover, so try not to worry so much, Annie."

I responded, "Yes, and don't they often get all these symptoms before they die, as well?"

Ellen reacted with a painful grimace and looked away.

Being there every waking moment and continually witnessing Bella's unabating anguish was taking a heavy toll. I was so focused on her health I had taken little notice of my own. Dr. Davis observed that I looked "thoroughly exhausted" and recommended that I take a few days of respite. Fortunately, respite was soon offered by Mrs. Sullivan. She had heard of Bella's illness and sent a note inviting Johnny and me to her home for the weekend. Edith fully understood how overwhelming it was to take care of a desperately sick child.

Though I was reluctant at first, I realized there was little I could do to help at home. Bella was far too ill to appreciate my reading, and her awareness was fleeting at best. Though her condition was still serious, the doctor felt it had stabilized enough to present some hope.

Before we left for the Sullivan's, I went into the summer kitchen and knelt beside the little invalid, assuring her that I would be back on Monday. She seemed to understand as she turned her head towards me and gave a light smile. Then, against the doctor's orders, I kissed her on her burning forehead, and took my leave.

Chapter 18

Theresa

—

harles brought us by wagon to the Sullivan home for a three-night stay, assuring us that if Bella took a turn for the worse he'd fetch us immediately. A weekend break would give the boys time to go hunting, and allow me the opportunity to rest and converse with Mrs. Sullivan.

I promised Edith that we would keep our distance, for fear of exposing her to the contagion. She responded in Spartan form, "If I were worried, I wouldn't have invited ya now, would I? So, not anot'er word about it!" she declared, dismissing the idea with a wave of her hand.

We began our time together by playing several games of chess. The change in atmosphere and activity helped me get my mind off things at home, which was a relief. To my utter amazement, I succeeded in capturing Edith's king in seven moves during our very first match.

"Edith, you let me win!" I asserted.

"You won on yer own, Annie Elizabeth. You're gettin' da hang of it, and I better sharpen up me skills if I'm gonna win ya!" she exclaimed, with conviction.

"If you're lying to me, you'll have to go to confession," I teased.

"My dear God! I swear on Oliver Plunkett's head d'at ya won fairly and squarely!" she growled, with feigned indignation.

"Who is Oliver Plunkett, and what does his head have to do with it?"

Once she had given me an Irish history lesson and the tragic details about Fr. Oliver Plunkett,[42] I didn't dare to doubt her assertion about my win. Of course, it was all in fun, anyway.

Our candid conversations eventually led to questions about Bella. I wanted to talk, and I needed to talk, but my ambivalence and feelings of guilt for having abandoned her were tugging at my heart. Nonetheless, I couldn't avoid the topic forever.

"How are ya doin', Annie?" asked Edith, with motherly concern.

"I'm all right; I'm just worried. Bella's desperately sick and I feel so helpless. I've been reading *The King of the Golden River* to her, but now she's just too ill to respond."

"Ya mustn't assume she's not aware, just because she can't respond."

"I hope you're right. There's not much else I can do for her."

"Oh, but yer givin' of yer time, yer energy, and yer heart. That's everyt'in'. Love is the best medicine, and the most precious of gifts."

There was a pause in the conversation. I could tell that there was something on her mind that she wished to disclose, but was hesitant to do so.

"What is it?" I asked, giving her the opening she needed.

"Well … ya know, I'm not altoget'er sure 'tis da right time to bring it up. But many years ago, I lost a little girl, named Maddie, to dipht'eria. But d'Almighty, in his goodness, gave us a special grace to cope. I was hopin' to share that wit' ya, seein' the sufferin' you're goin' t'rough now."

"Of course, Edith. I've been praying to hear more of your stories."

"Oh, be careful what ya pray for. Once I get a rollin' I can't keep me mout' shut! But anyway, I'll have to give ya a wee bit of family history, if d'ats ok wit' ya."

"Please do," I replied.

"All right d'en. I was born two years before d'is country, here, came into bein' … 1774. Can ya believe it?

"Me maiden name was Riley, da sixth livin' child of Brian and Aileen … two sons and four daughters; a lovely home. Papa was a saddler and Momma a seamstress. And bot' were strict Cat'olics, as ya might 'ave guessed.

"At sixteen, I married the love of me life, George Sullivan. He was near twice me age! D'at never really mattered to us. Oh, people gossiped, as d'ey will. 'He's robbin' da cradle!' d'ey say. Me husband was a cabinet maker, and a very good one! Learned his trade wit' da famous Hepplewhite in London.

"We had a good Christian marriage and five children who lived to maturity. Shauna, me youngest daughter, was born when I was close to forty-t'ree. Mikie was her only child. As ya know, she and her husband, Aidan Bryne, died from typhus durin' da blight. D'en George and I took the wee'un under our wing and changed his name to Sullivan when we got to da states.

"Oh, excuse me for ramblin' so. I was gonna tell ya 'bout Maddie and I got lost in da mix."

"Oh, I think that good story tellers always wander a bit, don't you? Please continue, and feel free to wander." I said.

Edith laughed heartily, "I t'ank you for permission, dearie, but I'm afraid, permission or no, I'm gonna wander!"

"Well, now, Maddie was one of da dearest children you could ask for, smart as a whip, t'oughtful and helpful, even at da tender age of t'ree. Da little girl was learnin' to read at da time she became ill. O, dear Mary, Mot'er of God, did d'at child suffer!" she interjected, reliving those vivid memories.

"It's a merciless disease," I muttered, with tears welling up in my eyes.

"Umm, it took its toll on our hearts, d'at's for sure. But somet'in' wonderful happened d'at helped us cope. Me father, Brian, or 'Granda', as we called him, passed away a few mont's earlier, and he was very close to da little girl.

"Well, one mornin', t'ree days before Christmas, I found Maddie sittin' up in her bed. She looked well for da first time in weeks. I said, 'Maddie, yer sittin' up, dear. Are ya feelin' better?' D'en she responded joyfully, '*Granda* came to me durin' da night. He's comin' to fetch me on Christmas Eve!' Needless to say, I was shaken to da core, and a cold chill run down me spine. And sure enough, at da stroke of midnight on Christmas Eve, wit' our family and da midwife as witnesses, she drew her last breat' … Granda came."

"Oh, Edith," I whispered ."If only I had your faith."

"Don't assume d'at me fait' was any different from yours when I was yer age. I have a good seventy-five years of life o'er ya, Annie Elizabeth. You and I? Our souls are cut outta da same fabric. I too had doubts 'n' struggles. I was never blind to da discouragin' ways of human life … d'injustice, da sufferin', da grief, and d'evil events d'at plague our time. So, don't canonize me just yet!"

"Canonize?" I asked.

Edith laughed with amusement, "I'm sorry, dear, d'at's when da Cat'olic Church declares some person to be a saint! Believe me, I'm not d'ere yet!"

She continued, "An important t'ing to remember is d'at da first treasure to be stolen from us when evil strikes, or tragedy overwhelms us, is da virtue of hope. Hope is da physician of every misery. Once we abandon it, we're left to da dark twilight of doubt, where d'ere is just enough shadow to make us stumble around aimlessly."

I nodded in agreement.

"I've been d'ere, too. What will often dispel da doubts are da graces received. D'ose blessings should never be stored away or forgotten. D'ey're meant to rekindle da fait' d'at lies just beneat' da surface. What was it we were discussion' durin' yer last visit?" she asked.

"Oh, the odds of things happening at the same time."

"Oh, yes! Statistics and timin'. D'at's right."

"You've had many blessings, haven't you, Edith?"

"Far more d'an I deserve, dear."

"But your faith is real faith; mine is fair weather faith. Sometimes, I pray for something and just the opposite happens. The other night, I prayed for two long hours that my sister would show some signs of improvement, and when I went back to check on her, she was worse than ever."

"Ah, but we have to allow Divinity to act as He choses. Fait' is not magic. St. Paul tells us d'at God works all t'ings together for da good, for d'ose who love Him. D'at means we have to trust and accept his decisions, even d'ough we can't see His reasonin' at da moment."

"But isn't that just another way of saying that life is mere chance, and we have to simply accept it and move on?" I asked.

"Oh, no! Chance assumes d'at d'ere is not'in' beyond our senses and d'at everythin' d'at happens is accidental. You told me of da tangle of t'reads of which yer pastor spoke. D'at tangle is how t'ings seem from here, but fait' lifts us beyond d'at. Our lives are not simply an arbitrary t'row of the dice. St. Paul is sayin' d'at all t'ings are interwoven wit'in a mysterious and great design. Connected. Christian trust is quite different from 'Eat, drink, and be merry, for tomorrow we die,' which was pagan Roman philosophy. Trustin' in God raises one's acceptance of a situation to a much higher level … a level of da cooperation of wills, divine and human. Wit' d'at comes da possibility of briefly glimpsin' da ot'er side of d'embroidery."

"Are you saying that trust is the reason these unusual things happen to us from time to time?" I asked.

"In part, but more importantly, trust helps us recognize da flip side; da graces, d'at is. God speaks to everyone. We're just not always payin' attention. But d'ere's somethin' more important d'an trust, and dat is love."

"Scripture says that God *is* love," I replied.

"Yes. But most of us would have a difficult time describin', in words, what love is. St. Paul describes d'attributes of everythin' d'at love *'is and isn't'* but falls short of a definition: Love is patient, love is kind, love is not boastful, and so forth. But let me add somethin' more. Love is readin' *The King of the Golden River* to Bella, love is prayin' two hours for her recovery, love is sneakin' in durin' da night and riskin' da contagion in order to comfort her, love is da weariness you feel right now from yer worry. And in d'end d'ere are t'ree things d'at last: fait', hope, and love, and da greatest of d'ese is love. When ya do d'ese for ot'ers out of love, ya enter into Divinity itself. Ya become a partner in da divine scheme of t'ings."

I had tears in my eyes and was doing everything possible not to burst into an emotional wreck.

"Let me show ya somethin', if I may. Do ya know what a matrix is?" asked Edith.

"I've heard the word before, but I don't know its meaning."

Mrs. Sullivan got up and went over to the mantel and brought back a rock for me to observe. "Do ya know what d'is is, Annie?"

"Yes, it's a fossil. They're shell impressions. We have a couple of these at the school house, and Charles has one. They're quite old."

"D'at they are, maybe even older d'an me," she said with a giggle. "But what I want to show ya is da matrix. D'at is the area of stone around the shell impression. It holds everythin' in place. Wit'out d'at matrix da fossil would disappear. Love is like d'at matrix. It is da key d'at holds the whole kit and caboodle in place. I often use d'is stone as a source of meditation on how love preserves our moments, our sorrows, our losses, and our joys. But unlike the dead imprints in da stone, love preserves t'ings alive and for all eternity."

Thankfully, I committed every word from this encounter to my journal. What a source of wisdom Edith Sullivan was.

Saturday was blustery and cold with clear skies and dazzling sunshine shimmering off the drifting snow. At this time of year, sunset occurs around 4:30 p.m., and darkness ensues rapidly. Shortly after dusk, Johnny and Sully arrived from their hunting exploits having shot two wild rabbits. The boys were quite proud of their stealthy tracking skills, and my brother helped Michael skin and clean the creatures, as he'd seen Father do many times before. Edith took the meat and began preparing a spicy rabbit and vegetable stew for Sunday's noon meal. Our hunters then tacked the hides to a board, used as a home-made frame to preserve and stretch the pelt. As much as I believed that women should have all the rights and opportunities that men have, I was all for leaving the skinning and cleaning to the males of our species.

Sunday's weather was a duplicate of the previous day. Edith was unable to attend mass on Sunday morning, due to the extreme cold. However, she did spend an hour in front of the crucifix, prayer beads in hand, in silent meditation. After the noon meal, the boys went hunting again, hoping to replicate the prizes they'd acquired the day before. Predictably, Edith and I settled in for some quiet games of chess and friendly conversation. No sooner had we lined up the pieces to do battle when there came a knock at the front door.

"Annie, would ya mind answerin'? I'm slow as a turtle." Edith cackled.

"Certainly," I replied, reaching the entry before she had finished her request.

The visitors were Daniel Allen and his wife Bonnie, neighbors from a quarter mile farther up the road, who were in need of a sitter for their two-year-old daughter, Theresa.

"I'm sorry to bother you, Edith," said Danny, respectfully, "but we're greatly in need of a sitter for Theresa until tomorrow evening. The two oldest boys are showing signs of illness and we're concerned that the toddler might become exposed. As yet, she hasn't been near the boys, but we're not taking chances."

"Of course!" responded Edith, without a second thought. "It would be a pleasure. I'll keep her as long as needed. After all, she does know me and we do get along fairly."

"Oh, thank you! The doctor will be paying us a visit tomorrow," added Bonnie. We'll be back to fetch her, probably sometime after six, if that's not too long?"

"Not a problem," she answered, with a smile.

"Edith," I interjected. "I practically raised my two little sisters. I'd love to help you."

"T'ank ya, dear, but you've come to rest, and rest ya shall. Besides, I've always wanted to have a wee'un at da yout'ful age of eighty-seven, and here's me chance!" she responded, with a hearty belly laugh.

Mrs. Sullivan continued, "Oh, Danny and Bon, d'is is me dear friend and mentor, Annie Goodwin, daughter of Captain John and his late wife, Sarah."

Both nodded, in acknowledgement.

"Pleased to meet you both, and you too, Miss Theresa," I responded, extending my hand to shake her tiny fingers. I then added, "Me, a mentor? Edith, Oh my! I'm afraid it's quite the reverse. Mrs. Sullivan is a great blessing to me."

"And to us, as well. And we expect to pay her for her kindness," added Dan.

"Now, d'ere'll be no talk of compensation," asserted Edith, with no room for compromise. "'Tis me Christian duty to help d'ose in need. I do t'ings outta love, or not at all!"

———

Theresa was a lively and intelligent child. She knew Edith from a few other visits, but had never stayed overnight at someone else's home or been away from her mother for more than a few hours. We were expecting a commotion at bed time, and we were not disappointed! I volunteered to stay with the infant, but Edith was adamant that she would be the one to take care of the child.

"After all, Annie," she said, with resolve, "ya came here to rest. I'll not put ya to work doin' the very t'ing ya came here to rest from. D'at's me final word on da subject."

I responded, firmly and decisively, "I will not risk the possibility that little Theresa might have already been exposed. You are eighty-seven, Edith, and though you may think you're immortal, it's the very young and elderly who are most likely to die from diptheria. You're like a grandmother to me, and I will tend to the little girl's needs. That is *my* final word on the subject. I've Irish blood too!"

Edith broke into a jovial belly laugh, "I surrender … I surrender! After all, we don't wanna have two Irish women lockin' horns, now do we?"

I had won the skirmish with her, but something she said had cut my heart to the quick. I felt ill, and thought I might either vomit, faint, or both. I pretended I needed to use the outhouse and excused myself.

I had abandoned my dear Bella at the hour of her greatest need, and now I was caring for a stranger's child. What insanity. Of course I was tired, everyone in my family was tired. Did that give me the right to go on holiday while my sister lay near death? No, I couldn't do anything to help her while she was so ill, but I could have been at her side at the very least. Now it was too late to change my plans. It was a frigid and windy night. Temperatures had dropped near zero, and I was needed to help comfort this child.

After composing myself, I returned to the parlor where Theresa, who had been sitting on the floor playing, now began to fret and fuss for her mama. As I sat down beside the distraught infant, Edith, who was sitting on the sofa, spoke, "Annie, dear, be at peace, all t'ings work toget'er for da good when done outta love."

I had said nothing, but she had read my heart like a book! Her words imparted a sense of calm. Well, at least until my new charge began to scream bloody murder! "Mama, Mama, I want Mama!" She wailed for nearly half-an-hour without interruption. We expected the little girl to be fussy, but we weren't anticipating the sacking of Rome. Johnny and Sully tried to pacify Theresa by handing her little playthings, but the tiny imp threw those objects right back at them with superb accuracy. Edith proposed that I attend to the child, alone, as all the unfamiliar faces might be overwhelming her. I agreed. Picking up the tantruming urchin, I carried her into the guest room and sat her down on the bed.

My first endeavor was to introduce the little girl to the classical art of vocal music. My opening arias of "Twinkle Twinkle Little Star," "Hush Little Baby," and "Mary Had a Little Lamb" were sung to perfection, but the audience was not placated. I was on the verge of tears and preparing to hand my charge back to Edith, when I remembered how Mother used to get the fussy twins to sleep. She would combine the song lyrics with hand and body motions. So I followed her example and added in the choreography. Although Theresa whimpered during the clumsily animated songs, her disposition changed swiftly from distraught to serious, serious to calm, and finally, calm to giggles. Success! I then read a few short stories and used the tried-and-true "hovering-tickle-troll" game, which brought about some much-needed laughter from the little girl. Finally, after a few more soft variations of "Hush Little Baby," she dozed off, obviously preferring opera to vocal recitals.

I was exhausted and slipped directly into winter hibernation; that is, until just before dawn, when my tiny roommate awoke screaming! The poor thing had no idea where she was. I got up, lit a lantern, and brought her into the kitchen where I sang softly and rocked her. It wasn't long before I realized she was in need of a change of diaper, a task for which I was highly qualified. After having finished the chore, we settled into Edith's old rocker, and I wrapped the both of us inside an enormous quilt.

Once we were both warm and cozy, she looked up at me with a smile and cooed, "Ann-nee, Ann-nee." She remembered my name!

"T'ree-sa, T'ree-sa." I replied, using her pitch and cadence. She giggled. After a few more rounds of the echo game, she fell back into a peaceful slumber.

Later that morning, Theresa's parents stopped in briefly, and the child was elated to see them. I feared another tantrum once they left, but by some maternal magic, Bonnie was able to reassure the little girl. Miraculously,

Theresa didn't even seem to notice their leaving, and was completely at ease, playing with blocks and some of Sully's old toys.

After our noonday meal, it was obvious that the toddler was sleepy, as she could barely keep her eyes open. I extended my hands, beckoning for her to come to me, which she did without any further coaxing. As we settled in, the rocker creaked in syncopation with the ticking clock, and that combination created a hypnotic pulse that soon lulled the tired little bundle into slumberland. It was as pleasant an afternoon as one could desire. The woodstove crackled and shared its generous warmth and aroma with everyone within its reach. With my head leaning gently against the crest of the rocker, I was perfectly positioned to enjoy the peaceful view of the hillside through the window. The sun peeked through the pine branches as they moved gracefully with the breeze in a winter dance.

I was beginning to doze when something beautiful passed right through me. It was warm, vibrant, and made me feel joyful, alive, and hopeful. I have never been able to find words to describe the moment. It was almost physical in nature. At that very instant, Theresa woke from a sound sleep, pulled herself up, wrapped her little arms around me, and gave me a delightful hug! Then, with equal swiftness, she slid back into her resting position and fell asleep as though nothing had happened. I looked over at the clock and it was 1:35. A paralyzing chill crept over me and I thought of Bella. "Something has happened to her," I thought. Tears began cascading down my cheeks. Silently, I continued to rock my little harbinger for the next hour or so, pondering the mysterious implications of what had just occurred.

At three o'clock Father came to fetch us as planned. He stood silently in the doorway for a moment and then burst into tears. Johnny and I latched on to him in a jumble of squeals and hugs. He whispered, "Bella's gone, children. She began gasping for air and then stopped breathin'. 'Twas over in a moment. Nothin' we could do." Mrs. Sullivan led us all into the parlor where we vented our sorrow.

"Father!" I cried out, through my tears. "She came to me! She came to me!"

"Who came to you, dear?" he asked, clearly puzzled by my words.

"Bella! She gave me her last hug through the arms of this little girl," I said, motioning to Theresa, who was playing quietly on the floor.

Understandably, Father, Edith, Johnny, and Sully turned their attention to me, with an air of silent bewilderment.

"Tell me, Papa," I asked, "she died this afternoon at exactly 1:35, didn't she?"

Father's mouth dropped. "Yes! Yes, how did ya know, Annie? How *could* ya know?"

I repeated in detail what had transpired, to the amazement of all present. After a few minutes of extended conversation, Johnny and I collected our belongings, said our goodbyes to Sully, and thanked Edith for her kindness. I then planted a gentle kiss on Theresa's forehead and whispered, "Thank you." She stopped playing and looked up at me with an adorable smile. We then parted company to prepare for another Goodwin funeral. It was January 21, 1861.

Chapter 19

Contrition

*P*art of my heart died with Bella on that wintery day, some thirty-nine years ago. Yet there was the consolation that something uniquely touching had occurred the moment she left this life. Charles's only comment was, "Interesting." I think his agnosticism made an about-face from that moment onward, but he would never have admitted it at the time.

The most amazing aspect was that Bella's spirit had found *me*! She was barely three-and-a-half and had never been to Edith's home, but she obviously didn't need a map to find the place. She was riding on the wings of something that instinctively knew the way.

But uncertainty never failed to intrude upon those rare moments of spiritual clarity, and the disquieting questions often followed. Did that essence that radiated from Bella's love for me live on? Or did it disappear into oblivion like smoke from an extinguished fire? Even that precious embrace was not enough to completely close the door on my recurrent doubts about God and the afterlife.

Early in the morning on the day of the service, Thomas Thwing, along with an assistant, arrived in order to take another photograph. What was most disagreeable to me was not the photograph itself, but that the image captured the most heartbreaking moment of all my memories of Bella. Why not one of her catching frogs, or throwing snow at Lilly, or falling asleep in my arms? I just wanted to remember that joyful, inquisitive, bundle of love in the thousands of other beautiful moments that had so touched my heart.

As Thomas was setting up his camera and other paraphernalia, he introduced us to his cousin, Susan Thwing Maxwell, who had come up from Bowdoinham. She was a photography enthusiast and knew a great deal about the newest, most advanced types that were now being used in the big cities. She informed us that daguerreotypes and ambrotypes would soon be outdated and replaced with less fragile, less expensive, and more easily replicated products, popularly known as tintypes.

Susan was petite, wore her brunette hair in ringlets, and was in her mid-thirties, and best of all, she was unmarried! Father seemed more energetic and talkative in her presence than he had for months. The Maxwells had been involved with all the maritime-related ventures in Bowdoinham and Bath for years, and Susan knew a fair number of Papa's sea-faring mates. He thought her to be a "kind-hearted, handsome, and intelligent woman." Charles and I couldn't help but notice a definite spark which added a welcome touch to the somber atmosphere.

Having already described our funeral traditions, I will simply say that Bella's was not much different from the others, with one exception. Because the ground was frozen, Bella's little coffin would be brought to a crypt in Hallowell to await the April thaw for burial.

"Wonderful," I declared to Father, in private. "We can all grieve now and refresh our sorrows again in three months." He glanced at me with a pained grimace, put on his coat, and wandered out to the barn. His response shifted my awareness. My attitude was becoming more cynical, and I felt it right to reassess the road down which my thoughts were wandering.

Our family, once again, was numb with grief piled upon grief. We responded to the funeral preparations in mechanical fashion and did what needed to be done in a blurry haze of routine. It had only been eight months since Mother's passing. With another death, it felt as though we were being punished for some unknown crime.

> The sense of guilt is enduring and tormenting, and can only die or be relieved by repentance, confession, amendment or atonement. It needs not that it be the theft, fraud or wrong, amounting to a thousand, ten, twenty, fifty, or a hundred thousand dollars, in order that the soul be oppressed by its burden; a twenty-five cent—*a quarter of a dollar sin*, may become larger than the globe, weightier than many worlds, with a punishment like the sin of Cain—unendurable.

Once again, the ever-shrinking breathing portion of the Goodwin family plodded through the emotional surge of bereavement. One week you're carefree, sliding down the hill in the snow with your little sister, and two weeks later, you're laying her lifeless body in a wooden box. Through this gauntlet of grief, I began to understand that the "Why?" questions would never be answered in this life. I needed to accept those chaotic tangles on the underside of the embroidery in hopes that the top side of the sampler would not be an eternal, empty void.

As the chaos and stress of the funeral finally abated, I was left with a deep, agonizing wound; an unshakable sense of shame for not being there with Bella. My sister's suffering was a dreadful thing to witness, and a part of me couldn't wait to get out of that house when Edith called. What compounded my guilt even more was the uncomfortable truth; the poor child, in her release from the bondage of suffering, flew to me. The irony! Was it truly her responsibility to seek me out after I made the choice to abandon her?

It took weeks for me to come to terms with my shame. Only after dragging Edith through all my lamentations did I find hope of recovering a sense of self-worth. She reminded me that if it hadn't been for my absence, I never would have known the degree of Bella's love, nor would I have experienced the grace of that last hug. She was convinced that everything happened the way it was supposed to happen.

"The Allen boys never got da contagion, ya know," declared the elderly sage. "Theresa came to me house for one purpose, and one purpose only, ta give ya Bella's last embrace."

After seeing that I was still downcast, she muttered a few words of frustration in Gaelic, and commanded me to try an experiment. "I want ya ta read *The King of the Golden River* to Bella," she asserted, looking at me like a doctor who was handing me a prescription. "D'at will do da trick."

That night, I took Edith's advice and audibly invited Bella's soul to sit at my side. As I read, questions popped into my mind as though she was there in the flesh, asking me to clarify or explain certain passages. Most likely, I simply knew Bella's mannerisms so well that I anticipated what she would have asked. Anyway, by the time I had finished the book, I was free from that awful curse.

———

Time moved along, and by my twelfth birthday, we were at war with eleven Southern states. On April 12, 1861, Confederates fired their artillery on a Union-held fortification called Sumpter in Charleston Harbor, South Carolina. Major Anderson, who was the commander of the fort, ended up surrendering. He did this, in part, because of the overwhelming barrage, but also because the defenders were starving. Father told me that Anderson[43] had been in charge of the arsenal right here in Augusta many years ago, which made that distant first battle somewhat more meaningful to me.

Every day, throughout the summer, Father purchased newspapers in order to follow the war effort. Anxiety was high, as regiments were starting to form in Maine and throughout every other state. Small rural areas were often the hardest hit, as nearly fifty percent of the army was composed of young farmers. A few of Charles's older friends had already enlisted and my brother continually talked about doing likewise. Fortunately, he was only sixteen, two years below the minimum induction age. Even so, the idea of my big brother becoming a soldier frightened me greatly. Hadn't three deaths been enough?

"This "so-called" war is going to be a romp in Capitol Park; everyone knows it!" he boasted. "As soon as those rebs hear our cannons roaring and look down the barrels of our fifty-eight caliber Springfields they'll hightail it all the way back to Richmond, tails b'tween their legs!"

"Dear God, Charles, when are you and your friends going to get some common sense?" I barked. "Papa says this war's gonna employ some of the most dreadful weapons ever invented. It's gonna make the Revolution look like a snowball fight."

"And you and all your female companions believe that hogwash? When are all you doomsday womenfolk gonna see this whole secession thing for what it really is?"

"And what's that, Charles?"

"A sand castle! The Confederacy's gonna be swept away by the tide."

"And what tide might that be, Charlie? A sanguine one, perhaps?" I countered, sarcastically. "I told you about Edith's dream. There's going to be untold bloodshed and…"

"Don't let the dream of an old Irish woman clutter up your mind, Annie."

"You don't know her, Charles. She's not just some old lady who's gone off the rails."

"I meant no offense to Mrs. Sullivan. It's just that you're overly dramatic! This thing's gonna blow over before I have time to enlist. So, why all the frettin'?

"Because I love you, Charles Andrew Goodwin! Even when you're bein' an idiot!"

"Do you think my desire to put an end to slavery is being an idiot? If there ever was a cause worthy of dyin' for, this is it. Sounds like you're the one bein' the idiot."

"Charles, this is not about the cause. Of course it's a righteous one, but … I can't take any more deaths." I began to cry, and Charles put his arm around me.

"Oh, come on now, Sis. You don't need to trouble yourself about me for at least two years. By that time, I'll have become such a nuisance, you'll beg me to enlist. Cheer up."

As usual, humor was his antidote for every challenge, be it physical, spiritual, or intellectual. However, if there was one thing I knew about Charles, it was his stubbornness. Once he got a notion in his head he pursued it to the very end of the trail.

In late July, the first major battle, involving thousands of troops, took place in an area called Bull Run[44] in Virginia. It was said that people in Washington, D.C., and the outlying areas were so sure of a Union victory that observers—men, women, and children alike—came out with picnic baskets, leisure attire, and comfortable blankets to enjoy the "festivities." Well, the Confederate army routed the Union forces, sending them and the shocked spectators back to Washington to lick their wounds and recuperate.

After reading an eye-witness account of the battle to Charles, I said, dryly, "Your Honor, I rest my case. It's not going to be a stroll in the park."

"Great, maybe I *will* get a chance to fight, after all," he responded.

I couldn't then, or even now, put into words what Charles meant to me. He had been my playmate and confidant throughout our early childhood, my fearless knight and protector from all evils, imagined or real. Everything he did was wondrous and he was my unsung hero. Even his imperfections often had positive repercussions with me. His tendency towards agnosticism could drive me crazy, but his skepticism helped drive my pugnacious desire to "know for certain." It was, in part, his gifted ability to laugh in the face of the grim reaper that elevated and mitigated my usual gloomy perspectives in those moments. I had no doubt that his death would bring about the onset of madness in me.

Chapter 20

The Music of Love

Music had long been a part of the Goodwin-Kean traditions. Irish and Scottish jigs, children's songs, sea shanties, patriotic songs, and popular tunes lulled me to sleep in Mother's arms during my infancy and toddler years. Our community made music, too. The neighbors would gather at our house at sunset with their fiddles, concertinas, and anything else that made noise, and our revelry would continue well into the night. My happiest memories come from those warm summer evenings, listening to the concert in our front yard.

Unfortunately, over the passage of time, the melodious art had been relegated to a position of unimportance, given our family's regrettable twists of fate. Festive occasions, when most families gave voice to song in celebration, were the very times that ghostly echoes of better days haunted us with a sense of nostalgic loss.

It's true I had no choice but to live my life within a world of empty chairs. However, I did have a choice as to *how* I would respond. Moping endlessly won't raise the dead, but a good tune can raise the spirits of the living.

If not for her rheumatism, Grandma would have enjoyed teaching me to play piano. However, even engaging for a minute or two caused her great difficulty. So, I asked Miss Hunt if she knew of anyone who could instruct me in the basics of the instrument. She hesitated and then reluctantly revealed that she played the piano but had never taught anyone else.

"Oh, Miss Hunt, please consider it!" I pleaded. "You make everything you teach entertaining. If you do not, I'm afraid I'll end up with some old witch who'll slap my hands every time I make a mistake. Grandma had a teacher just like that!"

"That's a good way to kill the love of music, right from the start," replied Miss Hunt.

"Truly! She quit after three lessons."

"I would have walked out right after the first slap."

"Me too. And I'd probably slap her right back! So, will you teach me? Please?"

"Very well. I'll give it a go. But don't expect too much of me, I'm not a qualified piano teacher."

"Thank you! Thank you! Thank you! I promise to practice every day."

"You had better!" she chuckled. "Or I might turn into an old witch!"

"Miss Hunt, I don't think there's any chance of that, no matter what kind of a musical dunce I turn out to be."

My first lesson, held at our home, was all about posture. To be honest, posture was never my *forte*. I learned the habit of slouching as a survival skill. After finishing supper, we children were expected to sit until dismissed by Father. While those long-winded, adult conversations were dragging on, Charles and I would sink slowly "into the sunset" until our faces had nearly dropped out of sight. This technique was highly effective in getting Papa's attention. With an annoyed glare, he'd silently motion for us to disappear, rather than interrupt his discussion by initiating a parental lecture on how slouching would cause the downfall of Western civilization. At long last, the piano gave me the motivation I needed to mend my evil ways.

My biggest challenge with learning to play was finger control. The digits have to be kept naturally curved while playing. However, my pinkies were almost my undoing. Because they're the tiniest and accustomed to working in connection with the ring finger, they don't like to work independently. In private, I would sometimes growl, "Curve, damn-you! Curve!" Gentle persuasion didn't work, but neither did my threats to amputate the useless appendages.

My second piano lesson was held at my teacher's home. A lovely Chickering & Sons square grand piano adorned her parlor, which to my delight, was in perfect tune. She talked at great length about the musical genius Mozart, whose music was just beginning to be played in American concert halls. She even played one of his beautiful sonatas for me! Her playing seemed flawless to my ear, though she was of a different opinion on the matter.

By the time the first crimson maple leaves appeared, I was playing piano with both hands together and working on my first recital piece.

Charles became my greatest devotee as well as my perpetual audience. Though I hit plenty of sour notes, he never made a sarcastic comment. Most likely that was because our piano was so badly out of tune that one couldn't distinguish between a mistake or the correct note. They all sounded equally wrong or equally right, depending on the amount of sleep you'd acquired the night before.

Then Miss Hunt ruined the illusion by hiring David Fuller,[45] a piano maker and tuner from West Gardiner, who came to our home and brought the groaning beast into proper pitch. Now my blunders stuck out like a pig in the parlor. The listener was no longer required to employ guesswork. But when the notes were played correctly on a nicely tuned instrument, it became a joy to sit at the keyboard. Soon, the entire family was present for our evening concerts, which often turned into sing-alongs, making those autumn evenings of 1861 some of the most enjoyable since the nostalgic days of my childhood.

In September of 1861, Father began courting Miss Maxwell. He and Susan had waited a few months more than the traditional year of bereavement, before beginning their romance. I must say, it was very enjoyable for Charles and me to observe the two of them together. Father was forty-five and Susan was thirty-six, but they carried on like a couple of infatuated school children. This was an aspect of Father that none of us had ever witnessed. It was sheer, delightful entertainment. He was her humble servant, and she, his princess in waiting. "Is there anything I can get for you, Susan? Would you like some more tea? Let me get your shawl, dear. Let me help you up into the carriage. Would you like to sit by the stove? You must be frozen." I even overheard them discussing the various details of photography, which normally would have lulled Father into a stupor, but now he sounded like an enthusiast. The Lord of the Sea was demonstrating his rarely observed gentlemanly side. Who was this refined man who looked so very much like my father?

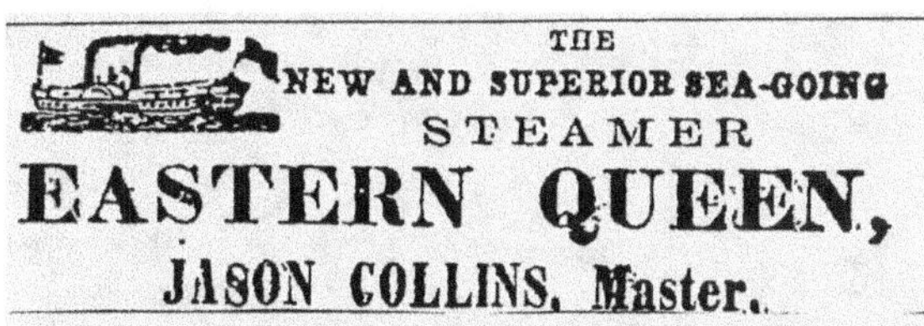

On an early October afternoon, with fall foliage ablaze with color, Father proposed to Susan during a romantic cruise on the *Eastern Queen*. The discussion of a wedding date seemed to be their only disagreement. Susan wanted to be married in the spring, with the harsh Maine winter behind them. Father, the practical man that he was (and always thinking in nautical terms), wanted to "tie the knot, as soon as possible, to stabilize the family vessel."

Presently our income was adequate, but with a civil war in progress who could say what the future might hold. Recently, the bank had foreclosed[46] on that large parcel of land we had acquired two years earlier. Papa had not been able to keep up with the mortgage payments. The untimely death of Mother, who had always been our accounting navigator, led to some monetary difficulties that might have otherwise been avoided.

How would we fare if the war moved to the northern states? Large forts like Fort George, Fort Popham, and Fort Knox were being constructed or remodeled, manned, and fortified along the Maine rivers and coastline "just in case." Even the arsenal in Augusta was on high alert, manufacturing munitions for the war effort. If Papa was called up for active duty, he wanted to make sure there was someone capable at home to take charge of the family should any of these what-ifs become reality. After some degree of compromising, the lovebirds decided on a December 24th morning nuptial, a common date for weddings at the time.

Wedding superstitions were every bit as plentiful as those of funerals and almost as bizarre. Grandma Kean described several for our amusement, which I committed to my journal.

May was an unlucky month and if you married in January your husband would die first. June, the most popular month, was the most "charmed" of the twelve, full of everlasting love. December, the month chosen by Father and Susan, promised a life full of love, not a bad month compared to some.

Once the intent to marry was proclaimed by invitation, the spirit of darkness would have greater power to disrupt the wedding. It was believed that the lovers should avoid quarreling and steer clear of dangerous situations, such as climbing ladders, walking too quickly down stairways, crossing streets, and riding on horseback.

Bad luck was also seen in the couple's future if one of them were to receive an unexpected telegram or letter on their way to the wedding.

Only an even number of guests should be at the wedding breakfast; odd numbers suggested a lack of parity or equilibrium in the marriage.

At the conclusion of the ceremony the bride should always step out of the church or room with the right foot. Hence, the phrase, "Starting out on the right foot."

Weddings at churches were just beginning to be fashionable, but most were still performed in private homes, especially in rural areas like Chelsea. The invitations were all done by hand, and often delivered in person rather than by post. Charles and I had the best script in the family, so we were assigned the task. We decided to make it into a competition and then ask the happy couple to choose the winner. They were to be worded as follows:

The Capt. John A. Goodwin family
Requests the pleasure of _________________ company
At the marriage of
Capt. John Andrew Goodwin and Susan Thwing Maxwell
Tuesday, the 24th of December at 11 o'clock
At the Goodwin family residence in Chelsea

Charles and I went off to write up our sample invitations. After we each had done three, we chose what we thought to be our best work and presented them to Father and Susan.

"The script is excellent on both of these," said Papa. "What do you think, Susan?"

"I would take either one, John," she remarked. "Do *we* have to decide?"

"Yes, you have to choose one. This is a contest between Charles and me," I explained.

"So one of you is going to hate me, perhaps?" chided Susan, with a smirk. "I'm not sure that's the best way for me to enter the family circle. John, you're going to have to decide this one."

Just then, Lilly came skipping in. "Ah, Lilly. Just in time!" Father said cheerfully. "Come on over here and pick the one you think is best."

"Father!" Charles and I exclaimed, simultaneously.

"You're not gonna let a three year old pick out your wedding invitations, are you?" pleaded Charles.

"I'm four!" grunted Lilly, with exasperation.

"And why not? The invitations are both beautifully done; let's let her choose," he handed our two samples to Lilly.

Lilly looked them over like a museum curator trying to decide which of two ancient Greek urns to display. She went from one to the other, describing attributes of each in her little girl way. "This one has a pretty 't', and this 'g' is lovely," she commented. Finally, she lifted one up to Father and said, "This is the one."

Since Charles and I were standing behind Lilly, we couldn't see which one she was holding up. Father then showed us her choice. It was Charle's invitation! Charles shot me an "I told you so" smirk. "Lilly, why did you choose his?" I growled.

"Because it's the prettiest," she said as she scampered away.

"Don't feel so bad, Annie; you came in second," laughed Charles.

"Lilly has no appreciation of great art," I mumbled to myself.

"OK, you two. We have twenty guests to invite. Annie, you do your ten and, Charles, you do yours," Father ordered. "No more fightin."

"But Lilly chose mine! I should do 'em all, like we agreed," pleaded Charles.

"I know, Charles, but our guests are not art experts like your baby sister. Ten each. That's my final word."

I gave Charles a "go eat worms!" smirk and we went off to finish the invitations.

———

Father, Charles, Johnny, and I spent an entire Saturday in early December traveling and distributing invitations. We met and socialized with every

Thwing and Maxwell on the planet, arriving back in Hallowell long after sunset. It was relaxing to be back home near the woodstove after traipsing all over Kennebec Valley. I was completely exhausted from the travel and from worrying about making this wedding perfect for Father and Susan, so I curled up in Father's comfortable wing chair and fell into a deep slumber.

———

It was the morning of the wedding and we were all running around getting ready for the guests to arrive. At one point, there was a loud knock at the front door, but by the time I answered it, no one was there. I looked around and noticed a sealed envelope laying on an outside step. Since it was addressed to the "Capt. J. A. Goodwin and Family," I opened it. To my disappointment, it was a note from Pastor Rogers sending his regrets that he couldn't perform the wedding but that a suitable replacement would arrive at the appointed time. I needed to find Father to relay the unwelcome news.

During my search, I noticed that guests were beginning to arrive and that they were all coming in through the side door. Well-dressed attendees were entering a shabby old woodshed, passing by a stinky outhouse, and then traversing two other rooms to reach the parlor! I was embarrassed. This was not a proper pathway for a formal event. When I inquired as to why they had not entered through the front, they responded, "We were instructed to use that entry."

I frantically searched every room in the house and eventually found Papa curry-combing the horses in the barn. He was dressed in his formal jacket and top hat. "Father, what on earth are you doing?" I said, gasping for breath. "Guests are arriving and you're out here doing chores. You have to get back in there, now! Your clothing is getting dirty and you're going to smell like a horse."

"Oh, Annie. Stop your dramatics. Bein' with the animals helps calm my nerves," he replied, matter-of-factly. "Besides, there's plenty of time."

"Papa, Reverend Rogers is unable to perform the ceremony; he just sent us a note!" I exclaimed. "He said he'd send a 'suitable replacement.' What does that mean?"

"No worry, dear. He's a man of his word. I'm sure someone'll be here to get the job done," he replied, confidentally.

"Also, there are people arriving, some that I don't remember inviting, and they're entering through the wood shed!"

"Oh, I'm sorry, we forgot to tell ya. It's been so hectic of late. We extended an open invitation, by word of mouth, to anyone else who might wish to come. It was Susan's idea. She didn't want to hurt any feelin's. And the wood shed? That's a good-luck tradition in her family, so I thought I'd just ride along with it. The Maxwells only use the front entry for funerals, and we don't want to put a spell on our wedding, now do we?"

"Papa, since when were you superstitious?"

"I'm not. But her family is."

"Very well, if that's the way she wants it, I guess. Papa, hurry up!"

"I'll be along, fairly."

I returned to the parlor and was greeted by a wondrous sight! It was impossible to count all the candles that adorned the tables, sills, and mantel, lighting up the parlor like the summer sunshine.

I approached Susan and asked, "Where did all these tapers come from?"

"Oh, the guests brought them, of course," she replied. "After all, tonight is Christmas Eve."

"Well, let there be light, then!" I jested, with mounting vexation from not being included in these last-minute changes. But there wasn't any time to sit and lick my prideful wounds. Moments later, there stood Father, dressed and groomed with Susan at his side.

The parlor and the adjacent rooms, now full of guests, grew silent as Charles proclaimed from the entry, "The minister has arrived with three bridesmaids."

The congregation stood and turned towards the doorway. The procession began and a trio of white-veiled figures entered the chamber, one adult and two children. Each proceeded separately towards the bridal couple in solemn step, carrying a lighted lantern that emanated from under the translucent material. Obviously, these were friends of Susan, another glaring wedding detail that I wasn't privy to. Papa was in for a list of complaints once this ceremony was over!

As the procession started, I began to feel faint. I attributed my malaise to the crowded room and the warmth from all the candles. As the first two bridesmaids walked by, my light-headedness was joined by a sense of exhaustion, as though I had just run a mile at full speed. "What's wrong with me?" I wondered, in dismay. I had no sooner begun to recover when my emotions all went awry. The sorrows of the past collided with the joys of the present and hit me like a brick wall. I was overcome and began to sob in silent gasps, lowering my head to avoid being noticed. But one individual did notice.

Out of the blue came a familiar, consoling voice, gently speaking my name, "Annie."

Gazing through the mist of tears, I raised my head and beheld the last of the veiled figures, standing before me.

I reached my hand out and gently parted the lace. A pretty little face looked up at me … Then my heart stopped!

"Bella!" I screamed.

I then awoke from the dream with a start, and tumbled off the chair onto the floor. My shrieking had jarred me back to consciousness, frightening my poor grandmother nearly to death. To my great disappointment, the vision of Bella was only a dream. But the warmth of seeing my dear sister's smile hovered around me for several days.

The actual wedding day dawned cloudy with a few flakes of snow meandering from the sky. It was, however, warmer than it had been during the previous week, which made traveling somewhat more pleasant for our guests.

Both Father and Susan wore black attire for the ceremony. Dark clothing was easier to keep clean and was worn at weddings, funerals, and other public functions. Though fashionable in cities, white was just not practical for the mud, dust, and horse dung of mid-nineteenth century Chelsea, Maine.

At 11 a.m., with all the invited present, the ceremony began with Rev. Rogers officiating. The wedding itself was brief, and the vows went as follows:

"Captain John Andrew Goodwin, wilt thou have this woman, Susan, to thy wedded wife, to live together after God's ordinance, in the holy estate of matrimony? Wilt thou love her, comfort her, honor and keep her in sickness and in health; and, forsaking all others, keep thee only unto her, so long as ye both shall live?"

Formal home wedding. Ca. 1860

"I will," responded Father.

Then turning to Susan the minister continued," Wilt thou have this man, John, to thy wedded husband, to live together after God's ordinance, in the holy estate of matrimony? Wilt thou obey him, serve him, love, honor, and keep him in sickness and in health; and, forsaking all others, keep thee only unto him, so long as ye both shall live?"

"I will," affirmed Susan.

———

During the 1860s, two-ring ceremonies were rare. It was common for the bride alone to receive a wedding ring from her spouse. In the earlier years of our century silver had been the common metal used for rings. Since the gold rush, however, the price of that precious metal had dropped significantly, making gold the standard of wedding bands. Father had his and Susan's initials inscribed on the inside surface.

At the appropriate time in the ceremony, Father took the ring off the satin cushion which Johnny was holding, and then placing the gleaming symbol on Susan's finger, he said, "Let this ring be an ongoing, outward sign of our union before the Almighty."

After Father had finished, the pastor concluded, "Therefore, what God has joined let no man put asunder. I now, in the sight of God and these witnesses here gathered, pronounce you husband and wife.

Chapter 21

Courting on the Sofa

Our memories love to linger o'er the joys of other days
Ere our hair is tipped with silver, and the care-lines marked our brow;
When our life was all before us, and our souls sang sweeter lays,
Whose burden was to live and love, in ever-present now.
With bounding heart and rosy cheeks, and pleasure-speaking eyes,
We walked the self-same pathway that all human beings tread;
But there's not among the treasures that our memories fondly prize,
Like courting on the sofa, when the old folks are in bed!
—*Gardiner Home Journal,* Aug. 21, 1862

By early 1862, the civil war had bogged down into a stalemate. This fratricidal conflict wasn't going to be brief by any stretch of the imagination. Although most of the headlines indicated "glorious" successes for the Union, further reading of the content exposed the truth of the matter. The southern armies were winning the lion's share of the victories. The North had the technology and the manpower, but the Confederacy had better commanders in the field. Poor Mr. Lincoln had so much worry on his shoulders. On top of the responsibility of managing and orchestrating a civil war, in February the dear man lost his third child, Willie, to typhoid fever.

The most captivating news we received about the war came from my uncle Eugene[47] (Gene), who was Father's next-to-the-youngest sibling (out of 10!). He wrote often to my Aunt Hannah Stinson, who lived in Hallowell, and she forwarded the letters to the rest of us.

In June 1861, Eugene was assigned to Company F of the 99th New York Volunteers and was witness to some iconic, historical events. We had already learned of his good fortune to attend President Lincoln's first inaugural address. He was also an eyewitness to the now-famous battle between the ironclads, the *Monitor* and the *Merrimac.* He wrote this about the battle:

First, it hammered the sloop-of-war, Cumberland, with its 10 powerful cannons. The Cumberland had no choice but to surrender. Then the iron monster turned its rage on the warship Congress, which it quickly disabled. By nightfall the Union vessel was ablaze, followed shortly after by the sound of a massive explosion as the powder magazine in the ship exploded!

The next day, March 9, there was an interesting turn of events as the Monitor, a Union ironclad, chugged into Hampton Roads. It had a novel, revolving gun turret, which was an improvement over the Merrimac's stationary cannons, which could only fire accurately by continually repositioning the vessel. The two iron beasts pulverized each other for about four hours, but the projectiles simply bounced off their targets. The noise inside those metal vaults must have been deafening as the cannon balls slammed into the iron siding. Rivets that held the iron vessels together were said to have sprung from their mounts by the impact, becoming dangerous projectiles for the crew. Despite the vicious interchange, the battle ended in a draw and the Merrimac steamed its way back home. I believe it is now sunset for the day of wooden warships.

On May 18, 1862, I turned thirteen years of age. This was also the year I became a young woman. Changes in my physical being and personality seemed to be happening at an alarming rate! I truly felt like I was in someone else's body. Not only did I sometimes move awkwardly, bump into things, and trip over who knows what; but my emotions were all at sea. One minute I was happy, the next angry, followed by a deep melancholy. I would "explode" without warning, at anything and anyone in my family for no apparent reason. Some things that came out of my mouth seemed to be beyond my ability to control. Papa was totally bewildered by my unpredictable moods, but Grandma reassured him and admonished him to be patient, as she had raised three daughters of her own, and knew all about this chapter of a young lady's development. I went to her often for counsel to discuss the mysterious trials and tribulations of my newly evolving feminine nature. Boys could still be terribly annoying to me and yet, incredibly interesting, all at the same time! What on earth was happening to me?

One conversation that I remember having with Charles, went something like this:

"Charles, have you seen the doll that Aunt Hannah gave me for my seventh birthday?"

"No, I gave up playing with dolls quite a while ago," he snickered. "What do you want it for, anyway? You're too big to be playin' with 'em yourself, and that thing's a wreck. Its head keeps falling off."

"Shhh … she might hear you," I scolded.

"The doll? Is your well running dry or something?"

"Not funny Charles! It may mean nothing to you but she comforts me when I'm upset," I responded.

"Does she talk to you?" he whispered, in a sarcastic tone.

"Well, if you must know, she does!" I replied, fuming at his mockery.

"Ooooo … and what does she say?" he asked, cocking one eyebrow.

At that moment I spied the doll on the piano, grabbed it and ran up to my room, yelling, "Go to hell Charlie Goodwin! Go straight to HELL!!" I slammed the door behind me, ran up to my room, laid down on my bed, and hugged my little doll, Miriam, with its adorable decapitated head, and cried myself to sleep.

It's not easy to be somewhere between a grown woman and a little girl. There are some things you know you will have to abandon by nature. But there are important things, learned in childhood, that you should never leave behind. I made up my mind I would never stop being a child at heart; I would always remain playful, inquisitive, unconceited, and opinionated. I had watched some of my older acquaintances turn away from all those wonderful attributes to become quiet, submissive, and boring, just to win the attention of boys. I was beginning to like boys too, but they'd have to meet me on my own ground.

My first beau was William Henry Runnels.[48] His father was Benjamin Runnels,[49] who owned a farm on the County Road. Willie was a handsome lad with sandy blond hair, a farmer's tanned complexion, and a stature that rose above my own by a hand. He always gave me a warm smile whenever he saw me, which was usually at the Old South. Our first meeting was, in fact, at a church fair in mid-August. Emma, who knew William very well, was the one who introduced us.

"Emma, do you know that boy over there? The one with the white shirt and hat, near the rose bush?" I asked, pretending this was the first time I'd ever laid eyes on him.

"Yes, Annie. And you can stop playin' dumb. You've been staring at him ever since we got here. Do ya wanna meet him?," she responded, bluntly. Though Emma was younger than me, she was highly perceptive and didn't put up with pretentiousness from anyone. Even worse, her voice was loud and carried above all the other nearby conversations. I was sure that Willie had heard her.

By now, I was blushing like a ripe tomato. Feeling clumsy and tongue tied, I didn't answer her question. I just wanted to go hide somewhere.

"Annie," she said, grabbing my arm and pulling me towards William, "let's go!"

Just as we got within a few feet of William, I tripped over an invisible object and went flying into a downward trajectory. My face-first collision with our planet was prevented only by throwing both hands out in front of me to break the fall. "If he didn't think me a fool before, I've left no doubt, now," I thought.

William helped me to my feet and I was mortified! Holding back an explosion of tears, I said, "I'm sorry, I'm so very clumsy!"

He just looked at me, recognizing my humiliation, and gave me that winning smile, saying, "It intrigues me, when a girl falls for me."

Thank God! His humor had broken the ice, and I began to laugh at my own adolescent awkwardness.

"Willie, this is Annie Goodwin," Emma announced. "She's my dearest friend, and the only person I know that thinks she can fly!"

I decided to go along with her jesting, and replied, "Yes, but I haven't been very successful yet, as you can see." I then curtsied politely, "Pleasure to meet you, William."

"Oh, the pleasure's all mine," he nodded with respect. "And if ya ever master the art of flight, I'd be delighted to have ya teach me. Always wanted to soar like a bird!"

"I wouldn't hold my breath, then," I chuckled. "My soaring is more like that of a penguin."

"Well, your landin' was quite impressive!"

"Hmm … perhaps, but I think we humans better stay with balloon navigation for now."

"Well, Miss Annie, it is always a good thing when we're able to laugh at ourselves, don't ya think?"

The three of us began to have a relaxed conversation about everything from farming to when we thought the Civil War would end. At one point during the conversation, Willie volunteered to fetch some cider and on his way back he tripped, nearly spilling the delicious nectar. Fortunately, by some miracle of physics, most of the liquid remained in the cups.

"Whoa!" he exclaimed. "Guess my flight feathers ain't fully developed, either. Can't get more embarrassin' than this."

"Oh, surely it can! My brother calls me a gifted halfwit," I giggled.

Emma broke in, excitedly, "We're all gifted halfwits! What's the stupidest thing you've ever done? Think hard or I'm going to win the prize!"

☞ A chemist in Connecticut is said to have made a discovery by which dirt can be converted into an article of wholesome diet. If this is really so, the cost of living hereafter will be made *dirt cheap.* B.

We started revealing those delightful, empty-headed moments of which all humans are prone, each trying to outdo the other. I started first.

"When I was about five," I began, "I told the pastor at our church that Jesus should never have healed the *leopards* just because they were carnivores, which was the only reason I could think of that would make the Son of God want to do such a thing.

"Before the Reverend could respond, I continued, in my very best "know-it-all" voice, to tell him how elegant and amazing these creatures were. And though they ate meat, they were only responding to the nature that God, Himself, had given them. The class broke into a roar of laughter, and I, for the life of me, couldn't figure out what was so funny. Even the pastor was cackling. Truthfully, once he explained what lepers were, I wanted to crawl into the nearest hole and never come out."

"Bravo! That was a corker!" said Emma. But mine's the worst, so Willie, you go next."

"OK, Em. But Annie, that's *nothin'* compared to my stupidity," said William. "I was nine! Old enough to know better, but common sense was nowhere to be found."

"Tell us!" Emma and I exclaimed.

"Well … if I must. Pappy and I were moose huntin' with uncle Joe up in Skowhegan. First day we was out on the trails, we come across a flurry o' moose tracks back in the woods. So the next day, I got up real early. I planned to track down a moose, shoot it, and surprise Pappy. So, I set out 'cross the open field, rifle in hand, climbed over a few fences, and wandered into the woods. 'Bout an hour later, out near a small clearin', I caught sight of that big ol' critter makin' its way through the brush. I aimed my rifle and fired, and it hightailed straight into cover of some nearby trees. Naturally, I trailed it for a ways, notin' the blood in small patches, here and there. Pretty sure I'd find it, but knew I'd need a lot o' help luggin' it back home.

"So, I went to fetch Pappy and Uncle Joe for assistance. We all returned to the kill site and spent the good part of an hour combin' the area. Finally, I heard Uncle Joe yell, 'Willie! Ben! … come 'ere!' We ran fast as lightnin' through the underbrush, followin' his jubilant shouts."

"Jiminy Christmas! Willie … Jiminy Christmas!" exclaimed Joe.

"Did ya find the moose, Uncle Joe? Is it a bull or a cow?" I hollered, with elation and hopin' it was a bull. I could already see them antlers hangin' over the hearth.

"Ah … It's a … It's a bull."

"How big are them antlers?" I yelled, convergin' on the site.

"Well …Jiminy Christmas! Ain't no antlers, Son."

"Thought ya said it was a bull?" I asked.

"Well …"

Finally, I set eyes on the prize. There it was! A huge kill with a ton o' meat! It *was* a bull and there weren't no antlers … but there *were* horns!"

Emma and I broke into hysterics!

"That's right, ladies, laugh away. 'Twas one of the neighbor's steer. Guess I crossed one too many fences. Needless to say my bottom was sore for a week, not to mention my pride."

"Did your father make you pay for the bull?" I asked, feeling both sorry and amused at once.

"Well, what happened was, I ended up workin' for that infuriated neighbor for an entire month. I did that as a recompense for my crime. Father paid off the rest. Pappy wasn't happy! And he swears to this day, he'll never let me go huntin' by myself again, and I mean never, like even when I'm fifty!"

Willie sighed with relief, having concluded his humiliating hunting saga. "That's 'nough o' my shenanigans. OK, Emma, your turn," said Willie. "Better be a good one. You've been doin' 'nough braggin' 'bout it."

"Oh, it won't disappoint. I promise," she responded.

"Now, let's see," she began. "I didn't shoot a bull … or heal the leopards," she said with a devilish grin.

"Come on, Emma. Quit stallin'," I snapped.

"Hold your horses, Annie. Let's see … It all started early one mornin', when one of our neighbors, Mr. Smith, came over, complaining about the smell that was comin' from our pig pen. Accordin' to him, the odor was traveling up the road durin' those hot, muggy, July afternoons. Father told him he would try to manage the stench by puttin' lime in the manure, which tempers the smell. But that suggestion didn't temper Smitty's temper. He stomped out of our house in a ranting rage, threatenin' to take legal action if we didn't get rid of the smell.

"Anyway, at the very moment he was takin' his leave, I was wakin' up. I walked over to the open window armed with a loaded chamberpot and drowsily fired the projectile of solids and liquids out the window, procuring a direct hit on top of old Smitty's head. Not to brag, but it would have impressed the Union artillery!"

"Oh, my God, Emma!" I whispered in astonishment, suppressing an eruption of guffaws.

"The rocket came down and the fella turned brown!" she added.

"Your father must have been furious!" I crowed.

"Well, normally he would'a tanned my hide, but under the circumstances, he saw the whole thing as divine justice. 'Hey, Smitty,' he yelled. 'Take care of that stench! I can't even smell my hogs any more!'"

"Emma, that's horrible!" I snorted, with convulsions of laughter that made my stomach ache. "You made that up, didn't you!"

"I swear to Almighty God on a stack of Bibles, that it's the truth, right down to the last stinky detail." she declared.

After awarding Emma a "trophy" of ginger cookies, the time came for us to leave for home. I was so elated by the way things had gone with William that I failed to discuss the most important topic of all, making arrangements to get together again!

"It's not your task to make plans, Annie. It's his!" asserted Emma. "Askin' a boy to meet you somewhere would be very, very forward, not becomin' for a young lady."

"And why not?" I demanded. "Who made up all these stupid rules and proprieties, anyway?"

"Annie Elizabeth! Those rules are there to protect a lady from makin' bad decisions."

"Well, of course!" I said sarcastically. "Men are incapable of making bad decisions, unless we

.A lady paying a visit to her daughter, who was a young widow, asked her why she wore the widow's garb so long.—"Dear mamma," replied the daughter, "it saves me the expense of advertising for a husband, as every gentleman can see for himself that I am for sale by private conract."

count slavery and every war since the beginning of time."

Emma chuckled, "You don't want to get the reputation of bein' immoral, do you?"

"How's asking somebody to make plans immoral?"

"It's just not done in polite society."

"What! Where's the logic, Em," I said, exasperated.

"It's not logical. It's the way God intended it."

"How did God get involved? This lunacy's not in the Bible."

"Oh, I'm sure it's in there somewhere."

"Well!" I consented, with a snotty air. "Whether I like it or not, I'm going to have to go along with these pretentious, absurd, "young lady" dictates, tedious expectations handed down from generation to generation, just to become another thread in the fabric of proper society."

"Where on earth did you get all those big words? I don't know what half of 'em mean!" admitted Emma.

"It's a quote from a novel. Anyway, I…"

"You're sayin' you're stuck. Right?"

"So, you really did understand me, after all. Yes, I'm stuck."

"Well, you won't be stuck long. Willie really likes you."

"We'll see," I replied, and ended the conversation with a forlorn sigh.

Chapter 22

Wisdom and Whiskey

——

A Modern Miracle —The Bangor Whig gives a curious story of an elopement which recently occurred in Aroostook, and the sudden restoration to speech and hearing of one of the parties, who was deaf and dumb, consequent upon the overtaking of the runaways by the father of the bride, who attempted to compel her to return home. In the words of the Whig; "Then was shown the miraculous power of the great passion … The deaf heard, and the dumb spake! There, at that supreme moment, ears opened and lips moved which had ever before been closed and silent. A miracle was performed: The mute declared in most plain English, and with very emphatic expletives, that 'the girl was his, and he would have her—father or no father!'"

—*Gardiner Home Journal,* Feb. 17, 1859

My head was filled with all those worries that thirteen-year-old girls have had since the fall of Adam. Did Willie really like me or was he just being polite? Does he think I'm a clumsy ox? Did he notice the scar over my eyebrow? Does he think I'm pretty? Am I too short, too fat, too skinny? Did I smell sweaty when he was near me? It was a very hot afternoon. With all these foolish questions racing through my brain, I suddenly remembered the promise I had made to myself not to become a slave to the desire for attention from boys.

Susan had been keeping an eye on me at the social and knew perfectly well what I was up to. Later, she informed Father that I was showing an interest in the Runnels boy. What I didn't know at the time, nor would it have made any difference, was that Grandpa Goodwin had been in a heated confrontation with Willie's grandfather over a boundary dispute which had caused hard feelings. The conflict almost got to the point of bloodshed, at least there were threats going back and forth between the families. Father told me the whole story, and for him it was all "water over the dam." But, he also admonished, "I'm not so sure how Ben will feel about his son takin' a fancy to a Goodwin girl. Old Runnels nods when he sees me, but never says much."

A few days after the social, I was sitting on our front steps, husking corn, when a splendid occurrence took place! William and his mother rode by the house in their wagon on their way home. I ran out to greet them.

"Hey, Annie," said Willie. "This is my mother, Naoma.[50] Momma, this is Annie Goodwin, the girl I been tellin' ya about."

"Good day, ma'am," I said, politely nodding.

"Very nice to meet you," she declared, extending her hand to greet mine. "I've heard many pleasant things about you over the past few days. Willie even mentioned the healing of the leopards."

"Oh, nice to make your acquaintance, as well. Yes, I should probably listen more and talk less, but I did finally learn the difference between lepers and leopards," I replied.

"And I learned the difference 'tween a moose and a steer, didn't I, Mamma?" added Willie.

"*I'll* say you did!" chuckled Naoma. "It was an expensive lesson."

"Well, I guess we learn best from our mistakes." I added, with a grin. "So, where are you folks headed?"

"We had some shopping to do in Hallowell. But I think my son may have had another errand on his mind, as well."

"Yes," agreed Willie. "It's such a glorious day I thought I'd take a secret excursion around the loop to see where ya live. But now the secret's out and I'm caught red-handed!" William jested.

"Well, if you wanted to be more discreet, you could have come by at midnight. I'm not usually sitting on the steps at that time."

"Yes, I know. Discretion just ain't one of my virtues. But I gotta let ya in on a secret."

"And what's that?' I asked.

"I was hopin' to be caught!" he replied, with a chuckle.

"Well, sometimes indiscretion is the best form of discretion," I remarked, grinning at my own "Charlesian" wit.

Mrs. Runnels smiled, amused by our adolescent exchanges.

There was an awkward pause in the conversation, but, eventually, Willie continued, "Annie. Ah … I hope ya don't think me too forward, but I'll be at the French's on Saturday. Sure would like some company, if ya have the time."

"I'd be happy to come. I'll need to get Father's permission, but that shouldn't be a problem."

"Excellent. Well, I'll see ya there, then."

"Great. Until Saturday. Nice meetin' you Mrs. Runnels."

"And a pleasure meeting you, Miss Goodwin. Enjoy the rest of your husking."

"Oh, I will, ma'am," I replied.

The two then drove away down the Blanchard Road, as I watched out of the corner of my eye, pretending not to be crazy with joy. Once they were out of earshot, my pent-up excitement erupted in a resounding "Yes!", which was probably heard up in Augusta.

I thought Saturday would never arrive. Mother had told me that "a watched pot never boils," but she forgot to tell me that a "watched clock dial never moves"! Finally, Saturday did make its appearance and I was up at daybreak, fixing my hair and trying on a number of different blouses and dresses. Mother had a beautiful, older dress in the closet that would have fit me, but Father reacted with a firm, "Absolutely not!"

I responded in an equally firm manner, "And why not? What good is it doing, rotting in the closet!"

Tears welled up in Papa's eyes, and I instantly regretted my abrasive words. I realized I was acting just like one of those young girls I despised for discarding their principles in order to be noticed by the opposite sex.

"Father. I'm so sorry. I can't believe the way I'm behaving … all because of a boy."

He gave me a hug and told me he was sure that Mother, if she were alive, would let me wear it. But now the dress was a family treasure that Father wished to safeguard as a cherished memory. Little did I realize that one day I would be the caretaker of this precious artifact, which, in fact, hangs in a closet beside me as I reflect on these, equally precious, journal entries.

By the time I was finished trying on every possible combination of clothing that I owned, I ended up choosing the very same ensemble that I'd started with! Second-guessing myself rarely worked.

Charlie brought me to the French's farm at half past ten that morning. Willie wasn't there yet, so Emma and I had time to do some riding. Her family owned two lovely horses that carried us all over the nearby trails and roads. A few leaves were starting to turn and the air was warm and still, creating an atmosphere of nostalgic, late-summer magic. The crickets were chirping their brief, captivating, transcendent aria, alerting us that the time of harvest was at hand.

"Annie, you look absolutely stunning!" Emma declared.

"Olive Emma French!" I giggled. 'Stunning' would take an act of God! I'll settle for something a notch above repulsive."

Emma laughed. "Boys are a waste of time. I'd never spend more than two seconds lookin' at myself in a mirror."

"We'll talk about this in a couple of years," I responded, with a patronizing air.

"I'll *never* change my mind. I'm not sayin' I'll never get married, but I won't jump all the fences you're jumpin' just to get the apple."

"Ha! You'll not only jump fences, you'll swim rivers, and climb mountains just to get a glimpse of the apple!"

"What?" she replied.

"Two years."

"You're crazy!"

"Yes!" I nodded affirmatively. "Maybe only one-and-a-half!"

"You're on, Miss Know-it-all!" she consented, extending her hand to seal the deal.

By noontime, Willie hadn't arrived and I was becoming distressed, and struggling not to disclose my fears. I tried to calm myself with an internal conversation as we rode quietly along the trails. "He came all the way to the house just to show his mother where I lived. Boys don't do that unless they like you. Then again, some boys are fickle. I've got to stop thinking like this; I'm driving myself crazy!"

Emma, insightful as always, read my silence correctly.

"Annie, I'm not sure why Willie's so late. He's usually here by now. Maybe he's makin' himself handsome for you," she said, sensing my troubled state.

"No. Boys don't "pretty themselves up" for anything. We have three in our family, and I doubt they even know how to use a mirror. I wonder if he's having second thoughts?"

"That's nonsense. He went clear 'round the back roads just to see you. Who does that unless they're smitten? I've known Willie all my life. He's not like that. It's somethin' else."

"Yeah, you're probably right. But what?" I entreated. I decided not to mention that ancient family feud, but the possibility of a problem with his father did cross my mind more than once.

The afternoon dragged along painfully. Every time a wagon traveled down the road, I would run out to see if it might be him. But he never came. Father fetched me at five o'clock and he could tell something was wrong.

"What happened, dearie?" He paused for a second, lit his pipe, and remarked, "He didn't show, huh?"

"Yeah," I mumbled, despondently.

"Well, ya know there's lots more fish in the sea."

"Papa, I hate it when you say that," I sighed. "I'm not tryin' to catch a fish."

"Well, sort like that, ain't it," he said with his best old-salt accent. "Ya pick some enticin' bait like ya did all mornin' long, fixin' and primpin'. Then you go to the fishin' hole ... in your case, Emma's house. Just cause the fish didn't show up don't mean the bait's no good. You just have to work on your castin' technique and try your luck again. Sunset's a good time. Always worked for me."

I rolled my eyes and sighed again. Father put his arm around me and commented, "You are the prettiest little thing this side of the Kennebec."

"Thanks, Papa," I replied. "Every father thinks their daughter is the most beautiful thing on God's green earth."

"Sure they do. But they don't know you."

"Yeah, I'm special," I said, with melancholic sarcasm.

"I know," he said, finally leaving me to my self-pity. "There's no better teacher than experience. You'll just have to find that out on your own, I'm afraid."

I heaved a big sigh. "Yup. I guess."

That night, I cried myself to sleep after hours of running and rerunning all the conversations and events of the past week through my tired brain. Even Charlie, who usually teased me about everything, was sympathetic. "Stop frettin'. It's all about that land grudge. You'll see!" he insisted.

The days passed and I was slipping into a gloomy state of mind. I dropped in on the French's twice that week to visit Em, but she hadn't heard anything from the Runnels either. I saw myself going down the rabbit hole of desperation that I had vowed never to enter. Thoughts of how I could change myself in order to become what Willie "wanted me to be" began to creep in; the very pretentious foolishness that I detested was rearing its ugly head!

Grieving over Bella's death was one thing, but grieving over a boy whom I'd only seen twice was ridiculous. After a few days of self-immolation, I began to come to my senses. This was all about someone else's free will and I couldn't control that. But I could control how I responded.

The following Saturday evening, I began reading *Les Miserables*, the now-celebrated novel by Victor Hugo, which Father had just purchased to help me to "get over my own misery." I was working my way through the first chapter when Charles asked me to join him in the parlor. I thought nothing of it and continued reading. He then returned, whispering in a suspiciously urgent tone, "Annie, please come down … now!" I grudgingly placed the open book face down on the bed and followed him. When I arrived downstairs, there sat Susan, Father, Johnny, and Willie!

"William!" I exclaimed. I couldn't think of anything else to say, though I'd rehearsed one hundred opening lines.

"Annie, I'm so sorry," he exclaimed. "Pappy wouldn't let me go to Emma's." Willie looked as though he wanted to cry.

Charles interjected, "He's here against his father's wishes and he's gonna catch hell for it. Ben's gonna figure this out and show up on our doorstep."

"We'll hide you, Willie. We can say we haven't seen you!" I shouted.

"Whoa … whoa, strike the sails!" interrupted Father. "Willie, is this all about that trouble between our families?

"Yes, sir. It is!" answered the boy, in a panic. "Crazy ain't it. Momma says he needs to drop it, but Father rules! No reasonin' at all with that man. Once he gets somethin' in his head he can't think straight. He'll see a dog, and'll swear it's a bear!"

"Well, this is gonna stop. I'll go talk to him," asserted Papa.

"Be careful, sir. He can be violent, sometimes."

"I can take care of myself, Willie,"

"Papa, please be careful," I pleaded.

"Don't worry about me," Father said with confidence, "I've weathered many a gale. Charles, go saddle up Riddle for me."

As Charles got up to do his father's bidding, Susan spoke, "John, there's someone here!" she peered out the window into the darkness. "Someone in a wagon."

"Pappy!" exclaimed Willie softly, with dread.

There was a firm knock at the door. Father commanded, "Everyone back in the summer kitchen and shut the door. I'm gonna talk to him."

Everyone did exactly as he said, except me. I wasn't going to miss this conversation for anything. I closed the parlor door and pressed my ear firmly against it. I soon realized that I could have been three farms away and still heard the conversation.

"John, where the hell's my son? You seen him?" shouted Ben, posturing himself for a fight.

"Yes, Ben, I've seen him. We need to talk!" Father fired back, with equal authority.

"Nothin' to talk about. I'm here to fetch him and bring him home. Where is he?"

"Not 'til you and I sit down, right here, right now, and talk," demanded Father.

"I'll go find him myself if you don't hand him over."

"Well, you'll have to get by me first, and that could be painful for both of us. And there's no need for that."

At this point, I was tempted to open the door and beg them to stop. Father and Ben were both big men and they could do real damage to each other. But there was a pause in the action and I assumed they were staring each other down to see who'd blink first. Then I heard Papa say, "Hey, Ben, ya like whiskey? Got some good stuff, straight outta Kentucky. Let's sit, have a drink or two, and talk this over."

"John, I just want my son."

"And you'll get him. Have a seat and try some of this stuff."

I could hear the clinking of glasses and the sound of pouring liquid.

"I know what this is all about," continued Father. "The boundary dispute. Hell, we don't even own that land any more! Let's let it go."

"John, there's loyalty," said Ben, sternly. "My pappy was right and yours was wrong. The Goodwins got the better end of the settlement."

"Well," said Father, in a more relaxed tone, "maybe they did."

"There ain't no maybe 'bout it, John!"

"So, how can I make it right with ya now, after thirty-plus years."

There was another pause in the action.

"I'm serious, Ben. There's enough war goin' 'round. Let's end this one.

How can I make it right?" asked Papa. "I've got five or six good acres that I've never broken with a plow. I'll share 'em with ya."

There was another long pause in the conversation. Then Ben spoke, "Well, I'll be damned. That's exceedingly generous of ya, John. Didn't expect that. I appreciate the peace offerin'."

"You can use Kean's portion of our farm, it's at the south end, nearer your place."

"Well, to be honest, got my hands full with my own. It's all I can handle at the moment," explained Mr. Runnels. "I will have another shot of that whiskey if ya don't mind."

"Sure thing," replied Father.

I couldn't believe what I was hearing. John Goodwin was not someone who gave in easily. He was stubborn by nature and almost always got in the last word. The evening turned from potential bloodshed to a night of fun and goodwill, all because of his love for me. The men talked late into the night, and though Willie and I never courted, our adolescent romance united our families in friendship. It was a time for rejoicing.

How I reveled in my newly acquired *joie de vie*! If only those moments could have lasted. But in the omniscient perspective of both writer and reader I can only dread the ensuing journal entries. Thank God these are but memories imprisoned in musty, scripted paper that may be put aside at will.

Chapter 23

Styx

Ravages of Scarlet Fever—No less than 403 persons, nearly all children, have died in Boston during 1857, of Scarlet Fever. This is the largest number that have died in that city of that disease for a similar period for many years, comprising fully one-tenth of the mortality of the year.

—*Gardiner Home Journal*, Jan. 21, 1858

*E*very year, the families of Chelsea and surrounding areas tried to dodge local epidemics. Fortunately, the great killer, smallpox, had lost much of its prevalence due to the development of an effective vaccine. But there were still plenty of contagions around whose names struck fear into the hearts of parents: measles, cholera, typhoid fever, diphtheria, influenza, pneumonia, and whooping cough, to mention a few. Perhaps the most dreaded was scarlet fever. It spread quickly and was no respecter of status. Rich and poor died from it. Even if one survived the illness, there could be life-long and life-threatening complications.

In the second week of September 1862, right at the beginning of harvest season, scarlet fever hit the French, Runnels, and Goodwin families with a vengeance. Since all three families had socialized during the previous weeks it was impossible to know which of us was the first to be exposed. The only persons spared the full brunt of the illness were Susan, who had a mild case, and Grandma, who, as usual, isolated herself in her room throughout the duration of the malady.

Initially, I paid no attention to my scratchy throat. I thought it was my seasonal spell of hay fever. Then the fearful symptoms appeared. Father, Charles, Lilly, and Johnny followed suit. The contagion could not have come at a worse time, as all of us were exceedingly ill and it was the busiest time of the year for farmers.

After my initial symptoms appeared, the malady ensued rapidly. The back of my throat was covered with a light-colored coating. This progressed to the classic "strawberry tongue" which became swollen and red just like the fruit. My whole body ached with fever. When I tried to get up out of my bed, I collapsed and nearly fell down the stairs. Thank God Susan was there to steady me and lead me back to my bed.

The scarlet rash soon followed. It started in the creases of my arms and legs and was rough to the touch. Susan tried to get me to drink liquids, but it was nearly impossible for me to swallow due to my swollen throat. At times, I'd hear Lilly or Johnny crying in the adjacent rooms, and their discomfort went on for hours. I felt so helpless.

I started to slip in and out of a feverish delirium. Mother appeared in ghostly form, beckoning for me to follow her. I would wake, gasping, drenched in my own sweat and battling a raging fever. At one point, Mrs. Sullivan materialized before me, praying something in Latin, over and over again. Then my deceased cat Sheba visited me. I was sure I was dying.

Finally, the fever visions stopped and there was nothing but a vague sense of light, like that of the moon struggling to pierce through a dense fog. I was wading at the shore of what can only be likened to the River Styx in the underworld of the dead. Gray boats with tillermen were traversing the gulf, as other-worldly voices wailed from afar. I tried to move but my feet became entangled and the tide began to rise up quickly around me. I struggled to yell for help, but no sound would come out. The water climbed higher, over my shoulders and up to my chin. I held my breath as the river engulfed me; I was drowning! Suddenly, the clouds parted and a great burst of wind gushed from the heavens. Air filled my lungs! I extended my arms and flew up, up, out of Hades and into the light. I was awake, and my fever had broken.

Slowly, but steadily, lucid memory began to replace my delirium. I was in my own little room. My possessions were all in their places. The sun was shining. I knew it was afternoon by the positioning of the shadows. Then the questions began. "What day is it? How long have I been ill? Where is my family?" The last question sent a bolt of terror through me! Everything was silent, yet it was daytime. No sounds of life. There was no crying in the other rooms, no sound of footsteps anywhere in the household. My heart was racing as I tried to drag myself out of bed. I was so weak that it took me a full minute to reach the door. "My God, please help me!" I cried, aloud. My door opened gently; it was Susan.

"Annie, oh, thank God!" she exclaimed. "John, Charles, get in here, Annie's awake."

Father rushed in weeping and embraced me. But his eyes were saying more than his tears. Charles followed, wearing a somber expression.

"Papa, what's wrong ... tell me," I cried.

"Oh, Annie, I'm so glad you came back to us!"

"Papa?"

There was a silent pause. He looked at me pitifully and whispered, "Little Johnny's gone, dear. He's with Momma." Then he added, "And Sarah Lilly ... she's at death's door," he croaked, his voice trailing off in a waver.

The Dying Child's Request.

A little daughter, ten years old, lay on her death-bed. It was hard parting with the pet of the household. The golden hair, the loving blue eyes, the bird-like voice—the truthful, affectionate, large-hearted, pious child! How could she be given up? Between this child and her father there had always existed not a relationship merely, but the love of congenial natures. He fell on his knees by his darling's bedside, and wept bitter tears. He strove to say, but could not, "Thy will be done!" It was a conflict between grace and nature, such as he had never before experienced. His sobs disturbed the child who had been lying apparently unconscious. She opened her eyes and looked distressed.

"Papa, dear papa," she said at length.

"What, my darling," answered her father striving for composure.

"Papa," she asked, in faint broken tones, "how much do I cost you every year?"

"Hush, dear, be quiet," he replied in great agitation, for he feared delirium was coming on.

"But please papa, how much do I cost you?"

To soothe her, he replied, though with a shaking voice:

"Well, dearest, perhaps two hundred dollars. What then, darling?"

"Because, papa, I thought—may be—you would lay it out this year for poor children——to remember me by."

I couldn't speak. The thought of Johnny, so young, so full of life, gone! I sat there, paralyzed. All I could think of was that horrible tangle of threads. Was God going to take away everything? Everyone? This time there were no signs or wonders, only death. I had promised that little boy that I would never abandon him. A sense of despair drove itself deep into my heart. My faith in a god of any kind was hanging by a thread attached to that wretched embroidery. And what about Lilly? That beautiful, playful, cuddly flower of life, now lying at the threshold of eternity. I had to get up! I wanted to be near her, if only to comfort myself in her last moments. I forced myself into an upright position in my bed.

"Annie, you can't get up, dear. You're far too weak. Rest," Susan admonished.

Father looked at me with compassion, "No, Annie, you mustn't get up. I can't lose you too! Promise me you won't try to get up. Promise me, dear heart."

I sighed. "Papa, would you put me in the bed next to Lilly? I won't get up but I need to be with my only sister. Please?"

"All right, dear. I'll carry you in." Father was so weak that my thin, emaciated body, which he normally could have lifted with one arm, gave him difficulty. He was out of breath by the time he'd completed his task.

"Thank you, Papa," I said. "What day is it?"

"It's Tuesday, September 30th. Then, anticipating my next question, he continued, "Johnny passed two days ago. Perhaps tomorrow you can pay your respects."

The next day I was feeling better, but very weak. Lilly was lying in the bed beside me, still breathing, burning with fever, and emitting a nasal whistling sound. I knelt at her bedside and made a short prayer. After that, being sick at heart, I wobbled to my feet and headed for the parlor. Holding the railing with both hands to keep my balance, I slowly made my way down the stairwell.

As I gazed upon my brother's lifeless body, I felt completely devoid of emotion. Though I sat there for more than an hour, no thoughts that I could latch onto entered my mind. At one point, Charles joined the vigil in silence. What could he say that would make any difference? If anyone was dead in that parlor it was me. Finally, I struggled my way back up the stairs and laid on the cot beside my gravely ill sister, staring at the water stains on the plaster ceiling until I fell into a restless sleep.

The next day, Charles, Father, Susan, and I rode in the wagon to the Chelsea Heights Cemetery for the fourth time in six years. As we made our way up the Hallowell Road with Johnny's coffin, a huge American eagle flew low, directly over the wagon, and continued to soar in circles above us. I had never seen a bald eagle so close while in flight.

"Maybe that's Johnny's spirit," said Papa.

Suddenly, I felt an avalanche of seething rage rising up within me. I wanted to scream at God, "You show us all these signs, but you can't even heal a little boy! You raised Lazarus from the dead? Fairy tales! Maybe you're not even there at all, and we see what we want to see, lingering, hoping against hope."

By the time we turned the corner onto the County Road, my anger had turned to disillusionment, but surprisingly, that thread of faith was strained but intact.

Mr. White, a gentle octogenarian and retired minister, greeted us at the gravesite. He said a few brief words and concluded with the Lord's Prayer. Then we buried another Goodwin child.

The next week was more trying than the previous. While being submerged in an ocean of grief, we now had to endure the waiting game for the outcome of Lilly's struggle for life. For five seemingly endless days, the poor little girl languished in a dreadful feverish delirium. At times, she would call out for Momma, Bella, and the rest of us.

In one rare, lucid moment she recognized me and asked a question that crushed my heart. "Annie," she whispered, "have I been a good little girl?"

"Of course you have, my sweet little flower," I responded, my voice quavering. I used every bit of my waning strength not to break down in front of her.

"Jesus is coming to fetch me soon," she whispered, with a slight smile on her parched lips. "I can't wait to see Momma."

Father overheard the conversation and pulled me gently away from my dying sister. "Go down with Susan, dear. Help her make some supper. Lilly needs to sleep. You can come see her later on, OK?"

"Yes," I murmured, my voice still shaking. I tore myself away from Lilly, sensing an explosion of sorrow building in my soul. Before I left the room, I noticed Father's distraught countenance and asked, "Papa, are you all right?"

"Yes, dear," he answered, forcing a smile to conceal the hopelessness in his eyes. Suddenly, he gasped, "This is more than a father should have to bear."

I threw my arms around him. Our tears cascaded, enjoining the autumn rain that was pattering against the sill of the open window.

———

After supper, I revisited my sister. She was not showing any more signs of awareness, but I was determined not to leave her side. Charles came in a couple of times and sat there quietly with me, attentively holding a small wooden horse that Johnny had carved as a gift for his seventeenth birthday. Lilly wasn't making any sounds but her breathing was becoming shallow and rapid; this was frighteningly all too familiar.

Sensing that this might be my sister's last night, I took courage, grabbed a pillow, and laid myself down beside her. I wanted her to feel the presence of human touch, so I snuggled up against her. The little girl had always been such a squirmy-worm whenever I slept with her. Now she was still, and her tiny form was barely distinguishable as it lay beneath the blanket.

From the lamplight, which flickered and danced from the mantel, tenebrous figures moved in a captivating exhibit, resembling a three-act shadow play. There were dancing figures and phantom creatures appearing here and there throughout the room. At times they would pause, as though intermission had been signaled. Soon, the action returned. The hypnotizing drama continued and eventually lulled me to sleep. I awoke twice during the wee hours to check on Lilly. She was still feverish, but she was calm and seemed to be resting peacefully.

At about five o'clock on the morning of October 7, I was awakened by a fragrant smell, something from my childhood. Something beautiful. I sat up, wondering if someone had brought flowers into the room, but the bed chamber was as it had been the night before. Then I touched Lilly's tiny hand. It was cold and lifeless and I knew she was gone! I screamed for Susan and Father, but Charles arrived first. Soon we were all gathered around her delicate little body. Only Charles noticed the powerful fragrance, which later contributed to many future discussions. For him, it was an awakening. For me, it was yet another enigmatic experience to help stem off my complete repudiation of everything sacred.

———

The sympathy for our tragic losses was remarkable. Letters and telegrams came in from all over, laden with heart-felt emotion and condolences. Some folks, whom we barely knew, sent flowers or stopped by in person to wish us well. There's something about the innocence of little children that touches the heart when death claims them.

We had all suffered greatly; there was no question. But Father was the one most visibly affected. He looked exhausted most of the time, and seemed to be aging prematurely. During the past two years, he had endured the loss of four family members, including his dear Sarah. He had defaulted on a large parcel of land and was shouldering the brunt of running a farm. His beard and hair were more white than brown, and he had lost weight during the contagion. Due to the fever, his voice was hoarse, softer, and even seemed gentler than before. There was now an element of deep sadness in his eyes that spoke of silent, courageous inner battles won at an exorbitant price.

We forwent a formal wake as we were overwhelmed and exhausted. Yet, there wasn't a moment when Lilly's earthly remains were left unattended. She was such a beautiful child, even in death.

Father and Susan drove the wagon that carried that gentle flower to her final resting place. Charles and I rode with Mr. Blanchard, who volunteered to escort us to the cemetery in our carriage. Grandma Kean was too overcome with grief to attend.

As we were traveling along the Hallowell Road, all at once, Charles burst into tears.

"Charles?" I asked with concern, placing my hand in his.

"I'm just remembering the evening before Lilly took sick," he moaned.

"What? Tell me."

"I'm so ashamed! So ashamed … Lilly came into my room and she was all excited about being able to write her alphabet in script. She was so proud! Annie, I sent her away, I didn't even look at what she was trying to show me. I told her, 'Not now Lilly, I'm busy. Stop bothering me.' And she did stop bothering me … She'll never bother me again." Charles gasped between sobs, "I sent her away … I can't believe how selfish I am. Forgive me Lilly!" Charles looked upward into the sky, as though hoping for some hint of consolation.

"Charles, it's OK. I abandoned Bella when she was dying. I felt horrible about it!"

"But she came to you, Annie. She let you know that you were forgiven."

"And Lilly came to you, too, Charles."

"What do you mean?"

"I've never had anything like that happen to me. And why should I? You risked getting sick just to see Bella! You read to her while she was dying. Why shouldn't her last thoughts be of you? … I did nothing for Lilly. I treated her like an annoyance."

"Charles, think. What did you experience when you entered the room on the morning she passed?"

"Flowers."

"And Father and Susan smelled nothing. They thought we were both crazy, remember?"

"Yes … it was strange."

"It wasn't just strange, Charles. It was Lilly's way of telling you and I how much she loved both of us. She forgave you and she wanted you to be sure of it."

Now silent, Charles closed his eyes, bowed his head, and folded his hands together during the last few minutes of the journey.

⸺

When we reached the cemetery, there stood dear Mr. White and a gathering of some thirty-five persons awaiting the opportunity to pay their respects. Charles asked Father and Susan if it would be proper for the two of us to carry Lilly's coffin from the wagon over to the gravesite. He saw no problem with our gesture. After we had performed that task of love, Charles knelt down on one knee, bent over and kissed the wooden box that held our sister, another flower to be planted in our garden of sorrows.

On the ride home, Charles and I looked at each other and spoke with our hearts alone. I believe that the translation of that internal conversation, refined now through years of reflection, would have gone something like this: "We are now the last two living children of the Goodwin household, first-born son and first-born-daughter, of seventeen and thirteen years, respectively. We are now sages of this human drama called life. We have stood paralyzed before the grave, and have run the gauntlet. Our souls are far more ancient than our few journeys around the sun. Life's paradoxes loom ominous before us; so planned, yet, so random; so purposeful, yet, meaningless; so hopeful, yet, despondent; so divinely conceived, yet, so naturally decayed. Is it divinity vs nature? Could it be both? And if both, what would be the underlying reason for such duality? Does suffering beckon to compassion? Does light have meaning without darkness? Does good define itself through the awareness of evil? Can faith exist without having experienced doubt? Should we chase the setting sun in the West, or face the deepening darkness in the East, in hopes of an eventual sunrise?"

Chapter 24

The Price of Freedom

Aside from all the grief that had assailed our family, there was one blessing, and that was the immeasurable bond that had fused between Charles and myself. Our respect and love for each other had grown, through the crucible of heartbreak. Where there had been a taunting, know-it-all, sarcastic boy, there now stood a young man with a humble and generous spirit! Thankfully, his ill-timed humor remained unscathed.

One desire that he had abandoned, much to my relief, was that of enlisting in the Union Army. Charles was loath to cause our ever-diminishing family any more grief. That worry put to rest, there was some troubling news that a military draft was on the horizon. We were quite certain that our need for him on the homefront would defer him from active service. It was beyond Father's ability to manage forty acres by himself, and we didn't have the resources to hire farmhands.

Our homestead farm was similar to most in Maine, save for the maritime aspect. Caring for it was a never-ending task. It could be laborious, boring, enjoyable, and challenging. Unexpected events could happen at any moment. Wells dried up, a fire once started in a cattle stall, animals got sick and needed to be tended to, machinery broke down, livestock sometimes wandered off, and late or early frosts could cause crop damage. There were occasional droughts, sudden spring storms that dislodged seedlings, and occasional, menacing infestations! We always had to be ready at a moment's notice to answer Father's battle cry, "All hands on deck!"

A SAD CASE. Mr. J. B. Winslow of Grafton, Me , was discharged from the 13th Maine regiment at New Orleans, for sickness. He arrived in New York, and so great was his anxiety to reach home that he rode night and day. He was taken out of the cars at Bethel, and cared for by kind friends, who desired him to remain and rest a little. With a consumptive's hopes, he declared that he felt better, though every one saw that he must soon die. Home was before him, and he must reach it that night. A friend accompanied him in the stage. He arrived within an hour's ride of his dear home where wife and children stood ready to receive him, when, unknown to his companion, his spirit took its flight from the body. It was a sad and touching sight. [Press.

Scarlet fever had visited us during school break, right at the start of the harvest. Papa and Charles were under the gun to bring in the crops, cover chores for the rest of us, and mourn our dead, all while enduring scarlet fever themselves! They accomplished this marathon of grief, stress, and grueling labor at a profound physical and emotional cost. Even with such above-and-beyond dedication, we barely made ends meet.

——◦——

The harvest was followed by the academic year of 1862 - 1863, my final one at the little schoolhouse. Again, our class was favored to have Octavia as our teacher. Every morning we explored the most important events happening in our world. We discussed the recent Battle at Antietam, the North's first major victory and the single bloodiest day in American history. We debated the unfair military-draft loophole that allowed the wealthy to pay $300 for a substitute to take a bullet in their stead. But the most striking piece of news was the preliminary Emancipation Proclamation announced on September 22. This proclamation would free all slaves in the rebelling states and would go into law on January 1, 1863. One pupil asked, "Why didn't President Lincoln free the slaves right at the onset of rebellion? Why wait until January?" Miss Hunt thought these were two excellent questions for investigation and she asked the older children to start conversations at home and collect thoughts for class discussion.

I posed the emancipation question at the supper table that evening, and Papa responded, "Well, here in the North, we say this war is all about preserving the Union. In the South it's all about states' rights. Somehow, slavery got taken outta the verbiage. I think the President just wants to get to the heart of the matter. The January date will give it time to simmer."

"Yes," I agreed. "Why do politicians always have to use words that side-step the truth?"

Charles jumped in, "Yeah, like the way people skirt around death. He kicked the bucket … gone beyond the veil … gone to a better place. They just don't wanna deal with it, so …"

"Oh, we've dealt with it plenty, Charles," I interrupted. "We get your point."

"Sorry, sis." Charles continued, "Old habits shuffle off their mortal coil with difficulty."

"You're hopeless, Charlie," I responded, shaking my head in feigned disgust.

"Where were we?" asked Father. "Oh yes, everyone knows the real issue is slavery, even those who try to disguise it. Lincoln's a brilliant man. Just like a prize fighter, he knows when to throw his next punch and just what kinda punch to throw."

"Exactly," affirmed Charles. "Look at *when* he decided to announce this emancipation business. Perfect timing."

"What timing?" I asked. "What does the date have to do with it?"

Charles continued, "Oh, the date's not important. It's just that he let the cat outta the bag after Antietam. Once you've got a victory in your pocket it's easier to get support for something as radical as freeing slaves. Kinda hard to emancipate if you can't even win a battle against their captors."

"Huzzah!" Susan exclaimed, with a grin, "Like running a race by yourself, then declaring yourself the winner."

"Great analogy, Susan," replied Charles, patting her on the shoulder. "Lincoln might be tryin' to call their bluff, too. Give 'em time to come back into the fold, so to speak. After all, he's not freein' border-state slaves. Those states are part of the Union."

"Well," retorted Father. "He knows how to play the cards, that's for sure."

The next morning, Miss Hunt asked us to present our thoughts on the timing of the Emancipation. Interestingly, the ideas collected by the nine children who remembered to do the assignment, were very similar to those we had discussed at the supper table. However, one scholar asked his uncle, a prominent lawyer in Augusta, for his thoughts. His uncle believed Lincoln didn't have legal authority to emancipate and was hoping to buy time to get the laws changed. In any case, the discussion was lively and interesting. Before we ended our exchange of views, we asked Miss Hunt to give us her scholarly opinion on the subject.

> SCHOOLS IN MAINE.—There are 4102 school districts in this State, 204,764 children between 4 and 21, and an average of $663,000 expended for school purposes.   [Age.

"Well, children," she began, "People are starting to lose heart over the horrible cost of stitching the Union back together for the sake of union. It's as mundane a reason for losing a son in battle as that of launching a thousand ships to fight over a beautiful woman. The President is raising the standard, and Antietam was the tipping point. He wants all that bloodshed to be sanctified, made holy by a noble quest … the freedom of an entire people. Lincoln has rightly legitimized this war as a struggle to end human bondage. Those are my thoughts," concluded Miss Hunt.

We all applauded!

John Collins,[51] another eighth-grade classmate of mine interjected, "You should run for President, Miss Hunt!"

"Sad to say, Johnny, I am not allowed … yet!" she asserted, with a smirk of rebellion.

In those days, the academic curriculum varied from schoolhouse to schoolhouse, in accordance with the schoolmaster's wishes. In some of the Chelsea schools, and there were nine[52] of them, it was all about morals and behavior. In those schools, children who misbehaved got the "switch," usually a piece of willow branch stripped of its bark that was applied to the bottom of the "problem child". Parents often encouraged teachers to use it whenever their child was naughty. Miss Hunt refused to employ corporal punishment, though her form of discipline was more terrorizing and more effective! Her method was to threaten to inform the parents of the misbehaving student. A punishment at home would be far worse than a few whacks from a willow branch.

Although she expected us to do our best work, Octavia saw her teaching role from an enlightened perspective. She, like Momma, had an older brother who was unable to learn some of the very basics that most children take for granted. The first day that she arrived she took the dunce cap and burned it in the woodstove right in front of us. Octavia understood that children have different abilities, learn at different rates, and have different interests, and she never tried to fit us all into the same mold.

English lessons were recited orally with our toes placed at a chalk line drawn on the floor. This was the one tradition that all teachers employed. It was called "toeing the line". We had to memorize many elements of our reading and present them to the class in this manner. Of course, there was history, science, spelling, grammar, definitions, interpretation, and arithmetic to round off the curriculum. During that final year, I learned to find square roots of non-perfect squares, how to solve quadratic equations, the Pythagorean theorem, and trigonometry. Using these skills, we learned to find the height of objects given its distance to the base and the angle with respect to its height. At one point, I was able to show off my mathematical skills in a practical way, which paid off in silver!

One afternoon, Father decided to cut down a very large white pine on our property that had been struck by lightning. I bragged that I could calculate its height within one foot, and he took me up on the challenge. He bet me a silver dollar that I couldn't do it. My penalty, if incorrect, would be to clean out the horse and pig stalls for a week. But the money was as good as in the bank!

First I measured off 100 feet, in a straight line, starting from the base of the tree. At that point I planted a stone to represent the vertex of the angle to be found. Then, from the stone, I measured the angle between the level ground and the top of the pine. This part was difficult, but I calculated it to be very close to 36 degrees. If I were off, even by a couple of degrees, I would surely lose the bet. Next, I looked up the tangent of 36 degrees and worked the mathematical magic to find the height.

"Father, the tree is seventy-two-and-a-half feet tall," I declared, proudly.

"Well there, smarty! I can finally take a breather from those stalls," he chided. "I'd say it's more like eighty feet. Go fetch Charles, and we'll cut this old-boy down and get a verdict."

It took nearly two hours to fell the giant, using a two-person saw, or "misery whip" as it was called. The blade continued to get hot and it would periodically stick firmly inside the cutting area. It was difficult for the two strong men to keep the blade straight, leading them deeper into "misery". There seemed to be an ongoing competition between my brother and father as to who could say the word "damn" with the most passion. Finally, the beast fell with a crash!

"Charles, you go and measure it," Papa demanded, "or Annie might finagle it to her likin'."

Finally, he came back with his numbers after taking measurements twice to ensure an accurate length.

"Ladies and gentlemen," he proclaimed, like a traveling medicine man, "the height of this behemoth is a whopping sixty-nine-and-a-half feet!"

"There … smarty! The stalls are yours," shouted Father, in jubilation.

"Wait a minute!" I yelled. "Charles, did you measure the stump?"

"Oh no! I didn't. I'll do it now."

I threw a know-it-all smirk at Papa.

Charles returned quickly and announced, "The stump is two-and-half feet in height."

"Yes!" I yelled. "If my addition is correct—and it is—sixty-nine-and-a-half plus two-and-a-half is seventy-two! Right on the money, Papa! And I mean *money*."

"Well, there!" said Papa, with a congratulatory tone, "You won this fair and square, my girl!" He then handed me a shiny new silver dollar, which was a lot of money at the time.

"Thank you, Captain," I said, saluting him. "I'll guard this treasure with my life!"

I was so excited with my accomplishment that I boasted to my teacher, who replied, "Well, Annie, I do think you are an excellent candidate for college. You've a sharp mind and an inquisitive nature, and you need to give the idea some serious thought."

"Oh, I have, Miss Hunt," I replied, enthusiastically. "I think about it all the time. But most of the colleges I've read about are either all male or just too expensive for a farm girl like me. I'm sure if I could find one that we could afford Papa and Susan would be all for it!"

"Well, that's one major hurdle overcome! We'll need to discuss this more in the future."

"I'll be looking forward to it!"

Chapter 25

Ice

As the winter drew on, our family was fortunate to avoid any more serious outbreaks of disease that were so common at that time of year. The miseries that had befallen our family had made us all the more reflective, serious, and compassionate. But, they had also given us a deep appreciation for the little joys that presented themselves, fleeting as they might be.

People are often surprised to hear about the frenzy that developed here during the war with regards to ice skating. It was not at all surprising to me, as we had a great natural resource, the Kennebec River, which often froze over with thick, smooth ice. There were times that one could skate from Hallowell down to Gardiner, or all the way to Richmond! On the river, there was no limit to motion or overcrowding as there was in a skating park.

[53]On Saturday, January 23, 1863, there was a grand skating tournament held in Gardiner. Charles, Susan, Willie, and I along with Emma and her family all attended. My brother was an excellent skater and had done the 15-mile river course from Hallowell to Richmond twice before. This time, he entered the speed race for the quarter mile in the 14 - 20-year-old boys' category, but didn't place. [54]Albion Still from Gardiner won first prize with a time of 2:29, but Charles had improved his time from the previous year by 15 seconds!

After the competitions, people crammed onto the frozen river to glide along with friends and family in order to take in the frozen wonderland. At times, two or three families might hold hands and glide together like a giant snake, side-winding their way up the river.

Willie and I, both average skaters, were by no means ready for competitions. But we did try some fancy couples' footwork that competitors had employed with "spellbinding grace on the ice." Charles lovingly referred to our method as "life-threatening terror on frozen water."

Initially, we skated together with some success, hands intertwined and doing wide full circles with simultaneous strides. As we gained confidence, I suggested we try our own rendition of a double circle-8, and Willie was game to give it a go. The double circle-8 is not like a single circle where you shift into a slight tilt and hold that position until you have completed the rotation. In the double-eight, nearing the completion of your first orbit, you begin shifting your body upright as you prepare to angle yourselves in the opposite direction to form the second circle which completes the lower portion of the "8". It's easy enough in theory, but a couple has to move *as one* to make the transition, rather than like two yoked oxen.

On one attempt, we maneuvered too closely to other skaters and accumulated too much speed to complete the task. As we tried to make the correction, the curved front tips of our skates locked together and down we went. Like a human bowling ball we slid into some nearby "pins", who just happened to be members of Gardiner's city council! Willie and I were mortified. But the two gentlemen simply picked themselves up, laughed, and asked us if we would mind demonstrating our technique, again.

I responded in a sheepish, apologetic tone, "I fear that could be dangerous, gentlemen. Next time we'd probably knock over the mayor."

One of the pair quipped, "That might actually do him some good. Maybe we could get something accomplished at our meetings."

The day had been a beautiful one, in spite of the misadventures. The *Gardiner Home Journal* recorded the day's events as follows:

Fairy Scene—We never witnessed a more beautiful sight than that presented from the principal street in Farmingdale, Saturday afternoon. The prize skating had brought together a great crowd of two to three thousand, most of whom were on skates, and their devious and multiform movements, so graceful and airy, presented a scene unlike anything we had ever before beheld. As we stood upon the railroad track, looking upon the crowds upon the ice, it seemed to us unlike anything in real life, and more like fantasy than like the movements of creatures of flesh and blood.

On arriving home, Susan, Charles, and I were greeted with an amazing sight. There, seated in the parlor, were Father, Grandma Kean, and a young black man conversing and drinking coffee.

"Oh my God!" yelled Charles. "Eli!"

I was stunned, not only by this unexpected visit, but by his general appearance. He was tall, well-dressed, and spoke with fluency and precision. There was but a slight accent in his speech, the only vestige of his years in bondage. Eli stood up immediately when he saw us, embracing first Charles and then me. It had been five long years since we had last seen him, and we all had a great deal to catch up on.

"I'm so sorry to hear about the passing of our dear Sarah. She this poor, black runaway like her own flesh and blood," he reminisced.

Charles and I stood there, still awed to encounter our blood-brother in the flesh.

He continued, "Poor little Bella … Johnny … Lilly. I wish I could have been here with you. So much loss." His voice quavered as he spoke.

"But you're here with us now, Eli, that's all that matters," I countered, trying to dodge those all-too-fresh memories.

"Well," he said, "I figured it was safe to come back. Lincoln's freed all the slaves in the rebelling states and it doesn't get more rebelling than South Carolina, does it?"

"Truly! And I hope you'll be staying with us for a while," remarked Charles.

"Well, I don't want to be a burden, but I was hoping to stay … maybe a week or two. I'm happy to help you, sir, if you need an extra hand around the farm," he responded, looking at Father.

"You can stay as long as ya like," Papa asserted. "But there is a chore involved."

"And what might that be, sir?"

"You'll have to tell us what's been goin' on in Canada over the past five years."

"My pleasure," replied Eli with a smile. "By the way, I *am* here on a mission."

"A mission?" I asked.

"Yes! To learn how to skate, of course."

There was a rumble of laughter.

"So, you think it's funny, do you?" he quipped. "A black man on skates. Imagine that!"

I jumped in, "If you learn to skate as quickly as you learned to read and write, you'll be doing figure-eights around us in no time!"

"Well, I'm thinking a bit more modestly. Perhaps, standing up on the ice for a few seconds?"

"Oh, there's nothin' to it," remarked Susan.

"Well, this is providential," interjected Father. "I'm takin' Annie and Charles up to C. A. William's in Skowhegan next week.[55] They've both out-grown their skates and we need to get 'em some new ones. We'll get you a pair, Eli. They make 'em right in front of ya!"

"Really? Sounds like fun," Eli responded. "Do you think they accept Canadian currency?"

"Hold onto your money, son! This is a gift. We've missed five of your birthdays. It's high time we pony up."

"Well, thank you, sir!"

"You are very welcome," replied Father, happily puffing away on his pipe.

I was thrilled that Eli was now free to come and go as he liked. My first inclination was to ask him to present the story of his riveting escape to our class, but I hesitated, knowing the grief he suffered. Surprisingly, out of the blue, he came up with the idea on his own and seemed delighted to share his experiences.

On Monday, Father, Charles, Eli, and I traveled by sleigh to the schoolhouse and asked Octavia if it would be permissible for Eli to speak to our classmates about his journey to freedom. She was not only intrigued, but delighted to have him recount his courageous personal saga. Charles began in typical form with, "Ya never know what you're gonna catch when ya go fishin.'" After presenting our captivating portion of the story, Eli began his gripping narrative.

The children were fascinated with the details of how the Underground Railroad worked in Maine. Every step of the way to Canada was methodically planned out. And there were backup plans if there was an impediment along the way.

Eli described one such scheme that nearly came to fruition.

"The last leg of the journey to Canada was the most dangerous," he asserted. "We got notice of a troupe of bounty hunters scouring the area near the border. Two runaways had already been caught that night, and I didn't wanna be number three. So, one of the conductors informed me that they might have to hide me in an empty coffin to get me over the border. I'm terrified of being forced into dark, cramped spaces. Terrified!"

> FRED DOUGLASS lectured in this city on Monday evening, on *The War—its Mission*. The eloquent orator seemed in his best tune—the house was densely packed—and his speech exceeded the utmost expectations of his audience. It is a shame to our city that we cannot have a hall that will accommodate half of our citizens, who wish to attend when such speakers address them. Mr. Douglass spoke under the auspices of a few gentlemen, who, we believe, will furnish our citizens with further lectures; and we hear it rumored that Wendell Phillips, Geo. Thompson, and other distinguished speakers will be employed to address Gardiner audiences.

The children all giggled in amusement at the suggestion.

"Oh, you all think that's funny, do ya," quipped Eli, mostly in jest.

"How'd you like to be locked in a cobweb-covered broom closet, overnight, just 'cause you forgot to sweep your master's floor?" Eli proposed. "They've got some deadly spiders in South Carolina. One bite from a black widow and you're a goner. Never got over it."

The chuckles had vanished as the wide-eyed scholars contemplated the terror of such a cruel punishment.

"It's all right, now," he continued, in a light hearted manner. "And thanks be to God, I was never forced into that coffin. The conductors located a sloop at Machias and smuggled me to a private dock east of St. John. Once past the slave hunters, I was free!

A few days after my arrival, because I could read and write like you're all learning to do, I obtained employment, apprenticing as a type-setter for a small abolitionist paper. From there I was able to keep track of the Underground Railroad in Canada and Maine.

But the most exciting thing to happen in my life was meeting a lovely young woman named Rebecca Kirkwood, who like myself, escaped from slavery. And I have every intention of marrying her once this cruel war is over," he remarked with joy.

"Bravo, Eli!" exclaimed Charles. "Hopefully, we'll be invited to the blessed event!"

"Charles, you will be my best man and Annie our maid of honor. Rebecca and I have already discussed it, and we're in total agreement."

"Wonderful!" I exclaimed. "But why wait 'til the war is over? You might be an old man by then," I jested.

There was a pregnant pause at this juncture of his presentation, as his features took on a deeply serious appearance.

"It's just that … before anything else, there is something I must do. I'm heading for Boston to enlist in the Union Army."

"Eli!" I gasped.

"Yes, Annie," he replied emphatically. "Let me explain."

He then began what appeared to be a very well-rehearsed speech.

"Young white boys are dying by the thousands for me. What's their reward for taking a miniball to the chest, and then pouring out their life's-blood on some God-forsaken piece of land, a thousand miles from home? What gain is acquired by those who must bear witness to a fallen comrade, begging for his mother, his wife, or his little girl, in the throes of a mortal wound. How does it profit a family who have proudly sent their sons to stare into the jaws of death, only to have to endure the grief of the empty chair? What is their recompence?"

Again there was a silent pause, begging an answer.

"Honor," replied Eli. "Honor. The cause is noble. It will be remembered in every history book long after our mortal hearts have ceased to beat. Future generations will stop and bend the knee whenever they pass one of those small marble headstones, beneath which lies the dust that once rose up to bring dignity to a people. Honor. I enlist for Sophie. I enlist for my people. I enlist for all those who have sacrificed everything for my freedom."

Miss Hunt and the children applauded. He had spoken with such eloquence, conviction and sound reasoning that our family considered it our sacred duty to support his decision in spite of our trepidation. And yes, we had good reason for worry. Black soldiers fighting for the Union, if caught by the rebels, were to be put to death without trial, and their white commanders would meet a similar fate. Eli was well aware of this Confederate mandate but looked beyond those risks to the lofty prize of freedom.

Three negroes from Bath were enlisted at the Provost Marshal's office in this city, Tuesday.— One of them was a slave in Alabama a few months since and arrived in Bath but a few weeks ago. In reply to a question if he did not fear he would lose his head if taken by the rebels, he said:—"Not till I've taken care of half a dozen of 'em." [Lewiston Journal.

Our blood-brother remained with us until mid-February, when a telegram arrived from Boston concerning the formation of the 54th Massachusetts Infantry Colored Regiment. Recruits would be under the command of a white officer named Colonel Robert Gould Shaw. Not wanting to be left out of such a righteous enterprise, he packed a few necessities and left early the next morning for Camp Meigs on the outskirts of Boston. Our goodbyes were heartfelt with many tears, mixed with a sense of humble pride. He assured us he would write when able.

Charles embraced Eli, and said, "Be careful my brother, don't be a dead hero."

Eli responded, in jest, "Charles, don't you worry, they probably won't accept me."

"Of course they'll accept you! Don't you have two opposing teeth?" quipped Charles, in his usual way of dealing with fear.

"What?" asked Eli, lifting one eyebrow in curiosity.

"Uncle Gene told me that if you don't have one tooth opposite another in your mouth they won't accept you. 'Cause when you're holding the musket in one hand you've got to be able to tear open the powder cartridge with the help of those two teeth. After that, you've gotta grip the miniball while you're pouring the powder into the barrel."

"Well, Charlie, I have a full set. My teeth were about the only part of my body I *didn't* injure while skating."

He left us to join that noble cause on Thursday, February 19. When or if we would ever see him again was the unspoken question that only time would answer.

———

We all hoped that 1863 would see an end to the war. The Union Army was now a mighty fighting force, and Lincoln had finally found a few generals who had "done the arithmetic". But once again, just before my fourteenth birthday, we lost another major battle. This one at Chancellorsville, Virginia, with thousands dead and wounded. How long would northern families continue to support a war with such a heavy cost? Some noisy politicians were calling for a truce to be signed, giving the Confederate States of America their independence to become a sovereign slave nation. Lincoln was determined not to allow that to happen, but again he needed a major victory to curtail the swell of disapproval.

My personal civil war was perpetually being fought just below the surface. Yes, I could laugh, act like a dimwit, joke, and display an attitude of nonchalance. Yet the most benign reminder could send me running off to my room in tears. Our casualties were mounting, too, and there was no easy peace to choose. The prospect of living, at once, in faith's freedom and in doubt's slavery was a daunting paradox. Though Edith and Pastor Rogers were reliable commanders who had done the spiritual math, I would need an unconditional surrender from the foe that dwelt not on a battlefield but in my very soul.

During this time, my sensitivity towards death took a clairvoyant turn. Once, in church, I had glanced over at a healthy, middle-aged woman, a relative of the Littlefields, and suddenly *knew* that her death was imminent. The premonition wasn't one of intuition but that of *knowledge*, like recognizing your own right hand. I tried to dismiss it as one of those random thoughts that pop into one's head for no particular reason, but the effect was too tenacious to dismiss. I told my brother about it and as one might expect, he replied, "Maybe you should buy a crystal ball and start a business." Ironically, it was Charles who later informed me that the lady had died suddenly at home on the very evening of my premonition!

Unusual manifestations punctuated the grief-stricken early years of my life. These events took my darkest hours and inoculated them with an elusive but ever-present pursuit of the eternal. They fortified that thin strand of hope that always seemed to be near the breaking point.

Even those formerly repugnant postmortem photos, frozen moments in the matrix of time, began to speak to me in their silent repose. As I gazed, I could sense each personality, nuance, and voice, everything that made up their uniqueness. Each of them irreplaceable, unrepeatable, singular visitors who had filled my life with love for a brief moment and then vanished. What was "self," that entity which casts off *its mortal coil*? Some would say it was simply a part of physical biology, nothing more; "It dies when the body dies." But, to me, its existence seemed far more mysterious than that.

I could never get beyond the riddle of my own unique existence. Why am I *me* and not *you*? What determined the *self* that I am amidst the billions that have been, are now, and will come to be? I am the only *me*; everyone else is *other*. What sort of magic took place to form *self* from two *others*? If I had a twin who was, atom for atom, identical to me, my uniqueness would remain intact. I would still be the only *me*. This enigma approaches an unfathomable intellectual wall that cannot be breached by reason alone. At this juncture, reason must surrender to something quite different, axiomatic, and akin to faith. This mystery imparted some hope of assurance, through all those deaths, the arid emptiness, and the doubt, that there was more to life than the obvious.

Chapter 26

The Heavy Artillery

"Are the Temperance men all dead in Gardiner?" To judge by the prosperity of the liquor business in this city we would certainly think that such was the case; but the all-absorbing interest in public matters has made many grow cold on the subject of Temperance. We hope to see a revival of its interests, especially among young men, for we fear intemperance is "marching along" with them, to an extent they little dream of—many of them.

—Gardiner Home Journal, Oct. 2, 1862

It was sometime in late June or early July that my brother made an alarming discovery in the little closet beneath the stairwell. It was there we kept pies, preserves, and other foods, so that pets and hungry children wouldn't be tempted. One morning, Charles was frantically trying to locate a jar of Grandma Kean's blackberry jam. He didn't find the preserves but he did happen to notice a panel of wood, far under the stairwell, that he'd never noticed before. It was a simple, wide, loose board propped against the ascending stairwell, which was easily removed, revealing fifteen full bottles of rum! Father usually kept his liquor in the corner hutch where there was, currently, the half bottle that had been there for the past week.

Maybe one of his shipmates had given it to him as a gift. But why would he hide it? Perhaps he was saving it for a family gathering. But, again, why would he want to conceal it? After all, the door was locked to protect anything we chose to place there; there was no need to doubly fortify it. Charles and I decided to keep this whole incident under wraps until we could get more information. Revealing it could cause an unnecessary uproar over something that had a benign explanation, and no one wanted that.

The next day, we checked behind the panel again and there were only fourteen bottles! Then we checked the hutch; there sat the same half-full bottle which we had observed the previous day. We observed Father's behavior and nothing seemed suspicious. Susan, Grandma, and Father came into the parlor around 7 p.m. He lit his pipe, opened a newspaper, and sat there until long after 9 p.m., which was the time that Charles and I usually went to our rooms. Susan often retired earlier than Father, so I decided to keep my door open, attentive to what was transpiring in the parlor. Shortly after ten, I discerned the soft tread of footsteps on the stairwell, which I identified as those of Susan on her way to retire for the night.

The small closet, housing Father's stash, was directly below us, so any sound coming from that area could easily be identified. As we waited, the silence became so acute that even the ticking pendulum seemed deafening. Shortly, there came a muted click that could only be that of a key turning. This was followed by a muffled clanking of bottles, a door shutting, and a lock being reset.

Charles, who had been listening as well, entered my room. "What do we do?" he asked with concern.

"You tell me, you're the genius in the family."

"Well, let's see if he stays in the parlor. Then I'll go down and pretend to use the outhouse."

"Then what? We can't confront him. This whole thing might be a misunderstanding."

"I'll act like it's any other night. If he's drinking, I'll smell it for sure."

Charles finally went down to appraise the situation. On returning, he informed me that Father was nowhere in the house and that he suspected he must have gone out to the barn.

"Let's find him," he said, in a soft, anxious tone.

I nodded in agreement.

We made our way down the stairwell in our nightclothes. We couldn't take a candle with us, so we had to feel our way through the dark house. There was one kerosene lamp still burning low in the parlor, but that was only bright enough to guide us to the doorway of the summer kitchen. Once inside, we maneuvered our way, blindly, around the table and chairs, into the woodshed, past the outhouse, and through a short hallway that led to the weathered, side entry of the barn. Fortunately, the wind was conspiring with us, so a few creaks and groans from that unlatched, heavy pine door would provide acoustic cover. Natural noises were plentiful, but the fewer we added to the collection the better. On entering, we noticed light coming from the other end of the barn. There was an abundance of loose hay, debris from the upper loft, which muffled our footsteps as we crept stealthily along in the flickering shadows. We finally reached some large rain barrels which became a perfect observation post.

Papa was seated on a stool with his back to us. The familiar silhouette of a rum bottle sat on a cutting block to his left, and his gaze was fixed on something he was holding in his hands. He then held it closer to the lantern and began to pour out heavy sobs. It was the postmortem photo of Mother! Charles and I were immobilized by the pitiful scene.

Over and over again, urged on by the bottle, he addressed each ghost aloud, "Sarah, my darling Sarah … Frankie, you were too young, so full of life … Bella, my dear little girl … and you, my little Lilly, sweet little flower … Johnny … " Then he erupted in a torrent of tears!

I looked over at my brother in the flickering light and noticed a big, solitary tear sliding down his face, like a raindrop on a window pane. We were witnessing something so sacred, that had it not been for our concern for Father, our presence would have seemed a shameful intrusion. After a few moments, Charles tapped me on the shoulder and motioned with his hand that we should leave. We made our way back into the house without being observed by anyone except our dog, George, who sensed that something was afoot. He quietly followed us both into my room, positioning himself between us on the floor, and repeatedly nuzzled against Charles and then me. The three of us sat there patiently awaiting Papa's return. Nearly an hour later, he lumbered his way up the stairwell and closed the door to his bedchamber. That night, in some novel way, we had met our father for the very first time.

In the morning, Charles and I tried to come to some agreement as to what could be done about the drinking.

"Perhaps we should talk to Grandma or maybe Susan," I ventured.

"No. That could open a hornets' nest. Susan may already know, but if she doesn't … Someone outside, maybe?"

"Pastor Rogers? He'll know what to do. I'm sure boozing isn't a new problem for any Hallowell minister."

"That's a fact. But he's at a convention in New York, I believe."

"Yup, well that's another one outta the henhouse."

"How about your Irish friend?"

"Sully?"

"Not Sully, silly … his grandmother. She always has the right words at the right time."

"You surprise me, Charlie. Are you finally beginning to see the light?"

"No, I'm hopeless," he shot back, with a grin.

"Oh, there's a glimmer of hope, somewhere underneath that pretentious, agnostic shell," I proclaimed, patting him on the shoulder.

"What were we talking about? My brain's gone to sleep," I sighed.

"Edith Sullivan," responded Charles.

"Of course," I assented, "Let's pay her a visit."

Later that morning, we headed up the road by wagon after finishing our chores. Susan had baked some fragrant apple pies, one of which she gave us to bring to the Sullivans. The pie gave us an excuse to show up on their doorstep, unannounced.

I hadn't seen Sully at school for a couple of days, which concerned me, as he was hardly ever absent. When we arrived, he quietly greeted us at the front door. "Good morning Annie," he whispered, greeting Charles with a friendly nod. "Grammy's been pretty sick … that's why I wasn't at school."

"Oh, I'm sorry to hear that. What's wrong?" I replied, in a secretive hush.

"She's been havin' real bad vertigo. She fell a couple of times durin' the night. That's why I need to be here. And … she's havin' trouble breathin'. I mean, she can't go up stairs without gettin' winded. I'm worried."

"Has she seen a doctor?" asked Charles.

"Yes … and he says it's just old age. Doctors are useless. Now she's tellin' me she's just fine, but she ain't. Just sayin' that to get me back to school. But she's sick as a dog. So pigheaded."

"Yeah. All us Irish are stubborn," piped Charles.

"Ya have no idea! She makes a mule look like a submissive creature!" he replied, with a smirk.

"Well, please tell her we hope she gets better soon. I need to talk to her … actually, both Charles and I …"

Charles, shot me a "shut up" look. I took the hint, and changed the subject mid-sentence, "… wanted. I wanted to give you this pie," I continued. "Fresh outta Susan's bakery this morning."

"Just for me?" Sully looked hopeful.

"No. But you can have a taste if Grammy says so," I admonished.

"Guess I'll have to abide by her wishes … as usual. Thank Susan for us, please.

"Michael! Who's there?" called a familiar voice. "Bring 'em in for heaven's sake!"

"Oh dear," said Sully, in a worried tone, "When she calls me Michael, she's serious. If she attaches "Sullivan" to it, I'm in trouble."

"Look," said Charles, "just tell her we came by for a moment, to drop off the pie."

"All right, but Edith's gonna be mad as hell when I tell her it was you, and I didn't bring you in!"

"Don't use that sweet old lady's name in the same sentence with the h-word," I teased.

"Michael Hazen Sullivan!" bellowed Edith. "Invite 'em in, for da love o' God!"

"Sweet ol' lady, eh?" he replied, with a sarcastic smirk. "I gotta go. Thanks!"

"Comin' Grammy," he hollered back.

Sully shut the door behind him, and we left for home.

———

Three bottles of rum later, Michael Sullivan returned to school. He informed us that Edith "was chompin' at the bit" to see me.

I hadn't visited the poor woman for over a month. There was no excuse for my negligence. Youth, such a selfish, frustrating interval!

On arriving at the Sullivans', Edith greeted us in an invalid chair which she mauvered with skill. In spite of her condition, she had managed to prepare a magnificent boiled dinner, topped off with blueberry pie, which she made from her own preserves. After the feast, we settled down at the kitchen table for some serious games of chess.

At some point, I mentioned that we needed to talk to her about something important. I wasn't quite sure how to approach the conversation so Charles just jumped right into the mire.

"Papa is drinking too much, and we don't know what to do about it," he began. "You seemed like the best person to consult."

"Oh, t'ank ya for yer trust, Charlie. Yes, I've plenty of boozers in me own family. Not an easy t'ing to surmount," she said, calmly. "Please forgive me for askin', but has he been hurtin' any of ya when he's tipsy?"

"No. In fact, I fear he's just hurting himself," I replied. "He only drinks in the evening, after everyone's in bed." We then explained our problem in detail; how we had found the ever diminishing number of bottles, Father's heartbreaking lamentations over his deceased loved ones, and our anxious indecision over how to get help.

"Oh, my," she whispered. "Dat poor, poor soul. Ya know, men like to present d'emselves as steel bastions of strengt'. But d'eir hearts are just like ours, Annie. D'ey can only wit'stand so much. For women, 'tis acceptable for us to display our anguish, even in public. Not so wit' men. D'ey're expected to keep it all tightly locked wit'in, as d'ough d'ey were marble statues."

Charles nodded in agreement.

Edith continued. "D'at's why so many, I believe, turn to d'is form of medication. Booze, d'at is. Takes away da pain for a while, and gives 'em some relief. Easier for 'em to express d'ose sentiments d'at d'ey try so hard to conceal."

"So what should we do?" I asked. "Should we tell Susan?"

"Oh, no," she said, with compassionate conviction. "D'at could end a marriage! Put yerself in her place. If Susan were to know of his lamentin' and callin' out for Sarah, she might assume d'at he didn't love her. And d'at's not true! He's tryin' to wrap his arms 'round da livin' and da dead."

Edith continued, as we sat there in deep reflection, "If Susan finds out on her own, well and good. D'en your papa will have t'explain himself. D'at's da way marriage works. Since he's not bein' abusive and da drinkin's mostly at night, it still can be mended."

"I hope so, Edith," responded Charles. "But if this "medication" makes him feel better, might he not come to depend on it?"

"Yes. He might. D'at's why we need to get out d'heavy artillery … Prayer!"

I smiled, and responded, "Somehow, I thought the conversation would lead there. But, you know, I've been praying and nothing is happening."

"And how do ya know?" she asked. "Prayer isn't a quick fix. It's a conversation wit' d'Almighty, an on-goin' relationship wit' the Divine Doctor. Here's a silly example. S'pose ya wanna learn algebra, but y'only know how to add and subtract. Ya beg Miss Hunt and she promises to teach ya. D'en, she shows ya how to multiply, but ya tell her, 'd'at's not what I wanna learn.' After d'at, ya study division, and again, ya protest. Yer beginnin' to get discouraged, but she begs ya to be patient. Finally, she teaches ya to solve a quadratic, and ya say, 'Well, it's 'bout time, I'm finally learnin' algebra.' And she replies, 'You've been learnin' algebra from da day ya first added two and two toget'er!'"

"Me point is d'at even d'ough ya don't see d'answers to yer prayers, 'mediately, or in da manner yer expectin', be sure d'at when ya pray t'ings are happenin'! Da Divinity is at work as we speak."

Edith asked us to join her in prayer for an end to "da good captain's romance wit' demon alcohol." She proposed a *novena*, a "nine day siege", she called it. We all agreed to pray at a set time, joining our hearts as one.

Charles thought the nine day thing was "typical Catholic malarkey" and Edith, perceptively, picked up on it. "Master Charlie," she posited, "I know exactly what yer t'inkin'. Da nine days come from da Good Book. It's da time from da Lord's ascension into heaven til da day of Pentecost, when da disciples united in prayer awaitin' the descent of d'Holy Ghost. However, da purpose of a set number of days is to denote perseverance, not superstition about numbers. It could be five days or twenty-five. Pick any number ya like."

Charles appeared embarrassed and looked over at me, sheepishly. Fortunately, Edith had done her homework and was able to explain things in a logical and undogmatic way. Charles didn't seem to have any problem going along with her suggestions and told me later that he appreciated her ability to foresee possible misunderstandings.

It was always a joy to be in her presence, but one didn't need special clairvoyance to see that her days on this earth were coming to a close. So, before we left, I made plans to visit with Edith on a regular basis, expounding on how much her counsel and friendship meant to me.

"Annie, dear, I love ya like me very own granddaughter. Ya never need an invitation!" she proclaimed.

I gave her a big hug and we parted ways to do battle with the spirits in the bottle.

We agreed on 7 p.m. as our prayer time. I must admit, kneeling beside my big brother was nothing less than awkward, terribly awkward! Outside of church, I don't think I'd seen him pray on his knees. The eloquence that normally flowed from my lips in private prayer was completely stunted to blabbering when Charles was in the room. It was strange. Maybe I was afraid my prayers would be analyzed by him for content, expression, and diction, as though I was giving an oration. Or it could have been that age-old reflex from all the teasing I got from him when I was young and gullible. But this time, the problem was mine. Charles took his mission seriously, never allowing his humorous side to impact the moment.

Every night, like sentinels, we waited for Papa's return to his bedchamber. The most challenging part for us was staying awake. Sometimes, it was past midnight when he staggered up the stairwell. It was as though we were the parents waiting for our wayward son to come home from a night of carousing. The next day we would check the number of bottles and sure enough, there was always one less.

One afternoon, Grandma Kean informed us that Susan wanted the family together in order to make an important announcement. I was sure that she'd found out about the drinking, or she might even be leaving Father!

Charles laughed at my lack of common sense. "That's ridiculous!" he said. "How many times have you ever heard of someone calling a family together to make a joyous 'Separation Proclamation'? She's not gonna secede from the union."

After dinner we congregated in the sitting room. Susan and Father walked in together, hand in hand, relieving whatever residual worries I may have entertained. Then she smiled lovingly at all of us and exclaimed, "Everyone, I am with child!"

Charles leaned over and whispered with a chuckle, "Addition, not subtraction, sis."

And that was the evening Papa stopped drinking. Charles and I counted the number of bottles that had disappeared since we found the original fifteen. Eleven bottles were in the closet on the day we visited Edith and there were two left. It had been exactly nine days since we began our prayers.

Chapter 27

Private Eli Goodwin

*Softly now! tenderly! Lift him with care,—this is a hero whose pale form ye
   bear.*
*Raise that right arm of his up to his side: look, here, that's where the ball
   struck when he died!*
*Brush back the hair from his pain moistened brow; cold enough,—Still
   enough—white enough now,*
*Lay his cap over it—gently—that's right, Cover his dead eyes away from the
   light.*

*Loosen his sword belt,—there, take it away; No blade is sheathed in the
   scabbard today.*
*Here, throw his flag o'er his poor wounded breast, Wrapped in its folds we
   will lay him to rest.*
*Only this morning, poor fellow ! He stood Smiling in front, gallant noble and
   good,*
*Cheering his comrades, himself at the head, Now they have killed him—we
   bear him here dead!*

*Some heart is longing and hoping for him; Some eyes must weep till their
   light has grown dim;*
*Some hand shall never more meet touch of his; No more shall his love hail
   those lips with a kiss.*
*There lay him down, in his lone hero grave—Throw the earth tenderly over
   the brave.*
*Now leave him sleeping—'tis all we can do—Love's work is o'er for him—
   life's journey through.*

—*Gardiner Home Journal*, July 2, 1863

While I was reading this sad, beautiful poem, I had no idea that the
Battle of Gettysburg was raging on into its second day. During that very
hour, Colonel Joshua Chamberlain and the 20th Maine were putting up

a ferocious fight on a rocky hill called Little Round Top. His men were at the very end of the Union line, and if he was unable to hold that position a huge portion of the Union army would collapse. I later learned that he ordered his men to make a last-ditch bayonet charge down the hill which saved the day for many of the Union forces there.

The most worrisome military news arrived by post, which we received near the end of July. It was from Eli and dated July 17, 1863.

Dear Family,

This is the first moment I have had the time to write a long-awaited and well-deserved letter to you. I apologize for the brevity of my first two. I am writing from the outskirts of Charleston, South Carolina, and I must say, I had forgotten how very hot it gets down here, in contrast to the Maritime climate. There are actually a few other Canadian soldiers here with me. One is from Quebec, who speaks fluent French and English. So far our letters haven't been censored, and I'm hoping this one will arrive intact.

In early June we were transported by train and then by boat to Hilton Head, S.C. From there we marched into Georgia where we were ordered, by the commander, to ransack and burn a small town which was of no military value; the most shameful experience of my life! Col. Shaw was furious. He asked for a transfer into active combat and threatened to report the incident to his father in Boston, who was a personal friend of the president. Not surprisingly, the transfer was granted. Thanks be to God!

We have two notables in our company; Charles and Lewis Douglass, sons of the now-famous Frederick Douglass. I have had the pleasure of conversing with them. They seem like fine fellows. There is a wide range of education among the soldiers as you may surmise. Some cannot even write their own name, and a few, like the Douglass boys and myself, can do so, with ease. I have been chosen by the men in my company to do much of the reading and writing of letters to and from home. It's an endless occupation, but one that I cherish. I can thank our beloved Sarah for that privilege.

At this moment most of the men are taking the opportunity to write home, for on the morrow some of us may meet eternity. The 54th has volunteered to spearhead the attack on the stronghold of Fort Wagner, which lies near the mouth of Charleston Harbor. The ironclads have been hammering the fort day and night with little effect. Shells simply hit the fort, embed themselves into the dirt, and throw off a little sand as they explode. The only way for it to be taken is through direct assault. Please remember me in your prayers.

That said, I am under no illusions. It may be my last day of life on this good earth. So, dear family, I wish to thank you for all you have done for me. You have given me freedom of body, and most of all, freedom of mind!

Through your love I have learned to read and write proficiently, and with that gift I have traveled the oceans, battled dragons, ascended the highest peaks, and journeyed to the outer reaches of the Solar System. I have met Shakespeare and Socrates, and known the wit of Benjamin Franklin. If I die tomorrow, loved ones, don't mourn me, for I have truly lived!

God's Peace,

Eli

After reading that portentous letter, we were anxious to learn the outcome of the battle; however, the victories at Gettysburg and Vicksburg overshadowed everything else. Finally, in early August, our three local papers published terrifying accounts of the assault. Though the fort was not taken, all agreed that the 54th had fought valiantly with terrible losses of life and limb! By the time it was over, two hundred seventy of the six hundred brave soldiers were dead or missing, including Col. Shaw.

The Confederates dug a huge pit near the fort and buried the dead there. An inquiry was sent to Fort Wagner by Union Commander Quincy Granville as to the disposition of Colonel Shaw's remains. The reply, intended as an insult, came back; *"He was buried with his niggers."* Though other Southern commanders wanted to respectfully exhume the Colonel's body and send it back to his loved ones, Shaw's father responded; *"We would not have his body removed from where it lies, surrounded by his brave and devoted soldiers … his remains may not be disturbed."* There was now no doubt that black soldiers were every bit as capable and courageous as their white brethren.

☞ The Bath Times says it is reported that a conscript in Gardiner cut off two of his fingers to secure exemption from military service. He ought to be branded as a coward, or sent to an idiotic institution.

But what became of Eli? Surely, if alive, he would have written to us by now. Father telegraphed the Adjutant General's Office in Washington, D.C., several times, before we got the disheartening news; Eli Goodwin was missing in action and presumed dead. His name appeared on the roster of those who stormed the fort on that fateful evening. I tried to accept his fate, but held onto a tiny glimmer of hope that he might still be alive … somewhere. During other battles there had been soldiers, thought to be dead, who were later found to be alive. Some of them had had the amusement of reading their own obituaries in the papers! But, realistically, we understood that Eli's body was probably buried near Colonel Shaw's on Morris Island.

Loss, for our family, seemed to be lurking in the darkened woods like a grim highwayman. Just when we thought we could find safety around the next bend, we were ambushed! The thieves didn't take everything at once. No, just a portion of our hearts at each assault. But unlike the robber who makes your pockets lighter, the angel of death hands you a weight that pulls you to your knees. If the burden of our grief had monetary value, our family would have been millionaires. For me, suffering could only make sense if there were an eternal, divine entity, who was the remedy to our short, difficult existence. In one of the September issues of the *Gardiner Home Journal*, I read this brief paragraph that summed up my darker thoughts.

Generation after generation have felt as we do now, and their lives were as active as our own. The heavens will be as bright over our graves as they are about our paths. Yet a little while, and all this will have happened. The throbbing heart will be stilled, and we shall be at rest. Our funeral will wend its way, and the prayers will be said, we shall be left in the darkness and silence of the tomb. And it may be but for a short time we shall be spoken of, but the things of life shall creep on and our names shall be forgotten. Days shall continue to move on, and laughter and songs will be heard in the room where we died; and the eyes that mourned for us be dry and animated with joy, and even our children will cease to think of us, and will remember to lisp our names no more.

—*Gardiner Home Journal*, Sept. 1863

The first time I read this passage, I felt the sting of that "sad longing for what once was," and wept like a baby. Then I read it again, and again, and began to realize the *wisdom* of death. What cruel individual would want grief to extend over her family for years and years, unabated? Who would want her children to experience heart-shattering sorrow every time they entered their home or the room of her passing? It is good that laughter and song can still find their way into the soul and joy can, once again, come calling. Isn't it less important that others remember us in the hereafter than we remember one another in the living years? That somber passage actually gave me some hope that I might, one day, experience real joy again.

Against the backdrop of our family's tragic losses, there still remained, for me, one earthly bright spot, my deep aspiration of attending college. During the summer, Papa and I spoke with Miss Hunt at length about my desire. Happily, she agreed to tutor me and design an accelerated curriculum that would allow me to pursue my dream. In mid-September, I began my first high school lessons.

"Annie, so nice to see you again. Your father informs me that you've located a college that you hope to attend in a few years, is that correct?" asked Miss Hunt.

"Yes, Ma'am, with your help. Of course, I'll need to pass the entrance exams, and I hear they're quite challenging."

"Well, most are. What school are you thinking of?"

"Mount Holyoke in Massachusetts is my first choice.[56] I've read some favorable things about it and that tuition is affordable."

"Where in Massachusetts is that?" asked Octavia.

"It's in South Hadley, Ma'am," I replied

"South Hadley, hmm," she whispered to herself. "That's not too far from my uncle's home in Worcester. Probably an hour or two by rail."

Octavia paused for a moment, and then a curious smile illuminated her countenance. "How would you like to visit the school?"

"I would love that!" I exclaimed.

"Do you think your father would allow it?"

"I'm sure we could work it out," I replied. "He wishes only for my happiness. A few years ago he wouldn't have been so willing, but after so much … Well, he wants Charles and I to follow our ambitions."

"You are fortunate, Annie. Many men are blind to the necessity of female education."

"Indeed," I replied. "But who will instruct while you're gone?"

Octavia thought, quietly, for a moment, "Well, Nellie Doyle has been looking for some temporary work. She used to teach at the schoolhouse on Davenport Road. I'm sure she'd be happy to substitute. Nellie is a teacher of integrity, but the children had better behave or else!" Octavia chuckled. "She won't put up with any shenanigans, and she's not afraid to use the switch!"

I chuckled, "I'm thankful you never used that horrid stick on our bottoms."

"Never!" she proclaimed. "It would cause you to dread teachers, despise school, and cripple any desire to learn."

"Everyone says you're the best instructor in Chelsea!" I exclaimed, with exuberance.

"Oh my, Miss Goodwin. Don't believe such nonsense. Miss Doyle is twice the instructor I am! Do you have any idea how often I venture off course on a whim?"

"But that's what makes your classes so interesting! You go deeper into things. You pull things out of the history books and make them come to life.

"Well, thank you dear," she replied, humbly.

I could see that she was a bit overwhelmed by my barrage of compliments. But what other teacher would be willing to accompany a fourteen-year-old farmgirl to visit a prestigious college two states away?

Chapter 28

Off to College

Father did agree to let me go, but not until after the harvest. We left on October 16 and took an early morning train out of Hallowell. I was more than a little excited about our journey and brought my journal with me, determined to record every moment. The rail cars were comfortable with cushioned seats, a dining car, toilet facilities, and sinks with running water! We switched railways in Portland, Portsmouth, and Boston with little difficulty.

At one point, near Boston, four negro soldiers got on the train and sat together in the seats in front of us. Two of them had deep Southern dialects. Thinking of Eli, I asked them which regiment they were from.

"Weez from da fifty-fifth colored regiment, missy," replied the tallest gentleman. "I's Jake and 'dese are my buddies, Paul, Joshua, and Washington, who we call Peanut, cause he's da tiniest man in da unit and don't resemble George Washington in height nor complexion."

We all laughed, and I responded, "I'm Annie, and this is my teacher, Miss Hunt. Pleased to make your acquaintances." We shook hands across the compartment seat.

I continued, "Do you know anyone from the fifty-fourth? I have a good friend, Eli Goodwin, from that regiment. He fought at Fort Wagner but we haven't heard from him since."

The four talked among themselves for a few moments. Joshua, the youngest-looking of the group, replied, "Sorry to say, missy, if you ain't heard from 'im by now, dat ain't a good sign. My cousin, Thomas James, was in da 54th, but he be home now. Lost d'arm at Wagner."

"Oh, I'm so sorry. I've read it was a gruesome battle."

"Well, he say he ne'er so frightened in all his life. He seen his buddy 'splode right front o'him, hit by some shell o'somethin'. But he keep movin' til da miniball laid 'im flat. God be praised, somebody drag 'im back, uttawise he be six feet unda."

"Oh, he's lucky to be alive," I muttered.

"No luck, missy. D'angel brought him back to d'encampment. No one see 'im come in. He swear on his momma's grave d'at d'angel pull 'im up off da ground. Anyway, whoeva' brought 'im back done save his life. He would'a bled to deat' on dat beach."

I sat there quietly, looking at them, not knowing what to say. Then one of the other soldiers said, in local tongue, "I'm sorry we can't help you. This is a terrible war and there are many broken hearts, I'm afraid. But we'll pray for your friend."

"Amen! Amen!" voiced the other three, nodding in agreement.

We continued our conversation with them until we reached our next stop, where we thanked them for their kindness and prayers and bid them a safe journey.

It was nearly nightfall when we reached Worcester Station. I was tired of locomotives and just wanted to fall asleep in a soft warm bed. Robert Hunt, Octivia's uncle, and her Aunt Bessie greeted us at the station. We then proceeded another quarter hour by coach over the cobblestones, until we reached their home on Cambridge Street. Their residence was a spacious, two-story, red brick dwelling that was built in the mid 1780s by a former Revolutionary War colonel, a great-uncle of Bessie. Much to my delight, Octavia's aunt and uncle were walking history books, and we talked late into the night. Somehow I forgot my fatigue.

The next morning we headed by rail to our destination, which took longer than expected. On arriving at the South Hadley station, we found ourselves still some distance from the school and had to employ a coach for the final seven miles. We arrived at the seminary just after 3 p.m. and were greeted by another Annie, a first-year named Annie James,[57] who hailed from Milburn, New Jersey.

She was a pleasant young lady, nearly my height, with sandy blond hair tied up in a bun and a slight but graceful build. On first encounter, Miss James gave the impression of being reserved by nature. However, after the formal introductions, she quickly revealed her vibrant and lively personality. She had volunteered to be our guide for the next few days, and her first duty was to escort us to the dormitory room, where we could unpack our bags and prepare to join the student body and teachers for the evening meal at 6 p.m.

The first thing that I noticed on entering the large dining hall was the organization. There were five girls setting tables, another group of five serving food, and after our meal, more groups of five gathered the dishes, another quintet washed them, and so forth.

Miss Hunt remarked, "I've never seen such efficiency."

"Oh, yes," agreed Miss James. "It teaches the girls to work as a team and gain discipline. Also, our tuition here is very low because we do most of the work ourselves, rather than having everything catered. Otherwise, many of us would never be able to afford the cost."[58]

"So, every chore is done as a team then?" I asked.

Mt. Holyoke Seminary

"Usually, but we switch chores monthly in order to get some variety. There are some duties that aren't much fun, as you can probably guess. While I'm thinking of it, are you both planning to stay through Monday?"

"We did want to experience a typical school day," replied Miss Hunt.

"Excellent! That will give you a far better sense of what life is like here."

Although Mount Holyoke had no affiliation with any particular church, prayer was a large part of the curriculum. The dorm rooms were each provided with two large closets for individual, quiet reflection. This activity occurred twice daily.

All meals were preceded by saying grace, and sometimes there was a short prayer of thanksgiving in conclusion. The students were all expected to attend prayer meetings, Bible studies, or spiritual lectures when they occurred. Exercise of the spirit was accompanied by exercise of the body, and there was a gymnasium providing many of those activities. A one-mile walk was required after breakfast to get the blood flowing and the mind activated.

On Sunday, we attended church services and spent the rest of the day with our guide, touring the grounds and facilities. We were able to meet many of the scholars, as well as a few of the professors. The grounds were beautiful and peaceful and reminded me very much of the rolling fields and hills in and around Chelsea. The weather was cooperating as it was warm and sunny during the day and cool at night, somewhat like late September in Maine.

On Monday, we were roused by a bell at 5 a.m. Miss James met us at the dining hall, and we followed her through the day. In order to keep the school running like a well-oiled machine, scholars were required to learn some seventy different rules by memory that needed to be strictly followed. When the seminary was originally founded, the girls had to memorize all their lessons and recite them, similar to what we did at our own little schoolhouse. Now, however, along with some recitation, new techniques were being employed, similar to those in the men's colleges. These included much written work, research, and the critiquing of various writings. The classes were done in small groups in order that each person could present her individual lesson and collect commentaries from the instructor. Every fifteen minutes a bell rang and each group moved to the next class or activity. The day proceeded like clockwork, and after a full sixteen hours, one was ready to retire.

On Tuesday morning, Annie J., Miss Hunt, and I were on mail duty. During the first few months of every new school year there was a great deal of homesickness, especially for the first-years, many of whom had never been more than a few miles from their own homes. The excitement of possibly getting a letter was palpable. As we walked the long corridors from room to room, Miss J. alerted me to our next postal customer, whose room was on the third floor. The young lady's name was Josephine; her home was in Hartford, less than an hour away by train. Her parents were said to be high-society individuals and were very, very wealthy. I was expecting a snobby, self-indulgent, nose-in-the-air would-be-princess!

Our guide knocked on the door, and someone replied, "Come in." The young woman with beautiful, wavy, waist-length red hair was at her writing desk near the window with her back facing the doorway. "It figures," I said to myself, "she's not even going to turn around to acknowledge us peasants." But she did turn around, and she was every bit as royal as I had imagined her.

Miss James handed me the letter to present to "her highness."

"Miss Josephine," I said, "I have a letter here for you from Hartford."

The "princess" reached over to the side of her desk and grabbed a wooden cane, painfully forced her way to her feet, and limped over to take the post from me.

"Oh, I'm sorry," I said, regretfully.

"N-not a problem. I have to m-move or my ankles … get … get stiff."

Josephine took the letter from me; her hands were shaking. She turned her back to us again and began to sob. I looked over at Annie J and Octavia and silently mouthed, "What's wrong?"

Josephine, who probably heard me, made her way to her bed and sat down. "This is the first l-letter I've received from home," she said tearfully, with a hint of anger. "The first one!"

Miss James suggested that we leave, so she could read in private. But

Josephine insisted that we stay. My preconceptions about this young woman had evaporated in less than two minutes; a lesson in humility taught.

"C-come sit with me, please," she asked, "I'm afraid to read it a-alone."

I pulled two chairs over to her bedside, and Miss Hunt sat next to her on the mattress. With her hands still trembling, Josephine opened the envelope and began to read it in a soft voice. It was a short, formal, and impersonal note expressing the hopes that she was enjoying her stay at the seminary. Her mother had signed it "All the best, Mother and Father." When she was done, she put the note back in the envelope and tore the whole thing to shreds and threw the pieces to the floor. Then she sat there staring silently out the window.

"Do you know why I'm here," she asked, still gazing away. "I'm here b-because I am an embarrassment. I'm a l-leper in their perfect world. Perhaps I should yell "Unclean!" like they did in the Bible."

"Oh, Josephine, I am so sorry!" I whispered, hanging my head from the weight of my previous assumptions.

She turned, looked at me, and smiled lightly. "It's true, you know. I am l-lame and I stutter like a parrot. But, I have learned much about myself in the last two m-months. I don't need their money … or their pr-prestige. I have l-learned to respect myself. This place, this is my real home. These girls are my family."

She continued, "When I was l-little and we had guests, Mother would send me to our neighbor's house, and their servants took c-care of me. My brothers were always getting into t-trouble … but they did not hide them.

"When I came here, I was afraid. But the girls t-treated me kindly. They let me be c-comfortable with who I am. I am a smart person," she blushed. "I can do things that are w-worthwhile, even with these infirmities."

"Well, Josephine," Miss James commented, "if your story doesn't bring Miss Goodwin into our fold, nothing will!"

"I am a good salesman, I think," she responded, with a grin.

The four of us continued to talk for over an hour. Josephine was brilliant in mind and in heart. Her parents must have never taken the time to look beyond the deformed leg or the stuttering to really get to know their remarkable daughter.

Before we departed for the station, I felt that I knew Josephine well enough to tell her anything. So I divulged my erroneous preconceptions.

"When Miss James told me of your parents' wealth, I imagined you to be a beautiful, vain, snobby, self-indulgent princess," I confessed, with a sheepish smirk.

"I'm s-sorry to disappoint you," she fired back, with a broad smile.

"Well, two of those assumptions were true, you know, I teased."

"Oh my! … Do pray tell … .Snobby and vain, p-perhaps?"

"How did you guess?" I replied, with a chuckle. "No! Of course not. You *are* a beautiful princess, and I pray that your family will wake up to the truth."

"Have you already forgotten, so s-soon? You are my family."

The four of us embraced and said our tearful good-byes. I sorely regretted having to leave this beautiful place, where part of my heart now resided. For me, there was no longer any doubt about it, I had made my decision. Now I would have to work diligently to gain the knowledge to pass those challenging entrance exams.

On our way back, I took time to reflect on all that I'd experienced at the seminary. My reminiscing always led me back to poor Josephine. During my all-too-brief encounter with her, I had shared some of my family's tragic losses, Bella's death in particular. I was taken aback by her response. She said she envied my "having had so many beautiful good-byes." I assured her that our grief was nothing to be coveted. She strongly disagreed and responded, "It is your family's enduring love, in life and in death, that is so tragically missing in my home. If I died, there would be no one in my family who would even want my last hug."

Chapter 29

Beyond the Door

———

$\mathcal{T}$he ride back to Hallowell was uneventful and the weather turned rainy and gusty throughout most of the trip. It was a perfect time to catch up on my reading and journaling, which I did for six long hours before falling asleep during the last hour from Portland. Papa met us, and we headed home, where I talked incessantly about the school! I was thrilled to find out that Miss Hunt had obtained a Latin primer as well as a copy of a previously administered entrance exam, so I could familiarize myself with the types of questions I would be asked. After some much-appreciated refreshments, Father brought Octavia home, amidst the blustery weather.

Wednesday was a rainy and dreary October day. I stayed in my room most of the time listening to the rain dripping into a pail through a leak in the roof. Father had promised to fix it before I returned from Massachusetts, but had been too busy taking care of a sick cow. Fortunately, she was well again, but the leak was still in need of medical attention. Returning home after those inspiring days of travel left me high and dry with a sense of melancholy. But this was no time for me to be lazy. First, I wrote a long letter to Josephine, then I read the first chapter of my Latin text, which was about as stimulating as watching water evaporate, and finally, I added another six pages of entries to my journal before the details were lost to the passage of time. At one point, Charles came in to discuss my college experience, which I was more than happy to revisit.

A while later, he came in again, followed by two adorable kittens that had shown up on our doorstep while I was away. I say kittens, but they were both nearly full grown yet full of kitty-ness. One had a soft, copious fur coat that was nearly completely black, save for a dash of white under its chin. The other was equally endowed with thick fur, but the torso was of a light gray hue that blended gradually to black on its face and other extremities.

12	CATALOGUE.

STUDIES OF THE JUNIOR CLASS.

Review of English Grammar, Latin (Exercises and Virgil,) History (Worcester's Elements, Goldsmith's Greece, Rome and England, and Grimshaw's France), Robinson's Algebra, Playfair's Euclid (old edition), and Wood's Botany commenced; also Smellie's Philosophy of Natural History,* and Marsh's Ecclesiastical History.

First year studies at Mt. Holyoke Seminary

"So, Charles, do they have names?" I asked, rolling a marble across the floor for the two ferocious predators to ambush.

"No, not yet. I thought you and I could have the honor of naming them. They're both girls."

"Hmm. That gray and black one is the same color as this dismal sky," I remarked.

"Yeah, but she's not drab. She has blue eyes."

"Oh, they are blue! Let's call her Sky. That fits, don't ya think?"

"Whatever hoists your sails, sis. What about the black one?"

"Well, she looks like she just jumped out of the woodstove. How about Soot? Or Sooty?"

"No. Everyone's got a cat named Sooty. Too common, too mundane, too lackluster, not to mention insipid," he responded, with a snobby, aristocratic flair.

"Ooo, expanding your vocabulary, Charlie! Four new adjectives! Good boy," I teased. "If my addition is correct, that should make six in all."

Charles cocked an eyebrow and responded, "Seven, if you include the word "damn."

"Shame, shame, brother. No cursing," I admonished, with levity.

"But it's the universal adjective! It describes everything perfectly, especially if you're in a prickly state of mind. Feed the damn dog. Plow the damn field. Saddle the damn horse. See how wonderfully it makes a dull sentence come to life?"

I sighed a huge sigh, and moved back to our original discussion, "Anyway, Charles, name the damn cat."

At this point, the crazy felines were knocking the marble all over my bare pine floor. We both sat there, pensively, for a few moments, when Sky and No-Name leaped up onto my bureau as though they had sprouted wings!

"I have it!" shouted my brother, vaulting dramatically onto my bed in the manner of a Shakespearian actor. "Hear ye, hear ye! Henceforth, throughout Christendom, yon mouser shall be called Night!"

"As in knights of the Round Table, O court jester?" I responded, in like dialect.

"No, ye fatuous damsel. *Night* as opposed to *day*!"

"Ah! Such a stimulating, stirring, intoxicating, and sensational name thou hast chosen for yon feline. Touché, Charles!"

"Touché thine self, O dimwitted numpty." He continued.

For a few minutes, my brother and I bantered back and forth in like form, playing with the kittens and trying to teach them their new names. However, Father needed help with remounting a wagon wheel, so Charles abandoned me to the unpredictable whims of Night and Sky. Those little demons loved to pounce on my stockinged feet and attack my unbraided hair or anything else that moved. In truth, they assaulted things that didn't move, as well: a bedpost; a chair leg; or in one instance, a door knob. Finally, tired from their antics, they yawned and stretched out on the floor.

The three of us were ready for a siesta, so I placed the little fur-balls on the bed and stretched out beside them. Soon I felt my eyes growing heavy. That annoying "drip-drip-drip" soon became my dearest friend, leading me gently into the land of Morpheus. Though I frequently had vivid dreams, the following one was exceptional.

I was standing near an ornate fountain, similar to the ones you might see in a city park, but far more elegant. There were flocks of brilliant bluebirds circling around, drinking from the basin and landing close to me. I picked one up and it wasn't the least bit startled. Behind me, in the autumn twilight, was the grand form of Mount Holyoke Seminary, radiant in the setting sunlight that cast an orange-red glow over everything.

I then heard my name being summoned. It was a familiar voice and seemed to come out of nowhere. I suddenly found myself floating effortlessly along a brick pathway that proceeded through a luminous green forest into a lush glade. The walkway led to a white-painted door, similar to the one in my bedchamber. There was nothing exceptional about the portal besides the anomaly that it was in a stationary position without visible support. I was beckoned on by the mysterious entrance. Or was it an exit?

I felt a sense of peace, even elation! There was no hesitancy on my part, as only goodness and beauty dwelt here. I pulled on the knob, and the door opened up onto a foggy landscape, from which a figure emerged out of the haze. As the apparition approached, it spoke to me, "Good day, Annie." It was Eli! I couldn't reply. I just stood there in disbelief. Now I understood that he had given his life at Fort Wagner and was coming from beyond the "door" to console me.

Suddenly, from behind the specter, emerged Charles. I was confused. Charles wasn't dead, so why was he with Eli? My brother came forward and reprimanded me, "Aren't you going to say hello to Eli?"

As I came to, I was standing upright, face-to-face with Charles, at my own bedchamber door. I had been sleep-walking again!

"Are you OK?" asked Charles. "You look like you've seen a ghost."

"Yes … " I exhaled. "Yes, I *have* seen a ghost."

Then Charles moved aside to reveal the living, breathing Eli, standing in full uniform!

I screamed, "Eli! It's really you … you're not a ghost! Oh, Eli!" I hugged him as tears ran in torrents down my cheeks. With my arms around him, I noticed the empty sleeve of his jacket. My mouth dropped. "Oh, Eli … you lost your arm!"

"Yes, Annie, but it could've been worse."

It took me a few moments to regain my composure, at least enough to distinguish reality from illusion. Finally, I was able to collect my thoughts enough to engage in conversation.

"What happened? I mean, … we thought you were dead. Father wrote to the Adjutant General's office in Washington; they said you were missing and presumed dead."

"Well, let me tell you everything. Everything I can remember, that is."

"Please, sit down," I said, sliding my desk chair over.

"Thank you. As I already mentioned to your brother, I lost my memory for a while and there are still some pieces of the puzzle that I can't seem to fit together, even now."

He began, "We marched out, at the double-quick, during twilight with the other members of the 54th. At first, we were well organized, and the cannon-shot from the fort simply flew behind us, harmlessly. We, wrongfully, believed the dirt walls could be easily breached and the battle would be over within an hour or so."

"We made it to within a few hundred yards of the fort and then, excuse my Latin, all hell broke loose! The flares went up from the fort and the muskets went off, a hundred at a time. The artillery was loaded with canister shot. Do you know what that is?"

I shook my head, and he proceeded to explain.

"They put thirty or forty round iron balls, about the size of large marbles, into a metal container packed with sawdust and fire it out of a cannon. The projectiles fan out, taking off arms, legs, and heads. Believe me, I've seen sights that I wish I could forget. My buddy, Tom, and I quickly dug a small pit in the sand with our hands and the butts of our rifles, laid low, and prayed out loud for God's mercy should we fall. For about a half an hour we waited. It seemed like an eternity, really. Finally the trumpet blurted out "Attack!" and we jumped up like madmen across the sand dunes. A few of our men did breach the parapet of the fortification. That's all I can remember.

THE EMPTY SLEEVE.

By the moon's pale light to this gazing throng,
Let me tell one tale, let me sing one song ;
'Tis a tale devoid of an aim or plan,
'Tis a simple song of a one armed man ;
Till this very hour I could ne'er believe,
What a tell-tale thing is an Empty Sleeve—
What a weird queer thing is an Empty Sleeve.

It tells in a silent tone to all,
Of a country's needs and a country's call,
Of a kiss and a tear for child and wife,
And a hurried march for a nation's life;
What a tell-tale thing is an Empty Sleeve—
What a weird, queer thing is an Empty Sleeve.

"From this point on, until I acquired my memory, the story comes from those who took care of me. I was told that a shell exploded between my friend and me, taking off Tom's right arm and shattering my left. I also lost most of my hearing in my left ear from the impact of the explosion. I ended up in the infirmary with an amputated arm. The worst part about my hospital stay was that I was unable to speak or even remember my name for nearly two months. Because I needed special attention, the army sent me north to a sanitarium in New York, where none of the aids or nurses knew me. Of course, the army being the army, they gave the doctors at the institution the wrong name. I became "Ian Goodrich" until my memory came back.

One morning, for no understandable reason, the memory trigger was pulled! The doctors say that at least ninety percent of mine has been restored. And bits and pieces are still trickling in over time.

Anyway, because of this army blunder, I was listed as missing and presumed dead and the sanitarium staff had no other records to go by. Finally, I was able to straighten out everything with the docs as well as the 54th, and I was given an honorable discharge.

"If I may, I'd like to add just one, rather queer footnote to my story. After I was released, I contacted my friend Thomas James, who lost his arm in that same explosion. I wanted to find out how he had fared, having heard that he was recovering at his home. Tom had a friend write back to me, as he can't read or write, and told me an angel had brought both of us back to the infirmary that night."

"This is amazing, Eli! I just realized where I had heard the name Thomas James before." I then walked over to my night stand and picked up my journal. "Look here," I said, thumbing through some twenty pages.

"There, look!"

It read: "Tonight we met some fine soldiers from the 55th Massachusetts colored regiment. I asked them if they knew Eli Goodwin of the 54th, who fought at Fort Wagner. They all said that they didn't know him, but one of them told us of his cousin, Thomas James, who lost an arm at Fort Wagner, and about an angel that saved his life."

"Well, that is one whopper of a coincidence, if I must say. Interesting how mysterious is the hand of the Divine!" declared Eli.

"Yes," I agreed. "It reminds me of a conversation I once had with Mrs. Sullivan. I think the statistics would put this event into the "more than coincidental" category."

"Here we go again," quipped Charles. "Annie's always looking for things that will tilt the completely natural into the supernatural realm."

"Charles," exclaimed Eli, "I thought you were a believer … are you not?"

"Well, yes! I believe in God. I'm just not so sure He spends His day doin' card tricks to keep my sister amused."

"Charles!"

"Now, Annie, don't go firin' up your engine! I'm just kiddin' around. What I mean is, well … for me, everything is miraculous. Existence is miraculous, life is miraculous … I don't have to weigh the odds every time somethin' happens. Annie's the real doubtin' Thomas, not me."

"Not everyone is the same, Charlie," replied Eli. "The most convincing arguments for God's existence often come from former skeptics. But … you're right. Blessed are they who have not seen, yet believe. Your unquestioning faith is enviable!"

"Well, I don't know about that. It's just the way I am," remarked Charles.

"But haven't our losses been enough to shake anyone's faith?" I implored.

"Yes, but I've come to accept that we all have an appointed time. Though I will say, Annie's experiences, along with the aroma of Easter lilies at our sister's death, have helped reinforce my trust even further. Those peculiarities do have their merit, especially when one considers their uncanny timing."

I smiled with some degree of unearned pride.

Eli stayed with us through Thanksgiving, which Lincoln had proclaimed a federal holiday. The country, on both sides of the Mason-Dixon Line, was turning towards God in hopes that these terrible times would cease. In response to our Nation's immense suffering, the words "In God We Trust" were to be stamped on the 2-cent pieces to be issued in 1864. Yes, 1863 had been a year of unprecedented carnage. However, the Battle at Gettysburg and the conquest of Vicksburg had turned the tide of the war and threatened to give a final death blow to slavery. It was a time to give thanks and take refuge in hope.

As November progressed into early December, we were joyfully preparing for the birth of little "Andrew" or "Andrea". Dr. Davis assured us that Susan was in excellent health and would likely come through the delivery without complications. By Christmas, Susan was a happy, healthy mother of a little boy, and Father seemed like a young man again. Baby Andrew sported a thin wisp of light brown hair and a red round face to complement. "He's the spittin' image of Charlie!" exclaimed Papa, though I'm not sure my brother was flattered. Finally, there was heartfelt laughter echoing through the house for the first time in years, while all the old favorite Christmas hymns were being hammered out by Grandma and me on our recently tuned piano. A cautious optimism settled over us.

The snowfall during the first two weeks of the new year was exceptional. Once again, winter outings took over our pastimes. The magnificent hills of Hallowell, with newly fallen snow, provided ample opportunities for some energetic coasting![59] All sledders were admonished to give pedestrians the right-of-way, and to proceed with great caution around vehicles, or else the constable could put an abrupt end to the merrymaking. Two Gardiner youths had already been tragically killed in a collision with an oncoming train.

The most popular slope for coasting was the Manchester Road in Hallowell. It's a half-mile climb to the summit, which descends at an exhilarating pace over ice-packed surfaces, rail tracks, across the main street, and to the river landing. If one is moving fast enough, according to some of my brother's less-than-mentally-sound friends, it might be possible to slide up onto the Hallowell bridge. Charles, myself, Emma, and Deborah Rollins[60] (one of Charlie's lady-friends, to whom he took a fancy), with little forethought, decided to give it a go! Emma, who was the most sane of the ensemble, hesitated, but finally gave in reluctantly.

Just walking up that slippery hill was a chore that took the better part of ten minutes. On arriving, and after the initial side-by-side, running push off, we were within speaking distance of one another, but after a few seconds, yelling distance only. Soon we were out of earshot of one another, as Charles took the lead and Deborah charged into second place. At breakneck speed, Charles and Deborah flew over the railroad tracks, crossed Water Street, and climbed the slight incline near the toll house, gliding safely under the bridge gate to a standstill. The toll keeper was less than impressed and charged each of them a dime for attempting to cross the bridge *"in a dangerous fashion on a vehicle."* Charles humbly promised never to attempt such a reckless feat again. That said, it would have been impossible to wipe the satisfaction off his face.

Emma and I were almost a hundred yards behind them, and I was slightly ahead of her. When I hit the tracks, I was airborne for a moment and narrowly escaped colliding with a parked wagon. In terror, I dug the tips of my boots into the ice-caked cobblestones to brake myself, stopping near the loading docks. But Emma flew under that same wagon, screaming her lungs out! She barely missed a pedestrian and bounced down an embankment onto the icy surface of the Kennebec. Woefully, she landed on a marked section of thin ice, a few feet from a small, but dangerous, patch of open water! She lay there on her sled, paralyzed.

"Emma, don't move!" I yelled.

"I'm not stupid!" she wailed, almost in tears.

"I'm gonna help you. Take hold of the sled rope, and when I get close enough, throw it across the ice. Then I'll pull you in really slow. Don't sit up, whatever you do."

"Annie! I'm scared! I can hear the ice crackling under me! I can't swim!"

By that point, Charles and Deborah had arrived on the scene, along with a few concerned bystanders.

"Don't panic. I'm coming," I replied calmly, my heart pounding like a hammer. "Remember," I continued, "you're on wood, and wood floats. You're not gonna sink."

In truth, I feared that the weight of the metal runners might pull the sled under the ice, and any sudden movement could mean disaster. I carefully shimmied flat against the ice to within a couple yards of my friend. The frozen surface was making its usual moans and groans, responding to the changing tide, which only added to her distress. Finally, she began rolling the rope over the ice like a whip. I pulled myself a little closer and finally grabbed the tip. Then, shimmying backwards, I began to pull gently on the cord. Inch by nerve-racking inch I pulled Emma over the frozen surface and finally grabbed her hand, pulling her to safety. Several observers applauded! I appreciated the recognition but that was enough heroics for one day.

When we arrived home, I was exhausted and retired to my room. A letter had just arrived from Annie James, so I took the time to read it and then enjoyed a short nap. After helping Susan with supper, I settled down to do the homework that Miss Hunt had assigned. The parlor, with its now closed-off fireplace, was well lit and cozy; the Franklin stove ushered away the winter chill. The refreshing ambience was enhanced even more as Grandma Kean softly played some old favorites on the piano in the other room. Brother Charles was in the summer kitchen, cleaning his fowling piece and attentively assembling all his paraphernalia, with the hopes of hunting wild turkeys in the morning. His friend Deborah and her brother had agreed to go with him, so he was preparing more enthusiastically than usual for the adventure. I'm not sure, however, if it was the pursuit of wild turkeys or some other game which was driving his enthusiasm. Finally, Susan entered, holding our precious little Andrew.

Just before 10 p.m., as I was preparing to turn in for the night, I glanced over at Susan and her sleeping child. I wasn't thinking about anything in particular when I was overcome with a wave of sheer terror. I knew at that very moment, baby Andrew was going to die! It was not a thought, but a *fait accompli* like what I had experienced with the lady at church. Tears began to flow as I gathered my things and fled in panic up the stairwell. My heart was pounding as though it might explode and I felt like I was going to vomit. I laid on my bed until the dizziness and nausea finally subsided. Then the questions came.

Why was this happening to me? What good is knowing something before it happens if you can't stop it? Wasn't death difficult enough to endure once it happened, or must I mourn baby Andrew while he's still alive?

Chapter 30

Scruples

I desperately needed to speak with Charles!

My brother was still working with his hunting supplies but had moved the jumble of gear to his room. I knew it was bad timing but I couldn't bear this burden alone.

"Charles, I'm sorry to bother you, but I need your help," I declared as I knocked and entered the room.

"In a few minutes," he responded, absentmindedly.

"Charles! You've gotta listen! It's important. Please stop working for a moment. I've had a premonition."

"Who is it this time? Me?" he replied, with a condescending smirk.

"No, Charles, not you. Baby Andrew." I teared up. "He is going to die, Charles."

"You've gotta get your mind off this hogwash or you're gonna end up *'away with the fairies'* as Edith would say. You're just worried about Andrew and thinking the worst."

"And what about the woman at our church? Did I have a reason to be worrying about her? I didn't even know her!"

"Lucky guess," he murmured, under his breath.

"No!" I bellowed, slamming my hand down on the bureau. "It wasn't a guess! It was an unalterable fact!" Then, in a calmer, pleading tone, I added, "Please, Charles?"

"Well," he responded, in a more serious tone, "we can't change predestination, can we?"

"No. And if I'm wrong, and I pray that I am, I promise I will never give in to such foolishness again. But, humor me for the time being, please."

"So, what can I do?"

"Well, if this is truly second sight, wouldn't there be a reason? Would such knowledge be given without purpose? I think not. We can't change it but we can prepare Papa and Susan."

"Well, just tell 'em straight, outright."

"No. They'll be more concerned about my sanity than anything else.

Hopefully, I still have enough time to think this through."

"Then, laying his hand gently on my shoulder, he admonished, "Go get some rest. I'll give it some thought and we can discuss it tomorrow at length. If it's really what you think it is, you'll be given the time you need."

I sighed, "Good night, Charlie. Thank you for listening."

"Of course. Night, sis."

I didn't sleep well for fear of something happening to little Andrew. I went in to check on him twice and he was resting quietly. What frightened me most was when the baby's room was too quiet. A noisy child is a living child. The dread of finding him dead in his crib was always on my mind. So, nap time and nighttime kept me vigilant and nearly sleepless.

———

Along with this new worry, our family had other burdens converging. Father and Susan were troubled by our household finances. Things began a downward slide in late 1861, when the bank foreclosed on the acreage Papa had purchased two years earlier. The fall harvest had brought in a third less than expected, and Papa was seriously contemplating another merchant voyage. Our faithful nag, Riddle, died during the summer, and Father had drained our resources to acquire two young replacements. Then, there were some outstanding payments for machinery, bought on time, which were coming due. We had nothing in reserve should an emergency arise.

Mother had always been the money manager in the family, but Susan, as she readily admitted, didn't have the accounting skills to keep the Goodwin "ship" afloat. So, Father knew he'd have to be resourceful. "Every choice in life is a gamble," he would often say. Well, he took a sizable gamble when he put Charles and me to work in an attempt to manage his accounts. He unwittingly believed us to be mathematical wizards. However, this task was not going to be like solving one of Miss Hunt's algebra problems or estimating the height of a tree, problems which one could either get right or wrong. These were complex issues that involved not only money, time, and speculation, but also Father's integrity, pride, and self-respect!

The thought of the task we were undertaking gave me a headache. Papa was now a 48-year-old sea captain and farmer, with a family and a new little mouth to feed. The idea of him going to sea, the stress of these financial woes, and the dreaded thought of losing little Andrew gave my mind no respite. I was too young to be so old. Thank God, I had Charles as my ally, whose free and easy attitude and sense of humor provided a cushion for my precarious sanity.

The most urgent question, for me, was how to express my dark

Notice of Foreclosure.

NOTICE is hereby given that John A. Goodwin, by deed of mortgage dated June 30th, A. D., 1859, conveyed to me a lot of land containing about one hundred acres, lying in Chelsea, Kennebec Co., on the second mile from Kennebec river, and bounded on the north by the town line between Chelsea and Augusta; on the east b the Cony road (so called); on the south by the Worromontogus road (so called); on the west by a stone wall at the end of the first mile. The condition in said mortgage has been broken, by reason whereof I claim a foreclosure of the same.   JOHN DAVIS.

Chelsea, Nov. 18, 1861.   3w48

premonition to a happy mother and jubilant father. For the next few nights, my brother and I continued to discuss the conundrum. However, all the solutions that came to mind were likely to be more harmful than not.

Early one morning, Charles appeared in the shadows of my bedchamber. "Annie, I figured out how you can tell Papa and Susan without scaring the living hell out of them."

"Charles," I responded drowsily, "don't curse."

"Did you hear what I said? I've figured it out."

"You've figured out what?"

"I know how you can tell 'em," he insisted, shaking me lightly.

"Charles … I was almost asleep … I'm exhausted. This better be important."

"It's ingenious!"

"Very humble … so tell me."

"You need an indirect approach."

"Indirect? Go on."

"Well, you're right, you can't tell 'em straight out or they'll think you're crazy as a loon."

"I know that, so what's so important that …"

"No, wait," he interrupted, "let me finish. You've got to tell them that this whatever-it-was came to you in a dream."

"Charles, it wasn't a dream … and I'd be lying if I said it was. That would be sinful."

"Oh, God help me! Think of it as a parable," he grumbled.

"What? What are you talking about?" I grunted, in sleepy annoyance.

"Jesus used parables, didn't he? Some of those tales might have been based on real events, but most weren't. They were metaphors … used to teach. It wasn't about the story, it was about the message."

"But Jesus wouldn't tell someone that he had a dream, if he hadn't, would he? What happened to me isn't a parable."

"Yes, Annie, but you're not Jesus, and if you really want to get the message to Father and Susan, you've got to do it in a subtle way. Stop bein' so scrupulous!"

Then Charles left me to my whirlwind of conflicting thoughts, interspersed with those compulsive visits to the infant's crib.

I didn't get up until ten-thirty the next morning. Why no one woke me I'll never know. I came down to the sitting room in my night clothes looking like I'd been dodging canister shot at Bull Run. And there sat Charles, wide awake, grinning at me.

"Susan, come in here quick!" he teased, "Look what George dragged in from under the barn!"

I plopped myself down on the sofa, glaring at Charles as though I wanted to strangle him. My less-than-charming appearance was entirely his fault!

"Annie, are you all right?"

I continued with my sour stare, not moving a muscle.

"Are you angry with me for something?"

I didn't even blink.

"Is it what we talked about last night?"

"You're getting warmer," I replied, barely moving my lips.

"Look," he whispered, " I just thought … well … I don't want to say this too loudly, but I think my idea is a good one, and I wanna discuss it some more. I wouldn't wake you at four …"

"Three!" I growled, scowling.

"OK, three … I wouldn't wake you at three if I didn't think it important. Don't be cross. I truly want to help you. You've got enough weight on your shoulders, sis," he asserted, compassionately.

At that moment, I recognized Charlie's good intentions and tears welled up in my eyes.

"Charles," I whispered, "can we go somewhere to speak in private? I'm afraid we'll be overheard."

"Of course. Let's go to your room."

"How about yours? Mine is right next to Susan's."

"Very well."

When we arrived in my brother's chamber we closed the door behind us for privacy. I didn't enter that room very often, and seeing Johnny's little bed sitting there, as though waiting for its owner to return, hit me hard. I put my head down between my hands and felt as though my heart was going to break. I then sighed heavily, raised my eyes to the heavens, and forced myself to fight off the tears.

"Oh, Charles. Thank you for your thoughtful ideas. But I can't lie. After you left the room," I continued, "my mind raced back and forth. After an hour or so, I finally dozed off, only to have an appalling nightmare. Little Andrew was lying there, dead in his cradle! The horror on Papa and Susan's faces! I awoke in a panic. I've made my decision, Charles. I can't lie … I just can't. I have to tell them the truth … even if they think I'm crazy."

"Annie, you don't have to lie," said Charles, looking at me with astonishment.

"What do you mean? If I tell them it was a dream …"

Charles interrupted, emphatically, "No! Listen … It was a dream!"

"What?"

"Didn't you just tell me that you dreamt of Andy's death?"

Suddenly, the implication of Charle's question came clear! "Yes … yes, I did!" I exclaimed, in triumph.

My mouth dropped in amazement. "Oh, Charles! I feel so much better!" I threw my arms around my brother and gave him a big kiss on the cheek. "Thank you! Thank you! You are a genius!"

"Finally, some recognition," he remarked.

I couldn't fault his ego this time. He had solved my scrupulous dilemma. Father and Susan could easily dismiss a dream. Although the content might be dismissed, it would also be remembered. Then, God forbid, when the child died, they would see the dream in a more providential light. It might, in some way, soften the terrible blow that I believed to be imminent.

I was very thankful that I wouldn't have to experience the guilt of lying. So, with Charles as my audience, I began to rehearse my presentation. I needed to skillfully present the dream in such a way so as to preserve my initial experience, and convey its impact. Too many words would obscure the message and too few would trivialize it. The desired effect would be to create a reasonable amount of concern and vigilance on their part, without terrorizing them."

At the supper table I, matter-of-factly, said that I had experienced a disturbing dream the previous night.

"What kind of a dream, dear? "asked Susan.

"Well, it was a very real and frightening dream about Andy. And, well … I feel uncomfortable sharing it with you, but I must. It will give me no peace to keep it within," I lamented.

"Go ahead, dear," prompted Susan.

"Very well," I replied, with resignation. "In the dream I was walking up the stairwell. It was late at night and I had a lantern in hand. When I got to the head of the stairs, I decided to kiss the baby goodnight. As I approached his crib and lifted up the blanket I noticed he wasn't breathing. I tried to wake him by touching his forehead; it was cold and lifeless! I screamed! Both you and Father got up out of bed and tried to revive him, but he was gone! I then awoke, in my own bed, my heart was pounding. It frightened me so very much. Do you think it means anything?" I pleaded.

"Well, Annie," said Father, "we've had our share of sadness in this house, haven't we? My guess is that ya deeply love your little brother and don't want anything to happen to him. That would make sense, don't ya think?"

"Yes, I hope that's all it means." I replied.

"Annie," Susan said, "we're not superstitious, and yet we know that God sometimes speaks through dreams. But I would have to agree with John. All this is probably a reflection of your love for Andy, combined with some of your own sorrowful experiences."

"I am sorry if I've upset either of you," I voiced with compassion. "I just couldn't keep it inside any longer. Charles knows about it too and he thought I should tell you."

Charles nodded in agreement.

"Annie," replied Father, "why would we be upset? If I had a dream like that I'd have to tell someone about it, as well."

"Don't worry," said Susan in a comforting tone, "I know how much you love that little boy … and he loves you too! Have you noticed how excited he gets whenever you enter the room?"

"Yes," I replied, almost in tears, "I just don't want anything to happen to him."

Susan smiled lovingly at me and placed her hand on mine.

"His cradle is right by my bed. But if it will make you feel better, dear, your father and I will be even more watchful. Would that help?" Susan inquired.

"Oh, yes. That *would* help … That dream was frightening."

She and Father smiled at me in a tender fashion. I knew that they had listened with concern and would do everything they could.

The next few days were, in some ways, worse than those that had followed the deaths of the other members of my family. Even though those hard times had been painful, they had been shared sufferings. Now, I was alone in my anticipation of something dreadful that I had no power to prevent. Charles was very supportive, but I would wager that deep down, even he believed that my foreboding was of natural origin.

I quarantined myself in my room during the evening hours in order to hear what was happening in the baby's chamber. But what if that fateful event were many days, weeks, or even months away? Could I survive the anxiety and sleepless nights? I was making myself sick in the process. After such ruminations, my thoughts would slide into the maelstrom of shame. What was I thinking? This was my infant brother's life. Did I really want his life shortened so I could get a little more sleep? How selfish! Charles admonished me to be at peace, and to stop reacting to every little noise that came from the baby's room as though it was a gunshot.

———

One night in late January, amidst the throes of restless sleep, I once again experienced that rare series of concentric circles of light pulsating in my mind's eye. As before, the circles of light began to wrap themselves around a central figure. Gradually, the figure became clear. It was Bella, smiling and holding little Andrew. Suddenly, I was overcome with a rush of emotion as reality devoured my joyful bliss. I awoke gasping, and sat straight up in my bed, covered in a cold sweat. I knew it was over.

From the next room, I heard sobbing and muffled, anxious voices. That moment gave way to the loud, frenzied wailing of the mother of a dead child! Charles, awakened by the mournful lamentations, preceded me into the dim morning light of my parents' room. Father looked at me in a pitiful manner, "You were right Annie. You were right." Charles and I joined their grief, each of us taking turns holding and caressing the lifeless infant. So many hopes and dreams had been swept away in the twinkling of an eye. It was January 31, 1864.

———

Baby Andrew had died of what would come to be known as "sudden infant cradle death." Finding your baby dead is truly the most terrifying experience that a mother or father can undergo. Susan was struck with the deepest melancholy and was confined to her bed for nearly a week. Father, in his tenderness, poured his heart and soul out to try to comfort her.

It took a few weeks before any of us were able to move into our normal routine. For Susan, the road was a long and painful one.

One morning, she confided, "I want to thank you Annie, for sharing your dream. It was a forerunner, and it helped prepare us for the trial."

"I'm so sorry to have added to your suffering," I confessed.

"No, dear. It made us vigilant and cushioned us, somewhat, for his passing. It gave us hope that his short life was not without purpose."

Chapter 31

The Nor

Little Andy's death coupled with the outstanding debts were causing more stress on Father than ever before. The ensuing cold, dark month of February seemed an unending purgation of body, mind, and spirit. Charles and I tried our best to help sort out the financial woes, but it was far beyond our abilities. By mid-month we were short on essentials like flour, sugar, and firewood. Times were hard and we began rationing what resources we had on hand. Our neighbor, Mr. Blanchard, kindly deposited two cord of seasoned wood in front of our barn one evening to keep us warm during the frigid nights. Father had tears in his eyes for his thoughtfulness, but he also considered such generosity a source of humiliation. Being the provider was *his* job.

One evening in late February, Papa made an important decision. He declared, "Even if I can't protect my family from illness and death, I can protect them from financial ruin. Susan and I have discussed this, and I've decided to go overseas once again. Three months at the helm is worth far more than three years behind the plow!" He then lit his pipe which heralded the end of any discussion on the matter.

Father decided to contract with a continental European shipping enterprise because of the possibility of an American (Union) ship being raided by the Confederates. There were some rumors that Great Britain might come to the aid of the Southern cause, and if they did then any U.S. merchant ship would be fair game.

"Father, do you honestly think that might happen?" I asked. "Queen Victoria is utterly opposed to slavery. She'd never support the Confederacy … ever!"

"That may be true, dear, but Parliament may see it differently. Some of their politicians are in the pockets of the cotton mill owners in Manchester, Birmingham, and other British mill towns. Many of those factories have shut down due to our blockade."

"Yes, but Her Majesty has signed a neutrality document, and she praised the Emancipation Proclamation. That should mean something."

"On the surface it does. But Her Majesty's more of a symbol of the vast British Empire than an omnipotent ruler. She reigns there but she doesn't hold the reins there, if ya get my drift," he replied, chuckling at his own wit. "There are plenty of wealthy Brits supportin' the Southern cause. I know this for a fact, as it's been reported by some trustworthy old salts who've just returned from the Isles."

"I believe what you say, Papa. But these rebel-supporters don't represent the British government."

"Oh, but many of them do! Parliament members as well. It's all under wraps … like shipworms eating away at the hull of a vessel."

I exhaled a heavy sigh and rejoined, "But Papa … "

"I don't want to argue with ya, Annie," he continued. "My mind's made up. I will neither contract with a Union vessel nor a British one, period … at least not while this infernal war is on. I don't wanna hear any more about it … understand?"

"Yes, Papa. I'm just worried about you. You're familiar with British and American shipping lines … but … "

"Look, dear, I'm an experienced mariner. I've sailed with crew members of every tongue on this good earth. I always do my homework, and I can sniff out a good crew and a reliable company from a hundred nautical miles with blinders on! I don't care if they're French, Indian, Dutch, or African … I know the sea, and I know the men of the sea. Now, no more talk."

"All right, Papa," I replied. "I trust *you*. I just don't trust that huge ocean out there."

"Annie, the sea and I are friends from way back. Now, no more frettin'," he replied. Then he winked at me, lit his pipe and that was that.

———

Papa contacted Bath, Boston, and New York City by telegram, requesting a foreign line with a position of captain or perhaps first mate, which also paid a fair wage. Early in March he heard back from New York that a Norwegian company was looking for a captain and crew. The vessel, named the *Nor,* was scheduled to sail out of New York in late April. After a few more exchanged telegrams, Father was given the position of captain. Though he didn't speak Norwegian, the first mate (who was also an American) spoke it fluently, as his family had immigrated from Norway when he was a youngster.

A Yankee Heroine. The schooner J. P. Ellicott, of Bucksport, Me., was recently captured by the pirate Retribution, and a prize crew put on board. The wife of the mate was left on board the brig, and she managed to get the prize master and his mate intoxicated, when she called on the prize crew, who were mostly negroes, to help her, and she actually handcuffed the officers, and took the vessel into St. Thomas, thus recapturing her from the pirates. Government should give her a commission.

Fortunately, Father convinced his creditors to give him until August 31 to pay off his loans, which gave him great relief. The rest of us appreciated the extension too, but we dreaded his going to sea in April. That month, in particular, is known to be fraught with bad weather, rapidly changing conditions and seasonable unpredictability, especially in the North Atlantic. The destinations of the voyage were St. John's, Newfoundland; Hull, England; Bergen, Norway; back to New York City, and finally, home. He would embark from New York on Wednesday, April 27, assuring us, "May is at hand, and the weather turns a favorable eye towards voyagers."

You might imagine that Charles and I were brimming with knowledge about sailing, having lived our entire lives with a mariner. Truth be told, we knew little about the commandeering of a ship. We had sailed to Boston with him, heard many of his adventures, but we were quite ignorant of some of the basics of that risky business. Oddly, Papa never encouraged my brother to pursue a life at sea, as his own father had done. He skillfully dodged the topic when it was raised by shipmates. After all our losses, he wanted his only living son to discover his own path.

John Andrew Goodwin was now approaching fifty, and both beard and hair were nearly white. Until this juncture, I had never perceived him as old. But now, his eyes looked weary, and though he smiled and joked as before, there was an air of a battle-worn commander. He had surrendered so many dreams and hopes in the wake of tragedy. Yet, there he sat, ready to go off again into the perilous unknown as though he were twenty. And he was doing it all for us.

If Charles and I had learned anything in our young lives, it was that we never knew which good-bye might be our last. So, with this three-month journey looming, we begged Father to tell us about the responsibilities of commandeering a trans-Atlantic voyage.

One evening before he embarked, Susan, Charles, myself, Emma, and Sully gathered in the parlor to hear tell of the challenging and often profitable world of an international merchant mariner.

Father lit our old whale-oil lamps and sat on the sofa beside Susan.

"Well, everyone, your wish is my command. What would ya like to know?"

"Everything," replied Charles. "Tell us about how you first became a sea captain."

"And whatever made ya wanna do somethin' so adventurous?" added Sully.

"Foolhardy, ya mean, Mr. Sullivan?" he chuckled. "All right. Well, ya know that my pappy was a mariner, and when I was a youngin, he would take me with him to sea. Never crossed the Atlantic with him, but we did sail from Bath to New York City. Once we went to Newfoundland. Now that, along with my prenuptial whalin' adventure, should have turned any sane person away from the seafarin' business."

"What happened?" I asked.

"Well, I was 'bout nine … or maybe ten at the time. We left Bath … 'twas this time of year. It was a cold and gusty mornin' when we set sail on the *Abigail*. We hadn't been out very long when we spied a mighty pod of humpback. Oh, there must have been at least forty of 'em. Amazin' sight. They were spoutin' from their blowholes and the ship and crew were saturated with brine!

"And that was the pleasant part of the journey," he joked.

"After that, the weather turned on us, and all that evenin' Pappy struggled to keep the vessel from bein' swamped. She was a 450-tonner, much like the *Macedonia* that I captained back in '54. By mornin' things had calmed down some, but 'twas bitter cold and everything was frozen solid. The deck had become a mirror of ice, like a skatin' park. The whole crew made a game of slidin' from the port to starboard while the ship moved along in the large swells. Of course, all their duties were bein' attended to durin' their merriment. In fact, they often sang when they were workin', which created a rhythm that kept the men synchronized like the gears of a human clock."

Then Father broke into an ancient shanty, to the tune of "Yankee Doodle", that I hadn't heard since my early childhood.

We are but poor mariners, We've newly come from sea
We spend our days in jeopardy, While others live at ease …
We care not for those martial men, Who do our states disdain
But we care for those merchant men, Who do our states sustain
Shall we go dance round and round, Come and pledge to me-O
Shall we go dance round and round, Come pledge me on this ground!

We all jumped in, clapping our hands in time, for another two or three rounds. Once we had finished our revelry, Father relit his ceramic pipe and continued with his saga.

"Where was I? … Oh yes, the weather cleared a bit durin' the afternoon but a huge fog bank crept in around dusk and swallowed us up. We had to proceed cautiously with the strikin' of the mainsail. At about 8 p.m., old *Abigail* jerked suddenly from the impact of somethin' slammin' into her hull. We'd been hammered by a large chunk of ice. Immediately, water began leaking in, and the men made a furious dash to plug the hole. After about an hour, the leak was secured but the hold had over a foot o' water in it, and she was riding low. Fortunately we had two large bilge pumps on the vessel, and after a long night of tedious work the crew brought the bark to its proper cruise level."

"What would have happened if you hadn't had those pumps?" asked Emma.

"Well, in that case we might've had to start a bucket brigade and possibly ballast would have to be discarded. Eventually, we would've gotten her up to proper water-line. We were carryin' a combination of ballast and cargo. Some cargo is light, like cotton, furniture, and goods packed in hay. Others are heavy, like coal, iron and metal tools, and so forth. The trick is to get the ship at optimum cruisin' level. If she rides too low, the pace will be sluggish. If she rides too high, she's more likely to be unstable in heavy seas.

Anyway, gettin' back to that hole in the hull. We made it to port and back on time and the damage was quickly repaired. But I was quite terrified by the experience."

"How'd ya get over your fear?" asked Sully.

"Simple! Pappy continued to drag me with him, screamin' and a-kickin', as it were. I guess that's the most effective manner of gettin' over any old trepidation, isn't it, Annie? Have her tell you 'bout her love of ferry boats sometime."

I smiled, sheepishly, nodding in agreement.

"But ya know," he continued, looking directly at Charles and me, "I really began to enjoy goin' to sea. Your momma used to say that my 'stair-well didn't go all the way to the second floor.'"

Susan smiled, winked, and nodded in agreement.

"Papa," asked Charles, "what about sailor superstitions?"

"All right, but you know I don't believe any of these … 'cept when I'm out to sea, of course," he grinned.

"Well, one of the most common ones is that you should never set sail on a Friday. Relates to Christ's crucifixion on Good Friday, but I don't subscribe to such nonsense. My whalin' voyage started on a Monday. It's all about the weather and the time of year … that's it.

Another old wives' tale was that there should never be any redheads aboard. Superstitious crews thought they'd cause trouble. Good God, if that be true, no man, woman, or child would have ever set sail from the Emerald Isle! Ain't that right, Mr. Sullivan?"

"To tell ya the truth, sir, I don't have to look for trouble. It seems to seek me out," quipped Sully.

"That's called prejudice, son. Pure and simple," replied Father. "But trouble on board a vessel depends more on rum consumption than hair color."

"The only other myth that comes to mind is that you should never rename a ship after it's been previously named. All started when several whalin' ships, after first bein' merchant vessels, were renamed and then lost at sea. Horse shenanigans! Merchant vessels are at sea for a few days, weeks, or at the very longest, a couple o' months. We stay closer to port, are often within sight of one another, and follow shippin' lanes. Whalin' vessels are usually ridin' the waves and chasin' their prey for *years*. They're out on deep water and often in uncharted seas; therefore, more at risk of bein' lost to the elements. Just common sense, not some deadly curse."

As always, Papa's knowledge and enthusiasm kept our interest well into the wee hours of the morning. It was nearly three before he called the curfew and we all reluctantly retired to our rooms.

On April 24, we escorted Father to the Hallowell rail station. Susan, who had recently suffered so much, was visibly shaken as the train pulled away on its first leg to New York City. Her lips were silent and her face was pale but resigned. It was all in God's hands.

Part III

Theresa Gervais

Chapter 32

Winter Fever

—

Charles took command of the farm after Father left. Well trained from years of experience, he understood all the latest machinery of the trade. If anything broke down he could fix it. His intuition concerning planting, the last frost of the winter, and weather patterns were nothing less than stellar. The sky, the wind direction, the thermometer, and the barometer were his scientific consultants. Since Charles was well aware of our less-than-advantageous financial situation, he attempted to do most of the work himself. Our two newly acquired horses, Abe and Ulysses, were sufficient for our needs, and keeping them in good health was a high priority. Susan appointed me as "equine custodian extraordinaire," or, in plain English, the horses' slave.

I had always loved horses. And who doesn't? Yet, I never realized how important it was, as caretaker, to develop a spiritual kinship with each, attending to their unique personalities and they to mine. Abe was gentle but easily startled, and once he became agitated it was difficult to calm him down. The trick that always worked for me was to change the tone of my voice. I would use quiet, low, gentle tones and give him a carrot or some other treat while speaking to him. Ulysses was playful and seemed to love human company. However, he could be very stubborn, especially if he didn't want to play the game that I wanted him to play such as "hitch me up to the wagon." It took me a couple of weeks to figure out his secret. After much experimentation, I found he could be coaxed into just about anything with a few hugs and a big kiss on the snout! Eventually, a whistle brought them both to my command, and we soon shared a mysterious inter-species form of language.

EARS OF THE HORSE. It is a good sign for a horse to carry one ear forward and the other backward when on a journey, because this stretching of the ears in contrary directions shows that he is attentive to every thing that is taking place around him; and while he is going he cannot be much fatigued, or likely soon to become so. Few horses sleep without pointing their ears as above, that they may receive notice of approach of objects in every direction. "When horses or mules," says Dr. Arnott, "march in company at night, those in front direct their ears forward, those in the rear direct them back, those in the centre turn them laterally or across; the whole troop seeming thus to be actuated by one feeling, which watches the general safety!"

Susan focused her time and energy on the art of cooking. It became an obsession, and a healthy one, at that. It took her mind off Father and gave the rest of us an experience akin to dining out every night.

One incident that confirms her culinary prowess was associated with Charles's abhorrence of lobster. He hated the taste and the looks of the arthropod, (which one can easily understand). The first time he tried this Maine specialty, he vomited! A few years later, Father encouraged him to give it another try. He vomited.

However, lobster was the only seafood that Charles truly disliked. He loved clams, scallops, oysters, and all manner of fish that could be obtained from salt or freshwater. With this in mind, Susan concocted a slight variation of her delicious haddock chowder, full of herbs, vegetables, and a few mild spices. But this time she added a secret ingredient ... lobster! She had mastered the fine art of culinary deception and Charles gobbled it down, went back for seconds, and would have had thirds if available. We never told him what he'd eaten or he would have been suspicious of every meal that his stepmother cooked and probably would have starved himself to death!

Grandma Kean was busy journaling her life's story. The poor woman could barely write due to her painful rheumatism but never complained nor let the discomfort get in her way. She could talk for hours, reminiscing about her children and their antics. Her family Bible, which is now in my possession, is filled with dozens of four-leaf clovers[61] that her children, nephews, nieces, and grandchildren picked for her; even a few of my own remain mingled amidst the generations.

One sorrowful chapter from her writings was that of her son James. He had been born late in Isabel's childbearing years, when she was forty-three. There were complications during delivery, and he was deemed mentally retarded. He had been labeled the "village idiot" by some ignorant, mean-spirited folk because of his slow intellect and inability to hold down a job. What piecemeal work he could manage was usually back-breaking and accompanied by skimpy pay.

I remember my uncle, who was barely seven years my senior, as a sweet, unassuming, generous soul who loved to play games with us. One time, our kitten Sheba went missing for several days. When the eleven-year-old boy heard about it, he was so distraught by my tears that he vowed to find her for me.

That very night there was a torrential downpour with gale-force winds that lasted well into the wee hours of the morning. In the midst of the tempest, there came a knock at our front door. It was Uncle Jimmy! He was drenched to the bone and holding our frightened little Sheba against his chest. That poor boy had kept his promise and had wandered about in the storm searching for the kitten. He found her shivering and crying beneath the Blanchard's barn. What an extraordinarily kind soul he was!

Jim was institutionalized several times throughout the years, so, regretfully, I never got to know him very well. His increasing isolation eventually led to his addiction to alcohol, which, undoubtedly, contributed to his death from heart and liver ailments. I pray he has found peace in eternity. "Blessed are the pure in heart, for they shall see God."

One afternoon in early May, my brother came back from the barn coughing uncontrollably. I asked him if he was all right, and he responded that it was just a reaction to the dust in the barn. But over the next few days, the coughing became more frequent, especially at night. Even Charles, who never worried about anything, started to show some minimal concern. One Saturday morning, the two of us, having gone into Hallowell for some shopping, ran into Dr. Davis, and Charles mentioned his persistent cough. The doctor invited the two of us to his residence on Second Street, where he had a small medical office located in the rear of the building.

"So, Charles, how long have you had this cough?" asked the doctor.

"Oh, for a couple of weeks. I think it began about the time Father left in late April, and it was just a light cough then. But it's starting to get worse. I mean, it wakes me up at night," he answered.

I interjected, "Yes … it often wakes the rest of the household, as well."

"Have you had any fever, Charles?" he asked.

"Well, I'm not really sure. I sometimes wake up in a sweat, even when the room is chilly."

The doctor put his hand on Charles's forehead. "Yes, I believe you are running a slight temperature. Let me listen to your lungs." He proceeded to his cabinet and took out a device called a stethoscope. I had seen an older version of this instrument, but this newer variety fit both ears, blocking out most of the background noise. Charles took off his shirt and the doctor placed the business end of the scope at various points on his back and chest. At each placement he would ask my brother to take a deep breath, and then he'd reposition the apparatus and ask him to breathe deeply again.

"Well," said Davis, "it seems like you've a case of winter fever, which in our profession we call pneumonia. Your lungs have some fluid in them, which I can hear clearly in the scope."

"Fluid?" asked Charles, with a hint of concern.

"Yes, but I wouldn't worry, son. Seems mild at the moment, and we wanna keep it that way. Would either of you like to take a listen?"

We both answered in the affirmative, and the doctor handed me the stethoscope. "Ladies first," he asserted, with a wink in Charles's direction.

I placed the ear-tips in both ears as the doctor placed the bell of the device on my brother's chest. At first, I wasn't quite sure what I was listening for. Then Charles took a deep breath and there was an unmistakable gurgling sound. "I think I hear it! It sounds like water trickling in a brook."

"Yup, that's it, Annie," he confirmed.

"Can I take a listen, too," asked Charles. "After all, it is *my* infirmity!"

"Here you go, Charles," said the doctor, handing my brother the scope.

"Oh my!" he interjected as he breathed deeply several times, "Sounds like a river!"

"Well, Charles," replied Davis, "I've heard oceans through that instrument. You will need to get plenty of rest, drink liquids, and I'll give you some cough medicine that might help you sleep at night. Pneumonia can be a very stubborn illness. And if you're anything like your father, you'll probably loathe having to stay quiet for a week or two. That's right. A week or two."

Charles nodded, grimacing in forced compliance.

"I don't wanna alarm you, Charles," interjected the doctor, sensing some reluctance from his patient, "but on occasion I've seen this ailment flare up and take lives. So, follow my instructions and I'll check in on you in a week or so."

"I will, Sir," he replied, with a bit more conviction.

The kind physician then opened his large medicine cabinet and took out the elixir and handed it to Charles. "Take two spoonfuls just before bed. But if you wake up coughing in the night, you can have one more spoonful, but that's it. Hopefully, it will help."

We thanked him warmly for his kindness and offered to pay him, but he declined. So, I deviously placed two quarter-dollars behind the inkwell on his desk. I knew he deserved more, but we had very little cash to spare.

Charles had been enjoying his "man of the house" status and predictably resisted the doctor's orders. However, on the days that he complied, he slept more soundly, and the coughing was less frequent and less severe. Nevertheless, the malady was frustratingly tenacious. Finally, Grandma, Susan and I had to implement direct action, demanding that he stop work and begin a period of complete rest. During this period of convalescence, the Blanchards, at Susan's request, again came to our rescue by having two of their farm hands work our fields for a few hours each day. We promised to repay them for their services once Father returned.

By the second week in May, a growing concern pervaded our thoughts; there was, as yet, no news from Father. We had received a telegram from New York on the 27th, and the *Nor* should have made a brief stop in Newfoundland, over a week ago. Although there was no telegraph from the island at that time, there would have been several stateside vessels returning to port with the mail.

If Charles and Papa weren't enough to occupy our thoughts, Michael Sullivan stopped in to notify us of more distressing news.

"Michael, how are you? Please come in." welcomed Susan.

"Thank you, ma'am. Is Annie here?" he asked, somewhat out of breath.

"Right here, Sully," I answered, coming to the front door from the kitchen. "What brings you to this tomb of gloom on such a lovely day?"

"Well, unfortunately, 'tomb of gloom' may be close to the mark."

"Oh no! Sully, is it Edith?" I asked, fearing the worst.

"Yes, she's still amongst the livin' … well, for the moment. She had a seizure two nights ago and now she won't eat. The woman's just bones to begin with," he added, his voice quavering with emotion. "The doctor says that old folks often just shut down before they pass. She may have a few days … or weeks, at best."

"Oh, my goodness," said Susan. "How are you faring with all this? You're all alone with her, aren't you?"

"Great-uncle Pat and Aunt Shannon are comin' up from Boston. But, for now, yes, I'm the only one with her. The Allens, little Theresa's folks, have been checkin' in on us every day, which has been a blessin'."

"If there's anything we can do, Michael, please don't hesitate to ask," Susan insisted.

"Well, to be honest, that's why I'm here, ma'am. Gram wants to see Annie."

"Oh, by all means!," exclaimed Susan. "Annie, go feed the livestock and you can head out, straight away."

"Thank you," responded Sully, with a smile. "Gram will be delighted to see her."

"I'll finish up my work. Shouldn't take more than fifteen minutes. You're welcome to come in and wait if you'd like."

"Sorry, but I get jittery leavin' her alone. Can Charlie bring ya?"

"Of course! Tell her I'll be there around eleven."

"Wonderful!" he replied. He turned to exit the front door, but suddenly stopped in his tracks. "Annie," he whispered.

"What is it?"

Edging back into the hallway, he continued in a hush, "I need to tell you something."

"Please," I responded, with intrigue.

"Well, after helping Grammy up off the floor, I got her to lie down on the sofa. Truly, I was frightened outta my wits. So, I asked her if there was anything I could do to help her, and she replied, 'Fetch Annie. I must see her before I leave this world.'"

A wave of emotion overwhelmed me. "Oh, Sully. I love her so much. I'm about to burst into a puddle of tears."

"Oh, don't do that!" he teased, attempting to lighten the moment. "She'll be mad as hell at me if you show up in a bucket!"

I forced a smile. "Well, I'll be along soon."

Chapter 33

Fáilte roimh an gclann

My head was spinning with worry as I mechanically attended to my chores. First it was Edith, then thoughts of Father would force their entry and hold me captive, only to be followed by the remembrance of Charles's frightening coughing fit during the night. One worry just replaced the next like guards taking shifts over my prison cell.

How does one stop the onslaught of ruminations? Staying busy used to help, but with so many bullets to deflect all at once, the situation seemed impossible. When people told me to "Just give it to God," I wanted to slap them! My frequent monologues with the Almighty were not leading to any semblance of inner peace. Just the opposite! The more I prayed, the more distressed I became. Prayer was an albatross, not a blessing. I wasn't able to separate my invocations from the myriad of possible outcomes that were forever surfacing in my brain. I asked myself, "What is prayer, anyway?"

After finishing my chores, I gathered my journal, overcoat, and some bread, freshly baked by Susan, to bring to the Sullivans. Charles was employing the horses, so I had no choice but to walk the mile and a half, up and over the hill, to the Sullivans' home. Perhaps some passerby would give me a lift. But it was of no consequence either way. The day was exceptionally beautiful and I needed a diversion.

While ascending Winter Hill[62] that swells beneath the Hallowell Road eastward, I was struck by the greenery that was resurrecting through the dead, brown fields. Nearing the summit, I was able to make out the hills of Hallowell, rising as a scenic background to our farm, and the rolling fields that extended for nearly a mile to the west. A sparkling rivulet that ran along the roadside sang its frolicking canticle, as a light breeze caressed my face, carrying the bewitching aromas of springtime. These fragrances stir the soul, connect the heart to life, and place therein a longing for something ancient, mysterious, and intangibly real. The journey was too enchanting to hasten through it. I might miss a chirping robin, a flower opening, or an emerging butterfly; or forfeit the never-ending changes in the shapes of those puffy clouds drifting from the west and vanishing over the eastern hills. A gentle warmth from both outside and within began to embrace me with the assurance that life was not simply an accident. During that miraculous transfiguration I was able to surrender to the moment with heartfelt gratitude. I journaled, "Perhaps, this experience *was* prayer."

It was a forty-minute walk to Edith's but I barely noticed the time. On arriving I gazed through the window and there she was, sitting up in her invalid chair and reading something. I gently knocked on the door and opened it slightly, "Edith, it's me, Annie."

"Oh, come in, dear," she replied with a shaky, but determined, voice.

I placed my things on the table, went into the parlor, and gave her a big hug.

"Oh, 'tis wonderful to see ya, Annie. Sit down and stay awhile, won't ya."

"Oh, I will. But don't let me tire you out. Michael tells me you haven't been well."

"Yes, I'm afraid d'is old mule's 'bout to be put out to pasture," she replied.

I smiled, "I'm sure you've a great many things left to do before that time comes."

"Oh, don't humor me, love. 'Tis my time and I'm not da least bit frightened. In fact, I am greatly lookin' forward to da blessed moment."

My eyes met hers, briefly, and then I put my head down. I didn't know how to react to her blatant acceptance of mortality.

"Dyin' is not an end, ya know. It's only a shift from da partial to da complete."

"I wish I understood it the way you do, Edith. I'd give anything to have your confidence. I just need to accept that I will never be certain until the door of this life closes behind me."

She then touched my hand gently, looked upward, closed her eyes, and declared, "Annie, before da guns of war are silenced, you will glimpse da hidden side of d'at embroidery."

I started to speak, but she touched my lips with her index finger, calling for my unfailing trust. Then slowly and with great emphasis, she spoke, "*I promise.*"

I didn't dare ask her anything else on the subject, but sat there quietly reflecting on her words.

Soon, we continued with normal conversation, but her assurance was etched deeply into my memory. We spoke of my worry for Father and Charles, and although Edith showed no particular clairvoyance in their regard, she did give me these maxims of spiritual wisdom to contemplate, which I entered into my journal:

Remember, earthly life and eternal life are two sides of the same coin. Death is but a flip of the coin.

Our mission in life should never be judged by human standards. Even the brief, seemingly insignificant life of an infant can have more value, in the sight of God, than that of a celebrated statesman who lives for a hundred years.

Lastly, let Love draw you where it will. Let go the reins and allow Love to be your master and guide. Accept everything with trust. Everything! That's what I have done, that's what you must do, and that's what every soul must do in order to be united to the heart of Divinity. These requirements are the ways of heaven; there are no hidden doors.

Then Edith told me that she wanted to give me something. She asked me to open the large wooden chest next to the hearth and take out the item that was wrapped in newspaper and sitting on the top of her quilts.

"Be careful, Annie," she said. "It's quite fragile."

I carried it over to the sofa, still wrapped in paper, and gently set it on the cushion beside me.

"Go ahead," she asserted, "take it out of da wrappin's."

As the mystery object revealed its identity, I sat there in amazement! It was a beautiful portrait of a very young Edith Sullivan, hand-painted on a ceramic plaque, framed in silver, and lying upon a wooden holder.

"Oh, Edith, it's beautiful!" I whispered, in awe.

"It's me. 'Twas a wedding gift to me husband from our family. He cherished it!"

"Oh … I'm sure he did!"

"Yes, I had to sit d'ere for two hours while d'artist did 'er work. I was twenty at da time."

"I love it! But who am I to receive such a treasure?"

"Who are you? Who are *you*? Yer da spittin' image of me when I was young. A seeker of Trut'! Someone willin' to wrestle with da demons of doubt. Someone who won't stop 'til she reaches her goal, … and," she said, in a slightly sorrowful tone, "someone acquainted wit' much grief. D'is gift is meant for you. Just say a prayer for me now and d'en."

"Of course. Oh, thank you, Edith. I will treasure it forever."

After a few more minutes, I could see that she was becoming fatigued, and I decided it was time to leave. Michael had just come in from outside and asked me if I would like a ride home. Had it not been for the beautiful, delicate masterpiece that was now in my possession I might have declined, but I wanted it to arrive safely. It was so difficult to force myself to leave this holy sanctuary. I knew I would might never see her again, and I wanted my last good-bye to be a joyful one. So, I plucked up my courage and, with a big smile, gave her a gentle but prolonged hug, thanking her for everything.

As I was walking tentatively towards the doorway, she called me with that Irish brogue, "Annie … We'll meet again in heaven. I'll greet ya at da gate!"

Holding back my tears, I replied, "I'll be looking forward to it, Edith!"

When I arrived home, I took the treasure to my room and placed it on its wooden stand. I then planted it on the mantle above my small stove for safe keeping. It was in a pleasant location and could be seen from my bed or from my desk.

Charles came up when he heard me arrive and became suddenly enraptured by Mrs. Sullivan's portrait!

"And who might this beautiful young lady be?" he questioned.

"Her name is Edith, and she's far too old and wise for you, Charles," I jested.

"I'll be hanged! That's Mrs. Sullivan, isn't it? What a beautiful woman she was!"

"Is!" I exclaimed, emphatically. "Her soul is far more beautiful than her physical being ever was. You men are all alike," I said, snidely.

"Well, excuse me, Sister Ann of Mount Holyoke, when did you enter the convent? I've seen the way you look at boys, and I'm not altogether sure it's their souls that interest you."

"Oh, Charles, I'm not the least bit interested in any of the boys around here, especially the ones that frequent your company."

"Lyin's a sin, Annie. I've seen the way you conveniently appear whenever Ryan comes over. You can't resist bein' within eyeshot of him."

"That is not true! I just happen to be in the house at the time."

"Is that why you're dressed to the nines when he comes 'round? Lord, you look like you're going to a wedding. Ryan even asked me if you always dress that way."

"He did not!"

"Oh, yes he did."

"He's never said more than two words to me. He's never even noticed me!"

"How can he *not* notice you? You saunter by him at least ten times, whenever he visits." Charles continued in a high-pitched, mocking voice,"Oh, excuse me, Ryan. Oh, I'm sorry to disturb you, Ryan. Oh, I forgot my Latin book. Would you like some tea, Ryan … or perhaps, me?"

"That's it!" I yelled and took my pillow and hit Charles over the head as hard as I could. And it was on! We ran into every room on the second floor grabbing pillows in a duel to the death. We ran downstairs, nearly trampling Grandma. I followed him into the summer kitchen swinging my weapon with exacting skill! He barely grazed my shoulder with a swing of his pillow, but I quickly ducked, battered him in the stomach, and slid under the table. George then got into the act and grabbed Charles's pillow and "killed" it! Feathers were flying everywhere. I quickly crawled my way into the dark shed near the outhouse and hid behind a kindling box.

Slowly, Charles crept in, "Annie … where are you?" He looked around, but the shadows were deep. I could hear his footsteps as he moved here and there in the shed. Finally, he opened the door to the outhouse and edged in slowly."

Slam! Bang! I shut the door and bolted it with a board that locked the "beast" in his rightful place. Grandma and Susan ran into the shed to see what the commotion was all about.

"Annie," yelled Susan, "What in God's name is going on here?"

"Critter in the shitter!" I yelled at the top of my lungs. Then I broke into hysterical laughter and slid to the floor with my back against the outhouse door. Charles was pounding, trying desperately to escape his stinky prison. After his unconditional surrender, I set him free, and we both spent the next half hour cleaning up the battlefield.

As we were restoring our feathery war zone, Charles began to cough uncontrollably. The fit became so violent that the dog took cover in the shed. My brother began to vomit up a quantity of phlegm and blood. He paused for a few seconds, and then continued to puke up the horrible mixture. This happened four of five times before he collapsed, exhausted on a nearby chair.

Susan felt his forehead. "He's burning with fever!"

"It's all my fault! I shouldn't have started this whole commotion. I'm so sorry!" I confessed, nearly in tears.

He looked at me and gave me a half-smile, "Aw, no, Annie. That was fun. Serves me right, I knew I shouldn't be gettin' riled up."

Susan interjected, "Charles, is this the first time you've coughed up blood?"

"No, I had some last week when I was pitching hay in the barn. I got overheated, that's all."

"We've got to get Dr. Davis. This sounds more serious than winter fever," she continued.

Grandma Kean joined us and asked what had happened. We then explained the situation. She just stood there, shaking her head in concern. "It sounds like consumption," she said with a grimace. "Charles, you look like you're losing weight, too. One of the signs."

"You are as skinny as a rail. You don't need to lose any more weight, Charles, or you'll be a skeleton," I added, trying to add a touch of humor.

"Well, you all know how to cheer a fella up, don't ya? This is "new-monia" or whatever Davis called it. It is *not* consumption. It's just when I get overheated."

"Well, you may be right, but we're calling on Davis in the morning, anyway!" affirmed Susan.

We helped Charles up and he went to his room to lie down.

Grandma called Susan and me aside and whispered, "I've seen this before. Belle *died* of it at eighteen. This is how it starts, then there's more weight loss. The body is "consumed", which is why it's named such. I fear for him."

"But, Grandma," I pleaded, "people can get better. I've read articles."

"Well, yes. A few can fight it off. Most who survive continue to have problems the rest of their days. Truthfully, most don't survive, dear. It's the great killer of young people. The plague of our time."

"But we mustn't show him that we've already surrendered him to the grave! He needs a proper diagnosis before we begin jumping to conclusions. We need to feed him hope, not despair," I asserted.

"Oh, Annie dear, what you're sayin' is true, but this illness is torture for patient and caretaker alike. It goes on and on for weeks, months, and sometimes years. Charles has the "graveyard cough" as we used to call it. He sounds like Belle did at the onset. But I pray, as we all do, that he will survive. I'm just an old, pessimistic woman."

Doctor Davis examined Charles the next evening. His diagnosis was inconclusive. The symptoms for pneumonia were prevalent, but consumption, also called tuberculosis, could not be eliminated as a possibility. He told us that Charles needed complete rest. He was to sit out of doors on clement days and get as much sun as possible. The cough medicine was strengthened to help him sleep—but, personally, I think a shot of whiskey would have done him more good. The doctor planned to call again in three or four days.

S ave your Doctor's Bills.—When Dr. Wistar's Balsam of Wild Cherry will *cure* coughs, colds, bleeding at the lungs, and arrest the fell destroyer Consumption, it does more than most Physicians can do. A single trial will satisfy the incredulous.

The elixir did help some. It made him drowsy so that he barely could recall his nightly coughing fits. Hacking up blood was becoming more frequent, but my brother continued to dismiss it as winter fever. That was just wishful thinking, and I knew it. From Miss Hunt's copy of *The Boston Medical and Surgical Journal,*[63] I had learned that coughing, with Pneumonia, was rarely accompanied by blood, except in the last mortal stages of the disease. Its victims were not prone to rapid weight loss as in my brother's case.

Dr. Davis visited Charles again, eight days later. The longer interval between visits was providential, as it allowed him to clearly observe the downward spiral of my brother's health. At this juncture, unable to find another reasonable medical alternative for my brother's condition, the doctor pronounced the dreaded diagnosis of tuberculosis. He tried to reassure us that the understanding and treatment of the illness had progressed since Auntie Belle's death nine years earlier. However, the prognosis was still unpredictable and often bleak. With proper care, Charles might enter remissive phases where the symptoms would diminish for a time.

During the next two weeks, Charles began to show some improvement, though the symptoms never completely left him. There were even a few nights that I wasn't awakened by coughing. The feature that frightened me most was his loss of muscle. He had always been thin but muscular. Now, of course, he couldn't work, and it was starting to show. His fever came on mainly at night and was not as high as before, but it was predictable and more persistent. There was never a day that he didn't cough, often spitting up blood into his handkerchief. He accepted his "cross" with resignation and never complained or lost his sense of humor. Fortunately, the warm weather was on his side and gave him great relief from his confinement during those cool spring days in Maine.

On May 25, my dear Edith Sullivan passed into eternity. On hearing the devastating news, I collapsed on the sofa and wept like an infant. Her death was expected, but there was a part of me that believed she'd always be there. It was as though I was drowning, and the lifeline I had been clinging to had suddenly snapped.

Sully stopped in to tell us about her last few moments.

"Who was with her when she passed?" I asked.

"Oh, she had quite a send-off, if you wanna call it that. Her nieces, Barbara and Abbie, her nephew Sean, Uncle Pat, Aunt Shannon, and me, we were all present. But in the confusion and swiftness of her passing, we failed to notify her beloved granddaughter so that she might be there as well."

"Well, people don't die by appointment, Sully. I'm sure the granddaughter will understand. Does she live in Boston?" I asked.

"No. She lives in this house."

My eyes welled up with tears, never having expected that answer.

Sully continued, "She instructed me, in no uncertain terms, and I quote, 'Tell her not to forget me promise.' I don't know what she was referrin' to, but I'm certain you must."

"Oh. I could never forget," I assured him. "She *was* a saint."

"She was *Love* itself," Michael added, with a wistful smile.

"Truly. Whenever I visited, I was lifted out of my confusion and sorrow. I was able to view life with different eyes. The sad twist of events in my little world seemed to make sense when she spoke."

"Her life was not an easy one, either. She lost so many friends and family during the blight. I don't know how that woman kept her faith. She would trudge off to mass every Sunday, with me in tow."

"She saw suffering in a different light than most, didn't she?"

"Yes. One time, some old bloke walked up to her after mass and asked, 'How can ya still believe after everythin' that's happened to ya?' She wasted no time with a response, "Well, me friend, if sufferin' didn't have value, why would our Lord go to the cross to endure so much of it?'"

"She turned sufferin' into prayer."

"I'm blessed to have known her. She calmed many a storm in my life. But, what's gonna happen to you now? Who's gonna … "

"Pat and Shannon are inheritin' the house. It's in Grammy's will. So, guess I won't be goin' too far. They like it here. More like Ireland. Boston's a mite too busy for their tastes."

"Well, I'm grateful for that. Friends like you are hard to come by, Sully."

Sully nodded with a shy smile. "Will you folks be comin' to the wake?"

"We certainly will," I replied. "At least Susan and I will be there. Maybe Charles. Is there a time that would be best?"

"You should know by now, our door is always open to ya."

The funeral mass for Edith Riley Sullivan was held at St. Mary's Catholic Church on State Street in Augusta, and at Sully's request, I attended. I felt very conspicuous as the only Protestant attending a Catholic funeral. There was just so much tension and mistrust circulating between those two Christian worlds. The local papers, with their insinuations and vague assumptions, continued to reinforce regional Protestant biases in their editorials, which mocked anything that smacked of Papistry. But I was in the minority there, surrounded by devout, life-long Irish Catholics. My apprehensions soon abated after meeting the priest, Reverend Charles Egan,[64] who was both warm and welcoming to me as a Congregationalist. He sensed my uneasiness and encouraged me in a lighthearted manner; "Just follow along with the rest of us old Micks, and you'll look like a seasoned veteran in no time."

Just when I was breathing a sigh of relief, the Sullivans were assigned to the very front pew! Thanks to Edith, I was better prepared than I would've been otherwise. I just followed the other mourners and stood, sat, and kneeled whenever they did. The entire service was in Latin, except for the sermon, but I'm happy to say I was able to understand a few of the Latin phrases from my studies. Michael let me use Edith's well-worn prayer book, which translated the Latin on the left-hand page into English on the right. The sanctuary was draped in black curtains and the coffin covered with a black pall embroidered with a white cross. It all seemed very formal, and somewhat spooky, in comparison to what I had experienced at the Old South.

Afterwards, we followed the funeral procession up to St. Mary's Cemetery at the top of Winthrop Hill and laid Edith to rest. The mourners were made up of Mulligans, Finnegans, O'Learys, Sullivans and every other Irish surname one can imagine, and that charming Irish brogue was ubiquitous!

I was continually being introduced as Edith's granddaughter. I felt honored to have that title and never sensed the need to correct the mistake. Fortunately, no one there asked me to render an account of my Sullivan ancestry! Even Sully, who was her only surviving grandchild in the States, said nothing to contradict this quickly-evolving myth. Aunt Shannon, happy to perpetuate the ruse, dug deeper into Irish folklore, looked over at me, smiled, and in fluent Gaelic, declared; "*Failte roimh an gclann, Annie … welcome to the clan!*"

After assembling around the gravesite, Fr. Eagan prayed a few words, read Psalm 23, and sprinkled the coffin with holy water. Edith's remains were then lowered into the ground to await resurrection on the Last Day. The mourners then left the site for the church rectory, where a small luncheon was provided by the local Irish community.

Oh my! Much to my great surprise and joy, the luncheon was anything but mournful. It was full of laughter, anecdotes, and singing. One might have easily mistaken it for a wedding! This was the perfect ending, or should I say *beginning,* of Edith's new life in the presence of the Divinity, to Whom she had dedicated her long life.

Chapter 34

A Friend of the Captain

Another week went by and Charles began to show some improvement. Susan and I brought out Father's wing chair, and Charles sat out on the lawn throughout most of the day, soaking in the warm sunshine. In addition, he soon required a small wooden stand, coffee, his slippers, and a hat. Yes, Charles was sick, but he wasn't an invalid and mild exercise was a part of his recovery. Probably because of our pampering, he began to slip into complacent entitlement and the litany of requirements grew by the day. With each new demand my temper rose like steam compression in a locomotive. One day he had the audacity to yell, "Annie, get me the Kennebec Journal, the one about the lunar eclipse!"

Finally, I blew my boiler!

"Charles," I barked, "we ain't yo slaves and you ain't da Massa! … so, get outta yo lazy-chair and fetch yo own newspapa' in da Big House, yo-self!"

He found my jesting in Uncle Tom dialect offensive. However, it did make him reflect on how he was treating us. From that point on his requests were somewhat more amiable.

A disturbing aspect of his illness was his loss of appetite. We often had to coerce him into eating, which was a drastic change from his former habit of devouring everything in sight. Since he was already an avid reader, we bribed him with weekly publications of *Scientific American* and by obtaining books on subjects of his choice. I told him, "If you want to read, you have to eat!"

His favorite topic, for the moment, was dinosaurs. He couldn't learn enough about the enormous fossilized skeletons being discovered in Europe and in the western U.S. This new field of study, called paleontology, was in its infancy but moving rapidly to become an indispensable science. Theories were sprouting like mushrooms about the characteristics of these huge beasts, how they looked when alive, and how long ago they lived. Some believed that they were animals that were wiped out in Noah's Great Flood. Others speculated that fossils were the manifestations of the Devil, designed to deceive "the elect."

There was a revolutionary new type of thinking among some scholars, initially proposed by the English naturalist, Charles Darwin, called *evolution*, which most of our church leaders wholeheartedly rejected. The theory proposed that the earth was not approximately 5000 years old, as reckoning from the Bible postulated, but many millions of years in age. It proposed that life developed and changed over the eons, adapting itself to variations in an ever-morphing environment. Evolution flew in the face of Biblical literalism, and many pastors condemned the "heresy" from the pulpit.

Mrs. Sullivan and I had discussed this topic, and she had not been the slightest bit alarmed. "One never need be afraid of science," she would say. "It reveals the genius and vastness of God's creation and how it all fits together. It will never explain away the Divinity, but through faith and reason, will affirm it."

Charlie was becoming a proponent of this new form of scientific thought and had engaged in several debates with Susan over the topic. Fortunately for my brother, she was used to Charles's know-it-all attitude and never took offense, in spite of her opposition to the theory.

Despite my brother's obsession with dinosaurs and the theory of evolution, he also maintained a deep and growing interest in spiritual matters. One day, out of the blue, he expressed a desire to read *The Imitation of Christ* by the 15th century author, Thomas à Kempis. Charles never read religious books other than the Bible, and even that was as rare as a two-headed budgie! Though never having heard of the celebrated work myself, I was not surprised to locate a copy in Edith Sullivan's book case. Sully gave it to me with the assurance that Edith would want it put to good use. And it was.

"Where did you hear about this book?" I asked my brother, handing him the copy.

"It was recommended Christian reading in the Kennebec Journal," he responded.

"This is a Catholic book, Charlie."

Immutability of Species.

We have absolute proof of the immutability of species, whether we search for it in historic or geological times. The cat and dog embalmed in Egypt four thousand years ago are the same as the cat and dog of the present day, and in the fossil remains of the pre-Adamite ages, there is not the slightest proof of any variations in the successive inhabitants of the earth. Mr. Darwin himself admits, to use his own words, "that this is the most obvious and grave objection to his theory;" but he conjectures that rocks still undiscovered, and myriads of years older than the Cambrian or azoic strata, may still bear testimony to his views.

"So what? It's esteemed by Christians of all types. Since when were you against reading Catholic books?"

"I'm not. I'm just surprised, that's all. I mean you never read religious books."

"True, and that's gonna change. It's a series of meditations. You, of all people, oughtta be shoutin' 'Hallelujah!' from the rooftops!"

"All right, then. Hallelujah!" I acquiesced. "But I'm not climbing onto the roof."

Charles grinned, "I need to prepare myself for that *last train to glory*."

"Must you always use those stupid death idioms? You're not dying!"

"Die today, die tomorrow. We're *all* gonna end up *on the wrong side of the grass*. No one has beat the odds yet, 'specially in this family.

I sighed.

"Oh my! Take a look at this, Annie," he declared, having just opened the book. "It's exactly what we've been talking about: 'What doth it profit to live long, when we amend so little? Ah! Long life doth not always amend, but often the more increaseth guilt … Happy is the man who hath the hour of his death always before his eyes, and daily prepareth himself for that hour.'"

"That's well and good for you, Charlie, but I don't wanna spend every waking moment thinking about death."

"But, you do, sis! And what's worse, you're not even sure there *is* an afterlife. I'll keep my cross; it's lighter than yours."

"Perhaps. But why *are* you and I so different? Why do I have to turn over every stone?"

"'Cause you're huntin' for treasure, Annie. If God put it in plain sight, you might never give it a second look."

———

Tuesday, May 31, 1864, dawned overcast and rather muggy for this time in the year. The cruel war was dragging deep into its 4th year with another major blood-bath at Cold Harbor resulting in thousands of Union and rebel casualties. It seemed, after the success at Gettysburg, that Robert E. Lee was continuing to outfox the persistent and aggressive Ulysses Grant. The lists of dead, injured, and missing were getting longer every week and the war appeared to be approaching a tipping point. Many voices were clamoring for "peace at any price," even if it meant the continuation of slavery. However, Lincoln had found some relentless fighters. Though not as intuitive as Lee, and not as successful in every encounter, General Grant had "done the arithmetic" of which Mr. Lincoln had so often spoken. He was ready to use all the resources at his disposal until the Gray Fox hoisted the white flag.

The Civil War itself, with the exception of Eli's unfortunate circumstances, had merely grazed our lives in comparison to what others were enduring. There were times when coffee and sugar were scarce, and cotton was nowhere to be found. But those things were of minimal consequence. Giving up cotton was almost considered a sacred duty in honor of those who had paid such a heavy price to pick and process the crop. From a distance, our family's tragic moments were nothing compared to the horrors of national fratricide. But we don't live our lives in an impersonal bubble from those we love, do we?

———

That afternoon, which was humid with threatening skies, Susan and I were cutting up vegetables for the evening meal when a knock came at the front door. I went to answer it. A handsome, lightly bearded gentleman with sandy brown hair, and dressed in formal apparel was standing on our brick walkway. The stranger, apparently sensing rain, had hitched his horse to a shade tree across the road from our dwelling. He seemed ill at ease and was fidgeting with what appeared to be a portfolio of some sort.

"Good day," I said. "May I help you?"

"Yes, my name is Alden Potter. I would like to talk with Susan Goodwin, if she is available."

"She is here," I replied. "I'll fetch her for you. Please, come in and make yourself at home. It looks like we're in for some weather."

"Oh, thank you," he replied, nervously. "Yes, there are a few rumbles out there … but a good shower might cool things off a bit."

"Yes, it would help," I replied, while walking away towards the kitchen.

I alerted Susan and she met our guest in the parlor. I introduced him and the three of us sat there quietly for a few awkward moments, as he fumbled with the contents of his leather satchel.

"Pardon me for my uneasiness," he began, "but what brings me here is an unsettling task. Are there other members of your family at home?"

"Yes," I replied. "My grandmother and brother are here."

"Well …" he continued, with hesitancy, "would you mind asking them to join us?"

"Surely," I responded, throwing a sideways glance of concern in Susan's direction.

I returned to the parlor with both Grandma and Charles. They were introduced to our guest and stood at the doorway, expectantly waiting for the visitor to speak.

Addressing Susan, Alden began, "Madam, I am Alden Potter, a seamer and pattern maker in Bath … A dear friend of your husband John." He hesitated, clearing his throat. "The news that I bear … is distressing. I'm sorry," he remarked, bowing his head towards the floor. "I would ask you all to … to please be seated." Charles and Isabel quickly obliged.

"Proceed, Mr. Potter, if you will," said Susan, whose face had already turned pale in anticipation.

"Very well, Mrs. Goodwin. Postponing my task will do no good," he began, emitting an anxious sigh. "We have learned from a British maritime report that the Norwegian barque, the *Nor*,[65] sank after hitting an iceberg during a squall in the North Atlantic, somewhere off Newfoundland. Regretfully, I must inform you that … save for two souls, all hands were lost."

The shock from the news left us mute.

After a pause and with a painful wince contracting across his brow, he continued, "And … regretfully, Captain John Goodwin[66] was not among those recovered."

Susan shrieked and fainted. I grasped her around the shoulders to keep her from falling to the floor. Charles applied smelling salts to help revive her. Within a minute or so she regained consciousness but was greatly shaken. Mr. Potter was visibly grieved by having to relay such heartbreaking news.

He turned toward Charles and I and whispered, "I've never before had to be the bearer of such tragic tidings, but as I was a close friend and shipmate of your father, I felt it my duty to do so." Alden looked over at me, and a big tear slid down his cheek, a tear that was quickly wiped away by his shirtsleeve. Apparently, Alden felt it improper of him to show such emotion. I felt quite the contrary.

"Mr. Potter," I pleaded between sobs, "Don't be ashamed to let your heart speak."

He looked over at me with an inquisitive expression. I'm not sure if he thought I was speaking from wisdom, stupidity, or that I was just an impudent country girl.

Poor Susan was so overcome with emotion that she was unable to converse for some time. We waited.

Eventually, my stepmother had recovered enough to speak. But Alden, sensing that his reporting of the details might be too much for the poor woman, proceeded with caution.

"Mrs. Goodwin," he voiced, respectfully, "if you're unable to bear this, I can simply give you the written report to read at your convenience."

"No, I've never run from the truth. Tell us everything. I need to know."

"Are you sure?"

"Yes, please continue."

"Very well." he consented. "As far as we know … Oh, yes, … here's a copy of the official report that we received from the British," he said, handing it to Charles.

"Where was I?" Mr. Potter took a breath. "The *Nor* struck an iceberg during a brief but violent squall, at about 1:00 a.m. on the 30th of April, last. The vessel had been successfully navigating ice all day long. But the sudden storm and the darkness of the hour made visibility and safe navigation impossible. A small but deadly rogue iceberg carved a mortal wound in the hull of the *Nor*, and she began to take on insurmountable volumes of water. The great surge made it impossible to manage with the pumps, though your father and his first mate gave their lives desperately trying to do so.

"As the ship foundered, flares were sent up, but the weather was too miserable for them to be seen by other vessels. Then your husband ordered several rounds of signal cannon be fired, but to no avail. Though there were vessels in the area, the noise of the storm muted the blasts. The berg had created such an enormous gash in her side that the crew, most of whom were below deck, had no time to escape. Regretfully, thirteen lives were lost.

"The two survivors, both Norweigans who managed to make it out of their bunks, jumped overboard and were saved by the miraculous appearance of a dislodged lifeboat. Both had severe frostbite and ended up losing several fingers and toes, but nevertheless, lived to tell the tale.

"The *Montezuma*, a British vessel, came upon the lifeboat at daybreak and rescued the pair. The water was extremely cold and … survival time … well … it was less than an hour in the frigid Atlantic. When the two were brought aboard they were near death … not expected to last the night. Providentially, they did survive and were able to give a detailed account of the disaster. The two "fortunates" spoke of selfless bravery, and credited their survival to your husband and the first mate, who did all they could to save life and limb."

Alden paused for a moment and turned towards Susan, "Mrs. Goodwin, your husband was a hero. John is responsible for the fact that those two are alive today. 'No greater love doth a man have than this, that he lay down his life for his friends,' so sayeth our Lord. I hope that knowledge gives you some solace … if not now, then perhaps, after the passage of time."

Grandma Kean got up and walked quietly to the south-facing window, staring out at the gathering storm clouds, whose ominous shadow was now beginning to absorb all the color in the room. Charles was distraught. He wasn't weeping, but his head was bowed with both hands wrapped against the back of his neck; a posture I had seen only once before, at Mother's passing. In a solitary moment, he had become the nineteen-year-old head of the family, stricken with a disease that might make this new mandate an impossible one.

An eerie stillness now pervaded the house. From the heavens came rumbles of thunder and an occasional flash of lightning, but no one spoke a word for what seemed an eternity. Even our pets joined us in hallowed reverence. The rain began to patter against the window as the five of us sat there like statues frozen in time. The ninety-year-old tall clock ticked away without concern for anything that might have happened on its watch. It took no responsibility nor interest in the deeds of mortals. Babies were born, children died, wars were fought, kings and presidents came and went, but the pendulum moved, unaffected: no tears, no remorse, no empathy, no guilt. It is we who mark the days against the unknown hour. It is we who immortalize one minute or another for whatever joy or sorrow. It is we who vow never to forget. How very mysterious is this life that we had no choice but to enter.

At some point, I began to wonder if Mr. Potter might be ill at ease with such grief-stricken, prolonged silence.

"Mr. Potter," I whispered, extending my hand. "I'm sorry, I never introduced myself. My name is …"

"Annie Elizabeth, correct?" he interjected, finishing my sentence.

"Yes, sir. Annie Elizabeth."

He seemed relieved that someone had finally broken the silence.

"Your father spoke of you often. We were mates, you know, on voyages to Boston, New York, and the Carolinas, several times. Business affairs, mainly." After a brief pause, he added with concern, "I understand your family has already been severely tried … and I'm afraid I have just added heavily to that burden."

Charles, overhearing, turned to him in response. "Sir, you have done the right thing. It wouldn't matter who brought us the news, we would be equally devastated. Better a friend of Father's than an impersonal telegram."

Observing that my stepmother was slowly recovering, and trying to distract my own painful thoughts, I asked, "Would anyone like some coffee or tea?"

"I would never impose on you, at such a moment," proclaimed Alden.

"Oh, it's no bother. Staying busy helps me to keep my mind off my troubles. Which would you prefer?"

"Coffee would be perfect. But, please make some for yourself, so I can pretend that it wasn't only on my behalf."

"Of course. Would anyone else like some, while I'm up?"

"I will, dear," replied Grandma. Coffee was her catharsis for any ill, physical or otherwise.

Our guest remained with us for another hour or so, conversing and reminiscing of his encounters with Father. Within that time, the storm had abated, the air was cooler, and the humidity had vanished. So, Alden took his leave and promised to stop by now and again. We assured him that any friend of Captain John Andrew Goodwin would always be welcome in our home.

There are, undoubtedly, details that I've forgotten concerning that fateful day. I experienced a certain anesthetizing numbness at the time. It was as though I was watching a tragic play about a family who had just lost a loved one at sea. I was a mere spectator! I went through the rest of the afternoon and evening as though it were just any other day. Sad faces surrounded me, but I was neither happy nor in mourning. My sleep that evening was undisturbed. It was strange.

Though different in its manifestation from Susan's, my mental paralysis was nothing less than a form of shock. By the next morning, however, reality began its slow sobering crescendo. The weight of losing Father to the depths of the sea didn't hit me all at once as when Mother died. Rather, it set in steadily, filling in all the nooks and crannies of my heart, like the water from the iceberg pouring through the cabins, archways, hold, and galley, taking the *Nor* into the abyss.

At some point during the next day, I realized that Father was truly gone. I would never see him again. Now, everything in my surroundings began to remind me of him. The house, the barns, and the fields, which he was so very proud of, were all there for us because of his hard work. All our worldly possessions had been given to us through his endeavors. I couldn't look at a chair, a clock, a spoon, or anything in our dwelling that I didn't associate with him. Like the heroes in Lincoln's Gettysburg Address, he had given us his "last full measure of devotion."

Although we wrote to our governor, Augusta native Samuel Cony, and the U.S. embassy in Norway concerning possible monetary compensation, we received only cursory statements, such as, "We'll look into the matter," which they probably never did. We were all rightfully outraged by the brevity and ineptitude of those in charge of relaying additional information to us. But we were at war. There were more important concerns for our government than the loss of a Norwegian merchant vessel with two Americans on board, while thousands of Americans were dying on the battlefields every week.

The person who assumed the heaviest burden was Susan. For more than two weeks, she shuttered herself in the master bed chamber, closed the curtains, and only ate small portions of the food that we brought to her. I attempted to talk with her but she was never willing to speak of her pain, even though we were all grieving the same terrible loss. Charles and I took turns emptying the bedpan and doing other unpleasant but necessary tasks on her behalf. She rarely thanked us, and we were getting worried, as it was not in her nature to be rude or ungrateful. Her face was becoming emaciated with a sickly pallor, and her hair was rarely groomed.

For the Gardiner Home Journal.

Despair Not.

Despair not, despair not, whatever betide;
  Though the storms of adversity dark,
O'erhanging the billows of Life's restless tide,
  Now threaten thy wavering bark.

Be firm at thy helm, for the waters afar
  Are strewn with the fast sinking wrecks
Of those, who, with thee, just commencing life's way,
  Trod too proudly their beautiful decks.

Be hopeful, despair not, the lightning-rift cloud
  Is lined with a silvery hue;
And wider, still wider, its radiance shall glow,
  And brighten the waters anew.   LINDA.

There was an ever-growing miasma that reeked of decay coming from her room. The sickening smell was finding its way into all the nooks and crannies of the second floor. No room was exempt from the stench. I was nominated to venture into that abyss, find the source of the godawful reek, and eliminate it. When I offered to clean it up, Susan, who must have lost all sense of smell, simply nodded and said, "Do as you wish." The odor was from several rotting meals of pork and fish that the cats had apparently scavenged and dragged under her bed. That noxious ooze of decaying flesh and maggots nearly made me vomit, but I held my breath and removed the stomach-turning morsels.

Afterwards, Charles and I took over, opening shutters, windows, and curtains to air out that putrid abode of despair. We would soon have to take drastic measures, as she had all but stopped eating and was losing the will to live. If our attempts didn't work, Grandma was preparing to seek professional help from Dr. Davis, which might result in a prolonged stay at the asylum in Augusta. We hoped to avoid having to take that step.

The day after our cleaning endeavor, I surprised myself at my own audacity. On entering her room, I found last night's supper untouched and my Irish temper rose to an explosive level. I used every bit of self-control I could muster and calmly but firmly declared, "Susan, you've got to get out of here. You're not eating, and this place is like a tomb!"

"It is my tomb, Annie," she replied, in a flat, defeated tone.

That was the last straw.

"Not on my watch!" I screamed. "Get the hell out of this room, now! Or Charles and I will drag you out, screaming and kicking!" I couldn't believe I had just cursed, but the shock-effect did get an emotional response.

"How dare you speak to me like that! You heartless brat!" she barked.

"Heartless? Do you think you're in more pain than the rest of us? Who do you think you are?" I bellowed. "Captain John Goodwin was my father! I loved him with all my heart! I've cried myself to sleep every damn night since we learned of his fate. And you sit in here, day after day, wallowing in your own self-pity. Well, go ahead! Starve yourself to death, because I won't be making any more meals for you until you climb out of this grave! The choice is yours!"

I stormed out of the room and slammed the door behind me. Charles had been eavesdropping and had heard every word. "Annie," he whispered, so as not to be heard by Susan, "I can't believe you spoke to her like that!"

"I'm sorry, but she's killing herself. I lost all self-restraint," I replied, still fuming from my encounter.

"I'll say you did! You were completely out of control … and It was wonderful!" he asserted, with a big grin. "Your gentle persuasion might have done some good."

"Gentle persuasion? More like the siege at Vicksburg."

"Well, it worked for Grant," chirped my brother, in predictable form.

"Let's hope," I concluded, looking upward for some help from above.

—◆—

At about eight p.m. the next evening, Susan emerged from her "crypt" with bedpan in hand. She silently brushed past me without so much as a sideways glance and journeyed to the outhouse to complete her mission. Afterwards, she came back into the parlor and sat down. Her head was bowed as I stood before her, waiting for her to speak.

All at once she began to weep. Her hands were shaking and her body wrenched with each sob. I sat down beside her with an impulse to reach for her hand. However, I thought better of the idea, remembering our heated exchange on the previous day.

Finally, the trembling ceased, and with the semblance of a soul on the brink of madness, she turned toward me and began her saga.

"Death and I were becoming friends, you know," she explained, smiling as though reminiscing about a cherished acquaintance. "Oh! To join in that eternal sleep … to walk with my beloved in that garden where suffering is denied entry."

"Every evening I prayed for the Almighty to separate my ravaged soul from this mortal body. But, every morning I awoke imprisoned, with no means of escape!"

"One evening a thought came to me," she continued, with a dreamy, incongruous expression, "I'll wander down to the bridge tonight and let the merciful river sweep away my misery from this vengeful earth. The waters that took away my beloved will return me to him! Poetic justice! But then again, might such a sinful act separate us, forever? … Patience! Only a few more weeks of anguish, and God or madness will sweep me away of its own accord."

Suddenly, Susan's demeanor turned to rage! She lunged and grabbed the collar of my blouse with both hands. "You and your cruel rebuke! You robbed me of my consolation!" she bellowed with contempt. "Bluebirds! Lilies! Hugs from beyond the grave!" she fumed.. "Where was *my* solace in this godforsaken house of death?"

Charles quickly appeared at the doorway in response to Susan's frightening display. He stood there, frozen, wondering whether or not to act. I shook my head lightly, indicating he should not intervene. He took the cue with guarded anticipation.

Susan paused, glanced over at Charles and gently released her grip on me. This was followed by a deep sigh, and then, as though sanity had finally taken hold, she continued, "This very evening, something began to stir within, a revelation that I was choosing my fate as surely as if I were to drown myself. I had made the decision not to decide. The hell that I was experiencing was, in good part, of my own making and I could no longer play the helpless victim of fate. If I were to die it would be my choice, not destiny. In every respect, it would be nothing less than premeditated suicide.

"I then walked over to the dormer, pulled back the shades, and opened the window. The setting sun was pouring a beautiful orange glow over the horizon. The air was that of the open ocean! Had I closed my eyes I would have thought myself to be at the seaside. Suddenly a brisk wind blew in through my bedchamber, lasting but a few seconds. And just as suddenly, all became still, as before. 'That was odd,' I thought. As I looked around the room I noticed that the only thing disturbed by the breeze was John's Bible. It was open. It was open to none other than the verses that John and I read together the night before he left, the Beatitudes."

Susan then looked up at me, with a smile of forgiveness and whispered, "'Blessed are they who mourn, for they shall be comforted!'"

Chapter 35

Madame V

Susan was out of the woods but certainly not immune to bouts of melancholy, loneliness, and grief. However, she never ventured back into that dark, dismal world of self-destruction. We reflected frequently on her enigmatic encounter with that ocean breeze, which helped bolster her hope.

In accordance with her wishes and improving mental disposition, we decided to hold a memorial service for Father sometime in July. She ordered a large marble headstone from the Monumental Masonry Company in Hallowell, to be erected during the ceremony. The inscription chosen was a short poem that she found in a volume lent to her by the stoneworkers. There were many fine examples to select from under the category of "Lost at Sea," as such tragedies were not uncommon.

The warm, early days of summer and the longer daylight hours helped ease the sad nostalgia that so often filled the empty rooms of the Goodwin abode. Charles seemed to be much improved and, once again, ventured out to work for an hour or two every day. Dr. Davis, understanding the importance of my brother's need to feel useful, had approved this undertaking barring the recurrence of hemorrhaging.

Another unexpected godsend was the leasing of twenty acres of our farmland and the rental of Grandma Kean's former dwelling to James Kebler,[67] an acquaintance of Father, who had moved up to Maine from Massachusetts to try his hand at raising sheep. He was willing to renovate and use the large old barn that had belonged to Grandpa, which stood idle, just above the stream that traversed our land. He also volunteered to help us with our own dire farming situation, covering many of the chores that Charles was unable to undertake. Though he wasn't paying us enough to cover all of our outstanding debts, it was a great help. Our financial woes were relieved somewhat by his monthly installments. Life, once again, seemed to be on an upswing.

Charles had taken on a growing interest in astronomy and was using one of Father's old nautical spy glasses to explore the heavens. He had constructed a tripod and attached the scope to a swivel adjoined to a copper mount to keep his focus steady.

One clear June evening, as we were attempting to observe Jupiter and a blurry speck of light beside it, Charles asked, "Can you imagine the existence of something that had no beginning?"

"Do you mean God?"

"No. Something else."

"There is nothing else, Charlie."

"Yes there is. Time. Along with the Creator, time is the only commodity that illustrates something which has always been. There's as much future time as there is past time."

"Do we really know that?" I asked. "The only time we actually experience is the present moment. The future is coming and the past is gone. Time is just an invention to organize passing *intervals* between events, a way of keeping track. You were born in '45 and I in '49."

"Well … let's discuss those *intervals*, shall we? Here's a thought; if time is just a construction of the human mind, could anything exist?"

"You're losing me."

"All right. This is a telescope. It has three dimensions. Agreed?"

"Of course."

"It has length, width, and depth, which by the way, are human inventions used to describe *real* dimensions of something. But there's another dimension, equally real; the most important of them all, *time!* A three-dimensional telescope which isn't present for any interval of time, doesn't exist at all. Time allows everything to exist. It's the fourth dimension, or maybe even the first! Time is a prerequisite to substance."

"That's very interesting Charles. You know, you actually do use that head of yours sometimes, don't you?"

"Yes, it's not just a beautiful ornament to enhance my shoulders." There was a brief pause in the conversation as Charles locked in on the planet and held the scope in place for me to get a glimpse of the giant planet's brightest satellite, Ganymede.

Charles continued in a soft voice, in concert with the moment, "I had another thought. Maybe you've thought of this too. If nothing ever existed to begin with, then nothing could ever begin to exist on its own, no matter how much time passed. Things come into being because other things kept the ball rolling. Cause and effect. Some *thing* that had no beginning had to commence the process in order for anything to be here. Aristotle called it a prime mover."

> When I gaze into the stars, they look down upon me with pity from their serene and silent spaces, like eyes glistening with tears, over the little lot of man. Thousands of generations, all as noisy as our own, have been swallowed up by time, and there remains no record of them any more; yet Arcturus and Orion, Sirius, and the Pleiades, are still shining in their courses, clear and young as when the shepherd first noticed them on the plains of Shinar.
> —*Carlyle.*

"Actually, I have thought about this, many times. This is the point at which philosophy, science, and religion meet on friendly terms," I responded.

"Well said, little sister. Every new discovery of science creates ten new mysteries to ponder."

"Well said, big brother," I said, patting him on the back.

We remained there, stargazing and contemplating the enigma of creation, until the moon crept over the eastern hills and overtook the intricate details of the cosmos.

———

In early July, we began to plan out Father's memorial service which was conducted at the Chelsea Heights Cemetery on a hot, overcast afternoon at the site of an ever-growing row of Goodwin headstones. But this grave was an empty one. Our new minister was unable to attend the service; therefore, Alden Potter agreed to read a scripture passage and lead the attendants in a short prayer. Susan, despite fears that she might not endure it, managed to surprise all of us by her composure. After the brief ceremony the white marble tombstone was laid in place. It read:

Capt.

JOHN A. GOODWIN

Lost at sea
Apr. 1864
Aet. 48

*No monument is left to trace
the time, the circumstance, or place
Where his dear body lies.
But God will guard his sleeping dust
And we'll resign the sacred trust
Till He shall bid him rise.*

The impact of Father's death grew within me like a malignant tumor. When you are with a loved one at their passing, you share their fate and unique circumstances. My greatest torment was not having been with him during his last moments. Envisioning him gasping for air as his limbs became paralyzed by the cold and drowning in the frigid North Atlantic or perhaps drifting on a wooden beam for hours while slowly freezing to death, tore at my soul. When someone is lost at sea, all you have is the multitude of circumstances to draw from. Endless variations of horror that display themselves to the imagination, and the curtain never closes.

Life had been so inexplicably cruel to us. It all felt like a random throw of the dice, yet the thread of hope lingered within my heart. I read accounts of people who had died and somehow came back to life, telling of deceased loved ones who greeted them in paradise. The opinion derived from most scientific journals was that such manifestations were merely the results of a dying brain, the last remembrances and desires of one about to enter oblivion. Naturally, the religious commentaries were all supportive of the supernaturality of such things. After reading all the favorable and unfavorable material I could get my hands on, I understood that no amount of literary study or anecdotal reports would be able to answer my core question. The proof was not to be found in them.

—

For a brief period of time, I became interested in spiritualism, the idea of communing with the dead through a human medium. It was all the rage in the 1860s! This religion, if I can use that term, had gained much popularity, especially during the war, when so many young men were giving up their spirits on the battlefields. To be truthful, our pastor, and those of the prominent denominations, frowned on the practice. However, given the burning question that had haunted me since my early childhood, I wanted no stone left unturned. I had no sooner decided to find a medium when a serendipitous event happened. Van Amburgh and Company's Mammoth Menagerie and Egyptian Caravan was coming to Gardiner on Saturday, the 25th of July! Emma had been to Van Amburgh's show the previous year, and a Gypsy fortune seer divined a message from beyond the grave. Emma's story was not only convincing, the accuracy was confirmed by her mother who had originally been quite a skeptic.

Em was delighted to go again, so we made plans. When we arrived, there was a bustle of people from all over the area and exotic animals were everywhere! My favorite was the giraffe who tried to nibble on my hat. Perhaps she thought it was made of acacia leaves. The poor creature must have been highly disappointed, as after one bite, she snorted, backed away, and shook her head in disgust! A noble Bengal tiger paced nervously in a large iron cage, and a pair of fierce looking water buffalo were strutting about in a tightly fenced-off area of the fairgrounds. There were some

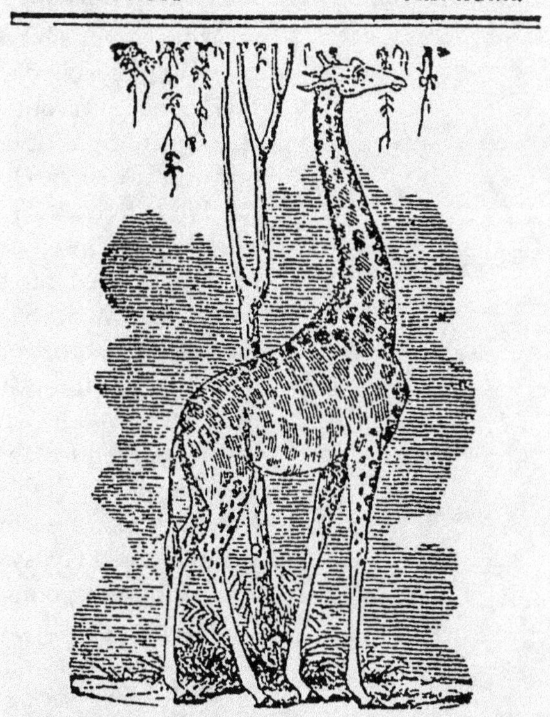

Nearly fourteen feet high. The only one on this Continent. The structure and history of this extraordinary animal have a high interest for the Naturalists.

beautiful, free-ranging peacocks that liked to show off their regal, feathery display to anyone and everyone. The caretaker, who noticed our interest in the birds, was kind enough to give each of us one of their exquisite, molted plumes to take home as souvenirs.

As we continued to wander around the fairground, we spied a small, circular tent, banked against a wooded area, which was about a stone's throw off the main trail. A large canvas sign along our pathway pointed to its location. It stated:

Within dwells the amazing spirit-medium Madame Vatesia!
The seer and medium of great renown who predicted the Battle of Gettysburg,
John Brown's revolt, The invention of the telegraph,
The Fort Tejon earthquake of 1857, The death of Little Willie Lincoln,
And much more!
Let her help you speak to your departed loved ones! $1.00 Admission.

"This is the person I saw last year, Annie!" said Emma excitedly. " She's amazing … but a bit creepy."

"Well," I replied, "being creepy kinda goes with her gift, wouldn't you say? It's not everyone who can summon the dead."

"You're right. It doesn't look like anyone's there except for that young boy near the entry. He was with her last year, too. I think it's her grandson."

We entered through the canvas flap followed by the youngster, who introduced himself as "Luca, assistant to the great Madam Vatesia." The tent was divided into two semicircular sections. The larger of the two compartments was at the entrance, which was edged with a single, plush sofa for waiting purposes. The smaller, enclosed section was where the medium practiced her trade. The boy asked us to be seated and informed us that Madame would be with us promptly.

We waited for about five minutes before the oilcloth doorway parted and out walked a tall, middle-aged woman with long, braided, gray-speckled, black hair, wearing a colorful head scarf, and sporting the traditional vestments of a Gypsy fortune teller.

"Goot afternoon, ladies. I am Madame Vatesia. What eez it dat you vant from me?" she began, with a strong Eastern European accent.

"I would like … " I hesitated, "to speak with my … deceased father."

"Oh, you poor dear … life can be so unkind." She then, slowly emphasizing each word, asserted, "Heese not dead … heese right here vit you, now. Trust vut I say."

After that proclamation, she continued speaking in a normal fashion, "You come in. Bote off you, but you must leef your baggage in dis vaiting area. It t'will be very safe. Luca vill vatch over it for you. For dat reeson, vee only allow t'ree persons at most."

"Madame, I don't want to seem impolite, but why must …"

"Vy must you leef your earthly possessions behind? Becoss you need to be free of da material tings to speak vit d'ose on dee utter side. Dey haff no possessions in dat vorld," she responded politely. "Luca vill vatch over your tings. You check d'em before you leef. No'ting vill be missing. I promise."

Emma and I looked at each other, hesitantly. Then we carefully set our belongings on the sofa and followed Madame Vatesia into her "ghost parlor." Her grandson watched us with quiet interest until the curtains closed, and we found ourselves seated at a small circular table adorned with an embroidered white cloth. In the center of the table was a bowl-sized stone, embedded with a number of beautiful purple crystals, the likes of which I had never seen before. A bronze, whale-oil lamp hanging from a tent pole was the only source of illumination.

"You look puzzeled," remarked Madame. "You ver expecting a kreestal ball?"

"Oh," Emma replied. "We've just never seen such beautiful crystals before."

"Ah … yes. Dose are vut vee call amet'ysts. Day are very rare and come from Brazil. I don't use kreestal ball. It eez made by man. Dis amet'yst eez made by heaven. It eez very powerful in da spirit world."

"Are vee ready to speak wit' your father?" she asked me, with a serious tone.

"Yes," I replied, nervously.

"Vee begin!" she proclaimed.

She asked us to place our hands on the table before us and close our eyes. We were cautioned not to open our eyes for any reason as it would break the spell. Madame explained that at one point during the encounter she would have to remove herself from the table when the spirit of my father entered her body. She said she needed to keep her distance to protect us from the possibility of becoming possessed by nearby evil spirits. It was all very spine-chilling. She then asked, again, "Are you bote ready?"

"Yes," we replied, simultaneously.

"Gif me your father's full name, pleese."

"Captain John Andrew Goodwin," I replied.

She then began the incantations. "Tia noo danna. Sumatio jabinna en kriah! Spirits of the departed, I beckon to thee. Come!" She seemed to be performing some unseen hand ritual as she tapped firmly on the table several times. "Tia noo danna … friendly spirits approach … evil spirits depart to your place of shame! Sumatio jabinna … Captain John Andrew Goodvin … "

There was a long pause of silence and then she rose from her chair. Although we were told not to open our eyes, we were able to follow her motion by the sound as she moved directly behind us and halted there, continuing with her eerie chanting. "Enter by the narrow gate, John. Enter by the narrow gate! Sentinels, guard his path! All others leave in peace."

I was completely overwhelmed with emotion as she was now speaking fluent English with no accent! Then there came another pause. She began to whisper softly to the spirits. "You are not John, no. You are Sarah. You may not enter through the gate, presently. Only your husband. Go back to your realm in peace."

Chills ran down my spine like icy spring water! How could she know my mother's name? I used every bit of strength within me to stop myself from shouting, "I want to speak with my mother!" I knew that if I did react, the spell might be broken and then I would talk with no one. I kept silent.

Madame came back, sat down at the table, and asked us all to touch hands with our eyes continuing to stay closed. Soon, from the depths of Vatesia's being, came the sound of a deep, raspy stirring that started softly, like the wind blowing through the pines. Then it grew in intensity and clarity until babble became words.

"Ahh-nee … Ann-nee … Annie, my wonderful girl."

"Father … is that you?" I cried. Tears were filling my closed eyes.

"Yes, my dear one," said the voice, again, with no discernible accent.

I was nearly hysterical with emotion. "Papa, I wish I could have been with you. I'm so sorry. I love you so very much!"

"I feel your love Annie … It is always surrounding me."

"Were you with Mother when Madame Vatesia summoned you?"

"Yes. We are always together, my sweet one. Always."

"Tell me, Papa, did you suffer greatly?"

"Oh, no dear. It doesn't hurt to die … it is like falling asleep into a new world. Then you are welcomed by those who have gone before you."

"How did it happen, Father?"

"The iceberg … Ahh-nee, the … ice … berg … " Then his voice trailed off and Madame Vatesia came back out of her trance and sat quietly for about a minute to restore her composure. Then she told us to open our eyes.

"Oh, Madame Vatesia! There was so much more I wanted to ask him. Why did he have to depart so quickly?"

"Miss Goodvin," she replied, in her previous accent, "He vas unable to stay longer, dear one. Da spirits move to da music off love. Ven day are called by da Great One, day must obey. All is love in dare vorld."

I was now at a complete loss for words. The realization of what had just happened was more than my mind could grasp, and I sat there enraptured. Finally, I came to my senses, realizing I was taking up Madame's time, and declared, "It was amazing! I can't wait to tell Charles! Thank you so very much."

"It vas my pleasure, dear one. I vill be here tomorrow, and vee can try to summon him, again, if you vish."

"That would be wonderful! I'll see if my brother can come with me … Oh, that reminds me. I need to pay you."

"Yes. Just leave da dollar vit Luca. I do not touch da money. T'ank you,

Miss Goodvin, and your young friend."

"Thank you, Madame. Farewell."

"Farewell," she replied.

Our belongings were sitting right where we left them, with Luca standing nearby on guard duty. Emma and I each gave him fifty cents. He smiled, courteously, and bowed to us in thanks. Before we exited the tent, we checked our purses and all was in order. We then left the fairground to catch the train for Hallowell.

On the ride home, I sat quietly beside Emma, awestruck and in deep thought. I had spoken with my father! And there were several things that Madame couldn't have known or learned about our family in such a short time, Mother's name, for instance. True, there are lots of Sarahs in the world, but it would have been a one-in-a-hundred long shot of a guess. And I never gave her *my* name, but Annie was the first word spoken by Papa. And finally, as he faded back into the next world, he spoke of the iceberg. I never mentioned that my father was lost at sea; however, the title "Captain" could have suggested it. Anyway, all of these things combined could not be lucky guesses on her part. I turned all the possibilities of deception over and over in my head. My conclusion was it was a real encounter with the supernatural and proof of life beyond the grave! Mrs. Sullivan was right. My prayers had been answered as she predicted. I should have never doubted.

When I returned home, my brother was sitting in his easy chair on the front lawn of our home. He was reading from his ever-growing library of religious and scientific books.

I was so excited I couldn't contain myself, "Charles! Charles! I've got to tell you what just happened!" I blurted out.

"Hi, Annie. How was the Menagerie?"

"It was wonderful. You would have loved it! But the best part was … well, don't tell Grandma or Susan, but Emma and I went to a medium!"

"You can do better than medium. Set your sights a little higher, sis," he chuckled.

"No, Charles, really! She was amazing. She let me speak to Father!"

"Ah … OK. This sounds interesting," he replied hesitantly, laying his book down on his lap.

"Let me tell you about Madame Vatesia."

I described our seance, moment by moment, in great detail. Charles listened quietly, without interrupting. He just sat there with a queer look on his face.

"So, Charles, what do you think?" I asked.

He looked at me and then looked away, as though he was debating how to respond.

"Annie," he asked, "was there a little boy there? Oh … about, say, nine or ten years old?"

"Yes, Charles. I forgot to mention him. His name was Luca. How did you know that? Are you clairvoyant, too?" I stuttered.

"No. I'm not a seer, and neither is Madame Vatesia."

"What do you mean, Charles, she told me things she couldn't possibly have known about our family … Mother, my name, the iceberg … "

"Well, my dear, duped sister, let me explain how she works her magic. That little boy, Luca, is … well, he's her partner in crime, you see. Do you remember Ryan?"

"Of course," I asserted.

"Yes, I'm sure you do … and fondly, if I'm correct."

"Stop it! Just finish what you were saying."

"OK, don't pop your cork. Anyway, his mother went to see this 'Madame V', as she called her. She wanted to make contact with Ryan's late grandmother from the Great Beyond. And, of course, like you she was amazed at the personal information that the 'Great V' was able to bring forth from the other side. Miraculous, was the term she used, when she described the experience to Ryan."

"Come on, Charles. Make your point, will you!" I barked.

"Patience is a virtue, Annie; one you need to work on. Again, I'm tryin' to tell you what happened. I let you finish your long-winded tale, now let me finish mine, please."

"OK, sorry."

"Well, Ryan waited outside for his mother. The tent was positioned in such a way that much of it was hidden in the brush, and for a good reason. Ryan, being suspicious by nature, found an observation post behind the brush, giving him an unobstructed view of the back of Madame V's spook house. After a few minutes, little Luca cautiously emerged from a side-slit in the canvas. The little conspirator had something in his hand that looked like a letter. Anyway, it was a piece of paper with something written on it. He dodged the thick bushes, went around to the very back of the tent, and waited. At one point he opened a small flap on the tent and handed the item to someone through the opening. He kept looking from side to side to make certain he wasn't being observed. After a couple of minutes, the item was then given back to him, he lowered the flap, and ran back into the tent with the paper."

Charles continued, "His mother returned, like you, overjoyed with what she had just heard from the medium. Apparently, the letter was taken from her purse by the boy, and it contained enough information to enable Madame V to perform some really convincing "spirit" shenanigans. His poor mother checked her purse and there was the very same letter, a note from her sister about her mother's passing.

I felt so stupid and dejected I began to cry. I wanted, so much, to believe that Father had spoken to me. My purse contained a small, leather note-book that I used to gather thoughts for my journal, and it held a wealth of personal information. The cherished little piece of Bella's funeral hem, that I used as a bookmark, was lying at the bottom of my purse. Because of the tight, leather buckle-strap, it couldn't have fallen out without Luca's help.

Charles could see how sad I was and he came to my rescue, as always. "Sorry, Annie. I feel sad that I had to tell you, but I know how much you really want to know the truth. I couldn't let you believe that what you experienced in that tent was really Father. But I do want you to know that not everything Madame Vatesia said was a lie."

"What do you mean, Charles?"

Charles, giving his best impersonation of Madame V, proclaimed, "Heese not dead. Heese right here vit you, now. Trust vut I say."

"I hope so, Charles," I responded. Charles rose from his chair and gave me a great big-brother hug. Tears were still rolling down my cheeks, now more out of embarrassment for my gullibility than sorrow.

☞ The music car of Van Amburg's Menagerie out through the planking, in crossing Jay bridge last Thursday. No harm was done except a delay of about half an hour. The elephant forded the river, and he liked the situation so well, that it was some hours before they could induce him to leave it. He would stand and fill his trunk with water, and blow it into the air, hugely enjoying the copious showers that would descend therefrom upon his dusky hide. It was a good chance for the spectators to "see the elephant."

Chapter 36

The Albemarle

The Civil War continued its ever-escalating blood baths. Cold Harbor and the Wilderness Campaign had been devastating to the Union forces. General Grant was striving diligently to solve the "arithmetic" problem that Old Abe had given him and was throwing everything he had at the rebels. Yet, the "Boys in Gray" were continuing to put up a withering assault. Robert E. Lee was proving himself, arguably, to be the best commander that the country had ever seen. Not only was Lee a brilliant general, but his men worshiped him.

However, the Confederacy's days were numbered. Since Gettysburg, the rebel armies had been pushed further and further back into home territory. And now, General Sherman was leveling everything in his path that might aid the rebellion, moving his huge army south from Tennessee. Thousands of former slaves were following him as he scorched a path through Georgia and closed in on his prize, the city of Atlanta.

A few days after my encounter with Madame V, Uncle Eugene,[68] who had witnessed the battle between the *Monitor* and *Merrimac* and had recently been mustered out of the army, came to Maine for a month in order to visit his family. On the 30th, along with a few other friends and relatives, we met at Uncle James's[69] mother-in-law's home in Hallowell. Uncle Gene, the youngest of my father's siblings, had not seen me since I was four, and I really had never known him. He had left home in his early twenties and became a school teacher in New Jersey. Now, at the ripe old age of thirty-four and still a handsome bachelor, he was about to return to New Jersey to resume his position there.

"I am so sorry to hear about your dear father, my elder brother, John," said Gene, empathetically. "He was a good man."

Charles and I nodded in agreement.

"I stopped at the cemetery to visit his grave and those of the other members of your family. You people have had such great losses since I've been away. Life is so precarious. Here I am, after serving several years in combat, returning basically unscathed. Doesn't seem fair does it?"

"Well," said Charles, "if we are trusting and resigned to His will, I'm sure we will see all things justly accomplished in the end."

"Amen, my dear nephew. Amen. But, sometimes that's hard to remember amidst the trials of this life, is it not?"

"And little Ann!" continued Uncle Gene. "Not so little anymore. A lovely young lady. When I saw you last, you were but a toddling youngster, running through the house following this young gentleman to wherever he might be going," he said, looking at Charles.

"Yes, and I'm not so sure following Charles was my wisest decision," I jested, triggering a few chuckles.

"I was only running so I could escape playing pony," said Charles on the rebuttal. "Of course, I was always the pony."

"Yes, and you were a good pony. Except once, when you bucked me and I hit my head on the piano leg!"

"And you milked that cow for all it was worth! Mother thought I had killed you by the way you carried on. There wasn't even a bump on your head."

"She used to love to get me into trouble," Charles complained, addressing the group. "Then Father would take her to Augusta and buy her a new doll to ease her suffering."

"Yes, I did make out pretty well on that one," I confessed, proudly.

"On a more serious note, Charlie, I hear you've been ill," interjected Gene.

"Yes, I'm afraid that's correct. But I must admit, the summer is paying me much benefit. On clement days, I sit out in our front yard and read."

I nodded. "Yes, and I am his devoted slave. Unfortunately, the emancipation didn't do anything for my bondage," I jested.

"Annie is very kind to me. But she does, at times, force me to eat," declared Charles, with more gratitude than I was expecting.

"Yes. I feed you in order to keep you alive."

"And I eat, despite the suffering it brings me, so that I might devour the books my sister brings me in compensation!" countered Charles, with his usual wit.

"That is our agreement. If he eats, I will find him some new literature."

"That sounds like a profitable exchange," quipped Uncle Gene. "Charles gets an education and you pay his tuition with food installments."

***

Shortly after this exchange, coffee, tea, and biscuits were served, and we all sat around in the parlor waiting to hear some of Uncle Gene's exploits.

He began by recounting his expedition to blow up the *Albemarle*,[70] the now-infamous rebel ironclad ram that was stationed on the Roanoke River. It had been causing a "tremendous amount of mischief" to Union vessels and needed to be put out of commission.

"Let me begin by starting at the end. We never did attack the *Albemarle*, and the behemoth is still lurking out there on that river. I know that's disappointing, but my story is far more entertaining than simply blowing up a Confederate ram.

"First off, we started out in late May, heading towards the mouth of the Roanoke River. There was a picket boat there to alert us, should the *Albemarle* venture into our area. That monster of a vessel had wreaked havoc on several of our ships and was able to traverse the entire river unchallenged. Our commander, Captain John C. Lee of Company I, no relation to Robert E., was considered an expert in torpedo designs and knew just about every type used by the Union or the Confederacy.

"A small ironclad torpedo boat was awaiting us near Roanoke Island. It was encased above the hull in iron, steam-powered, rode low in the water, had a small turret of a wheelhouse, and was easily commandeered by a crew of ten. Nearby lay a discarded wooden vessel, half submerged and lying on its side, our "practice" *Albemarle*.

"Well, these so-called torpedoes are nothing but an iron-encased, water-proof bomb with an inner triggering mechanism connected to a very long thin cable. The explosive device is attached to a long spar, 60 feet in length, which is affixed to the bow. At the tip of this contraption is a barbed spear to be driven into the wooden hull below the water line. After impaling its foe and leaving its "gift," the attacking vessel reverses direction, and when the torpedo boat is at the maximum length of its trigger-cable, the explosive is touched off, and the enemy ship is sent to Davy Jones's locker. At least that's the theory behind the madness. It's a little bit like trying to catch a bald eagle in a box with a stick connected to a pull-string; the only difference being, if something goes wrong, the box doesn't blow you to pieces.

"Just to make things more interesting, the whole mission has to be accomplished at night so as not to be seen by the crew of the *Albemarle*. That means, if there's not enough light from the moon, the operation shouldn't take place. So, Captain Lee decided we should practice with a live torpedo at night, as the moon was nearly full and the weather was mild. But first we needed to learn about the weapon itself.

"The payloads for these things weigh in at 50 to 80 pounds of explosives. In our case, it would need to be closer to 80, due to the hull thickness of our prey. The trigger system is similar to that of a caplock rifle, but modified for the job. Any mishandling can trip the device, so the lock system is never armed until an attack is imminent.

"If flirting with such a device isn't enough to get a sailor free room and board in a lunatic asylum, then operating the torpedo boat will do the trick. Ours was driven by a miniature steam engine that was louder than hell's bells! And, unless the crew of the *Albemarle* was stone-deaf, they'd hear us coming from a mile away. So, let's put this into perspective; in order to fulfill our mission, we needed either a deaf rebel crew or a full moonlit night during a massive thunderstorm. Definitely, a perplexing conundrum.

"After a few dry practice runs, we ate a sumptuous meal of weevils on hardtack and waited for the moon to ascend, so we could try an armed rehearsal. It truly was a glorious, quiet night, interrupted only with a chorus of crickets and bullfrogs. The serenity ended when we started up the *Tambora*, what we lovingly called our boat, named after the volcano whose eruption was heard from a thousand miles away.

"While the craft idled near the shoreline, we gingerly set the lock and trigger of the dangerous payload. One false move in the darkness would have afforded us a face-to-face encounter with Jesus. We advanced across the river, chugging along at a good clip. We could make out the shape of the wreck dead ahead of us in the shadows of the moonlight. Finally, the captain gave the order to let down the spar, which we carried out immediately. At about 50 yards out, Captain Lee tried to cut the engine but the thing wouldn't respond. The boat continued at full speed!

"We were now on a collision course with our target. We held onto anything we could find that was screwed down to brace for impact. The spar hit the wreck hard and snapped off its bracing, inadvertently snagging the trigger cable which caused the cap-lock system to fire. Two seconds later there was an enormous explosion from beneath us! The bow of the *Tambora* lifted several feet out of the water and came crashing down. Bits and pieces of our target flew about us as our vessel rocked precariously from side to side, threatening to capsize. Finally, the boat steadied without taking on water, and the crew, dazed and disoriented, started moving about the deck and down beneath, to check for damage. Fortunately, the only injury was to our pride, resulting from this foolhardy brand of naval warfare.

"The next day, orders came in to cancel our mission. Thanks be to God! Apparently, the rebel ram was at anchor a few miles upriver, and was surrounded by hundreds of logs, protecting it from such an attack.

"One odd thing that happened, proving to be providential, was that three large catfish were killed by the blast and floated to the surface. Two of them weighed more than ten pounds!

Destruction of the *Albemarle* by torpedo boat: Oct. 27, 1864

Needless to say, after ingesting the culinary horrors prior to our fiasco, we now had a feast fit for a king. If nothing else, torpedoes have proven themselves to be superb fishing gear."

The laughter and applause went on for nearly a minute. Papa's brothers all seemed to have his same innate gift for storytelling, a quality that must have captivated Uncle Gene's students in New Jersey.

Chapter 37

Female Soldiers

A female soldier from Maine: Yesterday, a rather perplexed-looking lass was discovered on Belle Isle, disguised, among the prisoners of war held there. She gave her name as Mary Jane Johnson, belonged to the 16th Maine Regiment and had been a prisoner some time … The heroine of a novel yet to be written in "Yankeedom" was considerably sunburned and roughened by the hardships she had encountered but still maintained marks of some womanly comeliness. Upon the discovery of her sex, Miss Johnson was removed from Belle Isle and is confined at Castle Thunder. She is about nineteen years of age.

—*Gardiner Home Journal*, Dec. 24, 1863

"There's no good reason that women can't vote!" I ranted. "I'd cast my ballot for Lincoln in a heartbeat. We can't allow this war to have been fought for nothing!"

"Annie, don't fret," replied Charles, calmly. "The American people will never vote Lincoln out. You know what he said; 'One shouldn't change horses mid-stream.'"

"Yeah, you'd think the voters would have common sense. But have you read some of the editorials? It frightens me. People are becoming weary and they're ready to compromise everything."

"Are you not weary, sis? Even Lincoln is weary," added Charles. "We just lost James Wellman and Gus Collins.[71] I knew them."

"Yes, Charlie, there's a terrible loss of life, but now's not the time to give up. And Pendleton and his Chicago platform want to drag us down that "peace at any price" rabbit hole. People are so stupid!" I barked.

"Careful who you're referrin' to," Charles declared, with a touch of indignation. "It's farm boys like me doing most of the dying, ya know. The draft lets the wealthy pay substitutes so they don't have to take a bullet: 'rich man's war, poor man's fight.' How'd you feel if I'd been drafted and died at Fredericksburg or at some other slaughterhouse?"

"We all know the draft is unfair," I rebutted, "but I wouldn't want your death to have been in vain! If Negro freedom is lost, then Gus and James *did* die for nothing!"

"I agree. But you need to put aside that tendency to generalize your contempt. Put yourself in the shoes of those grieving families. We Goodwins, of all people, should know what that feels like."

I sighed, "You're right. But this election is gonna change the whole course of history, for better or for worse. Eli's ability to move back to the States, reunite with his family, and live a happy life are all riding on it."

"You're preaching to the choir, sis."

"Yes, but who else can I preach to? I'm not yet sixteen. But even if I were sixty, I couldn't make a difference. Women are condemned to the bondage of womanhood!"

"Here we go again. Did you get up on the wrong side of the bed?"

"Yes, Charles. *Here we go again.* Where's all that empathy you're talking about? Try putting yourself in my shoes for once. By the way, my bed is against the wall, so there's only one side I *can* get up on; the 'enslaved-female' side!"

"Oh, kill the drama, sis. I agree, women should have the right to vote. But who do you think make up the majority of those who want peace at any cost? The women! They're the mothers, wives, and lovers who want their men back. They'd vote Lincoln out at the drop of a hat! They're the ones pushing their husbands to vote for McClellan. Don't delude yourself. And by the way, you can always move your bed away from the wall, so you *do* have a choice."

It always infuriated me when he joked about something that I was taking seriously.

"It's not about my bed, Charles. You're making me angry. Are you saying that fathers love their sons less than their mothers do? That the only reason a father might vote for a peace treaty would be to satisfy his nagging wife? That's insane!"

"No. I'm saying that men understand what's at stake more than women do."

"Oh, do they now? I think Mrs. Stowe has a fairly good understanding," I replied. "Let's face it; bad men created this war and other bad men will conclude it with a slave-holding handshake!"

"No, sis. Bad men did start this war, but as we speak, good men are dying to insure that doesn't happen."

"I hope you're right," I responded, with a deep sigh. "I'm just frustrated. I feel helpless."

"*You* feel helpless? Look at me! A consumptive, would-be soldier, a useless farmer who can barely walk to the barn without getting winded," he countered, with an uncharacteristic waver in his voice.

"Charlie, you had no choice. None of this is your fault. And I'm so glad you're here! I don't often say this, but I couldn't have made it without you and your tactless humor."

"Thanks, sis. And I couldn't have made it, either, if you hadn't been here to give me a source for my humor. Anyway," he continued, "rest assured that *I* will be voting for Lincoln."

"You're not old enough, Charles. They'll never let you vote!"

"They certainly will! I'm an adult and rightful heir to the Goodwin fortune," he retorted with a morsel of jest.

"Fortune? Mis-fortune, you mean," I fired back, sarcastically.

"I'm head of this household and a taxpayer," continued Charles.

"Yes, you paid our taxes with Susan's money!"

"They don't care whose money I used, sis. It's on the record. I'm a citizen with the right to vote."

I heaved a deep sigh. It was no use arguing with him.

Then, Charles put his arm around me and whispered, "It may be my last chance to do something of importance, Annie. I've got to vote … or die trying."

One night, a few days prior to the election, Susan and I were awakened by the sound of violent coughing coming from Charles's room. Rushing in, we were both startled to see him sitting on the side of his bed, doubled over a pail, vomiting up a whitish fluid intermingled with blood. We darted to his bedside to comfort him, as his body heaved forcefully, over and over again. Eventually the heaving stopped, followed by the gasping of one suffocating. Within a few minutes he was able to lie back down and I witnessed something I had never seen before, the look of dread on my brother's face.

"My God," he whispered. "My God."

His fever had returned, so I placed a cool, wet cloth on his forehead. Susan gave him some of Dr. Davis's medicine which seemed to relieve the coughing reflex.

Even after two or three days, Charles couldn't revive his appetite, which during the summer had only been mediocre at best. He had to force himself to eat and occasionally vomited up the food when his coughing fits commenced. The fever gradually subsided but his bodily deterioration was alarming. The decline was evidenced by the difficulty he experienced when doing what would normally be effortless tasks. He had trouble walking up the stairwell and had to hold tightly to the railing, became winded after strolling out to the apple trees, and had to ask for assistance when pumping water from the well. It was pitiful.

The most distressing aspect, from his perspective, was its effect on his self-worth. After all, he was still a young man. He felt it his solemn duty to carry on with all those traditional attributes associated with manhood and its responsibilities. Being unable to do farmwork was embarrassing enough, but having to ask someone else (worse still, a woman!) to help him carry two buckets of water from the well, was anathema!

One time, I was summoned to help him bring in some pieces of freshly cut wood to dry in the shed. On arriving at the indoor stack, he dropped the ones he was carrying to the floor. I laughed and said, "Perfect stacking, brother!" Then I followed suit and dropped mine where I stood. It was all in fun.

But Charles didn't find it humorous. He walked hurriedly to his room, slammed the door behind him, and broke into tears amidst terrible consumptive gasps. I rushed up after him and knocked on the door.

"Go away! Just go away!"

"Charlie … " I replied, "I'm sorry for whatever I did. Can I please come in?"

"I don't want to talk to anyone right now, sis. I'm not mad at you. I just need to be alone."

"Please? I wanna help. You're all I have now."

Something in that last interchange persuaded him to allow me to enter.

"What's wrong, big brother?" I asked, closing the door behind me.

"Annie, you'll never understand … you're not a man."

"Well, the latter part's true. But I've always been a good listener."

He sighed wearily. "I don't feel like a man anymore. Hell, I'm not even a little boy, for God's sake!"

"Of course, you're a man, Charles!"

"No, sis. I can't do anything. I can't work, I can't lift. Damn it, I can't even carry a few sticks of wood without losing my breath. That's not a man!"

"Yes! It's a man battling consumption; a man who loves his family; a man like Papa, who's facing a life-threatening foe!"

"Don't compare me to him. He was a hero. I'm nothing."

"What are you saying?" I asked, with exasperation.

"I'm here in the comfort of my home. I'm not out on the open ocean or fighting the rebels. I'm supposed to be managing a farm, but all I can do is sit around until my next coughing fit, and puke into a pail. Real heroic," he spouted, in self-contempt.

"We all have a cross and a mission, Charles. You've said so, yourself."

"I'm a burden, sis. I've become the family's cross, as if they needed another. So, where's the mission?"

"Maybe it's to help Susan, Grandma, and me to learn a deeper self-giving love than we might have known otherwise. Even Jesus had help with his cross."

Charles didn't respond, but his eyes expressed his reflective thoughts.

Early in the morning on Tuesday, November 8, 1864, I heard my brother stirring in his room, so I went in to see if he needed anything. I was stunned to see him up, dressed, and donning his winter coat and top hat.

"Charles Andrew Goodwin, where do you think you're going?" I asked with concern.

"I'm … going … to vote!" he replied, as he convulsively coughed out each word.

"You'll *die* on the way. You're too weak to even make it to the outhouse. No! Absolutely not!"

"Annie, you are not my master. It may be the last thing I do on this earth, but I am going to cast my ballot for Abe. If I die, so be it."

He pushed past me into the hallway and started down the stairwell. Midway, he became dizzy, lost his balance and fell the rest of the way, injuring his wrist and dislocating his right ring finger at the first joint. I nearly fainted when I saw it! I've assisted with the slaughtering of farm animals, and I've even cleaned up bloody vomit, but this was more than I could stand.

I sat down and covered my head with my hands to quiet the onset of nausea. After calm returned, I asked, "Charles, are you all right?" Then I heard a loud snap. I looked up and he was sitting on the floor in front of me, showing me the now-straightened digit.

"That was easy. Popped it right back into place. Feels a little numb, though."

"My God … Charles," I said, with disgust. Then I covered my head with my hands again and took a few more deep breaths.

"It was just a mite dislocated."

"A mite! The thing looked like a carpenter's square! I don't wanna think about it."

"I'm fine," he asserted, trying to rise to his feet and then tumbling back onto the floor. "Or I will be, once the dizziness stops."

I just shook my head. "You're not going anywhere."

Charles sighed in hopeless resignation. "The spirit is willing but the flesh is useless."

We both sat there, on the floor at the base of the stairs, looking at each other like two children that had just lost their favorite toy. Then the answer came to me in a flash, and I glanced over at Charles.

An opponent of Old Abe who was asked by a boy how long the President holds office, replied snappishly, "judging from the present style, I think they will keep old Abe there until hell freezes over." when up spoke the lad, "I guess, then, when Abraham leaves the chair you'll be found under the ice."

"All right, sis, I've seen that look before," he asserted.

"I have it! I'm going to the polls to cast your ballot."

"What?" he exclaimed, amidst more coughing. "Do you have squirrels in your attic? They'll never let you do it."

"Yes, yes they will."

I stood up and helped my brother to his feet. Together, we entered the parlor to compose a permission letter.

I continued, "I'll give the note to Mr. Davenport. He's overseeing the election at the schoolhouse, and he knows us … Well, at least he knew Papa quite well."

"He'll never agree, sis. You're a minor and a female."

"The soldiers are using proxy ballots, Charles, and so can you. Do you really think they care who delivers the votes to the ballot box?"

"Of course they care. Official couriers transfer the ballots, not their fifteen-year-old sisters."

"I am your official courier, dear brother, and you're a soldier battling an enemy. Just write it up, I'll hand over the note, and you will have added your voice to end slavery."

"Old Davenport is a rule follower and he won't go along with your scheme! And … I'm not sure I *can* write. My wrist is starting to ache. You write it, and I'll sign it."

I picked up a pen and in my very best cursive wrote the request, explaining Charles's situation in detail. The finished product looked like a legal document.

"Are you able to scribble your John Hancock on this thing?" I asked, handing him the note.

"Surely. But I think I should use my own name, don't you?" he replied in typical jest.

Then, holding the pen with his injured hand, he slowly signed it, *Charles Goodwin*.

"Annie, if my name's not on the list of voters, how will you convince them that I'm eligible?"

"I'm not sure I can, Charlie. And if they ask me your age, well, I can't lie about that."

My brother handed me the note and then grabbed it back out of my hand!

"You know," he added, thinking out loud, "Susan should be the one to do this. She's a woman, but she's also an adult, and she might actually get the job done!"

"What? If anyone can get it done, I can!" I barked. "I'm insulted! Besides, Susan would never have the gall. She's way too proper! If you want to cast your vote for Lincoln, you sure as hell better give me that note or it'll never happen!"

"That's it. I'll go saddle up and do it myself." Charles made a dash for the kitchen but lost his balance again and fell to the floor, stopping his fall with his injured hand, and almost hitting his head on the iron stove.

I helped him up and walked him over to the sofa. "Oh, Charlie, I'm sorry. This is my fault," I responded, sincerely rethinking my arrogance. "I know it doesn't matter to you how your vote is cast but it means the world to me. Susan *would* have a better chance. It's just that … I want to be a part of this election, too. Let me be your voice."

He demurred for a moment and then handed me the signed paper, "I wouldn't wanna deprive you of this opportunity, sis. Go and secure Eli's freedom!"

"Thank you, Charlie, and say a prayer for me."

Charles nodded, smiled, and settled down on the sofa to rest his aching body.

When I arrived at the schoolhouse, there were a few women and children waiting in carriages for their menfolk to finish voting. Five or six older gentlemen were standing outside the main entry, smoking pipes and conversing about the election. I had hoped to be inconspicuous, but that was impossible now. All eyes fell upon this brazen girl as she headed up the steps! One of the men was Emma's father, and I knew I was going to have to explain my presence to him and his friends. So, I took a deep breath and proceeded.

"Annie!" said Mr. French, "are you voting for Mr. Lincoln today?" The others laughed playfully at his suggestion.

"Yes, I am, sir. I thought it about time for young ladies to get in on the excitement," I replied, having decided to play along.

"Well, good for you!" he replied with a smile.

"Actually, my brother is quite ill, and I'm hoping to cast his ballot for him."

"Oh, I'm sorry to hear that. Emma thinks the world of him. I hope he recovers soon."

"Thank you, sir. I will give him your kind regards."

"Please do. And good luck in there with old man Davenport. He can be a real stickler when it comes to rules and all."

"I'll do my best."

"I'm sure you will, Annie. Take care now."

There was a short line of men approaching the two ballot boxes, with Mr. Davenport seated near them, watching every move. Ballots, at that time, were anything but secret; one box was for Lincoln and the Republicans, and the other was for McClellan and the Democratic Party. People could obviously see which person you were voting for. Also, you couldn't split your ticket and vote for one Democrat and one Republican, as these ballots were "unity tickets". You either voted straight Republican or Democrat. The 1864 election was the last unity-ticket election in our country.

It took less than a minute for the men ahead of me to cast their votes: three for Lincoln and two for McClellan. Then it was my turn to approach the formidable Mr. Davenport. Fortunately, no one had come in behind me, so I felt free to explain myself in a calm manner.

"And what can I do for you, miss?" he asked, with a formal tone.

"I've come to cast my brother's ballot for him, sir. He's very sick," I replied, in a pleading tone.

"Miss, I'm sorry, but I can't allow you to do that. Is your brother in uniform?"

"No, sir. He's sick at home. He attempted to come here this morning but collapsed on the stairwell." At that point my eyes were beginning to tear up. "He asked me to come here in his stead. Look, here's a note that I wrote for him. He was too weak to write it himself, but he did sign it."

Mr. Davenport pulled a pair of eyeglasses from his shirt pocket and perused the note.

"You're John Goodwin's daughter, aren't you?" he asked, still examining Charles's note. "A good man. Always willing to lend a hand when you need one."

"Yes, sir, he was. Regrettably, Father was lost at sea back in April."

"Yes, I heard, dear. A tragic loss."

Mr. Davenport picked up the ledger of Chelsea voters and began searching for my brother's name which I was sure wasn't on it. I held my breath as he turned the pages.

Finally, his index finger came to rest somewhere near the bottom of a page. He then looked up at me over his wired spectacles and asked, "And what is your brother's middle name?"

"Andrew, sir," I replied. "Charles Andrew Goodwin."

"Well, here he is," he said, turning the ledge towards me.

I was stunned with this revelation and my heart was beating like a military drum.

Mr. Davenport began looking cautiously around the room, as though scouting the horizon for prying eyes. Then he leaned over and whispered, "Put the ballot in the box, dear, and I'll cross your brother's name off the list."

"Oh, thank you, sir," I whispered back, with a deep sigh of relief. Then, with a trembling hand, I dropped a ballot into the receptacle marked Lincoln-Johnson. As I walked towards the exit, I turned to thank him with a big smile. He placed his index finger to his lips, implying the secrecy of our encounter, then returned the smile. On the way home I wept tears of joy. How Charlie's name ever came to appear on that roster I'll never know. But, I had just voted for Abraham Lincoln! It would be the first and last time in my life that I would have such a privilege.

Chapter 38

Cannon Fire

I was chomping at the bit to recount my "adventures in women's suffrage" to my brother. However, when I returned home, he had fallen asleep on the sofa, and his finger, hand, and forearm were wrapped in a makeshift bandage. Susan explained that the previously dislocated digit and wrist injury were swollen and aching. Thankfully, the wrist remained flexible and showed no signs of a break. Charles's breathing was heavy and often interrupted with intermittent snoring, but at least he was sleeping, a much needed respite from those frightening nocturnal coughing fits!

The next morning, at daybreak, we were awakened by the sound of cannon fire coming from the direction of the river. The window panes rattled with each burst. I ran into the hallway and opened the dormer window. Was the *Albemarle* coming up the Kennebec? Charles, who had put in another difficult night with his injuries and frequent coughing, joined Susan and me as we listened. Soon, fainter explosions were heard coming from Augusta, and then from the Gardiner area, then more from Hallowell.

We noticed Mr. William Searles, a former selectman, riding by the house.

"What is going on Mr. Searles, are the rebels attacking?" I yelled.

He gave a hearty laugh and shouted, "No, no, no … Mr. Lincoln won reelection! There's gonna be a humdinger of a celebration in Augusta this afternoon! The boys in blue pushed him over the top, thanks be to God!"

The three of us cheered and embraced one another! The relief and jubilation of that news was indescribable. My fear that Eli might have to remain a fugitive flew out the dormer window on that chilly November morning.

During the afternoon, Mr. Potter called to see how we were faring. He brought us some fresh bread and strawberry jam from Mean's Bakery in Hallowell. It was both a kind and timely gesture, as Susan and I were preparing to bake bread, having run out that morning. Our guest had just returned from the festivities in Augusta, and was clearly relieved by the outcome of the election. Predictably, our conversation centered around Lincoln's second term and my brother's relentless battle with tuberculosis. Charles, though exhausted, did manage to join us for a few minutes and then retired to his new, more convenient residence in the summer kitchen. There, he could lie down, absorb plenty of sunlight from the southern exposure, take care of necessities, and not have to risk falling on the stairwell again.

"Mrs. Goodwin," Alden inquired, "what is your opinion of Lincoln's choice for vice president?"

"Well, Mr. Potter … "

"Please … Call me Alden."

"Of course … and I prefer Susan, as well. We're in Chelsea. Formality is against the law here."

"Thank God! I spend my day in a shipyard. Formality and sometimes even clean conversation are rare birds … on the verge of extinction, I fear."

"Yes," she chuckled, "I'm well aware. But too much attention to propriety can inhibit self-expression, don't you think?" Susan asked.

"The men at my workplace have no inhibitions about self-expression, I assure you!" retorted Alden, smiling. "A few restraints might serve them better."

"Oh, I've lived my life among sailors … and when the rum is flowing freely … well …" she chuckled. "To answer your question, Alden, when this ordeal is over, there are going to be many changes in the wind. Millions of former slaves will need education, jobs, and homes. And there will be deep-seated wounds that must be healed. Abe will need a faithful Southerner like Andy Johnson at his side if he wants to bring about a "new birth of freedom" and if he wants to insure "that this government of, by, and for the people does not perish from the earth."

It seems to us that the result of the election must satisfy the rebels that there is no hope for them except in submission. Mr. Lincoln has certainly been elected on an uncompromising war platform, and of his opponents not a majority, we think, are for peace, except on the basis of a restored Union. We hope that now the excitement of this political contest is over, that the whole energies of the country will be united on a vigorous prosecution of the war, and that a speedy peace may gladden the hearts of both Democrats and Unionists.

"Yes, well said! You certainly *do* know your Lincoln."

"And shouldn't we all? Such a master of oratory."

"Without a doubt. And your assessment of Mr. Johnson is a fair one."

"To be honest," Susan reflected, candidly, "my selfish pride would have preferred our Hannibal Hamlin, being from Maine and all. But Lincoln does what's best for the country, not what pleases my whims."

Alden nodded.

Naturally, I had to jump into the conversation. Turning sideways and looking directly at Alden, I boasted, "I voted for Mr. Lincoln, yesterday!"

"What?" he responded, in a somewhat startled voice.

"Yes, sir." Susan affirmed. "She did cast a vote for Honest Abe … in a manner of speaking."

I then explained the whole incident to Alden, who thought it quite interesting, amusing, and a rather bold undertaking.

On finishing my story, he responded, "You know, Miss Annie, you really did cast a vote that never would have been counted otherwise. And your selectman was wise to allow you to do it."

"Yes, but my heart was beating out of my chest as I walked into that schoolhouse."

"But you did it! Something to be proud of."

Susan patted me on the back, and I glanced away with childish embarrassment. At that moment, Grandma entered in an unusually jovial mood, and greeted Alden. "Annie takes after her grandmother, she does. If a soldier falls in battle, she picks up the rifle and carries on! And I'd say it's 'bout time to feed the troops some of that bread and jam, wouldn't you?"

"Yes," replied Susan, "I was just going to make coffee."

"Let me help ya dear," insisted Grandma, who never allowed anyone else to make the brew if she was within a mile of the kitchen. Hers was the very best, and she'd tell you so!

I was somewhat uncomfortable being left alone in Mr. Potter's company, wondering what to talk about. But that concern was quickly remedied.

"So, Miss Annie, have you ever wondered about names?" asked Alden.

"I'm sorry, what?" I responded, somewhat bewildered.

He chuckled, "Oh, forgive me. I have a deplorable habit of wandering off the trail."

"Oh, please feel free to wander. Names? Hmm … less depressing than civil war, death, or consumption," I commented, with whimsical morosity.

Alden smiled at my feeble attempt at wit. Then he asked, "Have you ever thought how a surname often reflects a certain truth about the person who owns it?"

"Ahh … "

"Let me explain. Let's explore the possible roots of your family name, Goodwin. That could have been derived, centuries ago, perhaps, by sailors that depended on a 'good wind'. So, it might explain why many in your family are mariners, mightn't it?"

"A good guess, Mr. Potter … Alden," I replied, with a smirk. "I personally believe that the name Goodwin is a derivative from 'good' and 'wine'. We seem to have had our share of drunks and mariners. Some ancestors were gifted with both qualities!"

Alden smiled.

"And what about your last name?" I asked. "Are you a potter, Mr. Potter?"

"No, but there have been many ceramic artisans in my family."

"That *is* curious. But there are plenty of names that don't seem to describe anything at all, like Lincoln."

"It's not self-explanatory like Potter. But Abe's ancestors may have come from a place, such as Lincolnshire County in England. Some surnames might be contractions from one or more Old English words or have French origins that stem from the days of the Norman Conquest."

"Our neighbor, Mr. Blanchard, tells us his surname is common in Quebec, but his ancestors are all from the British Isles."

"Exactly."

"What about the Littlefields?" I proposed. "They originally owned all the land from the river to the County Road. I guess their name should have been 'Bigfields!'"

"Or, maybe the original name was Field, and soon Mrs. Field gave birth to some little Fields, and the name stuck!"

By the time we were done with this nonsense, our coffee, bread, and jam were ready, and we all headed to the kitchen table and enjoyed our small lunch.

"What are you two tee-heein' about?" asked Grandma. "Sounds like a coupl'a cacklin' hens! Not complainin' mind ya. Lord knows, laughter's been scarce as a five-leaf clover 'round here."

"We've been discussing how families get their surnames, like Potter, for instance. Alden has several ancestors who *were* potters. How about your middle name Susan? I'm sure Alden would like to make a guess as to its origin.

"Annie Elizabeth Goodwin! Shame on you! If you must know, Mr. Potter, my middle name is *Thwing*, Susan Thwing Goodwin. It was my mother's maiden name. That noble title was probably coined by some boozed-up coot who couldn't talk straight!"

We could all hear Charles laughing himself into a stupor from two rooms away. Susan yelled, "Charles Andrew Goodwin, shut your yap before I come in and do it for ya! You're supposed to be sick."

None of us were able to avoid the comical contagion of the moment. It was all in good fun, and Susan enjoyed playing it to the hilt. Then she set us straight on this noble surname.

"In all seriousness, *thwing* is a Viking word that comes from the East Yorkshire area of England. It means "a narrow strip of land". I hope you are all impressed with my scholarly research."

"That's fascinating. I am impressed!" I responded. "It's a common name around here. The pronunciation differs from family to family. The pronunciations I've heard are: Thwing, Thing, or Ting."

"Thank you for clearing that up, dear," remarked Susan. "But I'm not sure being a Thing is any better than being a Thwing."

Another roar of hysterical guffaws emanated from the infirmary.

The name game continued a while until Grandma changed the subject. "Perhaps Alden could tell us a bit about himself, now that we've revealed all our sordid family origins."

"About myself, hmm … Well, I was born in Georgetown, Maine, on Valentine's day. Unfortunately, like your beloved Sarah, my mother, Jane Morse Potter, died of childbed fever just a few weeks after giving birth to me, so I never knew her. She was only twenty-one." he said, pausing

Working in the interior of a vessel. *Harper's Monthly,* 1862

reminiscently. "My Papa says she was a beautiful woman in every way.

"The poor man had to raise me by himself, for the most part. However, four years later he remarried, Pamela Gilmore, a very kind soul and the only mother I've ever known. She bore me two sisters, Jennie and Sarah, and two brothers, Edward and William. Fortunately, they are all alive and in good health.

"My cousin Seth, a deepwater whaleman, helped pique my interest in seaworthy vessels. He knew a good ship when he saw one, right down to the last detail. I was already a fair carpenter, and through his influence, he brought me into the shipbuilding trade. I'm a joiner at William V. Moses & Sons in Bath, right at the bottom of Pearl Street. Easy to find, just follow the cussin'," chuckled Alden.

"So, Mr. Potter," I interrupted, "what is a joiner?"

"Oh, of course. Well, many think that I'm a carpenter, and I certainly do a great deal of carpentry. But a joiner is someone who uses wood, rather than metal, to bind wooden objects together. Older homes, for instance, are joined with wooden pegs and dovetailing techniques.

"My specialty is creating the wooden interiors of vessels. As you might imagine, each ship is different and has unique bends, curves, and angles for which structures must be precisely fitted. Wood is the best material for sailing crafts because it doesn't rust, swells as a unit when wet, and contracts as a unit when drying. And of course, there's plenty of fluctuating humidity on the ocean. If I must use nails of any kind, I use treenails made from the same wood as the rest of the structure that I'm constructing. Metal fasteners resist changes in the wood, and over time, can create cracks and loose joints. We don't want the living quarters of the crew to fall apart halfway across the Pacific! Then again, with the advent of ironclads, we may have to start thinking about ship-building in a different light. My skills may have to evolve.

"I'm currently doing an apprenticeship to become a pattern maker, which is a step up from joiner. It would mean better pay, and I would be designing aspects of the vessels and even creating wooden models to be approved by our master shipbuilder."

"Like an inventor?" asked Susan.

"More like a modifier. Making changes in ways that better adapt to the individual vessel we're constructing."

At that point, Alden realized he would have to leave soon or miss the train back to Bath.

We thanked him for his thoughtfulness and asked him to visit again. "Please feel free to drop in anytime," said Grandma, who had recovered her ability to laugh again during his stay. His presence had been a breath of fresh air for all of us. There was truly something singular about him.

Chapter 39

"I think I'm becoming a god!"

The next day, Charles was back in bed with a fever and heavy coughing. We had learned to distinguish the seriousness of his condition by the type of cough he was experiencing. There was the "barking," as I called it, which sounded somewhat like the yap of a dog. It was a sharp and percussive cough that usually happened when he was first waking, though it sometimes happened in the middle of the night. Although this type was alarming at first, it often ceased after a few minutes. The second type, which could be more serious, was the "wheezing" cough. This cough, though not as distressing to the ear, was accompanied by a hissing sound from deep in his chest. It meant that the airways to his lungs were partially blocked. When this happened he might need to change positions, or have to bend over completely, to clear out the tubes where the fluid was lodging. The last, and most severe, was subtle and started out sounding much like a steam engine starting up. It had a chugging, gurgling, hollow sound as Charles tried desperately to expel the fluid deep within his lungs. This was of the type where hemorrhaging and choking were most likely to occur. The most frightening aspect of this symptom was that his face sometimes turned blue from lack of oxygen, requiring us to pound on his back or chest to help clear the airways.

Susan, Grandma, and I listened carefully at night, keeping all the doors to our bedchambers open. Now that he was residing in the summer kitchen he was supplied with a hammer to summon us by pounding on the cast iron stove. At times he would surprise us and have a few days that approached normalcy. Then he would be back in bed with fever, sweats, and that horrible cough. Alarmingly, the frequency and duration of his good days were getting fewer and shorter.

I had grown exceedingly close to Charles, and I could feel the curtain closing on our time together. Our interests had converged over the years, and it is safe to say that he had become, in many ways, saintly. He never complained and, if anything, joked about his miserable condition.

One time he was reading about the Roman emperors and came across a section concerning the witty Vespasian who often made fun of the Roman populace who deified their rulers when they died. As the story goes, Vespasian was nearing death, and while sitting in the "imperial outhouse," he remarked, "I think I'm becoming a god!" From that point, every time Charles had a bad spell and wanted to cheer us up by minimizing his illness, he would say, "Don't worry, I'm becoming a god."

A telltale piece of evidence that illustrated his declining health was when he began asking me to read to him. Anything historical or religious was the perfect antidote for all ills. I could choose any book I wanted, until the last part of our session. The final selection had to be something for him to contemplate, often from *Holy Scripture* or *The Imitation of Christ*.

One night, in a moment of unusual candor, his eyes revealing an abyss of suffering and love, he turned and said, "Soon, I won't need the Imitation. I'll be with the real one."

His words thrust a dagger into my heart, and I fell to my knees at his bedside.

"What terrible sorrow we have known, big brother. What grief. Dear God, how much more?" I pleaded. "Seven empty places at the table, Charlie. Seven! What wrong have we done that we should be punished so thoroughly?"

Charles wrapped his bony arms around me. "Annie, hush … calm now. Don't forget the blessings that have been given, time after time with each passing. We have never gone through the fire without a quenching rain from the Divinity, as Edith would say."

"But were those truly from heaven, Charles?"

"You're frightening me, sis!" exclaimed Charles, forcing a grin. "You're sounding more and more like me, not so long ago. We didn't imagine smelling those flowers when Lilly died. That wasn't the power of suggestion. It was real and completely unexpected! That prodigy consumed my thoughts for weeks, and I was never able to dismiss it for anything other than what it was … a plain, bonafide miracle."

I sighed, tearfully. "It *was* extraordinary. But does such an event say anything about the existence of eternal life? See how pigheaded I am! These things are never quite enough." I sighed. "I don't know what it's gonna take, but I can't bear another loss … especially if it's you."

December, which used to be a festive time in the advent of Christmas, seemed bleak and almost meaningless. I often sat in my little room like a prisoner in her cell, watching the snowflakes glide to their anonymous destiny, their unique beauty, a veiled reminder of our own temporal flash of existence. The myriad of frost designs on my window that used to charm me, were now reminders of the cold, bitter earth, where we all, too soon, would abide. Darkness was creeping into my soul, and things that had formerly brought me joy became bitter reminders of cherished things lost. The war was dragging on with the interminable lists of deceased, wounded, and missing, written up in gory detail in every newspaper in the land. In some ways, I was beginning to envy the dead. The idea of eternal rest seemed comforting at times, with or without an afterlife.

The ever-present routine of daily chores was my only salvation from insanity. But even the thought of descending into a world of irreversible illusion was no longer frightening. It beckoned like a welcomed friend. Perhaps, for some individuals, bedlam is a better world than the stark, continuous horror that the sane must endure.

Milking the cows, feeding and exercising the horses, going to market with Susan, making meals, reading to Charles, journaling, and tidying up around the house, provided little distraction from the empty pain. Nighttime was the worst, when the shadows of what could have been returned as phantoms to guard the door of my soul, making sure that no light should enter. I couldn't run away from myself. Charles was convinced that I was undergoing the mystical Dark Night of the Soul, something alluded to in the *Imitation*. But, I believe it was just the perpetual umbra of death that plainly displayed itself in the expanding row of marble stones at Chelsea Heights.

My brother was spending more and more time in bed, and his body was wasting away. One afternoon, having been feverish and perspiring heavily, he took off his nightshirt revealing every bone in his back in anatomical detail. I couldn't erase that image from my mind. "That's what he'll look like in the grave," I thought. It reminded me of some disturbing images I'd seen in a Mathew Brady photo exhibit at the Augusta State House. Some were of soldiers who had been rescued from a Confederate prisoner-of-war encampment. Those poor souls were nothing more than two sunken eyes in a skull sitting atop of a skeleton. Yet, they were still alive, if you can call it that. My poor brother was beginning to resemble them, and it was heartbreaking. But his sense of humor and lovable personality had not been consumed! In fact, those qualities seemed to be growing richer in the soil of continual suffering. Such were the true markers of his deep faith. I wish I could have said as much for my own.

Providentially, my dear friend Emma began to be a regular visitor at our home and tried her best to cheer me. She sensed the worry and melancholy that gripped my spirit, and understood the pain, as she had also been twice touched by grief's cold hand. She willingly stayed overnight whenever possible, making those ghostly winter evenings bearable. We talked and reminisced about our adventures as youngsters, which seemed to have been in another lifetime.

Charles appreciated her presence and seemed disappointed when for one reason or another, she couldn't stay. Emma was helpful and often did my chores, voluntarily, so I could spend time reading to Charles. How very much I cherished those opportunities to be with my sickly brother, whose sands were quickly running out.

Just before Christmas, Charles had a very bad spell, and we were sure he would not live to see the arrival of 1865. He alerted us by banging the hammer against the stove. Emma and I awoke with a start and raced down the stairs, followed by Susan. Grandma arrived a few moments later. His pillow was drenched in sweat and blood and he was gasping for air, and there was a horrible sound in his chest that reminded me of the bellows of a furnace. Susan, Emma, and I flipped him over on his belly, as that position had given him some relief in the past. This time, however, it seemed to make things worse, so we moved him into an upright position on his bed. He started to turn blue right before our eyes! I, who had been composed during previous episodes, became a madwoman! I screamed at Emma and Susan, "Do something to help him, goddammit! Do something!" I began to pound my poor brother on the back to loosen up that vile substance that was strangling him. Then delirium began to set in. His fever was raging as I put my hand to his temple. Emma ran to get a cold, wet cloth to apply to his forehead. Nothing seemed to help him. He was leaving us.

"Where are you, God?" I screamed, as I drummed on Charle's back. "Is this what you call mercy! Is this how you treat your children?"

"Annie, don't say such things!" Emma reprimanded. " God hears you."

"Does He, Emma? Does He?"

Emma said nothing else. She and Susan held Charles at a slight angle while I, almost out of my mind, continued to hammer his back with the palms of my hands. Suddenly, his eyes began to roll in his head and his body became limp. He was going unconscious! We laid him on his side, and Susan ran to get smelling salts, hoping that might revive him. After placing the salts near his nostrils he began to gasp. A tremendous amount of fluid came out of his mouth, and he began to breathe again. For the moment, he was back among the living.

As soon as my brother was comfortable, I collapsed on the floor and began to rock back and forth, crying like a baby. "I'm so sorry. I'm so sorry," I moaned. Susan and Emma knelt down and wrapped their arms around me, telling me how much they loved me and that they understood.

"I cursed you," I cried, "when you've both been so kind to me and Charles. What's wrong with me? What's wrong with me? I even mocked our Lord!" I then felt a warm, gentle hand on my head. I turned around and it was my brother, reaching out to me from his sickbed. He smiled softly and looked me in the eye. "It's OK," he whispered. "He understands."

His touch absolved me of my crimes like a tiny raindrop being consumed in an ocean. It was unlike anything I have ever experienced before or since. We all retired for the night and the next thing I remember was waking up to a beautiful sunrise after an unusually peaceful sleep. It was Christmas Eve morning, and my brother had rallied again overnight in his tenacious struggle for life.

———

Like Scrooge, after his visit from the three spirits, I resolved to make this Christmas a meaningful one, especially for Charles. Being acutely aware that this might be his last one, Emma, Susan, and I cut down an elegant spruce and decorated it in complementary fashion. It was the fullest tree to ever adorn the interior of our home, and it looked as though it had been tended by a skilled arborist.

Charles did the honors of lighting the candles. Taking a match from the metal container, he applied the flame to each of the twenty-five tapers with his frail, trembling hand. The tree had a transcendent quality that seemed to unite past and present with love, joy, and continuity.

Inspired by the nostalgic glow, I walked over to the piano and sight-read my way through "O Tannenbaum." Even my brother tried to eke out a whisper of melody. Then we moved on to many of the old stand-bys. Though I'd never played most of them before, my fingers seemed to know just where to go! I was quite proud of myself.

We had only just begun singing the first verse of "O Come All Ye Faithful," when all at once, the present moment seemed to be suspended and the veil lifted! I could hear the voices of Bella and the rest of my siblings, along with Mother's sweet soprano voice, hovering high above Father's sonorous baritone. We each experienced the anomaly and looked at one another in curious wonder. It was probably a result of the acoustics or the familial similarity of our combined voices, but Charles was a believer. He stated, dryly, "Of course they were singing with us, it's Christmas Eve."

After the sing-along, we prepared for our traditional readings and sharings. For these festivities, Susan brought in some fancy frosted gingerbread cookies that she had baked, as well as some hot apple cider topped with cinnamon. Once settled in, Charles asked me to read Hans Christian Andersen's "Little Match Girl," which I found a most depressing tale, especially in light of my brother's unlikely prospects of recovery. But I had vowed to make this a special night for him, so I read the heart-wrenching story from beginning to end. While struggling through the last section of this disturbing tale, where the little girl lights the last match in her futile attempt to keep from freezing to death, my eyes were so clouded with tears I could barely make out the words on the page.

Afterwards, Susan lightened the atmosphere with her reading of *A Christmas Carol.* So many memories surround this story of repentance. I ca As my time n still hear Mother's gentle voice and Father's creepy moaning as the Ghost of Christmas Yet to Come. Even Grandpa Kean read it, the winter before Auntie Belle passed. Now it was Susan's turn.

On finishing that masterpiece of redemption, she asked us to discuss the character who spoke to us, and why. It was like one of Miss Hunt's assignments, but fortunately, there would be no marks attached. Susan broke out the wine, made a toast to 1865, and we took turns, in an abundance of good cheer, sharing our thoughts on the most meaningful Dickens' characters. But Charles seemed quietly distracted and never joined in, which was more than unusual during family gatherings.

"Charlie, are you all right," I asked, with some concern.

"Yes. I'm just thinking about what I'm gonna say."

"About the story?"

"Yes … and …" He stopped himself, and then added, "I have a lot on my mind, sis."

"Oh, I understand, big brother. You don't have to say anything if you don't want to."

"Annie, this is my hour. What I say tonight needs to be remembered."

The weight of those words left me without a response.

Finally, during a lull in the merriment, Charles began, "I'm sure it comes as no surprise that my choice would be Tiny Tim, but not for the reasons you might think," he began. "Yes, we both have life-threatening illnesses, but my affinity for this young lad is based on something deeper. It's his acceptance of illness that I envy. He's not angry or sad but, rather, sees his plight as an advantage. He wants his sufferings to bring others to Christ. And I wish that for my own, as well.

"As my time grows nearer, and let's not fool ourselves as it will be soon, I find myself willingly leaving behind more and more of the world and its treasures. And though I once feared the word *consumption* due to my attachment to this life, I can now say, 'Thy will be done.' I am not ignorant of what awaits me. I've read the medical journals and well remember our dear Auntie Belle's trial by fire. I'm ready. I've bought my train ticket and I know the destination."

Charles then made an unusual and touching request.

"I want to ask a favor of you," he began, acknowledging each of us with a smile. "I have mentioned this before, and I will ask again, as a reminder. If you should place a marker over my mortal remains, I only want five words written upon it."

"Charles!" I gasped, wrapping my arms around him.

My brother continued, "'He fell asleep in Jesus.' Nothing more, nothing less. Everything else is vanity to me now."

"I've written a little something for this occasion." He fumbled to put on his reading glasses, which had become necessary due to his failing vision. He then removed a piece of paper, unfolded it, and began to read.

In my heart I have knelt with the shepherds in the fields of Bethlehem and
 asked
what gift I should bring to lay before the Christ child. I prayed thus;
"Father in heaven, I will be a farmer and give the gift of my labor."
He replied, "No, that is not yours to give."
"Father in heaven, I will be a soldier and free the black man from slavery."
He replied, "No, that is not yours to give."
"Father in heaven, I will be a husband and raise a devout family."
Again, He replied, "No, that is not your gift to give."
In despair, I bowed my head, saying, "Father, I have nothing left to offer but
 my love and suffering."
And He replied, "Yes! That is your gift!
And a worthy offering it is!
For now you resemble my Son.
Go. Lay your gift before Him."

Grandma, Susan, and I sat there, speechless, overcome with emotion.

There followed a deep, blue silence that lasted a full minute as his words penetrated our hearts. He was trying to prepare us, knowing full well that I would be the one most shattered by his death. How I would miss his companionship, his love, and even those inappropriate, ill-timed jokes that he so loved to tell.

He must have been reading my thoughts when he finally broke the silence. Looking at me with a twinkle in his eye, he asked, "Annie, how does one make God laugh?"

"I don't know, Charlie," I replied. "How does one make God laugh?"

"Tell Him your plans, sis! Tell Him your plans."

Chapter 40

Smitten

———

*C*hristmas Day dawned with a magenta eastern sky. There had been a light snowfall overnight that gave our fields an unblemished coat of pure white satin. The only markings disturbing the pristine wonderland were the tracks of three deer that had passed by our doorstep sometime earlier. I quietly crept downstairs just after the tall clock struck half-past six. Blanket in hand, I curled up in Father's old wing chair. Though it was very cool in the house, it wasn't unbearably so, as some heat was coming in through the summer kitchen where Charles, being well enough, had stoked the wood-stove throughout the night. There was a small furnace in the parlor beside me, but I didn't want to start it up. It was just too cozy a moment to ruin it by the clanking of that iron door with one of my, often futile, attempts to get the thing started. Perhaps I was just lazy, but it was permissible to be lazy on Christmas morning. Sky jumped up on my lap, wrapped herself into a ball of fluff and fell asleep. She was probably exhausted from chasing the mice that were migrating indoors to live in the warm walls behind the stove. You could hear them scampering along the beams between the plastered walls. Occasionally, I heard the faint sound of sleigh bells jingling along the road in that outdoors wonderland. Soon, succumbing to this idyllic spell, I fell asleep.

The next thing I knew, the clock struck nine and there was a loud knocking at the side door. Susan, who was up and baking cookies, ran to the door, and I flew swiftly to my room so as not to be caught in my nightgown. While dressing, I could hear a muffled male voice which I could not, at first, identify. Soon, I recognized that it was Mr. Potter. After I finished making myself presentable, I went down to greet him in the sitting room. Both Grandma and Susan were there, as well.

"Merry Christmas, Miss Annie," he exclaimed. "I have some trifles that I picked up at Wight's in Augusta."

"Wights, that sounds familiar," reflected Susan.

"It's on the corner of Water and Bridge … the one near the railway. It's a millinery."

"Oh yes," remarked Susan, "Annie and I have been there. She's a very nice woman, with quite an abundance of beautiful merchandise, but no trifles that I can remember."

I nodded in agreement.

He had with him three medium-sized cardboard boxes, and he handed one to each of us. I opened mine ahead of the others.

After opening the box, I declared, "Oh my, Mr. Potter … This is far too lovely to adorn my head!"

"If anything, Miss Goodwin, it's far too plain. Hopefully, the size is correct, but I can always return it for modifications. And, please, call me Alden," he reminded me, with a smile.

"Oh yes, Alden … what a beautiful bonnet. It fits perfectly!" I exclaimed. "Thank you so very much."

The bonnet was a deep twilight blue and had a buckram brim covered with a silky floss. The crown was of a lighter blue silk and adorned with braids. The brim sat slightly forward of center on the wearer's head, which was the fashion of the time period. Susan and Grandma also received similar bonnets, but of different hues, burgundy and olive, respectively.

"Oh my goodness, Alden," said Susan, in an almost pleading tone, "Why on earth would you honor us so? These must have cost you a small fortune. They're exquisite."

"Thank you. I'm glad you like them. Don't worry about the price. They are much cheaper when you buy them by the dozen!" he chided. "Oh, yes. I have something for Charles, too."

"Oh, that's wonderful! He'll look splendid in one of these. Pink is his color," I said, laughing at the mental image.

"Oh dear," chuckled Alden, "I got him something else. Do you think he'll be disappointed?"

"I think he'll be relieved," I replied. "He's never liked to be conspicuous in a crowd."

"How is he faring?" whispered Alden, trying not to be overheard by Charles, who was just stirring in the kitchen.

"He's seen better days," answered Susan.

I added, "Yes, we nearly lost him a few nights ago."

"Oh my, I'm so sorry to hear that. He's such a wonderful young man. I brought him a book. Is he able to read, or perhaps, too frail?"

"Able, but not for extended periods, I'm afraid," Susan replied. "His eyesight fails him, at times."

"I read to him every day," I added. "He adores books, newspapers, anything that adds to his knowledge. It helps him keep his mind off his troubles."

"Wonderful! You are such a kind young lady. I hope he appreciates your affection."

"Oh he does. But, really, it's no chore; it's a privilege," I responded.

"Reading is a wonderful way to spend one's leisurely hours, don't you think?"

"Most certainly," he replied. "I read anything and everything I can find about seafaring. That's my passion."

"That goes along with your work, Mr. Potter," added Susan. "You're fortunate to be employed in a trade that you so much enjoy."

"Yes, I thank the good Lord everyday for His providence. I've acquaintances who work the mills from dawn 'til dusk for very little pay. They hate their work, but they have to eat. Even young children can be found operating dangerous machinery in these places. Seems like every week I read of some gruesome accident involving a little one. It's very troubling. But it's Christmas day, so I won't carry us down that melancholy track. It's a time for rejoicing with good company."

"So what book did you buy for our Charles?" inquired Grandma.

"Oh, it's right here. It is a new publication about the black race. Here, let me take it out of the wrappings. It's called *The Black Man: His antecedents, His genius, and His achievements* by William Wells Brown. Published last year, appropriately, with the Emancipation and all. I understand Charles has a very good friend who escaped slavery through the Underground, with your help."

"It was all my daughter's doin', God rest her," responded Isabel. "She was a devout member of the cause and knew every safe house in the area. But Charlie, well, he was the one who fished Eli out of the Kennebec. He was a keeper," joked Isabel.

"Mother taught him to read and write," I added. "By the time he left, he was quite articulate in his prose. His handwriting was nye as good as my own, all accomplished in a few short months! So much for blacks not being as gifted as whites."

"Good point. I would love to meet him sometime," remarked Alden.

As we were discussing Eli's involvement in the attack on Fort Wagner and his injuries, Charles entered the room and greeted Alden. I could see, by the expression on Mr. Potter's face, that he was taken aback by my brother's emaciated appearance. Charles, due to dizzy spells, had to guide his steps by securing his hand to the furniture, and occasionally employed a cane for balance. After carefully navigating his way to a cushioned chair he sat down with us.

"Charles, we could have come to your room," insisted Alden.

"Alden," replied Charles, as they greeted each other with a handshake, "it's good for me to get up and move around. The more I exercise, the longer I stay above ground."

Alden smiled, stifling a chuckle, at Charles's self-directed dark humor.

"Brother," I sighed, "you're so morbid."

"Feel free to laugh, Mr. Potter. My brother has a morose sense of humor, and he'd be highly disappointed if he didn't get a response of some kind."

"Well, I wasn't sure that I should."

Charles looked up at Alden with a sly smile and a nod of approval.

"Anyway, big brother, Alden has a gift for you."

Alden had rewrapped the book and gave it to Charles. "Oh, thank you, sir!" replied Charles with gratitude, removing the wrappings.

"Excellent! This book has been highly acclaimed!" declared Charles. "I had no idea it was available in this area."

"I picked it up in Bath," replied Alden. "The shopkeeper told me he was having a difficult time getting the book or keeping it on the shelves. I guess it's quite popular, at least here in the North."

"Well, that is good news. There are so many lies circulating. The biggest whopper is that blacks are not equal, in ability, to whites. I hope this will be widely read, especially by our deceived brethren."

"You can always pass it on once you've read it. Then others can come to their senses," asserted Susan.

Charles began to respond but, unexpectedly, went into a violent coughing fit that went on, continuously, for nearly five minutes! He spit up a small quantity of blood, mixed with the usual fluid that often clogged his breathing passageways. Finally, he stopped and normal breathing returned; though his face was gaunt and pallid.

"Charles, did you take your elixir?" I asked. Then turning to Alden, I continued, "His cough is never that severe this early in the morning."

"No, I'm all out."

"Why didn't you tell us?" asked Susan, with alarm.

"I just thought I could go a day or two without it."

"And today it's Christmas! The apothecary won't be available," I remarked, with consternation. "Perhaps Dr. Davis might still have a bottle or two. Charles, you've got to let us know when you're running low on your medicine."

"Sorry, I'll make sure of it in the future. But really, I'm fine now."

"Charles," I snapped, "people who are fine don't cough up blood!"

"Your sister makes a good point. I'll go into Hallowell and see if I can get more of that elixir," interjected Alden. "Would any of you ladies care to escort me to Dr. Davis' home? Or, if you prefer, you could just jot down the address. I'm quite familiar with the streets there."

"I'll go with you!" I responded, confidently. "I've been there before with Charles … if that's all right with you, Susan?"

"Of course, provided your brother doesn't need you," replied Susan.

"For the love of God! Why would I care either way?" growled Charles, with annoyance. "I'm feeling better, and I don't need my sister's constant attention."

"Well, we shouldn't be gone very long, a little over an hour, at most," noted Alden.

"Take five hours, if you like! … or all day, for that matter!" grunted my irate brother.

Grandma put her hands on her hips, bent over and looked him straight in the eye. "That's no way for you to speak to our guest, Charles Andrew Goodwin!"

Charles was mortified that his words had sounded so disrespectful. "I'm sorry, Mr. Potter," he said, with a humble tone. "I just don't like people fretting and fussing over me due to my own stupidity."

Alden patted Charles on the shoulder. "I understand completely. I'm the same way. And, Miss Annie, you're going to need a warm coat," Alden observed. The wind is brisk."

"Don't worry about me, sir, I'm a farm girl. I'm used to Maine winters."

Charles piped in, "I'll say! You'll never believe this, but my sister used to sleep with the window wide open in the middle of December. One time she woke up and there was half a foot of snow on top of her!"

"Don't stretch it, Charles; it was more like an inch, and it was on my blanket, not on me."

"Annie, you looked like an Eskimo peeking out of an igloo! It was the funniest thing I've ever seen!"

"I opened the window because that wood stove was blazing. I could have cooked bread on my desk! So, I shut the flue, opened the window, and fell asleep. It only happened once."

"Trust me, Alden, it happened all the time. Father got so mad at her he threatened to take away all her blankets, dismantle the stove, and give her a stall in the barn!"

"Charles, I hate it when you catastrophize a petty incident."

"What? Is there such a word? Catastrophize? Did you make that up?" asked Charles, in a skeptical tone.

"No, it's in the dictionary. Want me to prove it?" I yelled, exasperated.

"All right, you two," interrupted Susan. "Alden has better things to do than to listen to you two rant! Go get your coat and shawl, Annie."

"Oh!" I declared, in a moment of inspiration. "Perhaps I should show off my new bonnet."

"Perhaps you should," Alden responded.

"Are you sure you don't want to come with us, Susan?" I asked, starting to feel less courageous by the minute. "It might do you good to get out of the house."

"No, I need to do some baking. You go ahead. We'll get along fairly without you."

Alden had arrived in a small, pleasant carriage, which he'd borrowed from his cousin in Hallowell. I climbed aboard with him, both of us seated elbow to elbow in the narrow front seat. It was awkward … very awkward! I had boldly agreed to accompany him. What kind of young lady does such a thing? Certainly, not a respectable one. Now I was starting to feel anxious that I might be tongue-tied during our quarter-hour journey into town. I was with a grown man, albeit a handsome one, whom I scarcely knew. What was I thinking? I was starting to feel nauseous. Fortunately, Alden was never at a loss for words, and he caught me totally off guard.

"So, Miss Annie, what are you thinking about?" he began.

"My God," I thought. "If he only knew."

I finally replied, "Well, I guess honesty is the best policy. I was wondering if you were thinking me quite brazen for volunteering my company." I looked at him sheepishly.

"Nonsense! I was hoping you'd come with me so I could get to know you better. I invited you, after all.

"So, Annie, you and Charles are remarkably intelligent and inquisitive souls. Though, I shouldn't be surprised. Your father, God rest him, was likewise."

"I concede to Papa's intelligence and Charles's inquisitiveness, but how on earth did you come to that erroneous conclusion about me, might I ask?" (I was amazed at how quickly I had recovered my ability to talk!)

"Erroneous? Far from it! I've seen your growing library of books, experienced those witty conversations, and observed your interactions together. I am a very good judge of character and wit, and you are both in possession of plentiful amounts of each."

"Anyone can have things or say things that are meant to impress. I find that in most circumstances those "so-called" attributes are really nothing more than a veneer to cover up the painful truth."

"And what is the painful truth?" asked Alden, playfully.

"That things are not always what they seem, and first impressions, when considered in the mix, often leave one cold and disillusioned."

"And *that* kind of a response is precisely what I mean! You certainly can turn a phrase. It takes intelligence to think like that, and even more so to put it into words."

"Alden, there's nothing brilliant about what I said. It's just common sensical. But I must admit, I do love words. When I write prose, I always pretend I'm the reader. I want to make sure that what I'm writing is understood, precisely as I understand it, like a pure transfer of thought, or like the reflection of an image in a mirror."

I paused briefly, and continued, "Let me see if I can come up with an example. Hmm … Oh! I have an idea. Give me a sentence but don't accent any of the words … you know, like you're reading it off the page of a boring newspaper."

"Do you mean anything? … any sentence that comes to mind?"

"Yes, anything."

"All right," Alden replied. "Let me think. OK, I've got one. 'My barque is sailing on the morning tide.'"

"Oh, that's perfect. Let's see. By accenting any one word in that sentence, you can change its meaning. For example, if you say '*My* barque is sailing on the morning tide,' that means only your barque, not mine or Charles's or Father's is sailing. 'My *barque* is sailing on the morning tide' implies that you are not sailing your sloop, or your schooner, or your brig. And if you say 'My barque *is* sailing on the morning tide,' then you are emphasizing the affirmative, and there is absolutely no doubt that it will sail on the morning tide."

"Interesting," said Alden. "So the next word to be accented would be 'My barque is *sailing* on the morning tide.' I guess that would mean that it's not flying on the morning tide."

"Or sinking," I added, with a chuckle.

"I guess, one could apply *that* idea to almost any sentence," remarked Alden.

"Yes, one *could* apply that idea to almost any sentence," I quipped. We both broke into laughter and continued with "wordy" foolishness until we arrived at the apothecary.

The shop was not open, as we had surmised, so we headed over to visit Dr. Davis. Fortunately, he was home and managed to find one container of elixir in the very back of his medicine cabinet. He assured me he would order a few more in the morning, when the apothecary was in. I thanked him, profusely, and apologized for interrupting his Christmas morning activities with his family. As usual, he remarked with a pleasant response. "It's my mission to attend to the ill, one that I am happy to fulfill at any time of the day or night. Merry Christmas to the both of you, and give my best wishes to Charles."

On the way home, our conversation became more personal. He asked me how I was getting along with Charles being so sick and having lost so many family members. I mentioned some of the strange happenings surrounding their deaths and talked briefly about Mrs. Sullivan. He seemed quite interested in the supernatural and described a series of mysterious "forerunners" involving three familial deaths.

As we plodded upward along the first quarter mile of the Ferry Road, an interesting phenomenon took place; it started to snow. Having snow on Christmas day in Maine is nothing unusual, except when it's falling out of a blue, cloudless sky, which was actually the case! Flakes descended like beautiful little crystals that shimmered in the bright sunlight, creating a glittering fairyland, a veritable snow globe. Alden and I both looked at each other without speaking a word, astounded by the surreal event.

Predictably, I was the one to break the enchanting spell. "Have you ever seen anything like this before, Alden?"

"Once," he replied, still mesmerized by the twinkling diamonds that seemed to be spontaneously evolving out of nothing and then gliding to earth. "When I was about ten, I was at my aunt's home in Bowdoin. My uncle, who was only in his early thirties, had died suddenly and we were at the wake. Aunt Jenny was beside herself with grief and there was not a dry eye in the entire household. We children were ushered outside for some sledding, probably to take our young minds off the open coffin and all the grief. While out there, I silently asked God to let me know that Uncle Danny was in heaven. Well, it couldn't have been more than a minute before it started to snow, just like this, blue sky and everything. I accepted it as a "Yes" from God."

"That's a beautiful story," I remarked.

"Of course, now I understand that it was a rare but natural occurrence."

"Natural but quite well timed, wouldn't you say?"

"Yes, very much so. Somewhat like this little miracle that's surrounding us, presently."

There was another mutual, meditative pause in our discourse, as we basked in the aura of this remarkable event.

A few minutes later, as we turned onto the County Road, I again broke the tranquility of the moment. "You know, I greatly enjoy discussing these things with you. Most think I'm a lunatic."

THE MEMORY OF THE DEAD. It is an exquisite and beautiful thing in our nature, that when the heart is touched and softened by some tranquil happiness or affectionate feeling, the memory of the dead comes over it most powerfully and irresistibly. It would almost seem as though our better thoughts and sympathies were charms, in virtue of which the soul is enabled to hold some vague and mysterious intercourse with the spirits of those whom we dearly loved in life. Alas, how often and how long may those patient angels hover above us, watching for the spell which is so seldom uttered and soon forgotten!

"Well, let them think what they will, Miss Goodwin. I believe we're all meant to experience blessings, and they're given to be shared. How else are we to believe in the wonders proclaimed in Scripture if we cannot encounter the touch of Almighty in the present age?"

"True. But you've witnessed these singular wonders yourself. Might that explain your willingness to accept mine? Perhaps others receive such favors but fail to recognize them."

"Perhaps. But Scripture says, "Seek and ye shall find." Maybe things happen more often to those who seek? You've been seeking for a long time, from what you've told me, so why should you not find?"

I glanced at Alden and nodded with a reflective smile. His words sounded eerily reminiscent of Edith's wisdom.

By the time we reached my old schoolhouse, the snow had stopped and the blue sky continued to adorn the landscape. At that juncture, I had the country-girl audacity to ask him something that a city girl would never have dared, "Are you courting anyone?"

"Ha ha, Annie, you don't beat around the bush, do you!" he laughed.

"Forgive me, that was so impolite! Always putting my foot in my mouth." My face must have gone through three shades of red.

"Nonsense! You can ask me anything you like. Well, to answer your query, I was in a courtship not too long ago. But it all went sour. The young lady's hesitancy was financial, as she was from a fourth-generation of wealthy ship-builders, and her parents thought her to be marrying down."

"But you have a splendid trade," I added, somewhat bewildered.

"Well, not as splendid as they would have it. Her father inherited the money, the business, and the arrogance that often accompanies unearned wealth."

Alden continued, "You might be surprised to know that it was I who broke off the courtship … one year too late, I might add. Yet there are beneficial lessons that can be learned from our blunders. I don't regret my purgation with that family."

"Purgation? That's an interesting way to phrase it."

"Well, my ignorance and superficial infatuations were clearly revealed to me, if not purged."

"I'm afraid I always learn best from my howlers," I admitted.

"Don't we all! And I derived two valuable tenets from this doomed courtship. First, I will *not* live my life with someone who values me in proportion to my bank account. And second, I will marry for *love* or not at all."

We arrived at my home shortly. Before entering to bring Charles his medicine, Alden looked at me and said, "This has been a wonderful journey, together. I thank you for your charming and entertaining company."

"Alden, it's been my pleasure, completely. I'm so happy to have shared this time with you."

At that moment, I knew that I adored him.

Chapter 41

Anticipation

Let them think you care little for them or their love, and they will try hard to become worthy of your regard. Not flirt nor strive to wound their feelings—we don't mean that—humanity forbid! But don't make yourself cheap; just keep your own counsel; and the more hopelessly in love you are, the more do you guard the knowledge of that fact from your lover. Keep it down and in, all that you possibly can, till the magic words are said that make you one; then take off the bands, but do it gradually—"grow upon him;" show him by degrees the strength of the passion which he has awakened in your soul.

 —"Advice for Young Ladies," *Gardiner Home Journal*, Jan. 3, 1861

After he left for home, my affection for Alden hit me like an avalanche! In my naivety, I welcomed the onslaught and was unwittingly setting myself up for some insurmountable challenges. But who cares! When you first experience those longing pangs of desire, there doesn't seem to be a challenge in the world that cannot be overcome by a resolute will. My only concern was that he might not reciprocate the sentiment. And how would I know if he did? He had been kind and generous to all of us and had never shown partiality to me in particular. I rode with him because I volunteered, that's all. Yet, our conversations were deep, personal, and meaningful. There was something truly magical about that early Christmas morning excursion, and he'd looked at me in a manner that was totally new and disarming. Or was I just conjuring up what I wished to see? When you begin to care for someone, it's completely natural to try to interpret their every gesture, but it can also be deceiving and, in the end, erroneous and disappointing. I decided not to try unraveling their meanings, as it would certainly drive me mad.

But, try as I might, the thoughts surrounding those tender moments were always pushing their roots deeper into every corner of my little world. When I found myself alone, I would audibly command them to depart from my mind. Of course, they never listened. Within a few days, I came down with an irreversible plague, the dreaded disease of "love sickness," as

Charles called it. It was very much like having mild influenza, accompanied by a disordered mind. I couldn't sleep, couldn't focus on my chores and studies, lost my appetite, and truly felt feverish whenever those moments of anticipation and doubt collided in my heart.

There were no secrets between Charles and me. He was truly my best friend and confidant. Poor Emma also had to put up with my unhinged insecurities. Charles's main concern was the illusion of my mature physical appearance; I looked eighteen and carried myself with the grace and confidence of an adult. Even so, I knew that Susan would never consent to my courtship with anyone until I was of age. Invariably, my conversations with Charles were always contentious, as he usually played devil's advocate. He had great respect for Alden, but he loved me and wanted to present the opposite side of the coin, the side that I least fancied and most needed to take into account.

"Does Alden have any idea how old you are, Annie?" asked Charles in his usual interrogative tone.

"Charles, my age shouldn't matter. If Alden cares for me … well, it will work out."

"Your age certainly does matter. It's a matter of propriety. Alden Potter is a reputable man with a good future, and he probably thinks you *are* eighteen. All my friends thought you were my age until I set 'em straight!"

"Thanks, Charlie, for putting in the good word," I scoffed.

"That's supposed to be a compliment, dear sister. You carry yourself with poise and speak with intelligence, wit, and confidence, just like I trained you," he chuckled. "You could easily lie about your age without anyone suspecting the contrary. You're not going to entertain that possibility are you?"

"Well, first of all, thank you for your assessment of my attributes, which you had little or no hand in creating, and second of all, No! I would never lie. What good would it do? It would be a sin, and even worse, Susan would tell him and then he'd know he couldn't trust me. Once trust is gone, it's gone. But, to be honest, it did cross my mind for about two seconds."

"Well, don't consider it again. You're fifteen and not even close to courting age. You've just gotta make the best of it," asserted Charles, as he pushed the dagger of truth deeper.

"I'll be sixteen in May. Girls throughout history have courted and married at younger ages than that," I retorted.

"Sure, back when life expectancy was thirty," quipped Charles, with a know-it-all smirk.

"Well, Charlie, our family's life expectancy hasn't been all that great. Or haven't you been paying attention?"

"You've got a point there," he reflected. "But more importantly, what about Mount Holyoke? Your aspirations? Are those now of no consideration? Once you're married, and the babies start coming, you'll have no choice but to stay home and be a mother." Charles paused for a moment, and with a more compassionate tone asked, "So, how old is Alden? Do you even know? He could be twenty-five or thirty."

"He doesn't look anywhere near that old. He doesn't look any older than Ryan."

"No, he doesn't look it, but he sure sounds it! He's very mature and well spoken. But it wouldn't matter even if he was *your* age. Susan says eighteen is the earliest a young lady should even contemplate getting involved with a man. And, she's the boss!"

"I know," I mumbled, with discouragement. "But Susan knows Alden, and she thinks he's a saint. Maybe she could change her mind?"

"Hey, sis, Alden's a very kind and intelligent man and I can see why you care about him. Anyway, I think we're really just beating a dead horse here. Actually, there may not even be a horse to beat, as you don't even know if he reciprocates your feelings. If he does … well, your problems will have expanded exponentially."

"Thanks for the comforting words, Charlie."

"Anytime, Annie. Keep the faith. Everything will work out for the good."

As New Year's Day approached, Charles found himself more and more confined to bed. His cough was not much worse, but he began to experience pain in other areas of his body besides his chest. Pain in his back and frequent headaches were keeping him awake at night. It was clear to me that the disease was spreading into other organs. Dr. Davis was consulted and prescribed small doses of laudanum to relieve the suffering. This did help him sleep, but he was progressively requiring more frequent doses to keep his torments at bay. Once again, on New Year's Eve morning, we nearly lost him. Apparently, he had taken too much of the drug and was unable to wake himself enough to expel that asphyxiating fluid from his lungs. If Susan and I had not been there to pull him upright and pound on his back, he would have died. I was terrified, but this time I pulled myself together in true stoic form and managed to get my brother breathing again. Once awake, he asked us to cut the opium doses in half, as he figured it would be better to suffer pain and maintain consciousness than be unable to communicate.

"I don't want to enter paradise stumbling around like a drunkard!" he exclaimed.

Sunday, January 1, 1865, began cloudy with snow showers. By noon the sun was periodically peeking out from behind the clouds, but the wind was such that it made the outside temperature seem much colder than the twenty degrees displayed on our thermometer.

We had not seen Alden since his visit on Christmas morning, which was not unusual, as he lived an hour away by train. However, having been smitten by Cupid's fiery arrow, the days seemed like months. Normally, having too much time on my hands was a blessing, but lately it had become a curse! I wondered continuously about Mr. Potter's feelings towards me. My only remedy, though temporary, was to devote all my free time to Charles. When I did this, I was more able to keep my studying, chores, and piano practice moving along, as opposed to daydreaming and worrying about all the "what ifs" that dominate young love.

Spending time with my brother was always interesting, and I never knew what was going to come out of his mouth. He couldn't tolerate any display of worry on my face, and made sure to tell at least one morbid knee-slapper to brighten up my dismal attitude.

One afternoon, he tested my gullibility with this gem:

"Hey, Annie, did you know they just found Mozart's grave in Vienna?"

"No! That's exciting."

"Apparently, the gravediggers heard music coming from under-ground just before they found his skull!"

"My God!" I shrieked.

"He was de-composing!" Charles howled with laughter at my dimwitted naivety.

I should have seen that one coming!

———

Surprisingly, Charles's condition, once again, seemed to improve during the first week of January. He was able to sit up, do a little reading by himself, and venture into the other rooms for a change in scenery.

That week we received a thoughtful letter from Alden. It conveyed well-wishes to the family and hopes for Charles's improvement. There was no mention of me in it. However, on Friday, I received a note in the post with no return address. Assuming it to be from Josephine, who often omitted her return, I opened it casually and to my amazement it was from Alden! It relieved many of my worrisome fears and replaced them with a different, more realistic variety.

4 January, 1865
Dear Annie,

It is my fond hope that you and your family are well, and that Charles is improving. I am in hopes of visiting soon, and promise to bring some of that bakery bread that you all enjoyed so much.

I want to thank you again for your company on that enchanting journey into Hallowell! I contemplate those moments often. You are an exceptional young lady and I'm very much looking forward to spending more time getting to know you.

As always, I remain your dear friend and that of your beloved family!

Yours, most truly,

Alden

I was overjoyed and frightened out of my wits all at the same time. Now my dreams and fears had no choice but to meet! The fantasy was vaporizing. Would he be inclined to wait for someone to turn eighteen when there were so many young women who were of courting age? Might he not experience a sense of humiliation over the whole adventure, innocent though it was? Was I interpreting his note as reciprocity, when in fact it might merely be an expression of polite curiosity? I felt outgunned on all flanks. But I did have one powerful weapon at my command, my own deep affection for him.

Knowing that Alden worked a six-day week, leaving Sunday as the only time he could visit, provided me with time to put my thoughts in order. At this point, neither Susan nor Grandma needed to know anything. Perhaps I should write out my thoughts on how to begin the conversation with Alden, and then rehearse my approach to the most difficult topic, my age. Should I preface the whole ensuing conversation with that fact, leave it to the end, or drop it like a bombshell in the middle? To answer these questions, I needed to consult that wizard of all things sacred, scientific, and romantic … Charles.

My poor, emaciated brother fell asleep early on Friday evening. When such blessings came to pass, I always allowed him his much needed repose. The poor fellow had lost so much sleep in the last few nights. My opportunity to speak with him came late Saturday morning. As soon as I was sure that Susan was not within earshot, I handed Charles Alden's note.

"Oh, my, sis!" he whispered. "You're certainly in a pickle."

"What should I do, Charlie?"

My brother sighed, brushing his hair back off his face and pulling himself upright on his bed. "This won't sit well with Susan, you know."

"Oh, I'm very aware. But I'm only two years away from being able to make my own decisions. But, that's not what vexes most."

"What, then?" asked Charles.

"My age, of course."

"You can't help when you were born."

> "WANTED TO GO A COURTING" Two of the hands on board a schooner in Rockland harbor, on Sunday last, wanted to go on shore to do a little "courting." Unfortunately, the cook had left the vessel on Thursday and had taken the boat with him. Here was the dilemma! The "gals" would be expecting them, but how were they to get on shore? A bright thought struck them. They hoisted a signal of distress, and some boats from the wharf put off to the vessel, and being informed of the "state of things," brought the imprisoned mariners to the shore much to the gratification of their "sweethearts."

"I wish I could. Do you think he'll wait … I mean, does it sound like he really, truly cares for me, or am I just getting my hopes up only to be shot out of the sky like a duck?"

I looked at my brother, ready to hang onto every word that came from his mouth.

Charles realized, by my expression, that I needed a straight answer, though I'm sure he was contemplating something to say about the duck. He sat there for a minute thinking and reading the note again. Finally, after what seemed like forever, he looked at me and smiled. "It is my humble opinion that Alden cares a great deal."

I sighed an enormous sigh of relief.

Charles continued, "He sent you this, perhaps sensing that you might not be ready for courtship for one reason or another."

"What makes you think that?" I asked, perplexed.

"Well, he could have said all this in his previous note, but he didn't. He wanted it read by one pair of eyes, only. Yours. Also, there's no return address, which might have been deliberate. He's probably unsure and wants to be discreet. He's testing the depths of the water."

"Yeah, I hope I don't end up drowning in it."

"Annie, God did give you a particle of humor. There is hope," smirked Charles.

I sighed, put on my coat and shawl, and went outside into the barnyard to talk to the horses.

Courting in the 1860s was far more formal than in the ensuing years. Most men entered such a state more as a career choice than for love; though, it was usually the latter that drove both parties to the altar. The acceptable courting age for a young woman could start as early as sixteen, depending on her mother's preferences, but a chaperone would always have to be present when the two lovers were together. The process was usually lengthy and formal. Under normal circumstances, Alden and I would have never been allowed to ride alone together to fetch medicine for Charles, with or without romantic inclinations. The situation with Charles was dire and our family trusted Alden. It was a fortunate aberration of the norms in my case.

Our lives had collided due to my father's tragic death, and Alden had bridged more social hurdles in a few meetings with me than in a year of traditional formalities. Getting to know one another, even as well as we did now, would have been long and tedious. I would have had to be formally introduced to him, and we would have had to meet at multiple supervised social gatherings in order to get acquainted. Our freedom of conversational topics would also have been quite limited. Susan would have always had to be present, as the oldest female in the family and my stepmother. Discussing his previous relationship would have been out of the question!

Thank the good Lord that Alden and I were already miles ahead of this awkward, never-ending process, even though we were at present, merely friends. Age, in particular, the age of the young lady did often play a major role in the acceptability of the arrangement. She should be old enough to have completed her schooling, to bear children, and to be competent and mature enough to manage a family. Strangely, the man's age was of little concern. Men in their forties or fifties could, and often did, marry very young women, especially after the death of their wives.

By Saturday evening, I was a wreck, worrying about what might transpire on Sunday. My greatest concern was how I was going to speak with Alden in private. If everything went as usual, he would come to the house and be surrounded by all of us. Stealing away for a private moment would be nearly impossible. Perhaps, when Susan and Grandma went out to prepare some coffee and goodies, I could sneak in a word. Hopefully, Alden had thought about this as well. I would just have to wait for the right moment and take advantage of it when it came along. But how does one convey something so personal in a fleeting moment? No, there would have to be time, sustained time, uninterrupted time. That would be a trick.

Charles had another difficult, sleepless night. His coughing was of the sort that compelled me to sleep in the parlor to be close at hand should the situation become worse. By four a.m., he had finally fallen asleep. I, however, lay there with my eyes open counting the ticks of the clock. Sleep finally overcame my anxiety, but only for a couple of hours. I then realized it was useless to try to entice slumber, as it was a losing battle. I got up and made coffee.

By mid-morning, I planted myself in a chair next to the parlor window. Every time a wagon or rider went by I felt my stomach churning like a waterwheel. Susan noticed my preoccupation "with something" and asked if I was feeling well. I told her that my stomach was bothering me, which wasn't a lie.

"It's no wonder!" she chided. "You've had more coffee than Isabel drinks in a week!"

She was right. But I had to stay awake and alert. This was no time for me to be groggy and brainless.

Finally, at 2:47 in the afternoon, (Yes, I journaled the exact moment.), Alden pulled into the barnyard in that same borrowed wagon we had used on Christmas morning. My heart was pounding so hard I was sure others could hear it. I thought I was going to faint, but quickly talked myself out of such stupidity; "If you pass out, dimwit, you're certainly not ready to even think about courting." The change in attitude worked! I started to relax and accepted the moments as they unfolded. I would survive.

He greeted all of us with a big smile and a few fresh loaves of bread from the bakery.

"I had planned to be here sooner, but there was an accident at a crossing in Richmond. Apparently, some daredevil thought he could outrun our oncoming locomotive with his carriage."

"Oh my! Was anyone hurt?" asked Susan.

"No, … well, no people. Unfortunately the horse was badly injured and had to be put down. Very sad, an unnecessary loss of a beautiful animal. Poor thing. And the foolish driver only ended up with a few scratches."

"Such recklessness! Horses are not machines," I declared, "they're part of the family."

"Yes, and where would we be without them?" asserted Alden. He continued, "Well, I didn't mean to start a conversation on such a sad note, but that's the reason that I'm here later than planned."

"So, come in Mr. Potter," insisted Grandma.

"I will take you up on that invitation, Isabel," replied Alden. I grabbed his tophat and coat and hung them on the hook by the mudroom door. "Thank you, Miss Annie," he acknowledged.

We went directly into the parlor while Grandma took the bread to the kitchen to prepare some refreshments and a pot of coffee. Susan sat beside Alden on the sofa, and I on the adjacent chair, where I'd been seated all morning. This felt awkward to me, but anything would have seemed so at the moment. Alden wasn't displaying the least bit of discomfort, and his demeanor was relaxed, accompanied by his typical air of confidence.

"So how is our Charles doing," he inquired.

"Well … " Susan and I spoke simultaneously.

I laughed. "Go ahead, Susan."

"It varies from day to day." Then she whispered, "Between the three of us, I don't think he has much time left."

"It's very disheartening," I added. "He had a bad coughing spell last evening. I slept in the parlor to keep an eye on things."

"I guess that would be advisable, under the circumstances," replied Alden. "So sorry for the relentless series of trials that seem to be visiting this house. Please let me know if I can be of help."

Before we could reply, Isabel brought in some sliced bread, jam, and coffee for us to enjoy. I made it a point to avoid the coffee, so I wouldn't have to spend the rest of the day in the outhouse. We then spent an hour discussing the war, Lincoln's priorities for reconstruction, and whether Lee's surrender might be expected soon. Normally, these would have been intriguing topics of conversation for me, but this time it was more like watching mold grow. How or when would I have time alone with Alden?

Finally, Grandma excused herself, as she was tired and in need of her afternoon nap. "One away," I thought. Then Susan decided to start a new conversation about how Alden's apprenticeship was proceding, and that added another quarter hour to the torture. Just when I was about to give up the idea of talking privately with Alden, a miracle occurred. Alden asked if we could go in and see Charles. Susan told us to go ahead, as she had a couple of chores to do in the barn and would catch up with us in a few minutes.

"Yes! Two down!" I said to myself. "Now if I could only steal away with him for five minutes."

Charles was sitting up in bed, trying to force-feed himself some broth that Grandma had made, dipping a small piece of the bakery bread in the liquid in an attempt to ingest some solid food. He was getting noticeably weaker by the day, but his ever-morbid personality was as brazen as ever.

"Greetings, Alden," he whispered, coughing lightly. "Welcome to the Ninth Circle of Hell."

Alden smiled with amusement. "Well, I can see you've been reading Dante."

"No, I'm afraid my reading days are past. Staying *out* of the Inferno is my only endeavor now."

"Oh, Charles, will you ever stop with that ghastly humor?" I retorted.

"What am I supposed to do in my condition? Cry about it? I plan to laugh my way into paradise!" he replied, in his weak, raspy voice.

Then my brother caught both of us off guard, "So, have you two talked yet?"

"Charles!" I said, with hushed exasperation.

"Well, have you? Life is short … I oughta know. Go converse privately, somewhere. I'll even cover my ears."

I glared at Charles, then turned and looked sheepishly at Alden, who was wearing a look of bewilderment.

"Converse?" asked Alden, "About what?"

I shot a parting angry glance at my brother, who had just covered his head with the pillow. He peeked out of the covers and winked.

Alden and I went over to the corner table, where the late afternoon, January sun was beaming in. I put my head down in shame. I couldn't believe what my brother had just done. It was humiliating beyond words.

"Are you all right, Miss Annie?" whispered Alden.

"No, I'm afraid I just joined my brother in the Ninth Circle … or maybe the Tenth," I replied in an equally muted voice.

"Ah, I think Dante only described nine. What's the problem?"

I knew there was no escaping now, so I tried to collect my thoughts as best I could. This certainly was not going according to my dress rehearsals.

"Well … oh, how do I begin?" I paused for a moment. "I'm just going to have to be honest and take my chances."

"Oh, you're a gambler I see," he said, with a smile.

"Not usually, but, I guess this time. I have little choice in the matter."

"Well then, roll the dice."

I took a deep breath and began, "I loved your note. Thank you. I, too, had a wonderful time on our carriage ride into Hallowell. I guess that's putting it mildly." I put my head down, not daring to look at Alden. "I haven't been able to think of anything else … well, except for Charles. I don't know what to say, and I'm sounding like an imbecile." There was another pregnant pause and I continued, "But, I have to tell you something … I'm only fifteen. I won't even be sixteen until May."

"Well congratulations on your upcoming birthday!" Alden chuckled. He could see I was upset and tried to cheer me. "Annie, look up at me, please. I also have a confession to make. I'm thirty and I won't even be thirty-one until February!" he returned with a smile.

"Oh, my," I said. "I would never have guessed."

"I'm a fossil."

"No, no, no! I didn't mean you were old. It's just … well … "

"It's all right. I can see you are struggling for words. Let me explain, and then, perhaps you won't find our conversation so awkward from here on."

"First, let me say I was not proposing marriage in my letter, nor did I expect to court you. And I *did* know that you were younger than Charles, though how much younger was unclear to me, and frankly, unimportant. Your father was a dear, close friend of mine, and many of our conversations were of home and family. So, I knew much about you, vicariously.

"That being said," he continued, " I did very much enjoy our time together, and as I wrote, I do want to get to know you. It was a splendid Christmas morning ride, and in some ways, enigmatic. I have rarely spoken with anyone, male or female, young or old, who was equal in conversation to you. Rest assured, I would always try to walk in the ways of moral propriety." He then looked straight into my eyes. "So please accept my humble request for your treasured friendship. Where life will take us from here, well, we don't know. So smile and let us enjoy the time we are given."

"Thank you," I responded with relief. "Your presence will always be welcome in my home … and in my heart."

Alden then reached across the table and patted my hand, affectionately. "Do you have my address, so we can correspond? I believe it was applied to the previous note, if you still have it."

"Yes, I've already copied it to my journal."

I sighed with joyful reassurance. I wasn't sure whether to scream at Charles or to kiss him.

Chapter 42

Going Home

How much the heart may bear and yet not break!
How much the flesh may suffer and not die!
Of soul or body brings our end more nigh.
Death chooses its own time- till that is sworn
Lo! All things must be borne.
            —*Gardiner Home Journal*, Aug. 14, 1862

That afternoon passed in the blink of an eye! The remainder was spent in the parlor with Susan, while Alden and I played chess. I was the undefeated champion! After three triumphs in a row, I was tempted to let Alden win, but never gave in to the urge. After all, men need to know that women are as competent as anyone of their sex. Besides, my undefeated status was a manly challenge for him. With Susan and I as witnesses, he swore a solemn vow to eventually claim victory, which happily ensured his return!

I fetched his hat and shawl, and we said our good-byes at the doorway. "Thank you for the pleasant company, Susan, and give Charles and Isabel my highest regards." Then turning to me, he continued, "Congratulations on all your *good-wins*, Miss Annie. I promise to be more of a challenge when we meet again. Eventually, I *will* win!"

I thought to myself, "You already have, Mr. Potter."

I waited in the doorway with old George and watched Alden ascend the wagon. He looked over at me, tipped his hat, winked, and proceeded on his way.

I went immediately to pay a visit to my sharp-witted brother. He was lying back-to, and I thought he was sleeping. However, he heard me and turned over and insisted that I tell him all the "gory" details. What did Alden say? How did I respond? Did I think we might become more than friends? How did he react to my age, and I to his? It was kinda like being interrogated, but I enjoyed every minute of it!

Finally, after a lengthy discussion, I concluded, "I'm very pleased with the way things went today, Charles. I want to thank you, especially, for your bold, death-defying insistence that we speak, which led to my discussion with Alden. If you hadn't said anything, I doubt that we would have found an opportunity to be alone and talk. Then, I would have been doubly anxious for his next letter, or visit. You're a good soldier, Charles Goodwin."

"My pleasure, little sister. I like to march into battle and face the enemy head on." There was a solemn momentary pause, then Charles reached up and gently took hold of my hand. "I love you Annie," he remarked, tenderly, "from the bottom of my heart. Never ever forget it! Who knows if I'll live to see another day. You've made my misery almost tolerable," he said, trying to jest but with an emotional tremor in his voice.

I sat down on the bed and hugged him, and wept. This time, Charles didn't try to hold back or make jokes. He cried right along with me for a good long time. When we finally had exhausted all the tears, I gave him a kiss on his feverish forehead. He smiled and I let him take his repose. When I reached the kitchen doorway, I turned and looked back for a moment and he was still looking at me with that winsome smile. That image would be burnt into my heart forever.

And I saw the river over which every soul must pass to reach the Kingdom of Heaven, … and the name of that river was suffering … . And I saw a boat which carries souls across that river … and the name of that boat was Love.

—Attributed to St. John of the Cross

The next day, Charles's pain seemed to increase in great measure. It was becoming generalized. We continued to give him the laudanum, but he refused to take more than the minimal dose. When he slept, or tried to sleep (which was more often the case), he would moan terribly and my heart felt as though it would break. I knew I had to be strong for him; I needed to forget about myself and give it my all. By Tuesday, January 10, Charles began to slip in and out of consciousness. He would sometimes call out for me or one of the other siblings. At times he would recite shards of poetry that he had read, often mixing up one with another. Susan and I attended to him night and day. I set up a cot on the opposite end of the summer kitchen, and we took shifts keeping watch over my dying brother. My poor grandmother, who'd known so much sorrow, stayed in her room most of the time, dealing with her pain the only way she knew how.

On Tuesday, Charles recovered slightly, remaining conscious and in great pain throughout most of the day. He barely spoke, as even the slightest exertion exhausted him. At one point I could tell that he wanted to speak to me, so I pulled a chair over to his bedside.

"Annie," he said in a whisper, "is it nearly the end? Oh God. O my dear God! Let it be finished."

Tears were flowing so profusely from my eyes that I was temporarily blinded. "Yes, dear brother, it's very near the end. It won't be much longer, my love."

"Sis … " he gasped, reaching his hand out for mine, "forgive me … for all the teasing."

"Charlie, if you hadn't teased me, I wouldn't have thought you loved me. You … are … my very best … and dearest friend. I love you with all my heart," I blurted out between sobs.

"As much … as you love Alden?" he asked, jesting right up to the end.

"Yes, of course, you dimwit. Of course," I replied, laughing and crying at the same time.

"Good," he muttered. Then he drifted back into that semi-conscious world.

His suffering reminded me of Christ's agony on the cross. At one point he muttered repeatedly, "I forgive you. I forgive all of you." When I asked him who he was forgiving, he answered, cryptically, "the dying soldiers." On another evening of that week, he woke from his delirium and cried, "My God, My God, where are you?" and proceeded to recite portions of the 22nd Psalm, which I had no idea that he had ever memorized. It was eerie. By Friday, his body began to take on the grayish pallor of death. His chest made a gurgling sound with each breath as though his lungs were filling, but he was incapable of expelling the fluid. He was now near the close of life.

Alden sent us a note informing us that he would be unable to join us on the 15th but promised to be there on the following Sunday. I was deeply disappointed as we could have benefitted from his reassuring presence during this agonizing ordeal. I'm sure he didn't realize how much Charles's condition had deteriorated since his last visit. Emma was visiting her aunt in Wiscasset, and Sully was away in Boston, which left me alone with my dark thoughts.

The frigid weather kept us indoors, and forced us to make frequent trips to the woodshed. We were all living on the first floor in order to keep the warmth contained, and none of the rooms maintained their heat for very long during the Arctic blast. It was a never-ending battle with Old Man Winter in Maine.

One morning, the fire went out early in the sitting room, and the liquid left in cups from the previous night was frozen solid! Grandma, whose room was on that north side, now slept in the parlor, which was better insulated and had a southern exposure. Susan and I continued to take turns in four-hour shifts, from summer kitchen to sitting-room and back, in order to maintain our vigil over Charles and allow each other some undisturbed rest.

Along with the weariness, anxiety, and tension came fits of rage over little nothings. Susan and I would be screaming at each other, blaming each other for letting the fire go out in the parlor. Then Grandma would get in on the act and accuse both of us of taking her coffee away before she was done with it, only to find the half-finished cup on the mantle. In spite of our circumstantial rantings, by the end of the day there was no animosity; only three weary, battle-worn soldiers preparing for the next engagement with mortality.

On Sunday evening, Charles, again, regained momentary consciousness and reached his hand out to me. Before I could get to his bedside, he slipped back into the waiting chamber of eternity. He was an inferno of fever, and Susan and I continued to put cold, wet cloths on his forehead. Whether he felt any relief or not, we couldn't say, but we needed to do something in the face of such suffering in order to alleviate our own feelings of powerlessness. Our tireless vigil continued through the night. By Monday morning his fever had left, but now his hands and extremities were freezing. His breathing had become shallow but was not labored, and his pulse was very weak. I began to pray that death might come soon and peacefully to his consumption-wracked body.

The bitter cold continued, but the day was sunny. I went upstairs to my icebox of a bedchamber for a much-needed change of scenery. I started my tiny wood stove and began to tidy up my things. As I was sweeping my floor, the broom handle accidentally hit the shelf above the stove, knocking the priceless, porcelain image of Edith Sullivan to the floor, shattering it into a hundred pieces!

"My God, no!" I cried. "NO!" I fell to my knees in tears, heartbroken at my own clumsiness. As I glanced at the fragmented nightmare, I thought about Edith and all the wonderful things she'd shared with me. How she'd treasured that portrait! It was the only existing painting of her as a young woman, and, perhaps, the only image of her anywhere! I wept for a very long time, not only for the plaque, but also for all that was now taking place, and my anguish and fear of having to live in a world without Charles. It was as though the Divinity was trying to make it clear that nothing on this earth lasts forever. After my tears had run dry, I decided to collect every last miniscule piece of the plaque, with the thought that maybe someone could reassemble it. Perhaps Alden, familiar with ceramics, could bring it back to life. I placed the fragments carefully in a small jewelry box that I kept in the little built-in cupboard that Father had so thoughtfully made for me.

Throughout the day, my brother teetered between life and death. He was in a comatose state and nothing external seemed to affect him. His breathing fluctuated from heavy and labored to barely discernible. We laid him on his side to accommodate the coughing spasms that continued to plague him. His fever rose somewhat toward the evening, as usual, and we continued to apply the cold, wet cloths. Susan finished her shift at midnight, and I took my turn. Charles seemed to be breathing lightly and comfortably, and I was worn out from walking the tightrope between trying to sleep and stay vigilant, simultaneously.

I dosed off for a bit and awoke at the sound of the tall clock in the parlor striking two. There was something amiss in the summer kitchen. At first, in my groggy state, I couldn't quite discern what it was. Adjusting to my surroundings. I noticed a figure standing in the winter moonlight near one of the two south-facing windows. Its right hand was extended, pressed against the frosty glass window pane. Thinking it might be Susan, I asked in a whispering tone, "What are you doing up, Susan?"

The being turned towards me, and to my astonishment, it was Charles!

"Charles, oh my! Charles, what are you doing up, out of bed?"

He walked towards me, smiling in that familiar way, and put his bony hand in mine, never saying a word. Then he slowly walked back to his bed, climbed in, and soon returned to the state he had been in before, comatose, feverish, and breathing lightly.

Because I was so exhausted, I instantly fell back to sleep. At six, I changed places with Susan. By then, I assumed my experience with Charles during the night was nothing but a dream resulting from my emotional state. I did, however, recount the dream to Susan, and then went into the parlor, wrapped up in several comforters, and began to dose again. I no sooner had escaped into slumberland when I was awakened by Susan calling me into the summer kitchen. Worried that Charles had passed, I ran, stumbling like a drunkard.

On arriving, I saw Susan standing near the window and pointing to something. I thought she wanted me to look outside, so I went over to the other window and looked out.

"No, Annie. Right here … Look!"

There on the window pane was the long-fingered handprint of Charles, surrounded by the most beautiful, ornate frost formations I had ever seen! It had not been a dream after all! We looked at each other with sheer amazement. I had heard of people near death having a sudden surge of life and lucidity, but even with all the deaths I'd witnessed, this was the first time I'd seen it happen.

Tuesday was another blustery, freezing day, accompanied by furious snow squalls. One such squall left an inch of snow in less than five minutes. Then the sun returned to dazzle the eye with the sparkling-new, pristine blanket that covered the earth.

There was no change in Charles's condition, but we knew he wouldn't last much longer. I decided that I would take my shifts reading to Charles from the *Imitation of Christ*. Even though he wasn't conscious, I hoped his spirit to be so and that he might in some way benefit from my effort. The last passage that I read that evening was about wisdom.

This is the highest wisdom—to seek the kingdom of heaven through contempt of this world. It is vanity to seek and trust in riches that perish. It is vanity to court honor and give into pride. It is vanity to follow the lusts of the body and desire those things for which great punishment later must come. It is vanity to desire a long life and care not about a life well-spent. It is vanity to be concerned with the present time only and not provide for the things to come. It is vanity to care for what passes away quickly and not look forward to where unending joy abides. Remember; The eye is never satisfied with seeing nor the ear filled with hearing … Therefore, turn your heart from the love of visible things and bring to yourself to things invisible.

A sermon in four words on the vanity of earthly possessions: "Shrouds have no pockets."

After I finished the reading, I gently whispered, "Charles, you have given everything to follow your God. You have abandoned riches, honor, earthly desires, and a long life, and traded these for a life well spent. You have sought the kingdom of heaven and discarded the riches of this world for things invisible and eternal. I can only hope to do the same and one day have the same deep faith that you've demonstrated."

I then kissed him gently on the forehead.

Early during Susan's shift (from eight to midnight), Charles began having difficulty breathing. He tried to cough up the fluid in his lungs but barely had the strength. He managed to expel enough of it so he could breathe with some relief, but that didn't last long. Soon he was gasping for air! Susan called me in to help her lift him into a sitting position. I struggled to get him upright, but somehow managed to do so. I pounded on his back to loosen the horrible viscous liquid. Again, some phlegm-like substance came out mixed with blood and accompanied by an offensive odor. I knew that this couldn't go on forever, and I prayed for a peaceful end to my brother's suffering. The idea that he was probably unaware of what was happening gave me enough strength to continue my assistance in these trying, last moments.

"Please die, Charles," I silently prayed. "This is enough. Please, dear Lord, take him!"

I then dressed in my sleeping apparel and prepared for another restless night of vigilance. I curled up on the sofa in the cold, drafty sitting room and dozed off for a few moments. No sooner had I slipped into that much-needed land of dreams, when Susan's worried voice called me back into an exhausted state of consciousness. My brother was moaning and moving his limbs erratically, and his eyes were rolling in his head. The poor sufferer was having a dreadful seizure! Within a few minutes the horrible fit ended.

Susan looked at me with an anguished expression and whispered, "It won't be long now, Annie."

I replied, "Yes." And begged, "Please, God … soon … My poor brother."

"Why don't you go back and get some rest … I'll call you if anything changes."

"It's all right. I'll fetch a chair from the kitchen. I want to be with him."

"Of course, dear," replied Susan, sympathetically.

The wind was creating a mournful howl as the temperature dipped to its lowest point of the winter. The shutters creaked and rattled in the strong gusts, and George was whining and pacing nervously from one room to another. The waning gibbous moon scurried in and out from behind the translucent clouds, and the lanterns in the summer kitchen danced and flickered from the drafty currents that emanated from obscure crevices. Nature, itself, seemed to be preparing the appropriate environment for the parting of a beloved soul.

At 10:45 the death-rattle began in earnest. For a few minutes Charles moved about restlessly in his bed. Then suddenly becoming quiet, he took one last deep breath and the flame of life left him. It was 11:07 p.m., January 17, 1865.

Susan and I were both present. We crossed his arms, and she closed his eyes, which were partially open. I took on the painful task of alerting Grandma to his passing. In her typical, stoic manner, Isabel proclaimed, "God's will be done," then bowed her head, covering her face with her hands. I closed the door behind me to allow her the privacy she required. She had endured so much: two daughters, six grandchildren, a son-in-law, and a husband. There must be a special place in heaven for those who have been tried so in the crucible of suffering.

I then went back into the summer kitchen and sat there, alone. Susan had gone upstairs to find fresh attire in which to dress the body. The tall clock chimed the half-hour as though it were just any old half-hour. "How could that ancient timepiece be so inconsiderate," I thought to myself. I went into the parlor, stopped the pendulum, set the dials back to 11:07, and returned to my post beside my dead brother. George, who had sensed the approach of the gathering angel, began his otherworldly baying from out in the woodshed.

All at once, I noticed a slight tremor in both of my hands, which soon spread to my limbs, and then throughout my entire being. I tried to stop it, but the trembling continued without letup. The last five years of grief rushed forth and exploded within me, consuming my heart like an avalanche. One after another, the images of all my deceased family members invaded my mind. Their ghosts were everywhere! My dear youthful mother, my beautiful little siblings, Papa, and finally, Charles, my anchor, my North Star! I was all that remained of my family. It was too much to ask of a fifteen-year-old girl! I needed them! My shallow self-confidence, of which I so often prided myself, was annihilated in an instant! There was nothing here for me any more, and I just wanted to join them.

At that moment, something within me snapped, and with an insane, furious impulse, I rushed through the woodshed doorway out into the dark, freezing night, wearing only my nightgown. The wind blew like a gale and the newly-fallen snow was whipping up into mini-cyclones. I dashed across the open field towards the darkness with sheer abandon. "I want to go home!" I screamed, to the top of my lungs. "Don't leave me here!" I cried. "Momma! Papa! … Bella! I wanna come home! Charlie! I just wanna be with you! Please God! Please!"

I kept running, running with no destination but "home". My bare feet, bitten by the Arctic cold and cut by the bushes and stubble, were bleeding and aching. My face was numb from the ice-cold air and the merciless wind was beginning to quickly take its toll. I kept running, through snowbankings, across frozen streams, into the woodlands, and onward. The waning moon followed me with indifference, as it played its game of hide and seek among quickly moving clouds that lurked like icy phantoms in the night sky. I fell, got up, and kept moving into the blackness, then fell again, scratching my face and hands on the thorn bushes. I struggled to stand up and continued. My feet were beginning to succumb to the elements, but I pushed onward. Finally, I collapsed upon the icy ground with not even enough strength to pick myself up again. I was completely disoriented, and my energy was spent.

As I lay there, on a mound of frozen earth, strewn with patches of drifted snow, I realized that this desolate site in the middle of nowhere was my final resting place. I was going to freeze to death like the little match girl! The terrifying reality of my impulsive actions hit me, and I knew I didn't want to die. "My God! Help me!" I yelled in my hoarse, half frozen voice. But it seemed as though God was deaf to my plea, justifiably enraged with the mockery I had made of this precious gift of life.

His judgment fell upon me swiftly! From out of nowhere, a blinding snow squall began, making the situation even more hopeless. I was frightened beyond anything I had ever known. Where was I? Somewhere south of our farm. But where? I tried to pull myself up but my frozen limbs could barely move. I was able to crawl to what I thought looked like a small pine tree, in order to take shelter beneath its branches. I made it as far as the little shrub, but the cold was too extreme for anyone to survive for long, and I knew it. There were warm houses less than a half mile from wherever I was, but I could only move a few feet at best, and the elements conspired mercilessly. No one was even aware that I had left. Perhaps they thought I had gone to my room, needing some privacy to mourn my brother's death. Susan and Grandma might not even realize that I was missing for hours! By then, I would be no more.

Now I was going to die, not from disease or other natural cause, but by my own foolish hand. Grandma was going to lose another grandchild and Susan, a stepchild whom she'd grown to love as her own. If they were lucky enough to find my body before the scavengers got to it, I would then be laid to rest along that nice neat row of Goodwin graves at Chelsea Heights. Another name, another marble headstone, and another epitaph: *Here lies*

Annie Elizabeth Goodwin, daughter of Capt. John A. and Sarah, who died January 17, 1865, at the age of fifteen years and eight months.

I could see all of those stones in my mind, as though I was standing there before them. All the suffering, all the love, all the joys and adventures of those once living and breathing human beings, trying to make sense of their days on this planet. All forgotten. Perhaps the stones might be given a second glance by a passerby, not for who they were in life, but simply for the fact that they lived (and died) during the great Civil War. Remembered no more … but maybe it was for the best.

As the cold continued to suck the life from my body I no longer experienced it as "cold." Even the understanding of my desperate situation began to vanish. My thoughts began to move away from my mortal struggle to those of springtime, with all my family and friends present, alive and well. Vivid, pleasing memories began to flood my dying brain. Miss Hunt, Michael, Emma, and finally, Alden. I smiled. Then came quiet, moonlight, stars … slumber.

Chapter 43

The Prophecy

There is a form of girlish mold,
Under the spread of the branches old
At the well-known beechen tree,
With the sunset lighting her auburn hair,
And the breezes waving them, in fragrant air, waiting for me.

There is the sweet voice, with cadence deep,
Of one that singeth our babes asleep,
And often turns to see
How the stars through the lattice begin to peep,
And watches the lazy clock dial creep, waiting for me.

Long since those locks were laid in the clay,
Long since that voice has passed away,
On earth no more to be;
But still in the spirit world afar
She is the dearest of those that are waiting for me.
—Gardiner Home Journal

Deep, infinite, night … like the cosmos before the First Day. Nothingness weds itself to time; time unites with eternity, and eternity and existence exchange vows. In undulations their offspring wax, wane, and renew … radiating. Continuing uninterrupted. Gushing, pulsating in primordial rhythm. Suddenly, a single word rises from the void, stealing away the Destroyer's plunder. What *is* this? Thought? Yes!

Blessed thought! … Self!

Slowly, or perhaps, instantaneously, knowledge of my own existence revealed itself, but not like when one awakens from a night of restful slumber. As sensations returned, I found my entire being suspended like a fly trapped in a spider's web, or better still, in an invisible sea of jelly. Motion was sluggish at best and impossible at worst. Did I want to move? Perhaps, but it wasn't an overwhelming urge.

Though I was by no means awake, my mind's eye began to observe light, sporadic flashes which varied in intensity. Eventually, colors were emitted amongst the shimmering fireworks. Amorphic silhouettes began to appear. These ghostly visitors seemed to be striving, unsuccessfully, to evolve into definable form, but lacked the ability to do so. I was in no hurry. I was where I was, and there was no other place to be. Urgency had no meaning, as I had no awareness of time or responsibility.

The first truly formed images that I can remember were "presented" to me. It was as though I was watching the slow progression of figures from a *magic lantern*. The first mind's-eye display was that of unknown individuals. One would appear, fade, and the next would come into view until each had taken its turn. Then the mood of the show began to change. No longer were these living images but eerie phantoms, ghastly daguerreotypes of unknown dead, all in frightful poses. As each faded, the exiting corpse became animated, making cryptic motions with its bony hands, summoning my attention. Had my mind been of good health, this performance would have terrified me. However, I was more amused than anything else, viewing the drama as though it was some bizarre circus parade marching along Water Street.

Those visions were followed by the pleasant landscape of my home. I experienced the sensation of weightless flight! I soared above the fields, barns, houses, and livestock, free from the immobility of the matrix previously described. Whatever I chose to think became reality in my dreamscape. I flew like a bird at will. Oceans, sailing ships, and creatures of the deep were all there at my command. The colors were vivid and the sensations seemed palpable. Unfortunately, the darkness did reappear, and I found myself in that sea of immobility once again. This time, however, emotion gripped me! I was no longer an anonymous spectator, I was becoming Annie.

I believe that these transitions from pleasant psychic moments into the darker realms occurred several times. But my final vision, or dream, was the darkest and most heart-rending of all.

I found myself stranded on a battlefield in the aftermath of a great Civil War bloodbath. The dead were everywhere; wounded soldiers were moaning in agony and begging for death. Vultures by the hundreds had landed, feasting on a banquet of human flesh. Out of the smoke rode an apocalyptic figure wearing Confederate gray and seated on a gray horse. It was like a scene from the Book of Revelation. Slowly the rider approached. His face was ghastly in appearance, and I was frozen in dread. The specter appeared to be neither alive nor fully dead. Stopping directly before me, with his sunken eyes gazing into my own, it muttered, "Do you see this carnage? Look at it closely." The specter moved his hand panoramically over the devastation. "That's all there is. Don't fool yourself, Annie. There is nothing afterwards but worms, vultures, and decay." He then lifted his right hand towards the dark clouds and proceeded past me along the dark trail. The fact that this infernal creature knew my name terrified me! Then, after traveling but a short distance, the phantom stopped, turned slowly and stared me down. It was Charles!

I woke up shrieking in delirious horror! But thank God, Susan was right beside me to help me take the final step into consciousness!

"Annie? Annie? Can you hear me?" spoke a gentle, deep voice from above me.

My awareness at that point was strictly sensory, not yet interpretive, but I was able to open my eyes. There were several figures hovering nearby whom I couldn't yet recognize. Everything was hazy, but my mind was much relieved having escaped that hideous vision. I tried to communicate with words, but my speech was little more than a hodgepodge of sounds, garbled and unintelligible.

After traversing the world of the unconscious, my mind's entry into wakefulness was like a blank page. Slowly, names and faces began to associate through some mysterious property in my brain: Dr. Davis … Susan … Grandma. Within a few hours, I was able to talk, but my lack of clarity of mind made it a daunting, almost painful task.

By my second day of consciousness, things started to come back to me. In fact, too many memories flooded the vacancies in my head. My emotions ran so high with the onslaught of recollection, that Susan found it necessary to stay with me day and night in order to reassure and comfort me. However, one memory, an essential one, was still lurking in that enigmatic world of the subconscious.

Have you ever awoken from a fearful dream and, after a moment of blind relief, been confronted with a far worse nightmare in the here and now? As the gushing torrents of memory returned, my first and deepest impulse was to tell everyone of my mysterious sojourn in detail. But there was something unsettling about that desire. There was an ethereal vapor cloaking my memory; a veil, behind which, an entity was stirring. I seemed to be reaching for a peculiar object at the bottom of a murky pool … a thing I could feel but not identify. Then, in a flash, the debris settled and the horror was revealed … Charles was dead! I had watched him take his last breath! I would never tell him of my experience nor see him again in this life!

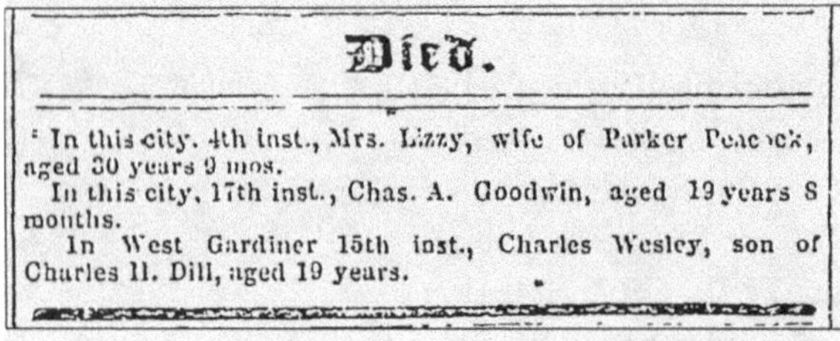

Died.

In this city. 4th inst., Mrs. Lizzy, wife of Parker Peacock, aged 30 years 9 mos.

In this city, 17th inst., Chas. A. Goodwin, aged 19 years 8 months.

In West Gardiner 15th inst., Charles Wesley, son of Charles H. Dill, aged 19 years.

This sudden, unforeseen realization left me gasping for breath and in a state of utter panic! The vivid memories of that fateful night exploded in full detail. I wasn't just remembering, I was being assailed from all sides by a barrage of images and emotions from Tuesday night. Tempted to scream for Susan, who had left the room, I prudently decided not to cause her more distress on my account. I didn't have the strength to run out into the frigid night again, even if I'd wanted to. There was no escape. I closed my eyes tightly and prayed. Immediately, a physical force struck a blow to my chest, as though my heart was going to explode! Startled, I opened my eyes, and to my great relief, my heart was quite intact. Sky was sitting on my sternum and looking at me curiously.

"Greetings, Sky," I said, in hysterical relief. "What are you doing on top of me?"

The animal—thankfully, considering my fragile sanity—didn't answer in words, but instead, curled up in a ball and began purring in contentment. That beautiful, peaceful hum was exactly what I needed to calm down from the emotional tempest. The battle, that I thought might rage for hours or days, was over in a few minutes, thanks to the curious little feline that Charles had brought into our home.

After peace returned, my mind wandered to more sobering thoughts concerning my impulsive race into that arctic night. I had been propelled into the abyss! Had my brother's death lit the fuse of an emotional powder keg that had been building up over the years? Was it the dread of abandonment? It wasn't rational thought that drove me out the door. In any case, Charles wouldn't have been very proud of such a deficit in character. He had been faithful and stoic right to the very end. I had been fickle in faith and a fair-weather friend to all those who loved me.

Adding insult to injury was the revelation that I had been unresponsive for nearly three days and had missed my brother's funeral! I was furious at my reckless behavior and all the unnecessary misery I had caused everyone. Had I been God, I would have let that ungrateful wench freeze to death! However, my demise wouldn't have benefited Susan or Grandma, even if I did deserve it. They had already experienced enough grief for several lifetimes. Their only wish was for my well-being, and that desire was soon granted. Within thirty-six hours, my mind was working at full capacity, and my body, though still afflicted, was showing signs of healing. In an attempt to piece together those missing three days, I began asking innumerable questions of everyone.

Dr. Davis informed us that it was miraculous that I had survived. He had never seen a case of such severe hypothermia where the patient had recovered full memory and not suffered irreversible frostbite or permanent brain damage. My toes were suspect for a few days but they recovered without treatment, or amputation.

According to Susan, I was found by a passerby near the stone bridge about a mile south of our farm. I assumed that I had run much further. However, being dressed in light clothing and bare feet, and with the elements so severe, life-threatening conditions quickly ensued. According to the newspaper, the temperature plunged to -18 degrees by midnight, and the wind was atrocious. After learning the basic facts of my rescue, I had more questions than ever. But since it was late in the evening and I was still suffering great fatigue, Susan insisted that I get some rest and promised to answer all my questions the next day.

Sunday morning, I awoke very much refreshed, but was still quite weak and very sore. At 9 a.m. my stepmother entered the room and demanded that I get up. Having watched my poor brother's body deteriorate from too little activity, I knew I had to start using my muscles before atrophy set in. So I willingly complied, but I did so too rapidly and ended up falling back onto my bed from a dizzy spell. On my second attempt, I was more careful and arose with no problem.

Susan asked me if I remembered Alden Potter? "Yes, of course. I love him!" I blurted out without thinking. Realizing how that might be interpreted, I added, "He's done so much to help our family."

Susan looked at me with one eyebrow cocked, "You have no idea. Well, anyway, he's coming to visit us today."

"Wonderful," I replied, oblivious to her enigmatic aside.

I had not moved about very much with the exception of having to use the chamber pot—a chore in itself! When I did glance in the mirror, I gasped in horror! My face was scratched and emaciated … and my hair! Dear God, what a mess. I've seen snarled fishing nets that were more easily untangled. My legs and feet were a real sight. Scratches, bruises, and cuts were everywhere, and my toes still had a purple tinge from frostbite. I couldn't let Alden see me like this. I was an animated corpse! So, I plucked up what courage I could gather, and with Susan's help, began to disguise my war-torn countenance.

"Oh, it hurts just to move. Even my aches have aches," I said, mournfully.

"Well, just thank God you're alive, young lady," retorted Susan. "The more you move around the better for your circulation and all."

"I know, but I'm wobbling like a penguin. And look at me! I look like I've been dragged through the field by a racehorse."

"We'll fix that all up. You'll look splendid when I'm done with you."

"That's impossible. I never looked splendid to begin with. Are you a magician?"

"Actually, I am," she replied. "You'll look like you belong in Harper's Weekly."

"Yeah, the aftermath of Fredericksberg,"

"Oh, Annie! It's good to see you haven't lost your sense of humor."

Susan got a jar of blemish cream and other toiletries from her room and began to brush some onto the visible scratches on my face. The stuff was lighter than my skin tone and made my countenance look like a drab, bleached sheet.

"What is that concoction, Susan? My face is turning into a field of white blotches," I asked with concern.

"No fretting! I'm not done. It's called zinc oxide, and it won't hurt you," she responded. "I'm just covering up the scratches and bruises, that's all. I need to blend it all together. You won't even know it's there when I've finished."

"How do you know it won't rot my face off? Some cosmetics have arsenic and lead in 'em."

"I've used this all my life and I'm not dead yet, so relax and let me work."

"If you put that stuff all over my face, I'm going to look like I really did die, for heaven's sake."

"Pale is a sign of nobility, girl. Don't you want to look noble?"

"I don't want to look like Queen Elizabeth, if that's what you mean. Did you know that her makeup was half an inch thick in places?"

"Yes, the poor woman had smallpox and had to cover those unsightly marks after she returned to good health."

"Oh, I wasn't aware. That's sad. But she could have selected a different hue! After all she was the queen."

"The idea behind the pale blush is to show that you are not a hired hand who works out-of-doors. That look was very popular in France and England and still is in some areas, especially among the upper classes. It distinguishes them from the others."

"Oh, the more I learn about this the more repulsive it gets. I'd rather be dirt poor and look like a human being, than be rich and look like a warmed-over corpse."

Susan chuckled, "Don't worry. Here, take the mirror and give me your opinion."

"Where did my freckles go? You covered 'em up."

"Yes, dear. But I also disguised your scratches and blemishes."

"Well, it certainly is an improvement, Susan. Thank you."

"Hopefully, you're not too white. I wouldn't want you to glow too brightly in front of our guest."

"There's little chance of that," I muttered.

After successfully making my appearance somewhat tolerable, I put on one of Susan's beautiful formal dresses, with hopes that it might offset the rest of me. Still weak and shaky from my ordeal, though I had been eating like a horse, I carefully descended the treacherous thirteen stairs at a snail's pace, holding onto both railings.

Having successfully navigated my way into the parlor, I plopped myself into Father's easy chair to take note of what I'd missed. There were three vases of rapidly wilting flowers raining down dried petals all over the mantle and floor, remnants from Charles's funeral. His mourning wreath, which had previously adorned the front door, now embellished the tall clock, hanging just below the face. The time of death, which I had set five evenings ago, was still in place. Adorning the Pembroke table, intermingled with the manger display, were several heart-felt sympathy notes.

Besides myself, that which remained of our little family consisted of a widowed stepmother and an elderly, widowed grandmother. Clearly, it would have been impossible for those poor unfortunates to manage the chaos of the last few days. The Blanchard family and Uncle James had handled many of the funeral details. The wake was shortened to a one-day affair due to my brother's deteriorated state, or at least that's what I was told. The truth be known, the brevity was likely due to the seriousness of my reprehensible, self-imposed plight and my subsequent need for continual care. My brother's mortal remains were now residing in the Hallowell crypt, awaiting the spring thaw. At least I would be able to attend his burial, which was a better kindness than I deserved.

Alden planned to arrive around noon, and although I was ready to talk about Charles, I dreaded recalling my lunatic, frigid, evening stroll. What would he think? *Crazy Annie!* That's what. Who would think otherwise? I wanted to avoid the topic, but knew I would gain nothing by postponing the inevitable. I was going to have to swallow my pride, which was a mouthful! Regardless, I was grateful to still be alive! Whatever others might think of me, Alden included, was inconsequential. I'd been given another chance at life, and that was worth more than all the small sacrifices I might have to concede to the virtue of humility.

Alden arrived right on time, bringing with him two bouquets of flowers. I assumed they were both acquired out of respect for Charles. He presented the larger of the two to Grandma and Susan on my brother's behalf. Then he turned to me, looked into my eyes, and said, "These are for you, my brokenhearted friend." Tears welled up in his eyes as well as my own, and I gave him a big hug. Susan then took the bouquets and went to find appropriate vessels in which to display them. Grandma, Alden, and I retired to the parlor. When Susan returned she stated, "I think Mr. Potter has a story he'd like you to hear, Annie."

I looked at Alden, somewhat puzzled, and then responded, "Well, I would love to hear your story. Please." I couldn't help but wonder why Susan had preempted my own bizarre tale for Alden's, but I was happy for the brief postponement.

"Well, let me start at the beginning, rather than in the middle as I so often do," he proposed, in that charming fashion of his. He looked over at me with a smile.

"On Tuesday last, I received a telegram from Susan here, telling me that Charles was believed to be near the close of life. She thought, if able, I might want to see him before he passed. Naturally, I very much wished to do so. I told our master builder about the situation, and he gave me his blessing to take leave for upward of three days.

"However, I couldn't leave until the end of my workday. I then boarded the 7 p.m. train to Hallowell. For reasons not worth mentioning, I didn't arrive until 9 p.m., and as you are aware, the weather early last week turned bitter-cold and windy. So, with the hour being late along with the inclement conditions, I decided to stay in Hallowell for the night, at the Pierces's home. I think our Captain John was friends with them, if I'm not mistaken."

"Yes, they were whalers, I believe," Grandma added.

"Of course, they've all retired now; the whaling industry not being what it was in the '40s. Anyway, I turned in shortly after I arrived, in order to get an early jump on the day."

"I'm not sure of the exact moment, but it had to be close to the time our dear Charles left this world …" recalled Alden, collecting his thoughts.

"Some time during that dark hour, I experienced a prodigy beyond description. My mind's eye beheld a frightening display! I found myself standing near a small stone bridge. Suddenly, you, Annie, were lying on the ground before me covered in snow and partially sheltered by a young pine tree. Then your frozen body began to fade into nothingness as an angel appeared to usher your spirit away! Simultaneously, a grave message was imparted without words, in simple, perfect knowledge,'*Go! There is no time to lose!'*

"I woke up with a start and understood, on impulse, what I had to do. The meaning was clear; you would soon be dead! I knew exactly where you were, though I had only passed the place once on my very first visit to your home!

"The only comparison I can make of this bizarre experience is that of an osprey returning to Maine from the Caribbean in the spring. It flies over the open ocean, follows no maps, or signals, or signs, but, miraculously, finds its way back to the nest it abandoned in the fall. I can't think of a better comparison from the natural world.

"Regardless of how these things transpired, the driving force within was overwhelming! It was as though I was a fireman rushing to a conflagration, knowing that you were trapped inside.

"I borrowed the Pierces's horse and a lantern and headed out into the frigid night. When I got to the Kennebec bridge, it was so cold that the toll-takers just ushered me on from the window. As there wasn't time to circumvent it, I then rode directly up Littlefield's hill, pushing the poor animal to his limit. When I reached your roadway, I knew I mustn't stop at your home; what I needed to find was not there. I quickly rode along, past the Blanchard's farm to the intersection. Then I turned left and traveled a short distance to that little stone bridge and stopped. I knew this was where I needed to be.

"I dismounted, lantern in hand, and walked about a hundred feet up a slight embankment, just west of the stream. By then the snow had stopped, and the moon was illuminating the blanketed area. Within a few seconds, like the osprey spotting its nest, I recognized the pine tree. It was still very gusty and the newfallen snow was whipping against my face, obscuring my vision. At first I couldn't see anything, but as I moved closer to the tree, with the help of the moonlight, I was able to make out a human form lying there. I quickly approached and realized it was your lifeless body, just as it had appeared in the forerunner!" Alden's voice began to choke with emotion. "You were lying on your side, covered with snow from the waist down, and your face and hands were under the tree, beneath its lower branches. I was terrified that you might already be dead! Placing my hand against your neck, I realized you still had a pulse and that there might be some hope."

At this point, Alden had to pause for a moment to gain his composure. "I picked you up and brushed you off, pulled you up onto the horse with me, and carried you back to your home. We had to get some warmth into your frozen body."

"Susan, would you mind taking over from here?" asked Alden, who was now overcome with emotion.

"Certainly … Well, Alden carried you up to your bed chamber, and we got a hot fire going in the woodstove. It was just such bedlam with Charles still lying on his deathbed and his sister about ready to join him."

"I'm so sorry!" I blurted out. "I caused everyone so much grief! I'm so sorry! Please forgive me!" I began to sob uncontrollably. "I'm so stupid! So very stupid!"

"Well, now, that's the understatement of the year! What in thunderation were you thinkin', girl?" quipped Grandma, with exasperation.

With that justified lambasting, my deep lamentations faded to a snivel and I glanced over at her, sporting a little grin amidst my tears. "Well, at least someone's got the courage to say it in plain English," I mumbled.

Alden smiled and winked at me in an attempt to avert my drowning in a sea of embarrassment.

After a few moments of silence, which was the equivalence of sheer torture, Susan continued. "Anyway, I got you out of your freezing wet clothing, robed you in some dry garments, and covered you with blankets."

I looked over at Alden in concern.

Alden laughed, having read my thoughts, "Oh, I wasn't in the room when she was changing your clothes, rest assured."

"Annie, Miss Prim and Proper!" exclaimed Susan. "You know me better than that! Anyway, Alden tended to your brother's remains, dressed him, and took care of procuring a coffin, with Edwin's assistance, so I could attend to you. Uncle James alerted friends, neighbors, and family members as to the times of the wake and service. They took care of everything."

"Really, it wasn't much trouble at all. An honor, in fact, to be of service at such a difficult moment," replied Alden. "I wish I could have done more."

"Ya saved the girl's life for heaven's sake!" exclaimed Isabel, with her wry wit. "How much more'd ya want?"

Alden smiled, modestly, and noted, "I had some assistance with that task. I only regret that I didn't come here directly after I got off the train in Hallowell."

"But the events happened the way they did for a reason," Susan responded.

"Yes, I'm sure," he replied.

Susan then continued with the story.

"Thursday, we had a small funeral service, and Alden presided with prayers and a scripture passage. Then Uncle James took the body into Hallowell, to the crypt to await spring burial.

"By Friday, your vital signs were stronger than ever and you were beginning to stir. Suddenly, you shrieked in terror, and we rushed to your bedside, alarmed by the frenzied outburst! However, after a few moments in that distressful state, you opened your eyes. We were all encouraged that the worst might be over. And Alden, he witnessed all of it. He stayed until he was convinced that you were out of harm's way."

"I wasn't aware that Mr. Potter was ever in the room," I remarked, with a perplexed look. "I had difficulty recognizing faces at first."

Alden continued, "Yes, I certainly was there, but only briefly after you came to. I had to return to my workplace as it had been a full three days. I promised I would come back today, and asked Susan to alert me by telegraph should any complications arise with your condition. Thank God, you seem to be very much on the mend!"

"That I am, thanks to you and everyone else, not to mention your remarkable encounter!"

"It's all true, every word of it!"

"When we were little, Charles and I used to make picnic lunches and go to that little bridge to fish. Much more pleasant in the summer, I assure you! But I had no idea that I was near it when I lost consciousness. I barely had the strength to pull myself under the tree branches. The moon was the only light source I had, and that was extinguished when the snow began to fall."

"Oh, that's another piece of the story that I nearly forgot to mention," Alden continued. "The doctor informed me that that inch of new snow may have saved your life, or at least, prolonged it. Apparently, the snow insulated your body from the extreme conditions, providing time for me to get there."

"I wasn't aware of that!" exclaimed Susan. "It does make sense, though. Eskimos use ice and snow to make homes. I understand they can be quite warm within."

"And I believed the snow to be my doom, that night," I responded. "Such irony."

"I have an apology to make," said Susan. "Alden wanted to relate this story to you himself, so Grandma and I had to promise not to tell you anything until he arrived. We sidestepped many of your questions for that reason."

"Oh, I'm relieved that you did. Painful memories were pouring into my mind like the opening of Pandora's Box. It would have been too much."

Considering what a hellish week it had been, the afternoon was refreshingly tranquil. Sometime during our conversations, Susan reminded me to ask Alden if he wouldn't mind gluing Mrs. Sullivan's plaque back together.

"Oh, Alden, in my clumsiness, I knocked over a treasured ceramic portrait of one of my dearest friends." I admitted. "Do you think you could take it back with you to your workplace and reassemble it? We'll gladly pay you for the effort."

"Nonsense! I would never accept a penny! I can fix it right here. Do you have glue?"

"We may have some out in the shed. I'll go check."

After a few minutes, I returned with the glue and the jewelry box of broken shards.

"That should do the trick," he assured me. "Let's go out into the summer kitchen so I don't get this all over your lovely furniture."

I felt a deep reluctance to revisit the ell. Seeing the empty cot there hit me hard. I paused for a moment, just staring at it, remembering. Alden stood beside me in silent respect. "Would it help if I removed it?" he asked, gently.

"No, I want to remember. I need to remember." I paused, thoughtfully, "Can I ask you a question, Alden?"

"Of course. Ask away!"

"Do you think I'll ever see my family again?"

"Goodness, Annie! Yes, of course, you'll see them again. All of them! After what we've just experienced, do you really have any doubt?"

"Honestly?" I replied, with some hesitation, "My mind always finds a morsel of doubt no matter how great the prodigy; and this one was truly mystifying! However, the osprey finding its nest is equally puzzling, yet we'd never refer to it as divine intervention or assert that it proves the existence of an afterlife. There are many things that the ancients believed to be miraculous, lightning, diseases, weather patterns, and so forth. They thought these events were brought about by the gods. *Might* we also be misattributing the mysteries of our own day in like manner?"

"Surely," Alden replied, "there are some things deemed miraculous today that will be better explained with the advancement of science. But nature's laws are predictable and repetitive under similar conditions. Science couldn't exist without that dependability. After all, millions of ospreys find their way home; it's the predictable natural outcome of being an osprey. So, wouldn't we expect what happened last Tuesday night to be a common event if it was brought on by natural forces? After all, nature follows its own laws. Wouldn't most people who are freezing to death in the wilderness be rescued at the last moment? But that's not the reality.

Save for those prodigious events, I would have slept until sunrise, been devastated by your disappearance, grieved your brother's death, and shattered by the eventual discovery of your frozen body. That would be the natural, predictable outcome."

"Yes. You're right. Something extraordinary took place, and I've been given a second chance at life. Why isn't that enough for this stubborn heart of mine?"

"Your tenacity is remarkable, Miss Goodwin. No stone left unturned. I do admire that quality."

"Quality?" I questioned, with trembling voice. "That quality drove me to insane desperation last Tuesday!"

Alden smiled, gently. "Well, take heart, Annie. Reflect on all these wonders and be assured that your sorrow will, one day, be turned to joy."

I shivered at his words. It was as though Edith had jumped into the conversation to admonish me. I wanted to tell him all about that dear old woman, but I knew it would have to wait. I took a deep breath and redirected my thoughts. We needed to get to work on the plaque if it were to be finished by evening.

Alden and I began piecing together the broken ceramic plate. It was a rather long, tedious process, as we had to wait five minutes for the glue to dry on one piece before we could add another. Finally, after nearly two hours, the bulk of the plate had been fixed into place. Now came the delicate portion of the process, putting the shards of the precious painted image back upon the restored plate. My greatest fear was that some smidgen might still be lying in a crevice on my bedroom floor.

Slowly, meticulously, and with a steady hand, Alden worked. These last pieces were so tiny and fragile that I felt it best to let him handle the task by himself. As each fell into place and the portrait began to emerge, Alden's face took on an air of trance-like fixation. I asked him if there was a problem, but he shook his head lightly and said nothing. It was as though he was in another world. Finally, he skillfully placed the last bit of portrait into position on the plaque and sat there, motionless, as though contemplating the finalization of a masterpiece.

"It's perfect!" I proclaimed, breaking the silence. "Thank you so much! I was worried that I might have left a fragment on the floor. Isn't she beautiful?"

He continued to stare at the image in amazement. Then he turned to me, and softly exclaimed, "It's her! … My God! … This is her!"

"Who?" I asked.

"She ushered you into eternity," he whispered in awe, as he leaned back to view the entire work.

"You mentioned an angel," I voiced, in bewilderment.

"I thought she *was* an angel," he replied, choking up with emotion and shaking his head in disbelief. "*She* saved your life!"

"But Edith's been dead for almost a year!" I stammered.

Alden then reached across the table and took my hand in his, declaring, "Oh, she's not dead. She's alive, young, and of unearthly beauty!"

Epilogue

What we really know about Annie Goodwin

According to the Kennebec County Registry of Deeds and Helen Taylor's *Chelsea, Maine History*, Captain John A. Goodwin, a merchant mariner, and his family lived in our home from 1844 until 1865. All the birth and death dates are as represented in the novel with the exception of Lilly and Bella's births which were gleaned from their gravestones. James Kean and his wife, Isabelle, were the maternal grandparents of our protagonist, Annie Elizabeth, and lived on the combined, forty-acre Kean-Goodwin property. The Maxwells, Frenches, Runnels, Blanchards, housekeeper Louisa Ricker, and Alden Potter were all real neighbors, relatives, and/or acquaintances of the Goodwins. Other characters are either real individuals who are referenced in footnotes or fictitious personages who were added to enhance the storyline.

Despite the fictional nature of the story there remains a tragic reality that underlies this novel. From the tender age of five Annie passed through a gauntlet of family deaths. By 1865 she was a real-life, sixteen-year-old "orphan Annie". The only records I have found for the causes leading to these tragic deaths are those of her mother, who died of "childbed fever" and her father, who was lost at sea in April 1864. All the other 'causes' are educated guess-work from researching local newspapers and noting the prevalence of certain illnesses mentioned in obituaries. Also, aside from the serendipitous acquisition of the Kean family bible and its artifacts, there are no actual diaries or journals of Annie or any other family member that have come to light.

Nineteen-year-old Charles, the last member of her immediate family and heir to the property, passed away in January 1865 leaving the large homestead farm unmanageable for the aging Isabelle Kean, Annie, and her widowed stepmother, Susan. The house, barns, and acreage were sold to James Kebler in September of that year for a sum of $1400. Annie, though still a minor, received $750 from the sale and Susan, the widow's portion, of $650.

Annie then went to live with her uncle James, her father's brother, who resided in Augusta. She later attended Mt. Holyoke Seminary and her name is listed in the school's enrollment documents for 1868 and 1869. On October 12, 1869, at age 20, she married Alden Potter, a ship joiner. They resided at 32 Oak Street in Bath, Maine and had two children, Edith and Fred. The 1880 census mentions Annie, Alden, Fred, Edith, and (grandmother) Isabelle Kean residing at that residence. Annie passed away in 1902, at the age of 53 from "malignancy of the uterus" and Alden died two years later at the age of 70, of enterocolitis.

Mrs. Sullivan is a joyful reflection of my own spiritual light, Pearle Edith Sullivan Gervais, my dear mom, to whom this book is dedicated. Through her 94 years, she was recipient of many graces from the Divinity, which I and our family members have witnessed with our own eyes. I have included variations of those occurrences throughout this narrative. °Her life was lived in unselfish love.

Artifacts found on the Goodwin-Kean property

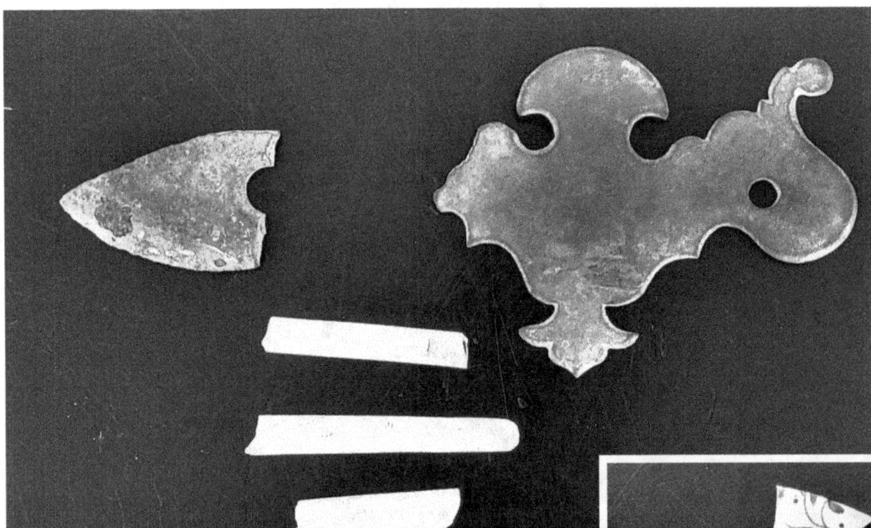

Top left; Part of gun lock plate
Top right: !8th century brass drawer pull
Bottom: Pieces of clay pipes

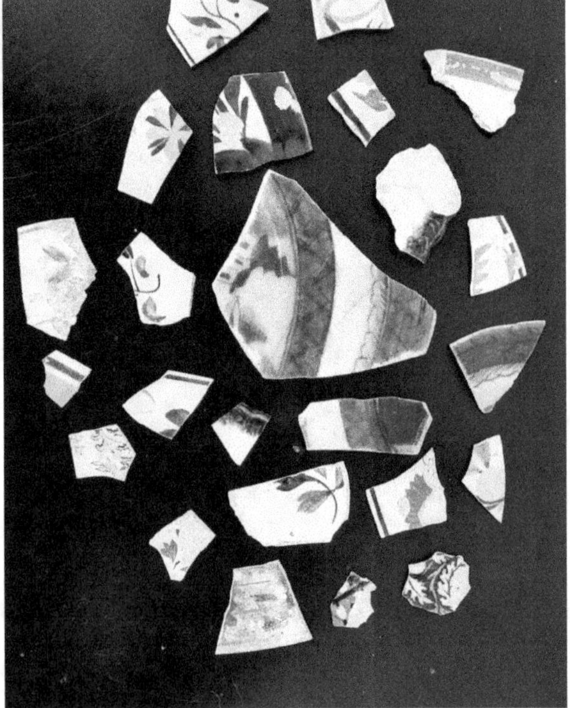

Period pottery shards

Acknowledgements

As a first-time author who began writing this work in the middle of the pandemic in 2020, I had no idea of the lengthy, challenging, yet exciting journey I had begun. Thanks to Barbara Bennett's consults, Laurel Dodge's editing skills, and Lindy Gifford's publishing advice and design expertise I have been able to navigate my way through the process.

My wife, Carrie, deserves a shout-out for her love, commitment, and patience with me for the many times I "disappeared" into my study, spending more time in the mid-nineteenth century than in the twenty-first.

I also want to acknowledge my adult children Theresa, Gabriel, and Ian for the wonderful memories I have of their childhood antics and unique personalities which contributed, vicariously, to help bring the Goodwin children to life.

Finally, I thank the Divinity for allowing me the time and inspiration to finish this work.

Notes

1 A version of this Hallowell legend was printed on March 12, 1887, in the *Hallowell Gazette,* and mentions the Goodwins and other local mariner families in its introduction.

2 Elisha H. Fisher left port on Apr. 22, 1840 and returned Feb. 20, 1842, with 2,413 barrels of oil.

3 From Augusta, ME. Registry of Deeds.

4 *Chelsea, Maine History* by Helen Taylor.

5 Found in the head of sperm whales and used in cosmetics, candles, and lubricants.

6 George Pollard, Jr. was the commander of the ill-fated Essex, which was attacked and sunk by an angry sperm whale. The book *In the Heart of the Sea,* (later followed by the movie of the same title), described that harrowing event. Pollard later captained the Hallowell-built whaling ship, Two-Brothers, which sank on the French Frigate Shoals. He, once again, survived the incident.

7 Born Dec. 17, 1815, of John Goodwin and Mary Springer.

8 Lieutenant James Kean (Maine Province) served in Stone's Massachusetts Militia during the War of 1812.

9 Born May 10, 1845.

10 Born May 31, 1818, son of John.

11 Born May 15, 1818, of James and Isabel Kean.

12 Mentioned in the *Hallowell Weekly Register,* March 17, 1900, in their historical account of the Old South. "… He came to us with 'holiness in the Lord' written on his brow … "

13 The Old South Congregational Church was, at first, a wooden structure built in 1796. It burned down in 1878 and was replaced by the present granite structure in the mid-eighteen-eighties.

14 Chelsea Heights Cemetery is on the west side of Route 9, near the Hallowell Rd. crossing in Chelsea.

15 Sarah Turner Kean, born June 17, 1820.

16 James Kean, born Nov. 29, 1842. (Isabel Kean, Annie's maternal grandmother, was 43 at the time.)

17 Twins Isabella and Sarah Lilly were born in April 1857. The precise day was not recorded in the documents.

18 Capt. James Kean died Jan.2, 1858, Age 71. (Born May 2, 1786.)

19 Became law on Sept. 18, 1850.

20 Served as a center for the UGR and as a local church for blacks. Built by free African-Americans on Newbury Street in Portland, ME. (ca. 1828) and is the third oldest of its type in the nation.

21 Israel Simpson Weeks' beautiful pillared mansion still stands today on Route 201 in Vassalboro, just beyond the town line.

22 Olive Emma French, born Oct. 10, 1850. Daughter of John and Aurelia (Littlefield).

23 A political group during the Civil War advocating restoration of the South with slavery left intact.

24 The 1860 census lists Isabel Kean at the Goodwin residence. She continued to own her home and likely rented it out to tenant farmers after the death of her husband, James, in 1858. The 1879 map of Chelsea continues to list her as owner of the property. The 1880 census states that she was then residing with Annie, in Bath, at 32 Oak Street. She died there in 1881 at the age of 82.

25 Now, Route 9.

26 Helen Taylor's *Chelsea, Maine History*

27 From *Chelsea, Maine History,* Taylor.

28 Mentioned in Helen Taylor's *Chelsea, Maine History* as: "one of our best teachers, and our scholars seemed to partake of that same spirit which animated the teacher … the teacher seemed to command respect by love"

29 *Chelsea, Maine History*: by Helen Taylor.

30 The *Gardiner Home Journal,* used frequently in this writing, was originally titled the *Cold Water Fountain,* (1840's) then, the *Northern Home Journal* (1850's), and finally, the *Gardiner Home Journal* (1858 onward). On occasion, the *Hallowell Gazette* and *Kennebec Journal* are referenced, as well.

31 Mentioned in Helen Taylor's *Chelsea, Maine History.* This area is now home to the Togus VA Medical Center.

32 Information from *Chelsea, Maine History* by Helen C. Taylor

33 A silver 3-cent piece.

34 Today it's called the Dr. Mann Road.

35 Information from *Chelsea, Maine History* by Helen C. Taylor

36 Its foreclosure is mentioned in the *Gardiner Home Journal,* Nov. 21, 1861.

37 The first station opened in Hallowell in 1851.

38 Medical records affirm that Sarah Goodwin died of childbed fever, May 17, 1860.

39 Louisa Ricker was mentioned as "housekeeper" for the Goodwin family in the 1860 census. Source: *Chelsea, Maine History*, Helen C. Taylor.

40 From Lincoln's Gettysburg Address.

41 By John Ruskin, UK author, 1841. First print in book form, 1851.

42 An Irish priest who was brutally martyred for his faith, July 1, 1681. Canonized in 1975, he is the country's patron saint of "peace and reconciliation". His mummified head is preserved at St. Peter's Church in Drogheda, Ireland.

43 Then Lieutenant Anderson commanded the arsenal from Nov. 1834 until May 1835. *History of Augusta,* James W. North.

44 July 21, 1861.

45 From *The Maine Register* for the Year 1855.

46 Cited in fig. 49

47 Learn more: Civil War-A Soldier's Diary. http://www.ioweb. com>civilwar>goodwin_diary

48 1860 census. *Chelsea, Maine History* by Helen C. Taylor.

49 1860 census. *Chelsea, Maine History* by Helen C. Taylor.

50 Naoma (Dearborn) Runnels. *Chelsea, Maine History* (personal paragraphs) by Helen C. Taylor.

51 Census, 1860. *Chelsea, Maine History* by Helen C. Taylor.

52 *Chelsea, Maine History* by Helen Taylor.

53 Event mentioned in detail in the *Gardiner Home Journal*, Jan. 29, 1863, p. 2.

54 *Gardiner Home Journal*, Jan. 29, 1863.

55 C. A. Williams company, of Skowheghan, was a prominent maker of ice skates from 1860-1870.

56 Annie is listed in the class roster of Mount Holyoke Seminary for the years 1868 and 1869.

57 Annie Sherman James Burling journaled her experiences at Mount Holyoke Seminary for the years 1863-1864. She eventually went on to become a school principal. She died in 1920.

58 Information taken from *Historical Sketch of Mount Holyoke Seminary,* by Mary O. Nutting, 1876.

59 Sledding.

60 Deborah H. Rollins, b. 05/26/1845. Daughter of George and Eliza. *Chelsea, Maine History*: Helen C. Taylor.

61 See photos at end of book.

62 This hill, with a summit of 415 feet, was named for the Winter family who owned that parcel of land.

63 *The New England Journal of Medicine.*

64 Pastor from 1856-1869. He also served communities in Brunswick, Bath, and Waterville.

65 The report states that after "being holed by ice", the vessel sank in the Grand Banks of Newfoundland, Apr. 30, 1864. All souls were lost save two that were rescued by the British vessel, Montezuma.

66 Despite multiple searches by this author and research done by Maine Maritime Museum personnel, Goodwin's vessel, circumstances, or whereabouts remain unknown. Neither is there any evidence that he was involved with the military. The only record of his demise is that written on his headstone stating he was lost at sea in April of 1864. Therefore, the Nor continues to remain a possible candidate.

67 James Kebler bought the Goodwin farm in August, 1865: Kennebec County Registry of Deeds.

68 Eugene Augustus Goodwin, mentioned previously. Born April 10, 1833 of John and Nancy.

69 James Oscar Goodwin born Dec. 2, 1818 of John and Nancy.

70 Mentioned in Eugene Goodwin's *Civil War-A Soldier's Diary.*

71 Both deceased are listed in *Chelsea, Maine History* by Helen C. Taylor.

www.ingramcontent.com/pod-product-compliance
Lightning Source LLC
Chambersburg PA
CBHW080604300726
48975CB00011B/2789